PRAISE FOR *Too Big To Miss*
BY SUE ANN JAFFARIAN

Plus-size reading pleasure—try this one on!

—Lee Child, *New York Times* bestselling author
of the Jack Reacher Mystery series

On one level, *Too Big To Miss* is a classic, fast-paced mystery; on
another, it's a passport into a world we either inhabit or live next-
door to, but rarely see in popular fiction. Sue Ann Jaffarian breaks
rules and breaks ground with humor, insight, and compassion.

—Harley Jane Kozak, author of *Dating Dead Men* and *Dating Is Murder*

Balancing her professional skills as a paralegal with her self-doubt
as a sleuth, Odelia is one of the most believable amateur detectives
in recent fiction. Beautifully plotted and carefully crafted, this is a
marvelous start to an exciting new series. Strongly recommended.

—*Library Journal*

Sue Ann Jaffarian does a bang-up job of portraying Odelia's world
(skillful paralegal who is adept at dealing with obnoxious lawyers);
loyal friend (refusing to accept the mystery of Sophie's death at
face value); and romantic lover (meeting an exceptional guy and
accepting him with his flaws). *Too Big To Miss* is touching, hilarious, has a killer plot that keeps winding round and round, and of
course has characters who feel real and struggle through their personal challenges.

—*Midwest Book Review*

There is a lot of humor and a fair amount of underlying angst in
this book, which serves to make the story realistic ... With a cast of
diverse characters, an intriguing plot, and a credible heroine, this is
an enjoyable read.

—*Mystery Scene Magazine*

SUE ANN
JAFFARIAN

AN ODELIA GREY MYSTERY

THE CURSE
OF THE
HOLY PAIL

MIDNIGHT INK
WOODBURY, MINNESOTA

FIRST EDITION
First Printing, 2007

Book design by Donna Burch
Cover design by Ellen L. Dahl
Editing and layout by Rebecca Zins

Midnight Ink, an imprint of Llewellyn Publications

Cover model(s) used for illustrative purposes only
and may not endorse or represent the book's subject

Library of Congress Cataloging-in-Publication Data
Jaffarian, Sue Ann, 1952–
    The curse of the holy pail / Sue Ann Jaffarian.—1st ed.
        p.   cm.—(An Odelia Grey Mystery)
    ISBN-13: 978-0-7387-0864-5
    ISBN-10: 0-7387-0864-X
    1. Overweight women—Fiction. 2. Murder—Fiction.
    [1. Lunchboxes—Fiction.] I. Title.

PS3610.A359C87 2007
813'.6—dc22

2006048706

Midnight Ink
2143 Wooddale Drive, Dept. 0-7387-0864-X
Woodbury, MN 55125-2989

www.midnightinkbooks.com

Printed in the United States of America

DEDICATION

For my nephew, Tom—one of the good guys.

ACKNOWLEDGMENTS

A big thank-you to "Team Odelia," which grows larger with each book, including my awesome agent, Whitney Lee of the Fielding Agency, and all the wonderful folks at Llewellyn Worldwide/Midnight Ink who continue, with their advice and support, to help me improve my craft.

A special thank-you to the Los Angeles chapter of Sisters In Crime.

And, of course, big hugs and thanks to my friends and family, who continue to lovingly support me in this madness.

AUTHOR'S NOTE

It has been suggested by several of my readers that I include recipes in my books, as is the custom of many other writers. After giving this some thought, I decided to share the following:

Odelia's Favorite Cookie Recipe

1. Wait until March;
2. Go to nearest supermarket;
3. Locate young girls in brown or green uniforms; they can be found in front of the store by a folding table, usually accompanied by a parental figure;
4. Purchase at least twelve boxes of Thin Mint cookies;
5. Place cookies in freezer, consuming no more than one box per month, preferably less;
6. Next March, repeat steps 1–5 above.

ONE

By the age of forty-seven, I had technically broken nine of the Ten Commandments—although I'm still a bit fuzzy about the whole "graven image" thing. For example, when I was eleven, on a dare, I stole several candy bars from a drugstore. And in high school, telling the fifth-period gym class that Sally Kipman was a lesbian would definitely be categorized as bearing false witness. But in my defense, it was only after she told everyone I was fat because I was pregnant.

Still, I always thought that I would make it to heaven with the sixth commandment intact; that going through life without killing another human being would be a piece of cake.

But I was wrong. And now here I am—ten for ten.

And it all started with my birthday.

I was born to be middle-aged. It fits me like comfy flannel pajamas that are worn and washed until they are faded and thin;

clothing with no eager need to prove anything or be something else—it just is.

Today is my birthday. As of 2:17 this afternoon, I, Odelia Patience Grey, wandered into my forty-seventh year as absentmindedly as someone who arrives at the supermarket only to realize that they really intended to go to the dry cleaners. I am comfortable with being forty-seven years of age and embrace it with enthusiasm.

I never felt young, not even when I was. When I was sixteen, my family claimed that I behaved more like a thirty-two-year-old. But it's easy to act older in a family suffering from arrested development. Given the choice, I would not go back and relive my life for anything. My time is now—and, from the looks of it, getting better with each passing year, every marching month.

I was examining my face in the bathroom mirror, sighing slightly as I took inventory of new wrinkles. Enduring crinkly lines on my face was one the few things I viewed as a downside to maturity. Admittedly, I am no great beauty, but neither would anyone mistake me for Medusa. My hair is medium brown, worn just below my chin. My eyes, inherited from my father, are green and close set. A slight bump and a spattering of freckles exist in harmony on my long nose. I'm told I'm cute, if one can still be considered cute at forty-seven.

The evening news drifted in from the television in the bedroom. I listened as I pulled, stretched, and smoothed my round face into alternative looks. A female newscaster was giving a follow-up report on the shootings three days prior at a community center. Five people had been injured, including three children.

Two later died. The shooter shot himself at the end, just before the police captured him. It had been a crime fueled by racial hate.

I stopped fussing with my face and looked into my eyes as they stared back from the mirror. The green was dulled with sadness. I could never understand how some people could treat life so cavalierly. Did they think that once the trigger was pulled, they could yell "cut!" and their targets would magically resurrect like TV actors between scenes?

A deep sigh crossed my lips, a barely audible prayer for the victims and their families.

The news program was turned off. A moment later, I felt a strong hand caress my fat behind through my slinky nightgown. As I leaned back into the warm palm, the hand stopped to cup the fullness, giving my bottom a familiar squeeze. I closed my eyes and smiled. This was love, and love always conquered hate.

"In some cultures," I said with sass, still not turning around, "you'd be forced to marry me after this."

"I think that's a sentence I could live with," my groper answered.

The fingers of his hand did a tickling tap dance on my left buttock, and one finger lovingly found the slight indentation left by a bullet last year—a bullet fired by a killer hell-bent on making me the next victim. Then the fingers went back to a loving caress. Since the shooting, Greg favored that side of my bottom. The hand on my butt moved up to encircle my thick waist and pull me close. Only then did I turn to look at him as he sat in his wheelchair next to where I stood.

Reaching down, I pushed Greg's longish brown hair out of his eyes. I love his hair. It's medium brown, nicely styled, and so silky to my touch. In the last few months he had grown a beard and mustache, which he kept closely trimmed. I had always thought him quite handsome, but now he was a bona fide babe. And he was mine. We had met fifteen months ago when a mutual friend died, and the fire still burned brightly between us. Out of the tragedy of Sophie London's death had come this glowing, healthy relationship. At thirty-seven, Greg Stevens is my junior by ten years.

I bent down and kissed him lightly on the lips, tasting something unusual but identifiable. "I can still taste the cigar you smoked tonight," I said, crinkling my nose. "No doubt you got it from Seth Washington."

Greg reached up his other hand and placed it on my other hip, turning me so that I fully faced him. "Don't blame Seth," he said, giving me his best puppy dog eyes, "I brought the cigars."

I bent down and kissed him again, this time a little longer and deeper, letting him know that I didn't *really* mind the cigar taste.

Greg had thrown me a birthday party tonight at one of our favorite Italian restaurants. Most of our friends had been there, including my closest friend, Zenobia Washington, better known as Zee, and her husband, Seth. Now it was just the two of us bedding down for the night at Greg's place—the best part of the day.

"Thank you for the party, Greg. It was wonderful."

"You're welcome, sweetheart," he said, taking one of my hands and kissing the palm. Holding it tightly, he turned the wheelchair and headed out the bathroom door, tugging me along. "Come to bed, Odelia. I have a big surprise for you."

I laughed. "I just bet you do."

If I had known that forty-seven was going to be this much fun, I would have done it years ago.

IT IS NOT AGAINST the law to be a nincompoop. If so, I would have a rap sheet as long as my arm.

Fortunately for me, no one was witnessing my most recent slide into childish stupidity and self-pity. I was wallowing alone like a pig in a mud puddle—or, in this case, a tub of chocolate pudding the size of a child's sand pail.

Now, there are comfort foods and then there are comfort foods. This particular item was my supreme tranquilizing grub. I had other favorites, but they were mere bandages eaten to soothe minor emotional aches and pains. But this, the one I fondly call "bucket-o-puddin'," was akin to full-strength, prescription-only drugs when it came to emotional eating.

When I was a little girl, my mother often made chocolate pudding. In those days, it came in a box and we cooked it on the stove. It began as a brown, sugary powder that was mixed with whole milk and then stirred constantly over low heat. That was my job, the stirring. With a wooden spoon I would gently stir and stir and stir, making sure that the precious brown mud did not stick to the bottom of the pan and scorch.

The pudding brand was My-T-Fine. I understand it's still made today, but I haven't seen it in years. My-T-Fine chocolate fudge pudding is one of those happy childhood memories that has disappeared from my life without explanation, just as my mother did when I was about sixteen.

Normally, I'm not that fond of pre-made puddings, but not long ago I stumbled across a new brand in the supermarket and decided to give it a whirl. It tastes almost, but not quite, like my beloved My-T-Fine.

I was sitting on my sofa, knee deep into the bucket-o-puddin', watching the movie *Robin Hood, Prince of Thieves*. It's one of my all-time favorites—not because it stars Kevin Costner, but because it boasts the British actor Alan Rickman cast as the Sheriff of Nottingham. I have a thing for Rickman. In my eyes, he is right up there with My-T-Fine chocolate fudge pudding.

Sitting patiently on the floor to my left was Wainwright, Greg's golden retriever. Greg was out of town and I was doggie sitting. To my right, ensconced regally on the sofa beside me, was my big, sassy cat Seamus. Seamus isn't much to look at. He has only one eye and both ears are raggedy, as if they had once, long ago, been a chew toy for some other animal. About a year and a half ago, his fur was tinted green by some local pre-teen hooligans wielding food coloring. It's now back to its original champagne color, but I swear that every now and then I still see a hint of emerald in the sunlight. As I studied my cat, he turned to look back at me with that one amber eye. It was a look of frank royal arrogance, leaving no doubt in my mind that cats have never forgotten they were once looked upon as gods.

After taking a big bite of pudding, I put a small glob on the spoon and fed it to Seamus. He licked it eagerly, almost as obsessed about it as his human mother. Knowing that chocolate was bad for dogs, I tossed Wainwright a Snausages treat from the bag resting on my lap. The animals seemed happy to join me in my comfort food binge.

The reason for this slide into chocolate sedation was the little black velvet box sitting on the coffee table in front of me. It was closed tight. Inside was a breathtaking diamond engagement ring.

Before leaving to attend a convention in Phoenix, Greg had asked me to marry him. He had popped the question in bed the night of my birthday, and was surprised and hurt when an eager reply did not gush forth immediately. We had talked about it into the wee hours of the morning, but I was still no closer to a decision. However, he had made it quite clear that he expected an answer when he got back Thursday, just four days from now. Truth is, I just wasn't sure. I mean, I love Greg and our relationship is wonderful, both physically and emotionally. But do we belong together for the long haul? That's the million-dollar question. As compatible as we are, I'm not sure that we want and need the same things to be happy over the next twenty years and beyond.

I put the dilemma and the pudding on hold long enough to shout at the TV. "Go ahead, Alan, cut out his heart with a spoon!"

The phone rang just as I was about to jam another load of pudding into my mouth. I put down the container and went to answer the cordless in the kitchen.

"Hello," I answered with little enthusiasm.

"What in the world is wrong with you?" the voice on the other end shouted.

"Hi, Seth, and good day to you, too," I responded calmly.

Seth is as much of a big brother to me as his wife is like a sister, and like most big brothers, he feels free to pass along unsolicited advice and comments. He's also an attorney and is used to thinking that his opinion is always the correct one.

"Do you have any idea what a good man Greg Stevens is?" His voice had lowered a bit, but it was still demanding.

"Gee, Seth, what do you think?" I snapped back. "I've only been dating and sleeping with the man for the past fifteen months."

I sighed, knowing that Zee had told her husband about the proposal and my reluctance to accept it.

"So why aren't you marrying him? He's crazy about you, Odelia. Marry him before he finds out he's just plain crazy."

I should have anticipated Seth's reaction. He loved me and thought the world of Greg. He only wanted what was best for both of us. So, damn it, just butt out.

"I never said I wasn't marrying him," I responded in a tight voice. "I just want to think it over. You know, make sure it's the right decision."

"Seth, you leave poor Odelia alone," another voice chimed in. It was Zee, obviously on an extension. "It's her decision. Odelia, honey, we're behind you one hundred percent, no matter what you decide."

"Thanks, Zee," I said into the phone.

"Christ."

"Seth Washington! You know better than to take the Lord's name in vain in this house."

Great, my marriage proposal was causing a battle in the Washington household.

"Like I said, Odelia," Zee continued, "whatever you decide, we're behind you all the way—both of us."

I heard an abrupt click and guessed that Seth had hung up.

"Zee, why couldn't he just leave things be?"

"Honey, Seth loves you. He's just worried about you. He doesn't want you to be alone."

"I don't mean Seth. I mean Greg. Why did he have to propose? Things are great just the way they are. Or were. Now he's changed everything."

"He loves you very much, Odelia."

"I know that," I said, my voice small. Greg's love was something I never doubted.

"It's only natural for him to want to marry you," Zee added. There was a pause and I knew what Zee was going to say next. "Greg isn't Frank, you know," she said in a soft, comforting tone.

Bingo. Right on the money.

Zee was referring to Franklin Powers, an attorney I was engaged to several years earlier. He was a seemingly charming man who had wooed and won me easily, maybe too easily. An attractive man a dozen years my senior, in time he revealed himself to be a control freak given to inflicting emotional torture mixed with violence. Although he never struck me, I had felt that those days were fast approaching. I broke off our engagement just two months before the wedding. The relationship had left me emotionally bruised and beaten and it had been three years before I could date again comfortably.

I answered Zee truthfully. "I'm not worried about that. I know he's nothing like Frank and would never hurt me that way." Now it was my turn to pause. "Greg wants children. I don't. You and I have talked about this before."

"But have you discussed it with him?"

"Yes, of course." I was tired and it came across in a cranky voice. I wanted to return to wallowing with the animals and rooting for the Sheriff of Nottingham. I was not ready to be grown up about this just yet, not even with my best friend.

"Zee, I don't really want to discuss this right now. Please understand."

"I do understand. And I'm here when you're ready to talk about it."

"Thanks."

"And Odelia?"

"Yeah?"

"Whatever you're eating, put it away. It's not going to help matters."

I frowned. Zee knows me too well. Like me, she's as wide as she is tall, both of us weighing in over two hundred pounds and wearing size 20.

"What are you talking about?" I asked, feigning ignorance.

She laughed. It was a smooth, sexy, throaty laugh. If My-T-Fine chocolate fudge pudding had a sound, this was it.

"Don't give me that," she scolded, still laughing. "Right now I'd say you were either up to your elbows in a pint of Cherry Garcia ice cream or a box of Thin Mints. Girl Scout cookie time is a long ways away, Odelia, better pace yourself." She laughed again.

"A lot you know. It's a container of chocolate pudding."

We laughed together and I felt immediately better. But then isn't that what best friends are for?

I hung up the phone and walked back into the living room.

"Oh … my … gawd!"

In the middle of the floor lay Wainwright, wolfing down Snausages from a torn package. On the coffee table was Seamus, his furry face buried deep into the bucket-o-puddin'. The cat looked up briefly, his usually creamy-colored snout brown, and then went back to his feast. The dog wagged his tail in welcome.

"Sheesh, I can't leave you guys alone for a minute." I scolded the dog, wagging my finger at him. "Your dad would kill me if he saw this." The happy animal thumped his tail again.

It was true. Greg was a loving but disciplined master when it came to Wainwright. And the dog was beautifully trained and loyal. But when the golden retriever stayed with me, I let him get away with murder, sometimes even letting him sleep on my big bed just as Seamus did. Greg tolerated the cat sleeping at the end of his bed when I took Seamus along for weekends, but he would never have broken Wainwright's training.

Seamus, on the other hand, was spoiled rotten and had the fussy disposition that went with such indulgence. Annoyed at my own stupidity of leaving animals alone with food, I grabbed Seamus, stuffed him under one arm and toted him, protesting, into the kitchen before he could get pudding on the furniture. I deposited him into the sink. Holding him by the scruff of the neck with one hand, I rinsed his face off with the other, accompanied all the time by kitty growls and squirming. Fortunately, no matter what indignities I foist upon him, Seamus never uses his claws or teeth on me. He seems to sense that whatever I do to him, it is for his own good. Near the end of the cleanup, the phone rang again. I snatched at the receiver, loosening my grip from the cat's neck. He used the opportunity to make a break for it and jumped down out of my reach. Oh well, now he was just wet, and water was harmless enough.

"Hello," I barked into the phone.

"I would have thought your disposition would be at least a little better at home," the person on the other end commented.

Damn, it was Mike Steele, one of the attorneys from the office. Correction: the attorney I *hated* from the office. Michael R. Steele, Esquire, was the poster boy for arrogance.

I am a paralegal in a firm called Wallace, Boer, Brown and Yates, nicknamed Woobie. I had worked for Wendell Wallace for nearly two decades, juggling legal secretarial duties for him in addition to being the firm's corporate paralegal. In recent years, I have done less for Mr. Wallace and more paralegal work. When Mr. Wallace retired, the transition to full-time paralegal was virtually seamless, except now I am assigned to Michael Steele, who recently made partner in the firm—as if he had not been egotistical enough as a senior associate. Another downside is that, although I now have my own private office, albeit a teeny-weeny one, it is just two doors down from Steele's office.

Michael Steele is the firm's problem child, a real pain in the ass to everyone, overly demanding and rude. His redemption is his brilliance in the field of law; in that, he is top notch. And while he does not like me any more than I like him, he, in turn, respects my knowledge and experience.

And here he was, calling me at home on a Sunday afternoon. Now I was really annoyed. This was beyond pudding therapy.

"What do you want, Steele?" I asked without ceremony.

He got to his purpose quickly. "I need you to stop in on Sterling Price tomorrow before coming to work. Take your notary stuff. He has some documents he wants notarized, in addition to giving you something to bring back to me. I told him you'd be happy to do it. Sounds like some simple acknowledgments."

"Gee, thanks, Steele, for asking me first," I said sarcastically.

Actually, I didn't mind, though I was not about to say that to Steele. I like Sterling Price. He is one of my favorite clients, and his office is not too far out of my way. I just wanted to give Steele some grief for not checking with me first.

"He's expecting you at eight sharp," Steele said curtly, then hung up.

Rats. That meant I would have to skip my usual morning walk with Reality Check, a support group for large people. My friend Sophie London began the group. When she died, I became the group's leader. Reality Check meets every two weeks to dispense advice, comfort, and support, and to cheer on its members in their daily struggles in an unkind world. Each weekday morning at six, a small band of us walks a section of the Back Bay in Newport Beach. It's a great way to start the day, even if it means dragging my lazy ass out of bed an hour earlier than necessary.

TWO

THE CORPORATE OFFICES OF Sterling Homes are located in Newport Beach just off of Von Karman. Unlike most buildings that house multimillion-dollar businesses, it's a two-story sprawling structure with redwood trim and a peaked roof. Set back from the busy street and surrounded by parklike grounds that included lots of trees and picnic tables, it has an attractive yet artificially rustic appearance. The company had spent a great deal of money going for the mountain retreat theme, which I found to be both refreshing and disturbing plunked down in the middle of the sterile architecture of Orange County. I pulled into the entrance and followed the driveway as it wound around behind the building to a large parking lot. It was just a few minutes to eight and the parking lot was mostly empty.

Once through the main entrance, I approached the receptionist. She looked as if she had just arrived. I waited patiently while she put away her purse, settled herself in her chair, and put on her headset. The receptionist was Latina, with pretty, dark eyes and long, dark brown, curly hair pulled back and held captive by a large faux tortoiseshell barrette. She wore very heavy eye makeup and her full lips were outlined in a color much darker than her lipstick. I fought the urge to pull a tube of lipstick out of my own purse and color inside the lines. Her clothes were clean, inexpensive, and hip. She looked to be in her mid-twenties. The aroma of fresh coffee wafted up from an odd-looking mug that sat on her desk. On the mug's side, MOMMY was painted in primary colors. After asking my name and checking her appointment book, she informed me with a smile that Mr. Price's office was upstairs and all the way down the hall to the left. He was expecting me, she said pleasantly, and, after having me sign in on a guest register, directed me to an area just past her desk where I had the choice of taking an elevator or stairs to the next floor. My body begged for the elevator, but since I had missed my usual morning walk, my conscience opted for the stairs.

Walking down the upstairs hall, I encountered no other employees. From a distance came the lonely sound of a single computer keyboard being put to use. It sounded like it was coming from the opposite direction. I found Price's office exactly where the receptionist had said it would be. The door was open. I poked my head in and saw Sterling Price busy at a small kitchenette that had been discretely hidden behind folding doors. I knocked gently on the doorjamb.

Price looked up and smiled. "Come on in, Odelia." He gestured toward a small conference table to the right side of the office. "Please have a seat. I won't be but a minute."

After placing my briefcase on the table, I unpacked my notary supplies and sat down to enjoy the view from the large picture windows that lined one wall. Price's office took up the whole end section of the second floor that looked out over the prettiest part of the grounds. From his office viewpoint, there was no sighting or even suggestion of the office buildings and traffic that hovered so close. Somehow I was sure that was not an accident.

I had never been here before. I had met Sterling Price many times, but usually in our office and once, recently, at Mr. Wallace's retirement party. He and my former boss were very old friends, having grown up together in Orange County when it was nothing more than miles and miles of orange groves. Like Mr. Wallace, Price was in his seventies. He was on the short side, a bit pudgy and slightly balding. He was also outgoing and charming. His brown eyes twinkled when he spoke, and his laugh and good humor came easily. But his easygoing nature aside, the man had built an empire in the construction and sale of upscale housing developments, garnering critics and even enemies along the way, most notably among those concerned with the disappearance of Orange County's natural wildlife and vegetation.

The other walls of his office were lined with attractive bookcases, many with glass doors. Here and there, a painting or a grouping of framed photographs interrupted the shelving. I scanned the shelves from where I sat and then did a double take of the glassed-in units.

"Would you like some coffee, Odelia? I just made a fresh pot, a special blend I make myself every morning, a combination of French Roast and Sumatra."

"No, thank you, Mr. Price."

"You don't know what you're missing," he said teasingly as he waved the pot at me. It was less than half full.

With one deep sniff of the rich aroma, I caved. "Sure, if you have enough. Black, please."

He gave me a not-to-worry gesture and poured some for me. "This was the end of a bag," he said, "but I'm sure there's more stashed away. Carmen never leaves me coffee impaired." We both laughed.

He carried two navy blue mugs emblazoned with the Sterling logo in bold silver to the conference table and settled into a chair to my right. The coffee smelled wonderful and tasted even better—a big improvement over what awaited me at my office.

"And please, Odelia, call me Sterling. Goodness, we've known each other many years now," he said, smiling. He lifted his mug up and took a big whiff of the rich steam before continuing. "My staff usually comes in around nine o'clock. I wanted to get this taken care of before I got buried in my daily routine," he explained between sips of coffee. "Thank you so much for coming here before going to your own office."

"It was no trouble at all … uhh … Sterling," I said, trying on his first name like a pair of narrow shoes. He smiled again. "Happy to do it for you. I'm just surprised that your assistant isn't a notary, with you being in real estate."

"Carmen is a notary, but she's taking a few vacation days off this week. Actually, we have a couple of notaries on our staff, but these papers are personal." He looked at me directly. "I'm sure you understand."

And I did. There was nothing like tidbits of the boss's personal life to fuel lunchroom gossip. It was the same in law firms.

My attention kept going back to the items behind the glass doors. "Um, are those lunchboxes?" I asked, pointing in a very unladylike way to the items on the shelves across the room.

Price looked over to where I indicated and gave a hearty laugh. "Yes, as a matter of fact, they are. I collect them. Have for years." I must have had a puzzled look on my face because he laughed again. "When we're done here, I'll give you a tour of my collection."

"If you have time," I said politely. "I don't want to take up too much of your morning."

"Nonsense." He gave me one of his twinkling looks. "Besides, I never miss a chance to show them off, especially the jewel of my collection."

We finalized the papers quickly. The notarizations were simple acknowledgments, just as Mike Steele had said they would be. Then Price indicated a couple good-sized stacks of expanding folders.

"I need Mike to go through these documents. No rush. But I'll have them sent over later. They're too much for you to carry."

I nodded my appreciation of his courtesy. Mike Steele, on the other hand, would have just loaded me up like a pack mule in a mining camp.

"I'm glad you're still working with Mike, Odelia," he said as I packed up my briefcase.

Well, that makes one of us, I thought.

"I'm sure he's no picnic to work under," Price added, much to my surprise.

Suddenly, I wondered if I had slipped and verbalized my comment, but I was pretty sure I had not.

"But he's a brilliant attorney and needs someone like you to keep him organized and in line."

"I do my best," I told him honestly, trying to keep sarcasm out of my tone.

"God knows you did wonders with Dell," he said, chuckling, referring to Wendell Wallace. "Now come along and let me show you one of the world's best lunchbox collections. Just leave your things there."

Following his instructions, I left my stuff on the conference table and followed him over to the glass cases where there were, indeed, lunchboxes—dozens of them. The shelves were filled with colorful metal boxes, most of which were adorned with pictures of cartoon characters, comic book heroes, and TV legends. They brought back memories, and I recognized many of the boxes childhood friends had carried to school every day.

"I didn't realize people collected old lunchboxes," I said in amazement.

"My dear, where have you been?" he teased. "It's a very popular hobby, especially among men. And it can be increasingly expensive as the years go by and these boxes become even rarer."

"Which one was your first?"

He smiled broadly and opened up a glass door to remove one particular lunchbox. It looked well used, with small dents and scratches. Adorning the front, back, and sides were scenes from the TV show *Gunsmoke*. On the box's front was Marshal Matt Dillon, jaw set and gun drawn. Price held the box lovingly, almost cradling it.

"This was my son Eldon's lunchbox when he was a boy," he explained. "He loved anything with a cowboy theme, particularly this TV show."

Something struck me as off. I racked my brain but could not remember a son named Eldon. In fact, I could have sworn Sterling Price's son was named Kyle. I had just seen the name Kyle Price on some of the documents I notarized. A son named Kyle and a daughter named Karla—twins; that's what my middle-aged memory bank was dredging up.

"I didn't realize you had another son."

Price looked at the lunchbox as he spoke, his voice in a monotone. "Yes, I had a son named Eldon. Unfortunately, he had an accident. Fell from a tree when he was eleven and broke his neck."

"I'm terribly sorry."

He nodded acknowledgment of my condolences and continued. "Years later, I was reading an article about the hobby of collecting lunchboxes and remembered that we had kept this stored away. That was the beginning. I have more than a hundred now, most of which I purchased after my wife's death about eight years ago. She thought it silly but always kept her eyes open for them like a good sport." He extended an arm toward the boxes lined up before us. "These are among my favorites in the collection."

"And this *Gunsmoke* one is your prize box?"

"Only for sentimental reasons, dear lady. Value wise, it's only worth about one hundred fifty to two hundred dollars. It would be worth more if it were in better condition."

I swallowed hard. Two hundred dollars for a kid's beat-up lunchbox that still reeked of sour milk seasoned with rust? Sheesh.

He put the lunchbox back in its place and picked up the one displayed next to it. "This ... this is my crown jewel; the ultimate lunchbox; every collector's dream acquisition."

Price held the box out for my inspection, holding it gingerly by the top and bottom as if it were made of glass. It did not look like much to me, but then what do I know? I tote my lunch in paper sacks and old Blockbuster Video bags.

Except for a dent on one of its corners, this particular lunchbox did not have the bumps and bruises of the one before it, but neither was it festooned with colorful pictures. It was rather plain, the metal painted a dark blue. On one side it sported a primitive watercolor of a cowboy riding a horse and twirling his lasso over his head. Around the horse's hooves were some quickly drawn grass tufts and in the background a few cactus plants. The picture was not even painted on the box but stuck on. The cowboy depicted in the drawing was unknown to me.

Okay, what was I missing here? I kept looking at the box, hoping a clue to its desirability would pop out of it like a genie from a magic lamp. My eyes traveled up to meet Price's smiling face, quite sure that I looked as dense as I felt.

"Is it safe to assume that this lunchbox is worth more than the *Gunsmoke* one?"

He gave a mischievous laugh, almost a childish giggle. It was plain to see that Price delighted in showing off this particular treasure.

"Would you believe, Odelia, at least a hundred times more?"

In my mind, I quickly threw a couple of zeros after the two-hundred-dollar figure. "Holy shit!" I gasped, then immediately slapped my hand over my mouth. *Holy shit,* I thought in horror, *did I really just say "holy shit" to a client, and an important one at that?*

Price let loose with a real guffaw.

21

Ashamed of my unprofessional behavior, I apologized. "Mr. Price, I am so sorry. That was very inappropriate of me."

He laughed, reached a hand up, and patted me warmly on my right shoulder. "Sterling, dear, remember? And actually, Odelia, that was very close to my exact words when I first learned of its value." He leaned toward me. I could smell the coffee on his breath. "I paid twenty-seven thousand, eight hundred dollars for this trinket," he confessed with a sly whisper. "Just over a year ago." He nudged me good-naturedly. "Go ahead, say it. Say what you really want to say."

"Holy shit," I said, this time with reverence and without apology.

Price laughed heartily. "You're probably too young to know this, but have you ever heard of the cowboy star Chappy Wheeler?" I shook my head. "His real name was Charles Borden and he was from Newark, New Jersey. In the 1940s, he found his way to Hollywood and eventually landed a TV series, appropriately called *The Chappy Wheeler Show*. It was one of the first shows of its kind, right up there with the more familiar classic cowboy genre shows like *Hopalong Cassidy*, *Roy Rogers,* and even *Gunsmoke*.

"This lunch pail," he explained, holding the box up for my inspection, "was the prototype for the first known children's lunch-boxes depicting TV stars. See the artist's signature at the bottom of the picture?"

I looked closer and saw what looked like a tiny "Art Bender" scrawled near a bit of prairie grass.

"This is an original drawing. This box, Odelia, started it all. Years ago, it was nicknamed the Holy Pail. Cute, eh?"

I was puzzled. I watched a lot of TV as a kid, but I could not remember a Chappy Wheeler, not even in reruns.

Price put the box back behind the protective glass and shut the door gently. "Wheeler was murdered in 1949," he explained, as if reading my confusion. "Found dead in his bungalow on the studio lot. His killer was never found. *The Chappy Wheeler Show* was canceled and the lunchbox never manufactured. This box is all that remains of that promotional dream. Supposedly, it's cursed." He laughed softly.

I found the story fascinating, though hardly worth nearly thirty thousand dollars. "So what did become the first children's TV-themed lunchbox?" I asked.

"This one," he said, pointing to a box behind another glass door. On it was a character I knew well—Hopalong Cassidy. "This box debuted in 1950."

I strolled along the shelves looking at the different boxes. Except for a few that appeared to be in pristine condition, most showed signs of minor wear and tear. Many, I was sure, had a history of being proudly carried to and from school in the saner, more innocent times of the '50s and '60s.

I stopped short in front of one of the cases and stared at a lunchbox. It was black. On the front was Zorro, my favorite childhood TV character. What can I say? Zorro and the Sheriff of Nottingham—I had a thing for men in knee-high riding boots even then.

I sensed Price coming up behind me. "Was that your lunchbox, Odelia?" he asked. "We're always drawn to our own."

I shook my head, more to clear my mind of memories. "No, it wasn't. But I wanted this one as a kid." I turned and looked at

Price. "My mother said it was a boy's lunchbox. She made me carry a pink one with flowers and ribbons on it." I made a face. "Ugh."

He chuckled. "Junior Miss."

"Excuse me?"

"Junior Miss. That's the name of the lunchbox you probably carried to school."

"Hmm. All I know is that it wasn't very cool."

Price laughed again. "You had good taste, Odelia. Too bad your mother didn't listen. Today the Zorro box is much more valuable than the Junior Miss."

Somehow I knew that without being told.

THREE

"A LUNCHBOX WORTH THIRTY thousand dollars! Are you kidding me?"

I shook my head and finished chewing the food in my mouth before speaking. "Nope, telling you the truth."

The question had come from Joan Nunez, a litigation paralegal in our firm. She and Kelsey Cavendish, the firm's librarian and research guru, were treating me to a birthday lunch at Jerry's Famous Deli. In between taking bites from a mammoth Rueben sandwich and slurps of iced tea, I filled them in on my morning introduction to lunchbox memorabilia.

"Amazing," Joan said slowly as she played with her fries, dragging one through a puddle of ketchup. She was around forty, small boned, with dark features and expressive eyes, and very proper in her demeanor.

Kelsey plucked at the sleeve of my blouse. "Pssst, hey, look over there," she whispered.

Joan and I moved our eyes in the direction Kelsey indicated with jerks of her chin. It took me a while, but finally my gaze focused on what Kelsey wanted us to see—Mike Steele. And he was not alone. He sat in a booth on the other side of the restaurant with Trudie Monroe, his latest in a long line of assistants. Trudie had only been working at Woobie for about three weeks. She was a sweet woman about thirty years of age with a pixie face, long coppery hair, and a cute figure. And knockers, *big* knockers. In addition to Steele, Trudie was assigned to Jolene McHugh, a senior associate at the firm. She also did work for me on occasion, though generally I found it faster and easier to do my own secretarial work.

When a paralegal shares a secretary with two busy attorneys, especially if one is a partner, and definitely if one of the attorneys is Michael Steele, she can bet her next vacation day that her work will end up at the bottom of the assistant's pile. Overall, I found Trudie capable but not overly bright. Yep, huge boobies and not too smart—just the way Mike Steele likes 'em.

"You think they got nekkid yet?" Kelsey asked, imitating her husband's Texas twang. Kelsey was a plain, tall, and angular woman in her mid-thirties with a firecracker wit. She had married Beau Cavendish four years earlier after a whirlwind online courtship. He was a teacher in Houston at the time and relocated to Southern California just before they married. Like Kelsey, he was delightfully funny and his accent added to his folksy charm.

"You mean *naked*," Joan corrected her.

"Naw, girl. I mean *nekkid*." Kelsey looked at both of us in mock disgust before explaining. "Naked is when you don't have any clothes on. Nekkid is when you don't have any clothes on *and* you're up to no good."

Joan looked over at the couple and frowned. "I'm sure Trudie told me during her first week at Woobie that she was married."

I took a big draw of iced tea from my straw and pondered the budding relationship of Steele and his new secretary.

"Hard to say if they've been nekkid yet," I said, "but I bet he's working on it."

Kelsey and I giggled. Joan's frown deepened.

Later that afternoon at the office, two boxes were delivered to me from Sterling Homes. One was quite large and addressed to Mike Steele; the other, a small one, was addressed to me personally. I opened the smaller box. Inside was a lunchbox, the very same Zorro box I had seen earlier in Price's office, along with a hand-written note.

> *Odelia,*
> *Every child should carry the lunchbox of her dreams.*
> *Warmest regards,*
> *Sterling*

I could not believe it. After running my hands over every inch of the box in disbelief and adoration, I picked my way through my Rolodex until I found the number for Sterling Homes. I was so excited and overwhelmed my fingers had trouble punching the numbers. The value of the lunchbox was anyone's guess. It was enough that this generous man had given it to me. I also had doubts about whether or not I should accept it. Woobie employees were not allowed to accept gifts from vendors, but there was nothing in the employee handbook about gifts from clients. The call went through, but the receptionist informed me that Mr. Price was not answering. I thought about asking for his assistant, then remembered that she was off for a few days. At my request, I was put through to his voice mail, where I left a stumbling and gushing thanks for the box. I also made a mental reminder to write a proper thank-you note later tonight.

"Cool lunchbox!"

I looked up at the enthusiastic comment and my eyes fell on Joe Bays, the firm's mail clerk and jack-of-all-trades. Being rather roly-poly, Joe filled every inch of the doorway as he stood staring at the Zorro lunchbox on the edge of my desk. I detected a hungry look in his eye.

"You know about lunchboxes, Joe?" I motioned for him to come in and sit in the small chair across from my desk.

"A bit," he said, still eyeing the Zorro box. He reached for it, hesitating slightly. "May I?"

"Sure. I just got it today. It was a gift."

He sat down and picked it up. Turning it gently in his stubby fingers, he rotated it to see all of the pictures on the front, back, and four sides of the box. He opened it and I heard the still-familiar click of the metal latch and the squeaking of hinges. Inside was a matching thermos that I had already discovered. Joe put the box down, twisted the plastic top off the thermos, and then followed suit with the stopper. He inspected both, then peered inside the glass-lined bottle as if looking through a telescope.

When I went to school, boys like Joe were branded as nerds. I imagine they still are. He was soft both in his body and in his face, which was youthful like a pubescent boy's, spotted with mild acne, and looked out of place on his tall, doughy, adult body. His eyes were small and held both intelligence and humor, though most of the time he kept them averted. His light brown, fine hair was short but always looked in need of a trim. Overall, his daily appearance reminded me of an unmade bed.

Occasionally, Joe attended our biweekly Reality Check meetings. In the world of BBW's—Big, Beautiful Women—he was a BHM—Big, Handsome Man—and needed the same support as his plus-size sisters. Over the past several months, Reality Check had been graced with several BHM members, though their attendance was more sporadic than their female counterparts. I suspected that many came to the group shopping for girlfriends with whom they could be comfortable.

"This is in fine condition," Joe pronounced when he was through. "Just a few dings here and there from use. Where'd you get it again?"

"It was a gift," I answered, "from Sterling Price. You know, our client Sterling Homes."

"Wow, nice gift. Might be worth a couple hundred bucks."

I almost swooned. Now I knew I had to give it back. It was too expensive a gift to accept from someone I hardly knew, especially a client. Since Joe obviously knew something about lunchboxes, I gave him a rundown of my trip to Sterling Homes that morning. When I mentioned the Holy Pail, his eyes widened and his mouth hung open, creating a fleshy tunnel in the middle of his boyish face.

"The Holy Pail," he said slowly, quietly, almost with reverence, more to himself than to me. He slumped back in his chair in disbelief. "Wow. You really saw it?"

I nodded. Obviously, Joe was not someone who needed an explanation about the Chappy Wheeler lunchbox. Joe had a quiet way about him. He was very shy and introverted, especially around the women in the office. He always seemed comfortable with me, though, and I assumed it was because I was old enough to be his mother.

"I saw it with my own eyes," I assured him.

He looked at me eagerly, like a puppy hoping for a treat. "You know, they say it's cursed. Bad luck for its owner."

Of their own accord, my eyes rolled in amused disbelief.

"Do you think Mr. Price would show it to me? Would you ask him, Odelia?"

I smiled at his excitement. "I don't know, Joe. But if I get the chance, I'll ask him."

"Not enough work to do, Bays?" The question came from Mike Steele, who now took his turn standing in my doorway. Steele was above average in height, nicely built, and sported a classic profile, and, as always, was immaculately clothed in a designer suit. I might consider Steele a very attractive man if I did not already find him odious.

Obviously intimidated, Joe jumped up and started to leave. Once he was out the door and behind Steele, he grinned his ear-to-ear thanks to me and left.

Mike Steele entered my office and picked up the lunchbox Joe had replaced on my desk.

"Things so tough at home, Grey, you can only afford a used lunchbox?"

"It was a gift, Steele, from Sterling Price."

He raised one trimmed eyebrow and looked me over. "Really? I thought the old boy was engaged." He snickered. "His fiancée might not like this, not to mention your own squeeze."

I chose to not dignify his comment with a comeback. Instead, I indicated the larger box that sat on the floor and said, "He also sent this box over with it. Documents for you to review, I believe."

"Wrong, Grey, documents for *you* to review. We're looking for anything that might help us break Sterling's contract with Howser Development should the need arise. Look for suspicious chinks in their paperwork." He caught me checking out the size of the box. "Don't worry, Grey, we don't need them right away. There's a dispute brewing between the two companies that may or may not turn into something. We just want to be prepared in the event it does turn ugly." He put the lunchbox down and turned to leave. "Just complete the review within the next two weeks. I wouldn't want it to interfere with your love life."

Grrr.

I decided to take the box of documents home, thinking I could look over a batch each evening and on the weekends. I had too much day-to-day work to do it justice at the office. After informing Steele of my plan and receiving his blessing to take the box home, I asked Joe to lug it down to my trunk. He was still babbling about the Holy Pail.

Lunchboxes. Who knew?

Once at home, I turned on the TV, stroked the cat, and promised the dog a walk after dinner. A short trip to the kitchen and I was back with a handful of Fig Newtons as a before-dinner appetizer.

To my surprise, the evening news was reporting on an event in Newport Beach. Usually, nothing very exciting happens in Orange County, except maybe exceptionally high surf or government corruption. I paid closer attention to the TV and saw a photograph of a familiar face plastered in the upper right-hand corner of the screen. At the bottom of the screen were the words *Breaking News*. A reporter, young, handsome, and mahogany colored, was on-screen, reporting live from the scene. In the background was the corporate headquarters of Sterling Homes.

I fumbled with the clicker and aimed it at the TV to turn up the volume.

"It has been confirmed," the reporter said with deliberation into the microphone held tightly in his hand, "that Sterling Price, CEO and founder of Sterling Homes, the prestigious real estate development company headquartered in Newport Beach, was found dead this afternoon in his private office."

Wainwright never let the falling cookies hit the floor.

FOUR

THE CLEAN, FRESH AIR of the Back Bay was tainted this morning with the odor of skunk. I twitched my nose and continued walking at a brisk pace. On a leash and trotting happily just in front of me was Wainwright. Beside me, dressed in a lightweight, pastel pink warm-up suit, was Zee. Ahead of us, and moving a bit faster, was a larger group of women from Reality Check. It was just past six o'clock in the morning, and a damp mist hung over the lower portions of the bay like gauze. Soon it would burn off, as would the haze overhead, and the day would turn sunny and warm.

It was here along the trail of the Back Bay that I had been shot by a lunatic fifteen months ago; not exactly where we were walking now, but nearer to the beginning of the trail. The group had offered to change the venue of our daily walks, but I had insisted we keep it the same. I needed to prove to myself that I could move on and put the ordeal behind me. So almost every morning I forced myself to walk along the place where I had nearly died. It was my daily dose of mortality. This morning, because of Sterling Price's death the day before, the location brought on more than just the usual little shudder.

Zee was only recently a regular on these daily walks. Like the little engine who could, she matched me stride for stride, her huffing and puffing lessening each day she walked. By nature, Zee was not a morning person, and in the past what early energy she could muster was spent getting her family out the door for the day. But these days her little nest was nearly empty, and she was in a funk. Hannah, her nineteen-year-old daughter, had just left to start her second year at Stanford. Her son Jacob, who was now sixteen, was off on an end-of-summer camping trip.

"Seems," Zee said, slightly out of breath, "like that man could have found something more important to do with thirty thousand dollars." We were just reaching the crest of a small hill that led to the parking lot and the end of our walk. "I hope he at least left some of it to charity in his will."

I had just finished telling Zee about Sterling Price's hobby. His death weighed heavily on my mind as I walked the trail robotically. I had just seen him the day before and now he was dead, another reminder of the impermanence of life. Here today, dead tomorrow.

It had almost happened to me, and it could happen to anyone at any time, including Zee. I shivered at my last thought and glanced over at her with frightened affection. The sight brought a smile to my face. In the warm-up suit, she looked like fluffy pink cotton candy wrapped around a fudge center. Losing Zee would be like losing a sister or even a limb, maybe worse. Yet loss was part of the price of living; just ask the families of those recently murdered people at the community center. It was just not a price I was willing to pay in cash. In my book, that kind of debt was still available on credit.

The TV news had reported that Sterling Price had died from heart failure. I reminded myself that he had been in his seventies, then thought of my father. Dad was in his eighties and still going strong. Automatically, I wrapped my knuckles lightly against my skull.

"Have you decided what to tell Greg?" Zee asked.

I stopped abruptly, yanking Wainwright back. I gave the animal a look of apology, then looked at Zee, then back at the dog, fuzzy about the topic at hand. Both looked at me expectantly. Then I refocused my thoughts and looked back again at Zee.

"I still don't know, Zee," I sighed. "I'm no closer to an answer than I was on Sunday."

We started walking again, this time in silence, and did not stop until we were at our cars. The other women were already in their vehicles and waving out the windows as they drove off. I bundled Wainwright into the back seat of my car and shut the door, being careful of his tail. I gave the cotton candy a quick hug, climbed into the front seat, and headed for home and my morning shower.

I HAD JUST RETRIEVED my second cup of coffee from the firm's kitchen when the phone in my office rang. I could see on the telephone display that it was Mike Steele. I got my groans out of the way quickly before picking up the receiver.

"Morning," I said, giving him my best Little Mary Sunshine impersonation.

"Get in here, Grey. Now." His voice was serious but lacked its usual sneer. I knew him well enough to know that that signaled a potential real problem and not just him playing God. I hung up, picked up a pen and a yellow legal pad, and headed straightaway to his office.

I popped into his sanctuary, expecting a briefing on some unexpected client crisis, and stopped dead in my tracks. Steele was not alone. Sitting across from him were two men. One was a stranger to me and one I knew well, but had not seen in a long time—Detective Devin Frye of the Newport Beach Police.

Detective Frye is a giant of a man. He stands well over six feet tall and is built like a solid, functional building. His age is somewhere in his fifties and he has a full head of curly hair cropped close to his skull, blond mixed with gray. His eyes are blue and his voice deep and gravelly. When he saw me, he stood up and offered me his huge right paw. I was reminded of Wainwright. We shook. Greg and I had gotten to know the detective when he was investigating the suspicious death of our friend Sophie London. We both thought him tops and occasionally ran into him around Orange County.

"Dev, what a surprise," I said, giving him a warm but slight smile.

Dev introduced me to the man at his side. "Odelia, this is my partner, Detective Kami Zarrabi."

Detective Zarrabi and I shook hands. He was a wiry man of average height with olive skin and big, deep brown eyes. His moustache and eyebrows were both bushy, like three black caterpillars marching parallel across his face. His shake was dry and confident.

Something was wrong. If Dev Frye was here, there must be a problem, a big one. He would not be in Steele's office if it were a social call. To my knowledge, he did not even know Mike Steele. I turned to Steele. He sat silent, his face pasty, brows knitted together. I had never seen him look so upset. I looked back to Dev and widened my eyes in question. Dev Frye worked homicide.

"We need to ask you some questions, Odelia," Frye said.

"About Price, Grey," Steele announced in an unusually subdued tone. "About his murder."

"I—uh … ahhh … ," I staggered a couple of feet and planted my behind hard into a chair across from Steele's desk. "But I thought he died from heart failure."

"It's just a formality, Odelia," Frye said. "About what time did you last see him?" I looked over at him and noted that he now held the small notebook that he kept in his jacket pocket. He was poised to scribble something in it.

"Murder?" I squeaked out, ignoring the comment about his presence being just a formality.

Frye continued. "Price was found by a secretary around four thirty. We know he returned from lunch around one."

"Murder?" I squeaked again, my brain stuck like a needle on an old vinyl record.

"Actually," Zarrabi chimed in, "we're not sure of the exact cause. We do know that he had a heart attack. He was found slumped in his private bathroom. The coroner's office will do an autopsy, of course."

Frye pulled up a chair near mine and sat down. Unfortunately, this would not be the first time he had found it necessary to question me about something horrible. I knew the drill.

"So, tell me, Odelia, when did you see Sterling Price last?"

I gave the detectives a full verbal report of my visit to Sterling Homes the day before, including the purpose of the visit, and ended with the gift of the lunchbox and my call to Price's office. Frye asked to see the Zorro lunchbox and followed me back to my office. We left Zarrabi with Mike Steele, who was slumped in his chair, staring vacantly out a window.

"Lunchboxes, who knew," Frye said, looking the Zorro lunchbox over, inside and out. I smiled slightly at the comment and tried to shake off the lingering shock the word *murder* had produced. "You said Price showed you his collection while you were there?"

"Yes, after our meeting. It was quite fascinating, actually."

"So it seems." With a simple hand gesture he invited me to sit in my own desk chair. He closed the door and sat in the visitor's chair across from me. In my small, cramped space, he appeared like a giant in a child's playhouse. "I was a Hopalong Cassidy fan myself," he said without emotion.

There was a pause in the conversation. He seemed to be thinking of something, but the set of his jaw told me it was not Sterling Price. I saw him glance over at the framed photo on my desk. It was of Greg and me, taken last Christmas.

"How is Mrs. Frye?" I asked. Dev's wife had been battling ovarian cancer for several years.

He looked directly into my eyes, then down at his huge hands, which still held the lunchbox. He gently put the box back on my desk.

"Janet died almost two months ago."

Tears sprang to my eyes. I had never met Janet Frye but I thought the world of her husband and daughter. I sniffled slightly to keep control and searched my brain for something comforting to say. But there was nothing to say beyond polite condolences.

"I'm very sorry, Dev. I didn't know."

He nodded slightly. "It was for the best. Near the end, she was so doped up on pain medication she wasn't really living. She did get to see her grandchild, though." In spite of his still-raw grief, he smiled.

"A grandbaby! How wonderful for you, Dev. Congratulations."

"Thanks." He pulled out his wallet and produced a small photo of his daughter holding a very young infant. "Her name is Michelle Janet. She's three months old now."

Smiling at the photo, I thought about how one life had replaced another in the Frye family. I wondered if anyone would replace Sterling Price in his.

Dev closed his wallet and put it back in his pocket. "Tell me, Odelia, do you know of any reason why someone would want to see Sterling Price dead?"

"So it's true—you do think it's murder."

"I think there are many possibilities. We won't be sure until the autopsy is complete, particularly the toxicology report."

"Toxicology? As in poison? But I thought you said he had a heart attack."

"Price was violently ill just before he expired, which, of course, doesn't necessarily mean foul play. And he did have a heart attack. I just want to look into other possibilities while I wait for the report." He brought out his notebook and became all business, putting away his personal sadness as simply as if he had tucked it away in his pocket with the photo of Michelle Janet. "I asked Mr. Steele the same questions," he continued. "In your acquaintance with Price, is there anyone you are aware of that might have wanted to harm him?"

Leaning back in my chair, I looked up at the ceiling and combed my memory for anything that could be of help.

"He was always battling the local environmentalists," I told him. "But I'm sure you already know that from the newspapers." Frye nodded. I was about to mention the potential problem with Howser Development but stopped myself short, worried about a breach of client confidentiality. Our client was dead, but the company, also our client, was still active. I wasn't sure what I could ethically say, so I said nothing about the matter. "Any questions having to do with his business affairs," I advised Frye, "will have to come from someone like Mike Steele."

"I understand," he said simply.

"You know, Dev," I said, leaning forward, my elbows on the desk. "I knew Sterling Price for many years, but I didn't *really* know him. He was a client and a friend of my former boss, Wendell Wallace. And except for polite pleasantries, we didn't really get very chummy. I'm not sure I can be of much help."

"But he did show you his lunchbox collection?" he asked with a raised eyebrow.

"Is that like showing me his etchings?"

"I didn't mean it in that way, Odelia," Dev said, chuckling and shaking his head in amusement. "But he did show you the boxes he kept in his office?"

I relaxed and smiled a little, comfortable with this particular cop. "Yes, in fact, he was very proud of them."

"And did he show you ... ," Dev flipped back in his notebook until he located the bit of information he needed. "Did he show you one called the Holy Pail? The box with the picture of Chappy Wheeler, the old TV cowboy star?"

"Why, yes," I answered. "In fact, he specifically called it the jewel of his collection. Told me he paid nearly thirty thousand dollars for it." I looked at Dev suspiciously. What would a lunchbox have to do with a possible murder? "Why?"

Dev ignored my question and continued his line of questioning. "So the Holy Pail was there yesterday morning when you left?"

I nodded, my curiosity rising. "He even took it out of the cabinet so I could get a closer look at it."

"Did you see Price put it back into the cabinet?"

"I think so." I closed my eyes and tried to summon up the exact order of events from yesterday morning. My memory played on the back of my closed eyelids like a movie on a screen. I saw the lunchbox and I saw Price replacing it on the shelf inside the glass cabinet. "Yes," I said, opening my eyes. "Definitely. He put it back just before I spotted this box." I indicated the Zorro lunchbox. "Why?" I asked again.

"According to the family, it's now missing."

"Missing?" I said incredulously, my mind whirring around the information, trying to quickly process it. "Do you think someone killed him to steal it?" He shrugged noncommittally. My mind kept grinding away like an overloaded hard drive. I heard Dev laugh quietly.

"You doing my job, Odelia?"

"Huh?"

"I can tell you're already trying to piece together the crime, if there is one."

"Just seems odd, doesn't it?" I shifted my mind into a higher gear. "Maybe someone took the box after he was discovered and before the authorities arrived. After all, it was worth a great deal of money."

"My job, Ms. Grey," he said, shaking his head slowly once again, "is to ask the questions and formulate theories based on fact. Yours is to answer the questions to the best of your ability."

I ignored his polite "butt out" and kept working the possible angles. "Was the secretary who found him the only person to enter his office after he was found?" My gray matter shifted upward again and I prayed my middle-aged transmission held out. "I know his personal assistant was out on vacation, but didn't anyone check on him during the whole afternoon? And what about visitors? Did you check with the receptionist to see if anyone logged in for an appointment?"

Detective Devin Frye stood up and looked at me with concerned amusement. "I'm going to have to call Greg and tell him to keep you under wraps for a few days. Handcuff you to his wheelchair if he has to."

"Greg's out of town." I said with attitude. "Besides, I'm just trying to help."

"You've already helped. You answered my questions." He pulled out his business card and handed it to me. "And if you think of anything else, call me."

We both rose and together walked from my office down the hall to the reception area, collecting Detective Zarrabi along the way. The offices of Wallace, Boer, Brown and Yates were tastefully decorated with modern watercolors hung on pastel-hued walls. It gave the offices an overall look of peacefulness, which belied the true hysteria that lurked within the walls of any busy law firm. Along the way, we passed attorney offices on our left and assistant bays on our right and were serenaded by the clack of keyboards. Most of the attorneys had their office doors open, and a glance showed the residents hard at work talking into dictation equipment or on the phone. Steele's office door was one of the only ones closed, but that was normal for him.

Once at the elevators, Dev looked directly into my eyes. I was wearing flat shoes today and he was so tall he had to tilt his head forward, nearly chin to chest, to accommodate my short stature.

He spoke sternly, but his blue eyes danced. "You're not to go looking into anything on your own, Odelia. That's an order."

My attitude about taking orders was clearly stamped on my face, but I answered dutifully. "Don't worry about that. I left my amateur sleuthing behind when I got shot. I've only got one good butt cheek left."

"Good," he said with finality and gave me a grin. Following a warm shake of my hand, he disappeared with his partner into an elevator.

The rest of the day went by slowly. No matter what I did to divert my attention, it kept coming back to the death of Sterling Price and the possibility that he had been murdered. Dev said he had been violently ill just before his death, yet he had looked robust and energetic that morning at our meeting. And the missing lunchbox, what about that? Shoot, I forgot to ask Dev if any of the other boxes were missing or disturbed. Now if I ask, he will think I'm snooping. But I'm not. I'm just curious.

Liar, liar, pants on fire.

FIVE

A GIGANTIC OREO COOKIE hung on the front entrance of the Sterling Homes corporate headquarters. I shook my head, removed my sunglasses, and did a double take. This time, I saw a huge, black funeral wreath. I made a mental note to call for an eye appointment. Soon. The black wreath stood sentry. Its full, curving, black satin bows guarded the dignity of the grief contained within the building's walls, warning visitors to subdue their actions and lower their voices.

At the front desk was the same receptionist I had met two days prior, but today she looked drawn and her eyes were puffy. Her curly dark hair was worn loose and wild around her face. She wore less eye makeup than before, and what little she had was smudged, adding to her stricken appearance. I juggled a large floral arrangement from my right arm to my left and signed the guest sheet. I had taken an early lunch today to bring by the flowers.

Okay, I know it seems terribly cold-hearted and manipulative to use flowers as a way back into Sterling Homes, and obviously

I am not above such trickery, but I really did want to do something nice for Price's staff. I would have done it yesterday, but the corporate offices had been closed down for one day, following the founder's death.

"I'd like to speak with whoever is filling in for Mr. Price's assistant," I said in a respectful whisper to the receptionist.

"Filling in?" the young woman asked, her own voice lowered. "But Mrs. Sepulveda is here today."

"Oh," I said with slight surprise. "I thought she was on vacation."

"She was, but she came back early because of ...," she let her words drift as she sniffed back the beginnings of fresh tears. "She came back because of Mr. Price, because of what happened."

I looked at her sadly. "I understand. Yes, if she's here, I'd like to see her. My name is Odelia Grey, I'm a paralegal from Wallace, Boer, Brown and Yates."

While she pressed buttons on her console to announce me to Carmen Sepulveda, I casually thumbed back through the guest register, looking for Monday's page. I kept flipping pages but could not find it; all the sheets were blank.

"I remember you, you know," the receptionist said quietly, pushing her unruly hair back behind her left ear. "You were here Monday to see Mr. Price. I'm very good at remembering people." She looked at my fingers traveling through the sign-in sheets. "The police took the visitor's list," she told me with a sigh.

"Yes, I figured as much. They came to see me about my appointment that day." I leaned in closer to her. "Do you remember who else was here Monday to see Mr. Price?"

"The police asked me that, too. They thought maybe someone had gotten by me without signing in. But you were the only visitor to see Mr. Price on Monday." She looked put out. "I take my job very seriously, you know," she told me, her voice rising slightly before she caught herself and lowered it again.

"I'm sure you do."

"The only time I'm not here is for my lunch hour and breaks, and then Amy fills in for me. Neither of us would ever let someone in without them signing the book. It's company policy, you know." Her phone rang and she answered it, still frowning at the suggestion that she might have slipped up on Monday. She said a few quiet words into the mouthpiece of her headset, then tilted her head back up to me.

"Carmen said she can see you now. Should she come get you, or do you remember the way?"

"I remember."

She said a few more words into the mouthpiece, then looked at me again. "You can go right on up. Carmen's desk is directly across from Mr. Price's office." Her eyes began to pool as she spoke his name.

I started toward the elevators, then stopped and turned back. "Miss ... uh ... I'm sorry, I don't know your name."

"Rosemary," she answered, giving me a small, sad smile, her even teeth framed in rose with a burgundy wine border.

I smiled back at her in sympathy. "Rosemary," I repeated, in an action meant to help me remember it later. "I'm very sorry for your loss—for the company's loss." Her mouth bravely tried to continue the smile but failed, and her large, dark eyes threatened to spill.

"Who was the unfortunate person to find Mr. Price?" I asked her quickly. "Do you know?"

"Sure I know," she answered, my question clearly insulting her. "It was Amy, Amy Chow, the girl who sits here during my breaks and lunchtime. I go to lunch every day from eleven thirty to twelve thirty. Amy has lunch from twelve thirty to one thirty."

"Does she work directly for Mr. Price?" I asked, trying not to appear too eager for the information.

Rosemary shook her head. "Not really. Carmen was gone and Amy was sitting at her desk, just in case Mr. Price needed anything. She's sort of a floater, you know. She fills in whenever anyone is out sick or on vacation."

I nodded slightly at Amy's job description. Law firms often employ individuals as floaters. "I understand Mr. Price wasn't found until after four—that no one saw him after lunch. Didn't Amy find that odd?"

I kept up with the questioning, asking each question in a soft, soothing voice. Rosemary did not seem to think it strange that I was so curious. The poor girl had probably told her story so many times to the authorities she could repeat it with the monotonous repetition of a pull-string doll.

"Not really." The young woman gave a light shrug of her slim shoulders. "Mr. Price often told us to hold calls and not disturb him. I think he liked working alone in his office, you know. It wasn't unusual at all."

"Thank you, Rosemary," I said, then continued to the elevators, digesting the information along the way.

She was right. A busy executive shutting himself up in his office to work was not all that unusual anywhere. Many of the attorneys at the firm did it, especially when faced with a court filing or trial preparation. Mike Steele did it often. Those were the times I treasured most.

I had never met Sterling Price's assistant, only spoken to her on the telephone over the years. Her greeting was formal but friendly.

"Odelia, how nice of you to come," she said softly, greeting me and extending her hand as I exited the elevator.

Carmen Sepulveda is a formidable, no-nonsense kind of woman pushing sixty. Efficiency glowed from her as if emphasized with a yellow Hi-Liter. Her dark hair was laced with steel gray and worn cropped short, close to her small, tidy head. Her body was trim and fit in her dark, severely cut business suit and durable, low-heeled pumps. She wore half-lens reading glasses that she peered over as she spoke. Only her brown eyes and the curve of her mouth, both surrounded by fine lines, spoke of warmth and kindness.

I handed her the flowers. "I wanted to deliver these in person and let you know how very sorry I am about Sterling's passing." She took the vase. "You might want to add a bit of water," I said. "I had to drain them for the trip here."

"How very thoughtful of you," she responded, genuinely touched.

She took the flowers and together we walked down the hall, not speaking until we reached the executive suites. She put the flowers down on a table in the small waiting area outside of Price's office and rotated the vase until she felt satisfied that the flowers had their best faces forward. Then she motioned for me to take a seat on the small L-shaped leather sofa. She sat on the other end.

"I'm afraid we'll have to chat out here. Sterling's office and conference room are still off-limits."

I looked at the large, black-lacquered double doors ahead of me with the engraved plaque "STERLING PRICE" set in the middle of the left door. There was still yellow crime-scene tape across it.

"Can I get you something, Odelia? Coffee, soft drink?"

"Thank you, but no. I'm fine." I looked at the woman and wondered how to begin. I was sure she was not going to gush information like the receptionist downstairs. Personal assistants like Carmen made careers out of discretion. "I don't mean to keep you, Carmen," I said, deciding to give truth a try. "But I'm upset and more than just a bit bewildered by all of this."

She nodded with a small downturned smile. "Yes, as we all are. I understand you saw Sterling on Monday morning."

"Yes, and he seemed fine to me. Perky, in fact."

"Yes, he was always a morning person. Liked to get in early before most of the staff."

"You worked for him a long time, didn't you?"

She sighed. "It would have been twenty-seven years next month." She gave a wry chuckle. "I was with Sterling Price longer than I was with my husband."

I smiled in understanding. "I was with Wendell Wallace a long time myself. It's kind of like a marriage, isn't it?"

"Yes," she said sadly, more to herself than to me. "I feel as if I've been widowed twice."

I reached over and touched her arm gently. "I'm glad it wasn't you who found him," I told her.

"I wish I had, Odelia." She spoke in a tone that struggled to stay even. "Maybe I would have looked in on him earlier and would have had time to get help. The poor girl who did discover his body was devastated. She's from our administrative department, just a clerk and very young."

Her surprising chattiness caused a tingle of excitement to run through me like low voltage. Maybe Carmen was going to give me some insight after all.

"The police told me," I said, hoping to loosen more information, "that he was very ill just before he died."

"That's what I was told," she said, tightening her lips and looking at the closed doors. "Apparently he had vomited a great deal just before … expiring. And he was soaked with perspiration." She looked back at me, her eyes wide with fresh grief. "Even though he had a heart attack, I know the police suspect poison," she said, the last word catching in her throat. "Who in God's name would want to poison that dear man?"

Quickly, and without a word, Carmen rose and picked up the flowers. She took them just a few steps down the hall. I got up and followed. She stopped in front of a small kitchenette built into the wall, similar to the one in Price's office. It was equipped with a coffee maker, the standard coffee pots—a brown pot for regular, an orange-collared pot for decaf—and a small sink and refrigerator. A dispenser for tea bags and hot chocolate packets stood on the counter. Carmen put the vase in the sink and began to add water to the arrangement.

"It was probably just a very bad case of food poisoning, that's all," she said in a barely composed voice as she fussed with the flowers. "He always liked eating in those small, dingy, out-of-the-way places."

"What about the lunchbox, Carmen? The missing box—the Holy Pail?"

She left the flowers alone and turned to me, surprisingly agitated. "I have no idea what happened to it, Odelia. And I don't care. That silly thing brought him nothing but aggravation, though he wouldn't admit it. In fact, I think he bought it just because of that stupid curse legend." She picked up the vase, wiped it off with a paper towel, and carried it back to the table.

I hurried after her, hoping not to upset her further with my questions. "What kind of aggravation?" I asked. "It was just a lunchbox, albeit an expensive one."

"Shortly after he bought it, Sterling was featured in a business magazine, a fluff piece about his acquisition of the lunchbox. You know, boys and their toys," she said with quiet sarcasm and a slight roll of her eyes, "that sort of thing. The article was called *The Curse of the Holy Pail—Fate or Fancy*. After the article was published, he got calls from all kinds of crackpots, many predicting his death and offering to take the box off his hands. Some for free—as a service, of course." She smiled cynically. "Others offered handsome profits." She straightened the front of her suit jacket and I could tell she was getting antsy. "Probably some fool took off with it before the police arrived," she continued. "After that article, everyone in the building knew about it and its worth."

"Do you have a copy of the article?" I asked. "I'd like to see it."

"Sorry, Odelia," she said, shaking her head slowly. "But the police took the only copy I had, as well as old phone message pads. I'm sure they're going to look into its disappearance and the crazies that called about it, though most of them never left messages, just voice mails that we erased. Fortunately, most gave up calling a while back."

In my head, I drafted a partial lie. "Carmen, if anyone else contacts you about the lunchbox, could you let me know? I have a friend at the office that is fascinated by the Holy Pail legend. I think he'd like to chat with others who are equally obsessed."

Carmen looked at me with sad amusement. "I'm afraid Sterling's death may bring the nuts back out of the woodwork, Odelia. So, sure, I'd be happy to re-route them someplace else."

I gathered my purse and held out my hand. I wanted to stay longer and ask her more questions, but Carmen looked long past weary. "Thank you for your time, Carmen. I'm sorry we had to meet under these circumstances."

"No, thank *you*, Odelia, for remembering us so graciously." She took my hand in one of hers and indicated the flowers with her other.

I started to walk toward the elevator but thought of something. I turned around.

"Carmen, I'm sorry, but one more thing." She smiled patiently, the emotional wear and tear of the past couple days plain on her face. "What about his family?" I asked. "Would one of them have taken the box?"

She shook her head and her face tightened. "They're the ones looking for it. They're the ones who originally noticed it missing, even before the body was cold. They know a quick and profitable liquidation when they see it."

"Money problems?" I asked.

"With them, always."

"And his fiancée? I understand he was engaged."

"*Was* is the correct word, Odelia. Sterling broke it off less than two weeks ago. He finally discovered he was being hoodwinked by a gold digger." She lifted her head in a defiant gesture. "Something I could have told him months ago."

SIX

I WAS IN COUNTDOWN for Greg's return. Knowing him, he would expect an answer to his proposal within minutes of seeing me. During the past three days, he had called every night before bed to say goodnight. Not once did he mention the engagement ring, but I could tell he was dying to question me about my pending answer. Greg had promised that he would give me these few days to think, and he always kept his promises. I knew my delay was killing him, but I just wasn't ready to give him an answer. Our nightly conversations had centered instead on the animals and Sterling Price's death. Like Detective Frye, Greg had admonished me to keep out of it.

In trying to come up with an answer for Greg, I had gone so nuts the night before as to draw up a pros and cons list, then tore it up when I realized that my answer could not be melted down into clinical categories. I was not trying to decide between a Ford and a Chevy. This was my life. This was Greg's life.

I did not have this much trouble saying yes to Franklin Powers. In fact, I had leapt to accept his ring. Maybe that was the problem. I had already chosen badly once. My heart had refused to read the red flags my head had seen and led me into a bad situation. Now my heart was asking my head for advice and getting the cold shoulder. In short, I was an emotional goulash.

Was love supposed to be this confusing? I love Greg. Why couldn't I just say yes to him? Why was I making this so torturous? I have never been happier. I adore the man. I lust for him. I like him as a person. Couldn't our other differences be ironed out later?

Tonight was a Reality Check night and my mind was elsewhere. The Reality Check meetings were usually held at Zee's house. When the weather was nice, which was most of the time in Orange County, we held them on her back patio.

Before each meeting the group enjoys refreshments and a bit of socializing. I took my paper plate of fruit kabobs and cheese and moved away from the others to sit in a lounge chair near the swimming pool. I stared into the blue water, the plate in my hand forgotten. The underwater lights gave it an ethereal look, as if heaven itself floated in the depths, just within, yet still beyond, my grasp. It had been here that I had met Greg Stevens for the first time. Right here, in this very spot, by this very pool. Sigh.

"Don't jump, 'cause I can't swim," I heard a voice behind me say. I turned to see Joe Bays standing near my chair, holding a red plastic tumbler. He smiled shyly down at me. I smiled back and motioned with my head toward the chair next to me.

"Hey, Joe, glad you're here tonight."

"Thanks. Always enjoy the meetings. By the way, who's that new girl, the one with the long, curly, red hair?"

I thought a minute, then turned to study the people gathered in the main patio area until I focused on who he was speaking about. I smiled. Joe had good taste.

"Her name's Sharon. She's twenty-four, a graduate of UC Irvine, and currently lives in Laguna Beach, where she's an artist. Pottery, I believe. This is only her second meeting."

"You got all that in just her first meeting?" he asked, teasing, but I could tell he was thankful for the information. I watched him as he studied the pretty woman. His look was appreciative of her ample charms, but not vulgar. He had a slightly silly grin plastered on his face when he turned his attention back to me.

"Is it true, Odelia, that the Holy Pail is missing?" he asked.

"That's what I understand."

He whistled. "Wow, it's worth a lot of money to someone."

"Joe," I asked, forming my question as I spoke, "how easy would it be for someone to resell something like that? I mean, especially since it's not rightfully theirs and is well known to collectors?"

He took a sip of his drink and leaned back in his chair to think about my question.

"Depends on how fast someone wants to dump it, I suppose. The quicker the sale, the less bidding there'll be, the lower the price," he explained. "It's stolen, so it's not likely to show up on eBay or be associated with a well-known auction house. The major collectors may already know about Price's death. News like that spreads fast in such a tight and specialized community. For sure, they'll be on the lookout for it and will take note of who's selling it if anyone does try."

"So why would someone buy it, knowing it's stolen? They can't display it or show it off."

"Why do collectors buy stolen art masterpieces?" he countered, answering my question with a question. Joe took a drink and cast another glance at the cute redhead before continuing. "It's an ego trip," he explained, "the pride of secret ownership. For some, it doesn't matter that they can't tell anyone. It's more titillating that they can't—like a private joke played on the world. It's quite possible that the Holy Pail is already in the hands of a collector."

"That fast?" I asked, surprised.

"That fast," he answered with a snap of his fingers. "It's one of a kind and irreplaceable. When the rich want something, they usually get it."

I thought about that as I turned my eyes back to the glowing, blue water. "The police think Price might have been murdered," I said to Joe as I continued to stare into the water. I turned to look at him and saw his small eyes bulging at the news. "You don't think anyone would kill him for a lunchbox, do you?"

Recovering quickly from his shock, he shot me an amused look. "People have killed for a lot less than that."

I shook my head sadly. He was right. People killed for senseless reasons every day. The daily news bore witness of that.

I thought about Carmen Sepulveda and how outraged she had been at the idea of someone wanting to poison Sterling Price. What was it she had said? "Who in God's name would want to poison that dear man?" Let's see, for starters: a cast-off fiancée, a money-hungry family, environmentalists, lunchbox connoisseurs. It was beginning to look like a ticket holder's line at a sold-out performance.

Zee was calling out that the Reality Check meeting was about to start. Joe and I both got up and started toward the others. I put a hand on his arm and stopped him.

"Joe, I know this was before your time, but what do you know about Chappy Wheeler and the Holy Pail? Anything beyond the fact that the box is valuable?"

He smiled at the question and looked down at the ground. Something told me he knew a lot about the subject.

"I'm a bit of a TV historian," he said, blushing. "I know that sounds kind of geeky, but it's a hobby of mine."

"It's not geeky, lots of people follow TV and film," I said reassuringly. "Was *The Chappy Wheeler Show* on the air long?"

"Nope, only about a year and a half, I think. But it was very popular. First show of its kind. It ended when Wheeler was murdered. I don't think they ever found his killer."

That was pretty much what Sterling Price had told me. "Do you have any information on him and the show?"

He lit up like a hundred-watt bulb at my interest. "Sure I do. I have articles, posters, stuff like that. And I can get you more, if you like. In fact, just today there was a small article in the *L.A. Times* about lunchboxes. I'll get you a copy of that, as well."

We started walking in the direction of the meeting. "That would be great, Joe. Thanks."

After a few steps, Joe stopped again. I halted with him. He seemed to be making up his mind about something.

"Be careful, Odelia," he finally said in a hushed voice. "The Holy Pail really is cursed."

A chill ran up my spine like a squirrel scurrying up a tree. "You don't really believe that, do you?" I said with a nervous giggle, trying to shake the creepy feeling off.

"Listen to me," he said, looking straight at me, his shyness gone. "Every owner of the Holy Pail has died."

"Joe," I said in a plea of frustration, "it's just a damn lunchbox!"

CURSED OR NOT, JOE came through with the information about the Holy Pail and Chappy Wheeler. I found a box of stuff over a half-foot high in the middle of my desk when I arrived at the office the next morning. On the very top were printouts from websites devoted to collecting lunchboxes. The sites that included the history of the hobby all mentioned Chappy Wheeler and the Holy Pail. Just under the loose papers was a magazine with a yellow sticky note on the front. *O—Please read the article on page 23!* Joe had printed precisely on the Post-It. The items under the magazine were about Chappy Wheeler, aka Charles Borden, mostly articles and promos designed to feed the active fan base of his heyday. The magazine was a past copy of *American Executive*. I leafed through it until I found page twenty-three, then I blessed Joe. Here in my hands was the article about Sterling Price and his lunchbox collection. There was even a photo of him proudly holding the Chappy Wheeler lunchbox. Price's mischievous eyes twinkled out at me from the glossy pages. He looked more like an aging boy than an elderly, big-business tycoon.

It made me sad. Then it made me mad. Four days ago, this man was alive and was a small part of my life. Someone had wanted him dead and had carried it out. It was probably none of my business, but I wanted to know who and why.

I looked at my watch. It was nine fifteen in the morning. Greg would be back this afternoon. His parents were picking him up at the airport and taking him home. The plan was for him to come down to my place to pick up Wainwright and take me to dinner. I'm sure he hoped it would be a celebration dinner. My phone rang and I was glad for the interruption, even if the display did show the caller was Mike Steele.

"Yes?" I said into the receiver in a voice that even I thought was a bit too edgy.

"Grey?" he asked.

"Who'd you expect?"

"Gawd, you sound like you're hung over. Have a bad night?"

"Is it any of your business if I did?" I knew this was not the tone I should be taking with a superior, but I didn't care. I looked down again at the magazine. Sterling Price's inner child leaped out from the slick paper. Senseless deaths make me cranky.

"Only if it affects your work, Grey." Steele paused, waiting for a smart-ass volley from my side of the net. When he did not get one, he continued, but sounded disappointed. "Hold off on that Sterling Homes document review job."

"Okay. Haven't started it yet," I told him, trying to even out my tone of voice. "I was going to this weekend."

"Nah, don't do anything for now," Steele said. "I just heard from Jackson Blake, Sterling's senior VP. No further work is to be done on anything until he reviews all of the company's outstanding projects and gives a summary to the board."

Steele was on his speakerphone. I could hear his chair squeaking in a steady pattern and knew he was sitting and swinging it from side to side like a little kid. It was a habit of his when he was lost in thought.

"Just sit tight until you hear otherwise."

"Sounds good to me," I answered, glad to have some of my work put on hold. "I was planning on attending Sterling Price's funeral this afternoon, if you don't mind."

Of course he would mind. Steele always minded anything that unshackled me from my desk and took me out of his reach. After the service, I planned on heading straight home. It would give me a chance to pull myself together before I saw Greg. I was semi-seriously considering flipping a coin to arrive at my decision about his proposal.

"Good idea. I was going to go to the service on behalf of the firm, but you can go in my place." Squeak ... squeak ... "I hate funerals. Don't even plan on going to my own, if I can help it."

I filed that tidbit of information away, thinking that if he kept that promise, Steele's funeral might be one worth attending.

"Besides," he continued, "your old buddy Wendell Wallace will be there. The firm will be well represented."

"I probably won't come back to the office after the funeral," I said casually, hoping to slip it by him.

The squeaking stopped abruptly, followed by silence. I braced myself. If Steele crabbed even one tiny bit about billable hours, I was going to remind him loudly that mine were among some of the highest in the firm. The squeaking started up again, and I breathed easier.

"No problem, Grey. I'll see you tomorrow morning. Bright and early."

I almost fell over. No problem? Did he really say no problem?

Stunned, I replaced the receiver and turned my attention back to the magazine article. I skimmed it casually. It was unremarkable in both the writing and the content, basically restating what Sterling Price had told me a few days ago about how he started collecting lunchboxes, how many he owned, and how he had recently acquired the Holy Pail. However, two-thirds of the way through the piece, I froze. I read several paragraphs over and over before picking up a pen and jotting a few names from the article down on a legal pad. I circled them.

> *Jasper Kellogg*
> *Ivan Fisher*
> *William Proctor*

They were the names of some of the prior owners of the Chappy Wheeler lunchbox, and they all had something in common—they were all dead. More importantly, according to the article, they had all died while still in possession of the Holy Pail. I thought Joe had been kidding, trying to scare me like a Halloween goblin.

I picked up my phone and punched in another extension at the firm.

"Joe?" I said into the phone, the magazine shaking in my hands. "What else do you have on these dead guys?"

SEVEN

STERLING PRICE'S FUNERAL WAS remarkable only by its brevity. The eulogy was given by Price's good friend and my former boss, Wendell Wallace. He stood straight and regal at the podium as he spoke of his many years of friendship with the deceased and of Price's accomplishments and loving family.

While I did want to pay my last respects to Sterling Price, the urge to check out the cast of characters that made up his life loomed large in my mind. From my seat about midway on the left- hand side of the filled chapel, I craned my neck to get a glimpse of the family, but it was useless. They were seated in a special area along the left wall, shielded by a dark one-way screen for privacy. I had never met any of Sterling Price's family and wanted to put faces to some of the names I knew. I did spot Carmen Sepulveda seated in the second pew on the right. Her head dropped down every so often during the service and I assumed she was wiping her eyes with tissue.

The graveside portion of the service was just as brief. When it was over, I made my way over to the Price home for the reception. It was located in Newport Coast, a very expensive housing development in Newport Beach featuring meandering streets, manicured lawns, and celebrity neighbors. Perched on the hillside, many residents had spectacular views of the Pacific Ocean. It was not a Sterling Homes development.

The home was elegant and large, with a design that reminded me of a Mediterranean villa. I had barely stepped inside when someone gently took my elbow. It was Mr. Wallace. Standing next to him was his lovely wife of forty-seven years, Hilda. Mr. Wallace smiled down at me from his six-foot-three frame, which was unbent by time. Mrs. Wallace leaned in and gave me an affectionate hug. I had last seen them at my birthday party a few days prior. They had popped in for a few moments before another engagement, and I was touched both by their attendance and by Greg's thoughtfulness in inviting them.

"Glad to see you here, Odelia," Mr. Wallace said. "Sterling always liked you." His voice vibrated slightly in grief and I saw his wife place a hand warmly on his arm.

"I wanted to be here," I said, and felt my own voice shake a bit at seeing Mr. Wallace's loss etched into his face. "Did you know that I saw him the day he died?"

"Yes, Mike Steele told me." Mr. Wallace looked around. "Where is Mike? Thought he'd be here."

"He decided not to come since both you and I would be here," I said. When I saw Mr. Wallace shake his head slowly in disapproval, I quickly added, "Steele was pretty shaken up by this, Mr. Wallace. I'm not sure he does funerals very well."

I could not believe my own ears. I was actually defending Steele, a man I detested, to Wendell Wallace, a man I adored. Something was wrong with me—something I intended to blame on middle-aged hormones.

For whatever reason, I had always referred to Wendell Wallace as Mr. Wallace, even though I had spent most of my years at Woobie working closely with him. It was never something he demanded; he was not that type of person. I never referred to any of the other attorneys at the firm by Mr. or Ms. unless speaking in front of clients. The atmosphere at Woobie was casual, and usually we all addressed each other by first names, except, of course, Mike Steele. He referred to everyone—superior, equal, and subordinate—in military fashion by their last name, and he was the only attorney I referred to in that manner.

"Odelia, how is that wonderful beau of yours?" Mrs. Wallace asked.

"Greg's fine, thank you. He's been out of town, but he's returning tonight."

She looked at me slyly and smiled. "And will we soon be hearing some exciting news?"

I felt my cheeks grow hot with embarrassment. I am definitely not some twenty-something maiden, but at the same time I felt girlish and wanted to giggle. For a surprising second, I wished I had the ring to flash at the Wallaces right here and now, no matter what my answer would be to Greg. I blamed this, too, on hormones.

"Hilda," Mr. Wallace chided gently, with a wink to me, "leave the poor woman alone. I'm sure Odelia will tell us when the time comes."

"Mr. Wallace, could you point out Mr. Price's family?" I asked, changing the subject. "I'd like to pay my respects."

As Hilda Wallace excused herself to go speak with several ladies who had gathered near a piano placed in front of a huge bay window, Mr. Wallace guided me into the large formal living room where several people were holding court seated on two matching sofas done in hunter green leather. They were all speaking in hushed chatter to each other as we approached.

A rather handsome, dark-haired man standing next to the sofa to my left turned his attention to us first and stuck out his hand to Mr. Wallace. "Dell, beautiful eulogy."

Mr. Wallace took the offered hand. "Thank you, Jackson," he replied, pumping the man's hand firmly.

The name sounded familiar to me. In a flash of recall, I remembered that Steele had mentioned a Jackson Blake who was a senior vice president at Sterling Homes. I would have bet my next meal this was the same person. I didn't have to wait long to know I wouldn't have to go hungry.

"Jackson, I'd like you to meet Odelia Grey, the paralegal at my firm that handles most of the corporate work for your company."

I thrust out my hand and we shook. Jackson Blake was about six feet tall, with an athletic build, and somewhere in his mid forties. Up close, his dark hair appeared more salt and pepper, and his eyes were dark and piercing, like he was taking a photo of everything, including me, and storing it away in his memory bank. He wore a beautifully cut dark suit, similar in style to those Steele preferred.

Earlier today when Steele had mentioned this man's name it had struck me as odd that I could not recall hearing it before. I had drafted the minutes of both the board of directors meetings and the shareholders meetings of the privately held Sterling Homes for years and could not recall any officer named Jackson Blake. Of course, I thought, I could simply be forgetting, but it still nagged at a corner of my brain like a pesky hangnail. Sterling Homes was not that big of a company in its operation, only in its profits.

A blond, petite, and very chic woman sat on the sofa next to where Jackson Blake stood. She was very pretty, with the sort of fashion magazine looks that money and a good surgeon could maintain for years. Mr. Wallace bent down and kissed her cheek.

"Oh, Uncle Dell," she murmured quietly. She dabbed at the corners of her flawlessly made-up eyes with a linen handkerchief.

Mr. Wallace shook his head in helpless silence as he introduced me to her, then he turned to me. "Odelia, this is Karla Blake, Jackson's wife and Sterling's daughter." He next focused on a slightly built man sitting next to Karla. "And this is Kyle Price, Sterling's son."

Next to her brother, Karla started sniffling. Jackson put a comforting hand on her shoulder, which was no bigger than a child's, and I saw her discretely shrug it off. He withdrew his hand and I looked up in time to see him shoot a quick, cold look to the back of her head. Geez, now there's a happy couple.

Karla Blake, or rather Karla Price, I did know, by name only, from the corporate minutes of Sterling Homes. She sat on the board of directors, though her brother did not, and was the chief financial officer of the company. The woman seemed brittle and pale dressed in a costly and unwrinkled black sheath, with her light honey hair pulled back in an immaculate chignon. Then Karla's look turned to me and I saw that in spite of her dabbing, her eyes were as clear and dry as a desert sky and just as blue. They pierced me with the same inspection and calculation as her husband's eyes had before her. In silent self-conscious response, my hands reached down to smooth out the many creases in my limp, lightweight navy and white two-piece dress purchased over two years ago on sale.

In turn, Karla and Kyle each politely took my hand and nodded as I gave short but sincere condolences. They appeared to be in their mid to late thirties.

Kyle Price was not as well-turned-out as his twin sister and her husband. He wore a plain white shirt, khaki pants, and an out-of-date tie that had been pulled away from his neck, exposing his considerable Adam's apple. His brown sports jacket bunched in the shoulders. He was clean shaven and wore his hair long, but not well cut like Greg's. He had the same light eyes as his sister, but they lacked the intensity. He gave me a small, sad smile as he acknowledged my condolences. Kyle Price looked ill at ease and fidgety, like a nervous horse ready to bolt.

From the corner of my eye, I saw Karla Blake lean toward her husband, who bent down stiffly to hear her words. "What's she doing here?" I heard her whisper tightly to Jackson.

For a brief moment I thought she was referring to me, and then I noticed Jackson looking beyond me to someone else.

"She still lives here, Karla," he whispered back calmly. "She has until the end of the month."

As I walked away with Mr. Wallace, I glanced discretely in the direction of their attention and noted a middle-aged woman standing by the archway leading into the formal dining room. For the most part, the woman stood alone. Occasionally, someone approached her, said a few words, and received a sad, forlorn smile and nod in return. She was very attractive, medium in height, tiny in the waist, suggestively full in the hips and breasts. She had a true old-fashioned hourglass figure, which her conservative gray dress and matching pumps tried hard to downplay. Her dark blond hair was threaded with subtle highlights and curved gently at the ends, framing her face just below her chin in a becoming manner.

I plucked gently on Mr. Wallace's coat sleeve. "Who's that?" I asked, indicating the woman by the dining room doorway.

"That's Stella, Stella Hughes. She was engaged to Sterling until recently."

So that was the gold-digging fiancée, I said silently to myself. Since my idea of a gold digger is a young, hot babe in a miniskirt sporting fake boobs, I looked at Stella Hughes with great curiosity. But then again, anyone could woo someone for their money. To my knowledge, there were no education or licensing standards for the job, like a doctor or lawyer. And although far from young, Stella Hughes was very sexy.

"What happened?" I asked Mr. Wallace, hoping to get the scoop.

He shrugged and hesitated. The combined gestures put me on alert. He was about to claim far less information than he really knew. You don't work for a man for umpteen years and not learn his habits and stall tactics.

"Not sure," he lied. My eyes pleaded with him in silence and he grudgingly continued. "The breakup was very recent."

"She lives here?" I asked casually, hoping to prod more information from the Wallace vault.

"Yes, at least for a few more weeks. Sterling let her stay on to give her time to relocate."

How civil, I thought to myself, remembering with a shiver the same offer from Franklin Powers when I ended our engagement, relationship, and live-in arrangement. Franklin had been sadly sweet in his offer to let me stay in a guest room of his house while I located and purchased a place of my own. He cited that it would be easier than moving my things twice. His argument, presented with all of his lawyerly skill, was a good one, and I had accepted. After less than two weeks of pure torture, with Franklin swinging between guilt and abuse in his bid to change my mind about marrying him, I fled.

A man I recognized as another of Mr. Wallace's longtime cronies strode over and greeted us, cutting off my questions. Mr. Wallace seemed relieved. It saved him from having to tell me to mind my own business. As the men spoke of golf, I excused myself and headed for the buffet set out in the dining room. I set my path accidentally on purpose to take me directly past Stella Hughes.

Daintily, I picked at the sandwiches, selecting two. They were the kind rolled jelly-roll style in flat Middle-Eastern bread and sliced into pinwheels. I had worked through lunch, grabbing only a vegetable-flavored Cup-a-Soup along the way. Looking at the filled table, my stomach was not shy about reminding me of that fact. I silently reminded it back that Greg was taking us out to dinner in a few hours. Internal discussion ended, I also chose two mini quiches and topped off my plate with some cherry tomatoes and a couple of carrot sticks. When I failed to see peanut butter, I passed on the celery. Rounding out my snack was a small glass of chilled white wine served to me by a waiter.

Stella Hughes was still standing by the entrance to the dining room when I completed filling my plate. She seemed to have staked out that spot as her territory. A couple stopped to give her a few quick words of comfort and moved on. No one seemed to be hovering around her like they were the family members. Nonchalantly,

I sidled over to where she stood. I was beginning to think the wine was a mistake as I worried about juggling the glass while trying to eat. Then, spotting a small hutch near the doorway and just to the side of Stella, I moved in and set my wine down, turning the unsuspecting table into a good excuse to stay near my prey.

Stella Hughes' uninterested glance passed over me no longer than a sigh. Up close, I could see under her carefully applied make-up the fine lines and dulling skin of aging, and that at one time she had been a true beauty, undoubtedly a blond bombshell. She smelled faintly of Joy, a fragrance I loved on most people but not on me. Quick as a bunny, I polished off a quiche the size of a half-dollar and took a sip of wine.

"Joy," I said simply and in her direction.

"Excuse me?" Stella Hughes asked, giving me a smidgen of attention.

"Joy. You're wearing Joy."

She looked at me, puzzled, then smiled slightly as she caught my drift. "Why yes, I am." Her voice was deep and sexy, the kind of voice you would expect to hear on the other end of one of those 900 numbers.

"One of my favorites," I told her. "You wear it well."

She turned so that she was looking directly at me, her expression and body language now inviting conversation. "Thank you," she replied. "I'm sorry, but I'm afraid I don't know you."

It is so easy to start up a conversation with a strange woman. Men have no idea. Just compliment a woman on her perfume, shoes, or hair, and you have an instant buddy. Ask about her kids and you make bonus points. Asking about grandchildren gets you invited to Thanksgiving.

I put my plate down on top of the hutch and wiped my fingers on a napkin, then extended my clean right hand. "Odelia Grey. I'm a paralegal. I work for Sterling Homes' attorneys."

"Stella Hughes."

"Sterling's fiancée?" I asked.

Stella stuck out her chin ever so slightly, presenting a look that invited a challenge. "Former fiancée," she corrected me in throaty tones. The woman appraised me with her eyes, which were dark and calculating. For the third time in just a few minutes, I felt like I was under a microscope. This certainly was not a trustful bunch.

"I'm sorry," I apologized. "For both that and for your recent loss. It still must be very difficult for you."

"Thank you, Odelia," she said, her husky voice fringed with grief that may or may not have been real. "A lot of people here don't understand that." She looked at the family cluster, then back at me. "We only just broke up, and it wasn't at all acrimonious."

A mean-spirited, low cackle popped out from between my lips, surprising me. "I once broke off an engagement myself and thought at the time that it had ended friendly," I told Stella. "Imagine my surprise when I discovered the opposite."

Geez, I thought, *maybe Franklin did haunt my relationship with Greg*. I picked up my wine glass and knocked back the tangy beverage like a shot of NyQuil.

"That bad?" Stella asked. I looked at her in surprise, suddenly realizing that she had witnessed my frenzied downing of alcohol. She was surveying me now with a look of frank amusement.

"Better than anything you've seen on the Lifetime channel," I told her with a wry grin.

Stella Hughes produced a laugh that bordered on a small snort. Seeing her shoulders relax, I decided to harvest her new comfort level.

"He was a regular Dr. Jekyll and Mr. Hyde," I shared. Stella closed her eyes for a second. When she opened them, she seemed far away, like her inner self had just departed on a short vacation.

"It wasn't like that with us," she said quietly. "He was wonderful. Sterling broke up with me."

"I'm sorry," I said simply, hoping she'd tell me the reason.

She shook her head. "It's okay. But it's why almost no one is speaking with me today. I'm *persona non grata* at this shindig."

She leaned in closer to me, and when she spoke, I could almost feel the low vibration from her deep voice. It reminded me of Seamus' kitty growls.

"I know I've upset the family by being here today. But I still live in this house, and I'm not going anywhere until I'm damn good and ready."

As I was listening, I noticed from the corner of my eye Carmen Sepulveda striding purposefully over to us from across the large living room. Her face showed a mix of anger and concern. Stella spotted her, too. When Carmen was within earshot, Stella took my arm.

"Come, Odelia," she said, her voice back to its normal pitch, "would you like to see the rest of the house?"

Thinking quickly, I said, "I'd really love to see the rest of Mr. Price's lunchbox collection. I've only seen the boxes at his office."

EIGHT

With all the friendliness of two grizzly bears facing off over a single salmon, Stella and Carmen eyed each other suspiciously before Stella spirited me off down a hallway. We were heading toward the back of the two-story sprawling abode with Stella giving me a mini tour along the way. We passed through a spacious kitchen sparkling with silver appliances and bustling with catering staff. Along one wall were French doors open to the patio. From there, we passed into an enormous family room with a pool table, wet bar, and a large-screen TV on which a Disney video was being played for the children in attendance. The far wall was a bank of more French doors facing the back. I could see a large garden area and a pool beyond the open doors. More people were congregating there, and there was another small buffet set up under the patio covering. A gray cloud hovered over a small group to the right of the pool, announcing the smoking section.

My guide took me through a closed door near the bar area and up a flight of back stairs. In this part of the house it was quiet and no mourners other than the two of us were present. Stella opened another door and we stepped into a cool and quiet book-lined room.

"This was Sterling's private study," Stella told me.

I liked the room instantly and could easily picture Price seated in the leather chair behind the big antique desk. There were large windows beyond the desk with a view of the back yard and pool, and I realized that this room was directly over a portion of the family room downstairs. The walls were paneled in warm, buttery wood the color of caramel and the shutters at the windows were stained to match. The whole space emanated a strong, cultured masculinity.

A large section of bookshelves had glass doors, and behind those doors were the remaining specimens of Sterling Price's beloved lunchbox collection, displayed much as their fellow boxes were in his office. I walked over and scanned them, recognizing again many of the boxes carried by childhood friends. I laughed when I saw an example of my detested Junior Miss lunchbox.

I pointed to it. "This was the box I had when I was in school," I told Stella. "Well, not the exact box, but the same. You know what I mean."

Stella came up behind me and pointed to a box a few shelves above and to the left of the Junior Miss. "That's my favorite." Pictured on the box were Dale Evans and her horse Buttercup.

I strolled along the glass enclosure slowly taking in the boxes. I saw another Zorro box, but it was different from the one Price had given me.

"Sterling gave me a lunchbox the day he died," I said, turning to her.

It was not lost on me that Stella Hughes paled at my words. Although her face was frozen in a polite smile, her eyes widened and lit up as if she had been goosed from behind. She stayed that way for a few seconds and I began to wonder if she had suffered a mild stroke.

"Really?" she finally said, her face relaxing into a feline grin.

"Yes, I had a meeting with him that morning. Afterwards, we discussed his collection, and he gave me the one lunchbox I had always wanted as a kid but never got."

"And that was?" she asked, drawing out the last word. Her upper body leaned slightly toward me in anticipation of my answer.

"Zorro," I answered matter-of-factly and pointed to the box on the shelf. "Like that box, but a bit different. He sent it over to my office later that day with another box that was filled with corporate documents. I was very surprised and touched by his generosity."

"You're sure it was a box with Zorro on it?" she asked. "And not one showing Chappy Wheeler? The one called the Holy Pail."

"I'm sure," I answered calmly. "And I'd be happy to give it back, especially under the circumstances."

Stella held up a hand, palm out, and waved it gently. "No, no, don't even think about it. It's just—" she started to say something, then stopped herself.

"It's just that the Holy Pail is missing and you thought maybe he'd given it to me," I said, completing the sentence with my dimestore psychic powers.

Her cheeks reddened slightly. "Yes, that's exactly what I was going to say." She seated herself in a nearby leather reading chair. "How did you know about the missing lunchbox?"

"The detective told me when he questioned me about my morning meeting with Sterling," I explained. "He even asked to see the Zorro box when I told him about the gift." I left out that Dev Frye and I were previously acquainted.

I discretely tried to look Stella over, calculating that she had already seen the big five-o come and go, and not recently. That would make her about twenty years younger than Sterling Price. Franklin had been a lot older than me, but not two decades. At forty-seven, I could not imagine marrying a man in his seventies. I could barely imagine marrying a man in his thirties. Hell, I was 'gator wrestling with the whole idea of being married, period.

Looking at her sitting in his well-appointed study, it made me wonder about their relationship. How did they meet? How long ago? And the big question—why did they break up? Was she really the gold digger Carmen claimed? I wondered if Stella would discuss such personal matters with me and decided not, at least not at the moment.

"Sorry, but I can't help you," I told her. "The Chappy Wheeler lunchbox was in Price's office the first and only time I saw it." My pumps were beginning to kill my feet so I dropped myself down in a chair that matched hers. "You ... none of you ... have absolutely no idea where that lunchbox is?" I asked.

She moved her head side to side, her head down, her thoughts lost in the deep pile of the carpet. "It's just disappeared," she said.

"Maybe he gave it to someone that day, like he gave me the Zorro box." There was no response. "Maybe he sold it to another collector," I ventured further.

Both theories sounded hollow coming out of my mouth. I had seen the man's eyes glow when he showed me the prized metal box.

The only way someone would ever take possession of the Holy Pail from Sterling Price was to pry it from his dead, cold fingers. Perhaps someone had.

Something else struck me as odd about this situation. I watched Stella closely. A man had been murdered—and not just any man, but a man this woman supposedly loved and wanted to marry. True, the lunchbox was worth a lot of money, but why was its whereabouts taking the forefront so soon after Price's death? Was the murder the outcome of a theft, or was the murder a convenience for someone to grab the box and run?

Thinking about it, the first possibility was unlikely. If Price had fallen prey to a thief, he probably would not have been poisoned. Instead he would have been struck or shot, or something similar. Poison was not a weapon of quick convenience or passionate anger, but of premeditation. And most likely Sterling was poisoned by someone who knew him, someone who could get close enough to administer it without suspicion. With this in mind, I was leaning heavily toward the second possibility, and one Carmen Sepulveda also had voiced. Simply put, someone saw an opportunity to grab the valuable lunchbox. Someone in the company, hearing all the commotion, came in to see what was going on and quickly saw an opportunity to make some serious money. I made a mental note to look up Amy Chow, the employee who found the body. Maybe she could recall who had come into the room immediately after she made the discovery.

"Stella, I know this is none of my business," I began. *None of your business, Odelia,* my inner voice said. *Listen to yourself and pay attention.* As usual, I ignored it.

Stella looked up at me with curious, hard eyes that reminded me of ball bearings.

"But why is that box so important at this moment? Besides its worth, I mean? It was probably just a simple theft that will be solved soon enough, surely as soon as someone tries to sell it. Don't you and the family have enough to worry about right now?"

Stella continued to study me. I fidgeted under her gaze and tried hard to determine what was going on in her head. To give my discomfort a break, I cocked my left wrist and checked my watch. It was almost four o'clock.

"I should check my office voice mail," I said out loud but not particularly to her. When I looked back at Stella, her eyes had softened. Silently, she stood up and went to the window to look out at the pool and the people milling below.

I opened my purse and grabbed my cell phone. *Drat,* I said to myself, realizing my battery was dead. I really should remember to recharge it. Greg was always on me about it.

"Stella, my phone is out. May I use yours?"

"Of course," she said, turning to me once again with the broad, catlike smile. She pointed to the phone on the large desk. "Use this one." Her words held the same false politeness a youngster uses when his mother has ordered him to be nice to the neighborhood misfit; a tone I remembered far too well from my experience as the fattest girl on Milton Avenue.

Hmm, interesting, I thought to myself as I straightened my posture and approached the desk, giving her my own fake smile. In the short time I had been with Stella Hughes, she had run the gamut of emotions. But which, if any, did she really feel and mean? I picked up the phone and began dialing the office, watching her out of the corner of my eye. Being somewhat of an underdog myself, a part of me wanted to like this deep-voiced woman with the jutting chin and defiant stance, but another part of me was suspicious and skeptical of her motives. But then, I was also highly skeptical of the entire Price family, not having seen anything even remotely like earnest grief being displayed by any of them.

"I'm going back downstairs, Odelia," Stella said as she headed for the door. "Please don't hesitate to ask if you need anything else."

"Thanks," I said. "It was nice meeting you, and, again, I'm sorry about your loss." She gave me another plastic smile and left.

There were four voice mails for me at the office. I listened to them all. The first two were from Mike Steele, asking me questions on some pending work. Hitting the appropriate buttons to leave a response, I answered each dutifully and in order, knowing that he would be both pleased and dismayed at my speedy response; dismayed only because he would not be able to rag on me tomorrow about my absence from the office this afternoon. The last was from a client, who left some information I had requested. The third was from Greg.

I listened to Greg's message again, coming back to it after hearing the one from the client. The first time, I listened to the content of the message. The second time, I paid attention to his tone, which told me that he was tired and edgy. Even though Greg was strong and athletic, traveling with his disability could be trying and exhausting for him. This trip, he had taken Boomer, his college-aged right-hand man from his shop, Ocean Breeze Graphics. I felt better when Boomer traveled with Greg, knowing that the young man would run interference for his boss. He was devoted to Greg, who had taken a chance on the intelligent yet alternative-looking boy several years ago and mentored him when others only took note of the multiple facial piercings and Kool-Aid colored hair.

Greg's message was that something had come up and he would not be coming home as planned. He said he would leave messages at my home and on my cell phone to make sure he would catch me.

I drank in the sound of Greg's voice, slurping down each syllable like a cherry slushy. Even in exhaustion, his voice held a tone of mischief and a promise of forever. Without further delay, I dialed Greg's cell phone. He picked it up on the second ring.

"Greg Stevens," he answered. The fatigue in his voice was standing at attention.

"Hi, honey," I said, virtually purring into the phone. What can I say? The man simply had that effect on me.

"Hiiiiiiiii," he responded slowly, his voice turning sweet but not gaining in energy.

"Hiiiiiiiii," I said back and giggled like a silly school girl. Franklin Powers never made me giggle.

"Where are you?" he asked. "I don't recognize the phone number on my display."

"I'm at Sterling Price's house," I explained. "I went to the funeral and now I'm about to head home."

"And I bet you forgot to charge your cell, didn't you?"

I looked down at the dead cell phone on the desk and twitched my nose in annoyance at his correct assumption. "No comment," I said.

He laughed quietly. Suddenly, I was overcome with the urge to crawl through the phone and lay my head on his chest to feel the vibration.

"So why aren't you coming home?" I asked, surprised to find the words hard to get out. I missed Greg; missed him right down to the run in the toe of my right nylon stocking. And I wanted him home—now.

There was a pause before Greg answered me. "Uncle Stu died, Odelia."

"What? Oh, Greg, no. When? How?" The words gushed from my shocked lips.

Greg was referring to his mother's brother, Stuart Foster, a retired engineer who lived in Minnesota, in Bloomington, near the Mall of America. Greg had been close to his uncle. His whole family, both immediate and extended, seemed to live in close emotional harmony with each other—a situation I found difficult to believe, given my own dysfunctional family, until I witnessed it on many occasions for myself. Greg's parents were supportive and loving, like the mom and dad from a family values sitcom. According to Greg, they had raised their two sons and single daughter with a very firm but fair hand. My own parents had believed in better parenting through ignorance.

I had met Greg's uncle Stu four months earlier when he and his wife landed in California during a tour across America in an RV. Greg's mother had hosted a huge barbecue in their honor during their visit, and even Greg and I got into the act by taking them to dinner and the theater in Hollywood.

Now I was crying in earnest. I liked Uncle Stu and his homey, gentle wife, Esther, who was a retired elementary school teacher.

"Poor Esther," I said quietly into the phone. "What happened, Greg?"

"Heart attack, just this morning," he said. "He was fishing with some buddies at the lake. Happened so fast, no one could help."

"You're flying to Minnesota, aren't you?"

"Yes, sweetheart. I'm sorry."

"Don't be sorry, Greg," I told him while I located a tissue in my purse and wiped my eyes and nose for the millionth time that afternoon. "It can't be helped. How's your mother doing? Anything I can help with?"

"No, sweetheart, but thanks. Mom and Dad are already on their way there. The rest of the clan will fly out tomorrow. Mom's hanging in there. Dad's actually more shook up than she is. He and Uncle Stu were the same age."

His voice was winding down even more. I wanted to put my arms around him to transfer some strength.

"My plane leaves Phoenix in an hour. I'm at the airport right now. Boomer's putting me on the plane and taking a later flight home. I'll be home as soon as I can." He took a deep breath. "Sorry about sticking you with Wainwright for so long."

"Don't worry about that, Greg. He's a good guest." I made a mental note to pick up more Snausages. Wainwright would be thoroughly, if not irretrievably, spoiled by the time Greg returned. "Be with your family and give them my love. I'll be here when you get back."

"You promise?"

"Yes, Greg, I promise," I told him softly. "Unless, of course, Alan Rickman swoops in and kidnaps me. Then all bets are off."

Greg laughed and gave me a loud, sloppy kiss through the receiver. He knew all about my obsession with Rickman.

NINE

AFTER TALKING TO GREG, I grabbed my purse and went in search of a bathroom. I didn't have to look far. There was a small one located just a few steps from the study. A couple of quick repairs to my makeup, a little lipstick, and I would be on my way. But to where? My dinner plans had been altered by a family crisis in Minnesota.

Loneliness for Greg shot through my body like a rampaging fever. I didn't feel like being alone tonight. Maybe I should give Zee a call—might even be able to wrangle a dinner invitation from her. Zee was a great cook, not gourmet, but the type of cooking that stuck to your ribs. And hips. And bottom. And—well, you get the picture. She made a mean chicken and dumplings, my personal favorite of her dishes. The thought of a home-cooked, sit-down meal with people I love almost made me swoon with anticipation. Even the good possibility of being nagged by Seth didn't dampen my hopes for a salvaged evening.

Before I left the bathroom, I pawed around in my bag for my cell phone. My eyes rolled around in my head at the realization of two problems. One, the phone was dead. Two, I had left it on Price's desk in the study. Taking one last futile look in the mirror, I stepped to the door, stopping short before opening it. Voices were being raised on the other side. Not right outside the door, but in the hallway between the bathroom and the study. I pressed my ear against the cool, white enameled door and made out what sounded like two men arguing in low voices. Not exactly yelling, but I could tell that both were vocalizing with a restrained tenseness, though I could not tell what they were saying. I pressed my ear tight against the door and held my breath.

The voices began moving away. I concentrated on the direction the sounds were heading and decided they were moving into the study. Opening the door as quietly as possible, I peeked out. With only one eye to the small crack, I could see just inside the doorway to the study. It looked to me like the backside of a man's dark suit coat retreating into the room. I could not see the other person.

With as much stealth as I could muster, I opened the bathroom door and eased out into the hallway. Sucking in my gut and pressing my big butt against the wall, I attempted to flatten myself out of view, hoping to make myself invisible merely by willing it so.

The doors to the study were of the double variety and whoever was in the room had not shut them completely. Moving slowly away from the wall, I peered through the crack between the doors. I could make out two people—a man in a dark suit and a woman in a gray dress. Once again I heard what I thought were two male voices and realized that one of the people was Stella Hughes. I squinted through the crack and saw Stella grab the man by both his arms and try to pull him to her.

The man pulled away and turned, giving me a good look at his face. It was Jackson Blake.

"Not here," he told Stella gruffly.

"Yes, here," she demanded. "It's been days since I've seen you."

She pulled him back to her and pressed her lips to his urgently. Jackson did not pull away immediately, but kissed back, their lips locked in passion. I watched as she lifted one of his hands to a breast. He fondled it as they kissed. Finally, he broke off and retreated from her.

"No," he said. He walked a few paces away from her and ran a hand through his hair. "Everyone's here. I can't afford for Karla to find out about us. She already suspects something."

"I don't care if she knows," Stella hissed. "The old man's gone. You're in charge of the company now. Isn't this what you wanted? Wasn't this what we planned? To be together?"

Jackson looked at her a long time, his face registering no emotion that I could see from my perch. With an audible sigh, he moved to face her, taking her hands in his.

"Yes, and we will be together," he said in a soothing voice. "I promise. Just not yet. Maybe in a few months, when this all settles down. I may be running Sterling Homes, but the board of directors controls it. And, if you'll remember, Karla is an officer and board member."

Stella jerked her hands from his and turned her back to him. He came up behind her and put his hands on her shoulders.

"If we were together now, darling, people would be suspicious," he told her, his voice oozing like honey on warm biscuits. "We have to let the dust settle. If we're patient, it will all fall into place. Everything we want." He nuzzled her ear. Stella's stiff shoulders relaxed.

Cautiously, I moved closer to the door, trying to hear and see better. I was worried that I would get overanxious and fall through the partially open doors right into the middle of the room. Ta da! Here I am, folks, eavesdropping.

"I might know something about the lunchbox," Stella told him.

He turned her to face him. "Really?"

She nodded. "That woman, the fat one from his lawyers', may know something."

Jackson raised his face to the ceiling, mulling this piece of news over. "Hmm," he said, looking back at Stella. "I understand she was one of the last people to see Sterling alive."

Nothing. I know nothing! I wanted to stamp my foot and shout it at them, but I held my tongue and my place at the crack between the doors.

"She told me Sterling gave her a Zorro lunchbox as a gift," Stella said. As soon as she said it, she stretched to rub her cheek against his.

"The police told me about the Zorro lunchbox and said they checked it out," Jackson said. "Maybe the old man also gave her the Holy Pail and she's keeping quiet about it. Maybe she intends to sell it on her own."

"Maybe," Stella purred in her kitty-growl voice. "I haven't figured out yet if she's that smart. But I intend to."

Excuse me! It was difficult, but I reined in my indignation and forced myself to keep still behind the door.

One of Stella's hands reached around to feel Jackson's buns under his suit jacket. "Mmm. I sure do miss you, Jackson."

Jackson Blake chuckled. "I know you do, baby." They stood there awhile, cheek to cheek, with Stella groping his other cheeks. "Soon, I promise," he assured her again.

"Soon's not soon enough," she said in a sultry voice, moving her hand from his butt to the front of his pants.

Jackson grabbed her wrist and playfully pulled her hand away from his privates. "We can't, Stella, not here."

"Shit, Jackson, you're no fun," she teased. "Think how exciting it could be with Karla and everyone else right downstairs." She started for his fly again, but this time he pushed her away firmly.

"No, Stella. I mean it. I have to get back before she wonders where I am."

Stella stood in the middle of the room, her arms crossed in front of her chest. "Go then, go back to your little tight-assed heiress." Her voice was no longer a purr but a snarl.

"Stella, please," Jackson pleaded.

"I said go, Jackson."

With that, Jackson shook his head and headed for the door. My heart stopped in fear of being discovered. But suddenly, Stella seemed to change her mind. She grabbed Jackson's arm and turned him toward her. I siezed the opportunity to tiptoe back into the bathroom. Silently, I shut the door and pressed my ear to it once more. I heard Jackson walk by, his stride confident even on the carpet. I held my breath, hoping that Stella would follow him soon and not need to use the bathroom on her way back downstairs. I waited so long I began to think she had walked by without my hearing. Finally, I heard her footsteps and waited until she was down the staircase before I moved a muscle.

Breathing a sigh of relief, I grabbed my purse, which I had left on the vanity, and slowly opened the bathroom door. First, I looked down the hallway. Next, I glanced toward the study. Both doors were wide open now, and there was no sound of anyone nearby. Quickly, I made a dash for the study.

I originally had planned to call Zee from there, but now I just wanted to get out of the house. I grabbed my phone, but before I could leave, I heard people coming up the back staircase. They were talking low. Crap, there was no time to run for the bathroom. Near me was a door. Opening it, I found a small closet and squeezed in. It was very stuffy and held mostly office supplies and storage boxes. I kept the door open a crack for air and to know when the coast was clear. From it, I had a clear view of the desk.

Odelia, I told myself silently, *you should have just told whoever is coming that you had come back for your phone. After all, it was the truth. But no, you didn't think of that, did you? You had to hide, making it impossible now to get out of this gracefully.*

Sheesh. I could be such a nag. Stella would not have to wonder too long or hard about my intelligence, that's for sure.

Through the crack of the closet door, I saw Stella come into the study. Behind her was a man, but this time it was definitely not Jackson Blake. With her was Kyle Price, Sterling Price's son. And this time, if my ears guessed correctly, they closed the doors to the study behind them.

"Why haven't you returned my calls, Stella?" I heard Kyle Price say before he came into my line of vision. His voice was nowhere near as deep as Stella's. Instead, it was a nasal whine, somewhere between the tones of a petulant child and a bored teenager.

"I told you, Kyle, that we need to keep our distance or people would become suspicious," Stella answered impatiently. She walked over to the desk and turned to lean against it while facing him. From my hiding place, I saw mostly her back and a bit of her left side.

Kyle came into view now. As soon as he stood in front of her, he leaned in to kiss her. She coyly moved her head away.

"What's wrong?" he asked.

"Nothing. I just think we need to cool it until this settles down."

Kyle Price slid his arms around Stella's waist and leaned in again for a kiss. This time she let him follow through, allowing him to kiss her long and deep. I heard him say to her, "God, baby, I miss you." One of his hands squeezed her left breast as he kissed her again.

Were my ears deceiving me, or was this similar to the conversation I had just overheard between Stella and Jackson, but in reverse roles?

Stella still seemed hesitant about Kyle's amorous advances. She put her hands on his chest and held him back while she studied him. After a few moments, she reached up a hand and outlined his waiting lips with a single finger.

"I'm supposed to move out of this house in two weeks," she told him, her voice shifting back into purr mode. "But I don't have anywhere to go." Now she rubbed both of her hands up and down his chest. "Maybe I can stay with you until I find something?"

Kyle smiled at her. "You may not have to move, Stella. This is my house now."

"What?" she asked, pulling away to look at him better.

"This is my house," he repeated proudly. "Dad put me on as joint tenant. Now that he's dead, it's mine and I'm moving in. He also just bought the Center, which also becomes mine now, free and clear. He signed those papers the day he died."

Immediately, my mind went back to the papers I notarized for Price. I could not remember exactly what they were, but they did have Kyle's name on them. I wrote a mental note to myself to check my notary journal for the types of documents Price had signed.

"But why, Kyle?" Stella asked. "Why would he do that?"

"Because he wanted us to be happy, Stella. You and me." He kissed her lightly again while she mulled his words over. "I told him about us," he told her between kisses.

"You *what?*" She sounded shocked.

"I told him about us. That the baby was mine."

"No, Kyle, you shouldn't have." Stella said, growing agitated.

Baby? I clutched a hand over my mouth to keep from gasping from the news. Stella Hughes was pregnant? Menopause, maybe. But pregnant? Suddenly I was glad I had stuffed myself into the closet. Geez, the Price family was better than the stuff that won Emmys for daytime drama.

"Don't worry, Stella. He was only mad at first." Kyle was dotting her face with little kisses as he spoke. "Besides, I had some good leverage. It was in his best interest to do it."

Stella seemed speechless. She pulled her face away from Kyle's lips and looked directly at him a long time. "What do you mean?" she asked warily. "What leverage?"

"Information, Stella. Information the old man needed." Kyle lifted her hands to his lips and kissed her knuckles. "Information he was happy to pay for." He let go of Stella's hands and started

90

unbuttoning the front of her dress as he talked, his voice becoming more nasally as he spoke. "Let's just say I finally managed to kick my sister off her golden pedestal."

Well, this was an interesting development. Kyle seemed pretty meek to me when I met him downstairs. What information could he have sold to his father in exchange for a house and the Center, whatever that was?

Stella remained silent as Kyle continued working her buttons. I wanted desperately to see the look on her face, but all I saw was the side of her head tilted up to him. The little bit of her face I could see reflected no emotion. She and Jackson seemed to both have a talent for blank faces when the need arose. Kyle looked back at her with slavish adoration.

Silently, and still looking at Kyle, Stella finished undoing the front of her dress and lowered it. Then she unhooked her bra and released her full breasts. Kyle wasted no time moving his mouth to one naked nipple, then to the other. Stella's hands moved to grasp his butt, as she had done to the unwilling Jackson. She said something to him I didn't catch, but it caused Kyle to lift his face from her boobs and glance at the doors. Straightening up, he walked out of my view. I heard the study doors open and shut and thought he had left—hoped he had left. Then I heard a faint click that sounded like a lock. Kyle returned to Stella, who had now shimmied out of her dress and was working on removing her hose.

"Everyone's downstairs," she told him in her husky voice. "No one will come up here today."

Oh, yeah? Personally, I felt the study was seeing far too much traffic.

TEN

"Are you out of your mind?" Zee nearly shouted at me from across our table at Mi Casa. A few people from neighboring booths glanced over at us briefly, then went back to stuffing their faces with enchiladas and burritos.

Following Stella and Kyle's copulation in the study, during which I did a fairly good imitation of the see-no-evil, hear-no-evil, speak-no-evil apes, I made sure the coast was clear and skedaddled out of there. Downstairs, I said my goodbyes to the Wallaces and headed for the front door, my car, and fresh air. I needed to slough off the sleazy feeling that covered me like morning film on teeth.

"Odelia," I heard someone call just as I reached the foyer.

It was Stella Hughes, moving toward me from the living room. Once she was in front of me, I found it difficult to look her in the eye. I mean, what do you say to a woman you just witnessed being bent over a desk with her knickers around her ankles?

"Odelia, I did so enjoy meeting you. Perhaps we can have lunch sometime?" she asked, again wearing the plastic smile.

Apparently, Stella was wasting no time getting to the bottom of my intelligence level. Glancing quickly at her face, but still avoiding her eyes, I mumbled something like, "Yeah, sure. Call me at the office." Then I fled.

Zee's home was closer to the Price house than my place, but I decided to go straight home. From there I called Zee. Seth was at a meeting and not expected for dinner, she told me, so we agreed to meet at Mi Casa in an hour. So much for my fantasy of chicken and dumplings or anything else homemade. But I do love Mexican food, and Mi Casa has great stuff. Before going to the restaurant, I changed into loose shorts and a cotton shirt and gave Wainwright a quick walk, apologizing the whole way for Greg's continued absence.

Instead of responding to Zee's outburst, I ignored her and continued munching on tortilla chips and salsa like a power saw at a lumberjack competition. There's something very satisfying about food that goes crunch. It's almost therapeutic the way it appeals to both the sense of sound and of touch, with taste thrown in as a bonus.

I buzzed through one chip, then another, until Zee grabbed the bowl and moved it out of my reach.

"What?" I said to her irritably.

"What? Did you just ask me *what?*" she asked, trying to keep her voice down. "You just announced that you spent the good part of an hour in a closet spying on a couple having sex, and you ask me *what?*"

I shrugged, attempting to be nonchalant about the spying accusation. "But I think I got some info about Sterling Price's murder, at least some possible motives. And I'm dying to know what dirt Kyle has on his sister."

"Dear Lord," Zee said, addressing a piñata shaped like a burro hanging over our table, "she is out of her mind." She looked back at me. "Didn't we go through this when you decided to stick your nose into Sophie's murder?"

I said nothing, but waved to a busboy to bring more chips.

"Wasn't getting shot in the behind—almost killed, mind you—" she continued, "enough warning to stay out of this sort of thing?"

I looked at my friend and started to say something, but our food arrived. I clammed up until our waitress, dressed in a white off-the-shoulder embroidered peasant blouse and full red skirt, left our table. Next, the busboy showed up with a new bowl of chips and fresh salsa.

"But don't you think it's odd that the Holy Pail disappeared the same day Sterling Price died?" I asked Zee. "The very same day I first saw it?"

Zee said nothing. She was in the middle of her usual food ritual of making sure everything was just so. We had both ordered enchiladas rancheros, but hers were both chicken while one of mine was shredded beef and the other pork. First, she scraped the sour cream off her food and plopped it on my plate, then followed suit with the guacamole, both of which I was happy to receive. Next, she scattered the chopped tomatoes, cilantro, and onions that were on one side of the plate evenly over the enchiladas. Finally, she daintily scooped up salsa from the bowl in the middle of the table with a spoon and sprinkled it over everything, including her rice and beans.

I simply smeared the extra guacamole and sour cream over my enchiladas like Spackle, dug in, and waited for her response.

"I do think it's odd," she said before taking her first bite, "that the lunchbox is missing. But that doesn't mean you should be sticking your big nose into it."

I chewed the food in my mouth before answering. "But don't you see? They, whoever *they* are, think I have the stupid box."

"But you don't, do you?"

"No, of course not."

"So what's the problem?" Zee took another bite, chewed and swallowed before going on. "Just let the police do their job. They really don't need you, Odelia. Especially that nice Detective Frye. Doesn't he have enough on his mind without worrying about you again?"

Earlier, I had told Zee about Dev Frye being on the case and about his wife's recent passing.

We ate in silence for a while before I started up again. When I latch onto an idea, I'm like a starving dog with a soup bone.

"But don't you think it's odd that all those previous owners of the Holy Pail died?"

"Odelia, there are such things as coincidences. I bet if you look into those deaths you'll find a reasonable explanation for each of them. After all," she said, getting agitated, "it's just a silly lunch-box!"

My thoughts exactly.

Joe had not been able to provide me with further information on the three dead men mentioned in the *American Executive* article about the Holy Pail and Sterling Price, so all I had was the magazine's brief account of each. According to the article, Jasper

Kellogg, a resident of a small town in upstate New York, had died from a heart attack at the age of sixty-eight; Ivan Fisher was fifty-six when he was killed in a car accident on an icy road outside of Chicago; and William Proctor, the owner prior to Price, had been lost at sea during a storm, along with his wife. He had been forty-two and his sailboat was discovered battered and abandoned off the western coast of Mexico. Zee may be right.

"A more important discussion," Zee continued, "is what you're going to tell Greg when he gets home. Seems to me you're more concerned about this silly lunchbox and those crazy people than you are about your own problems."

I took another bite and washed it down with iced tea before answering. Okay, I'll admit it: I was using the whole Price thing and Uncle Stu's tragic death to buy me more time to obsess about Greg's proposal. And I seriously doubted if this extra time was a good thing.

"I think Greg and I need to have another heart-to-heart talk before I give him my answer," I told my best friend. Zee nodded, her big, soulful eyes beacons of understanding in her dark brown face. "I won't be able to say yes until I know for sure he's okay about not having kids. I mean, truly okay with it."

I started playing with my remaining rice with the tines of my fork, looking at them and concentrating on the individual grains. "When I heard his voice today on the phone, I knew I couldn't bear to lose him." I put my fork down and looked up at Zee. "But I'm not sure I'm ready for marriage. Maybe we should just live together, try it out."

Zee sighed. "Well, you know my thoughts about couples living together before marriage. But that aside, do you really think that will give you the information you need to make a decision? Don't you know Greg well enough by now?"

"Yes, Zee," I said, feeling tears start to well up in my eyes. "I do know him well enough. And that's the problem. I know that I want him in my life. But I also know that having a family is a big dream of his. But it's not my dream. I'm forty-seven years old. I don't want children at this point in my life." Suddenly, Stella Hughes crossed my mind, and I wondered if she wanted the baby she was carrying. Odds were, she didn't.

I wiped at an escaping tear with one hand. "It's just the onions," I told Zee quickly when I noticed her own eyes begin to pool.

"Don't you see," I said, continuing, my voice strained, "for Greg and me to get married, one of us is going to have to sacrifice what we want or don't want on this issue. One of us will always feel like they settled or gave in. Is that how a marriage should start out?" I paused and waited for Zee to answer, but she just looked at me in helpless frustration. "This isn't a difference over whether the bathroom towels should be green or beige," I continued, "this is about children, other human beings."

"So what are you going to do?" Zee asked in a small voice.

"Right now," I said, motioning to our waitress, "I'm going to order flan."

I INSPECTED MY NAILS as the phone on the other end of my call rang—one, two, three times. A manicure was clearly in my future. On the fourth ring I would be automatically kicked into Mike Steele's voice mail. It was eight o'clock in the evening. I was full of enchiladas, flan, and questions, and I needed to digest them all.

Steele often worked late. I was calling him in the hope that he could give me some answers tonight, before I had to resort to Pepto-Bismol. The fourth ring began. I was about to hang up, thinking I would ask Steele my questions in the morning, when someone answered just before it rolled over into voice mail. It was Steele, and he sounded a tad winded. Probably ran in from another office or the library, I thought.

"It's me—Odelia," I announced to him.

"Jesus, Grey," he said impatiently, "what do you want at this hour? Another half-day off?"

I kicked myself for even thinking of calling, but now that I had him on the phone, I might as well go ahead. "I have a few questions about Sterling Homes and didn't want to wait until morning," I began. "But if you're busy, it can wait."

"Of course I'm busy," he responded with irritation. He paused. I almost said goodbye and hung up. Then he added, "Talk to me, Grey. What's on your mind?"

"Well," I began, "I met Jackson Blake this afternoon."

"Goody for you," Steele said sarcastically.

I rolled my eyes and continued. "I don't remember him being elected as a senior vice president of Sterling Homes. But I could be wrong." I waited, knowing that Steele was thinking this over before answering.

"You're correct, as usual, Grey. You wouldn't have remembered the minutes from that board of directors meeting, because our firm didn't prepare them." Steele cleared his throat. "Jackson Blake was recently elected senior vice president by unanimous consent of the board. Sterling told me this just a few days before he died. About two weeks ago, his assistant drafted the consent using one of the previous consents we prepared as a form. She was supposed to send the original to us for the corporate minute book as soon as it was signed by all of the directors."

Okay, now it made sense to me why I didn't remember the directors of Sterling Homes electing Jackson Blake. A corporation's board of directors is allowed to approve decisions and take action on them without a formal meeting, as long as all of the directors approve and sign a document to that effect. The document is usually called something like "Unanimous Consent By Board of Directors in Lieu of Meeting." Normally, it's a fairly short document that can be easily prepared using a previous one as a guideline.

I moved on to my next question. "So who is Jackson Blake, besides Karla's husband? And why have I not heard of him before? It's not that big of an organization, and I've worked with most of the upper management over the years."

Steele chuckled. "You answered your own question, Grey. He's Karla's husband. Originally, Blake was a field manager, an engineer, for Sterling Homes. Been with them for years. He and Karla met just over a year ago, a year and a half maybe, and married quickly. Daddy found his little girl's hubby a corporate desk job starting as a department head, and—whammo—senior VP almost overnight. He does seem to be highly competent, though. In fact, Jackson Blake has spearheaded some of the company's better decisions in recent months.

"And here's another bulletin for you, Grey," Steele said, continuing.

I took note that his tone had switched from annoyance to interest. He seemed to forget whatever he was involved in when I called and was really getting into the juicy gossip concerning Sterling Homes.

"At that same time, Jackson Blake was also elected as a director to replace Kirby Baylor, who retired from the board about two months ago."

"Is he in charge now that Price is gone?"

"Seems that way," Steele said. "At least for now and probably with the full backing of his wife."

I thought about this last bit of information. The board of directors of Sterling Homes had only five members. The chairman of the board was Sterling Price, and now with him gone there would be only four members, one of them Karla, another Jackson. They would hold fifty percent of the voting power on the board, and without the fifth board member there could be possible deadlocks on board decisions.

"But Karla's an officer," I pointed out to Steele, "and a capable one. Why didn't she just take the reins? Why her husband?"

"Because he pees standing up, Grey," Steele said in an amused tone. "The remaining board members are as old as Price. I've attended some of those board meetings and, believe me, those old guys don't always see eye-to-eye with the young, ambitious daughter of their business partner. One of Blake's considerable talents is wooing the board and smoothing the way for new ideas. Until Blake got on the board, Sterling Homes was fast becoming stuck in a time warp. Good thing Price liked him and listened to him, or the company might have sunk into a pool of stagnation. They would never have listened to new ideas from Karla."

I stored all this away for later consideration and followed up with my next concern. "What about Kyle Price? Do you know what 'the Center' is?"

Steele sighed, his signature sign of impatience, and I heard the squeaking of his chair. I was losing him, his interest in the topic wearing thin in his fickleness. Soon he'd cut me off, telling me he had to get back to work. "The Center is the Good Life Center—a touchy-feely spa where Kyle is the manager."

"Were you aware that Price recently bought the Center for Kyle?"

"Jesus, Grey, what's with all the questions?" Steele asked. Almost immediately, the high-pitched squeaking of his chair stopped. "Shit, no! You're playing amateur detective again, aren't you?"

"Uh—" I began, but he interrupted me.

"You think you're going to solve Price's murder, don't you?"

"Well—" I began again.

"Damn it, Grey, stay out of it. You got lucky with that porn queen's murder, but you almost got yourself killed, too."

"Awww, gee, Steele," I said in a sing-song voice, "I didn't know you cared."

He hung up with a bang.

ELEVEN

GREG CALLED JUST AFTER nine thirty to let me know that he had arrived safely in Minnesota. As with that afternoon, the sound of his voice caused me both sadness and pleasure; a common occurrence, which made me wonder if one could ever experience one emotion without the other. Were sadness and pleasure joined together like Siamese twins, never to be separated without the risk of loss?

He was staying at a hotel just a few miles from his uncle's place. Greg usually stayed in hotels when he traveled, even when visiting relatives. It was easier for him to maneuver in the specially equipped hotel rooms for wheelchair guests than in private homes. He gave me the hotel's phone number and the number at his uncle's house and promised to call again tomorrow night.

When Greg called, I was up to my elbows in the information about Chappy Wheeler and the Holy Pail that Joe Bays had provided. After we talked, I went right back to the task at hand, using the activity to keep my mind off my loneliness for Greg and my indecision about our future.

According to the various articles, *The Chappy Wheeler Show* was first broadcast over the radio in the mid 1940s and made the historic jump to television in 1948. The TV show was into its second season when Wheeler was killed. Charles Borden had changed his name to Chappy Wheeler in 1942 when he had taken up the guitar, learned to ride a horse, and headed to Hollywood to make his fortune as a musical cowboy. He was thirty-one years old when he was found dead in his private bungalow on the studio lot. The cause of death was a couple of hard blows to his right temple with a heavy object. Neither the killer nor the weapon was ever found. There had been evidence of a struggle but nothing pointing to any particular individual. No one saw anyone or heard anything.

Armed with a pot of chamomile tea, I sat at my kitchen table and read each article carefully. Small sticky flags were placed on the edges of pages I felt held important information. I also had a trusty yellow legal pad at my side and jotted down tidbits of information that I hoped, when carefully folded together like ingredients for a soufflé, would yield some clue as to the Holy Pail's curse and its eventual connection to Sterling Price's death, if there was one.

Included in several articles were photographs of the cast of *The Chappy Wheeler Show*. Like most TV cowboys, Chappy Wheeler was portrayed as a mysterious and soft-spoken loner with a sometimes sidekick; in this instance, a dwarf named Hiram Miller, better known as Hi. Hi's character, I learned from reading further, had given up circus life and settled in the fictitious town of Cold Water to run the local newspaper. Chappy Wheeler was the sheriff of the small town of Cold Water, which was supposedly situated on the edge of the desert in Arizona. There was also the requisite lady friend whose relationship with Chappy was purposely kept ambivalent to maintain sexual tension, such as it was depicted in the late 1940s, and to keep the audience guessing and returning. Her name was Lorna Love and she was the town's schoolteacher. Figures. The women who loved the cowboy in the white hat were always either teachers or saloon keepers and were considered old maids for their time. If this show had been broadcast today, Lorna and Chappy would have been humping in the dirt under the bored gaze of his trusty horse. Or having a threesome with the dwarf. Or both.

There were bios and information about some of the other regular cast members, but it was very obvious that the three main principals of *The Chappy Wheeler Show* were Chappy, Lorna, and Hi.

I studied one publicity photo of the cast taken on the set. Charles Borden had been, as they say, a tall drink of water. At least he appeared so in the photo. But after considering he was standing between a dwarf and a petite, rosy young woman, I decided that he was probably in actuality only average in height. He was a slim golden boy with blond hair, a strong chin, and deep, dark eyes. His fair skin was pulled tight over his lean face, and his look was one of serious contemplation. Lorna Love and Hi Miller were smiling for the camera.

Lorna Love was also blond and fair skinned. According to one old fan magazine, she was played by an actress named Catherine Matthews and was only twenty when the show was last broadcast. She looked docile and proper in her costume with the long, dark, heavy skirt and white blouse buttoned to the chin. Looking first at her face and then scanning Borden's, I couldn't help but wonder how much skin cancer had gone undiagnosed in the scorching heat of the real Old West, especially considering all those pale faces arriving from the East and Midwest.

The character of Hi was portrayed by Lester Miles. He was darker than Chappy and Lorna, with dark hair and a full beard. No age was given for Lester Miles, but he looked middle-aged.

Chappy Wheeler had been killed more than fifty years ago. Catherine Matthews would be in her seventies today and Lester Miles somewhere in his eighties or even nineties. I wondered if either was still around.

I continued rummaging through the stacks of articles, looking for more tidbits about this once-popular show. The goal was to complete my initial review before going to bed. To my surprise, I noted that many articles and magazines were not copies, but originals dating back over the past fifty years and kept in protective plastic slip sheets. I handled each carefully by the edges, touching them only as much as I needed. Joe told me that most of the information about Chappy Wheeler had come from a friend of his who was primarily interested in old television westerns. Holding a magazine from 1951 in my hand, I wondered about its monetary value to collectors of such memorabilia.

I was about two-thirds through the large pile of information when I noticed something odd. I had sorted the articles into three stacks—one for articles still needing to be reviewed, one for articles containing information I wanted to revisit, and the third for articles that contained nothing useful to my purpose. This was how I usually reviewed documents at my job.

I stopped and studied the third pile with curiosity. Pushing aside the other two mounds of documents, I moved the third stack, the cast-off pile, in front of me and started re-reading the articles. From that group, I created a sub-pile, which grew surprisingly fast. Almost all of these articles were about one, and only one, cast member of *The Chappy Wheeler Show*, and it was not Chappy Wheeler. When the documents had been mixed together, I had not noticed it.

I glanced at the kitchen clock. It was 10:20, too late to place a call. It would have to wait until morning. *Go to bed, Odelia,* I told myself. *Nothing is going to happen between now and nine A.M.*

I picked up my teacup and matching two-cup-size teapot and carried them to the kitchen sink. Midway, the phone rang. Only three people called me this late—Greg, Zee, and my father. Greg had already called. Zee, knowing my usual bedtime was eleven, sometimes called when she had trouble getting to sleep. I prayed the caller was not my father or stepmother, because it would mean something was very wrong. *Please let it be Zee,* I thought as I put the teapot and cup down on the counter and picked up the phone.

The man's voice on the phone threw me for a loop. It was Joe Bays, the very person I was thinking of calling a few minutes earlier.

"Odelia," he said in a hurried voice as soon as he heard my hello, "did you hear?"

"Joe?"

"Yeah, it's me. I hope I didn't wake you."

"No," I said, "in fact, I was just thinking of calling you, but thought it might be too late."

"Did you hear yet?" he asked again.

"Hear what?"

"About the office. About Steele."

I felt my eyes widen and almost pop out of my head with concern. "What about the office and Steele?"

I carried the cordless phone into the living room and sat down heavily on the sofa. Wainwright followed me from a snug corner of the kitchen and stretched out at my feet. Seamus meowed, hopped up on the sofa next to me, and began butting my free hand for attention.

"What, Joe? What?" I asked impatiently when he hesitated.

"Someone broke into Woobie tonight," he said.

"What?" I asked in a pitch loud enough to make the dog lift his head in alert.

"Someone broke into the firm tonight. Tina just called me to come down now 'cause they ransacked the file room pretty bad." Tina was the firm's office manager. "She said the police are there. She said they messed up some of the offices, too."

"What?" I said again in the same high pitch. Now Wainwright was on his feet and looking worried, no doubt scouting for something from which to protect me. "And Steele? What about Steele?"

"Mike Steele was taken to the hospital," Joe announced excitedly. "Tina said he must have surprised the intruder and was knocked unconscious."

My mind was spinning at the news. I had just talked to Steele a couple of hours ago.

"Who found him?" I asked.

"Dunno," Joe said. "Tina was real closed-mouth about details."

My call waiting beeped. "Hold on, Joe," I said to him and hit the flash button on the phone.

"Hello," I said to the other caller.

"Odelia, it's Tina Swanson. Thank God, you're still up. Something terrible has happened."

"Hold on, Tina, I was on the other line." I clicked back over to Joe. "Joe, I have to go. Tina's calling me."

"Okay. I'm on my way to the office now. But don't tell Tina I told you anything, okay?"

"No problem," I assured him and clicked back to Tina.

"What's up, Tina?" I asked, trying to sound relaxed.

"Odelia, someone broke into the firm tonight."

"What?" I asked, but this time the word lacked the hysterical surprise of a moment ago.

"Someone broke into Wallace, Boer tonight," Tina said in a rush.

Christina Swanson never referred to the firm as Woobie. She was a tall, nervous woman close to my age who had come on board as our office manager about six years ago. She managed the staff professionally, fairly, and competently, which was not easy with all the different personalities housed at Woobie, and half of them attorneys at that. But in spite of her expert handling of her job, Tina never seemed relaxed. Her eyes always displayed a bit of wild fright, not unlike a small animal trapped on the edge of a high cliff by a pack of hyenas.

I never envied Tina her job. The partners had offered it to me when the last manager left, but I declined and stayed with Mr. Wallace and my paralegal work. I got a snoot full of management woes working for Mr. Wallace, and I was unofficially Tina's understudy when she went on vacation. I definitely did not want that kind of stress full time.

"Why?" I asked her.

"Who knows," she said, still forcing the words out in a torrent, "but they really trashed the file room and work areas, especially your office, Odelia. It happened around nine thirty. I'm at the office now."

"What?" I said once again, the shocked tone of earlier returning. I was careful with my next words. "Was anyone there at the time?"

"Yes, Mike Steele. He must have surprised him or them, because he was hit and knocked unconscious." Tina's voice became shaky. "He was taken to the emergency room with a nasty cut on the back of his head and a broken forearm. They're going to keep him a day or two."

I did an involuntary intake of breath, and Tina must have heard it.

"Don't worry, Odelia, they just want to make sure he's okay."

"Who called you and the police?" I asked her. "I spoke with Steele tonight about eight. He was working late. Who else was there?"

Tina hesitated a long time. My imagination ran wild, and I prayed I was wrong.

"Someone from the firm called me at home, Odelia," she finally said, slowing her speech down from frenetic to almost normal. "I called the police."

I took a deep breath before asking my next question. "Was Trudie there with him, Tina?"

Again Tina paused a long time.

"Damn you, Steele," I whispered into the air with a hand over the phone.

"Tina, was Trudie there with Mike Steele?" I asked again, even though I already knew my answer.

"Yes," Tina finally admitted. "They were working late. Trudie said Mr. Steele had a filing due in court tomorrow. After it happened, she called me and I called the police."

Steele's calendar was closely linked to mine. I always checked them both, as well as the firm's main calendar, carefully and daily to keep track of deadlines that were on the horizon. Steele did not have a court filing due until the end of the following week. And he never worked on anything very far ahead of time.

"The only briefs they were working on were Steele's designer briefs," I told Tina in disgust.

There was a big pause following my comment.

"Odelia," Tina finally said, "I know I don't need to tell you how important it is to keep rumors from flying." She tried to keep her voice very low and professional, but her anxiety flavored it with a slight hysterical whine. "Your utmost discretion is a must."

I thought about that. "I agree, Tina. Do you want me to come down to the office tonight?"

"No, I've called Joe in since most of the damage was to the file room. But could you come in early tomorrow? And you'll need to dress casually. Also, I would like to meet with you first thing to discuss the ... uh ... the sensitive situation."

What she meant was damage control.

TWELVE

IT WAS SEVEN A.M. on the dot when, dressed in jeans and a pullover knit shirt, I stepped off the elevator and into the foyer of Woobie. My eyes were barely open. I held a cup of designer coffee in one hand and a bagel with cream cheese in the other. Immediately, I was intercepted by a private security guard. He was a surly older man whose gunmetal gray uniform barely covered his well-rounded gut. While he inspected my Woobie photo ID and my face to make sure they matched, he rocked his weight back and forth on his feet like they were killing him. Giving a slight snorting sound, he handed the identification back and grunted his approval for me to pass into the main part of the office. It made me feel better to note that fastened on his belt was a truncheon but not a gun.

I walked cautiously down the hall toward my office. There appeared to be no one around. My first clue that something was amiss, besides the not-so-secure security guard, was that the closer I got to my little office, the more disheveled the overall office appeared. Files that were once lined up on counters and shelves like sentries were helter-skelter, and loose papers, thousands of them, were piled in hasty stacks on the counters bordering the secretarial bays. Although a mess, it did not look like anything a vandal would take the time to do, and I suspected that during the night someone had picked up a great deal of the mess.

The door to my office was open, giving me a glimpse of the chaos awaiting me. I broke into a trot the last few yards, sloshing coffee as I went and not caring that the special brew had cost me almost as much as a half tank of gas.

Unlike the outer work spaces, no one had attempted to clean up the mess inside my office. The destruction was so complete that there was hardly any room for me to step inside. The open door was partially blocked by a putty-colored four-drawer steel filing cabinet. When I left yesterday for Price's funeral, the cabinet had been upright and standing in a corner of my office. Now it was turned on its side, its contents spilled like the guts of fresh road kill. My bulletin board was askew, my desk drawers open and emptied, and my small bookcase, on which I stored more files on racks, tipped. Even my one plant had been upended and its soil scattered. The only item that seemed undisturbed was my name plate, fastened on the wall just outside the office, to the left of the doorway.

"Pretty bad, isn't it?" a voice behind me said, causing me to jump out of my skin and spill more coffee.

"Oh, Joe," I said, almost crying, "what a mess!" I put the cup down on a counter and grabbed a tissue from a box on a nearby desk to wipe my hands.

Joe was a mess himself. He was dressed in jeans and a faded black T-shirt displaying a rock band logo. Under his eyes were half moons of gray, and he looked as disheveled as the office.

"Were you here all night?" I asked.

He nodded as he ran his hands over his face in a dry scrubbing motion. "Yep," he answered. "Tina asked me to clean up the file room and the stuff from the floor before anyone got in today. I grabbed a couple hours of sleep on Boer's couch." He pointed to the piles of loose papers. "It was so bad it looked like we'd been hit by a blizzard of gigantic snowflakes. The file room was completely trashed, like your office. But other than that, they just emptied files onto the floor. Nothing seems stolen or broken. The computers weren't even touched. Odd, huh?" I stared around in disbelief as he described the vandalism. "Fortunately, the other side of the office wasn't bothered at all," he said, "just this section."

Woobie's offices occupied one very large floor of a modern office building near South Coast Plaza, one of the largest shopping malls in the country. The office was planned in concentric squares, with attorneys occupying the large outside offices with windows. Assistants occupied the inside second tier and were housed in ergonomic secretarial bays with storage for working files. The very inner core of the office held the file room, kitchen, library, copy center, elevators, and reception area. Scattered throughout both the outside ring and inner areas were conference rooms and tiny, windowless, private offices like mine for paralegals and law clerks. When Joe said the other side was not touched, he meant the other sides of the square that comprised our firm's floor space.

"But who would do such a thing?" I asked in complete bewilderment.

Joe shrugged in response. "Lucky for the firm Steele interrupted them. Otherwise the entire place might look like this."

"But why didn't Steele hear the commotion before they did this much damage?"

"From what I can gather, and from what I overheard some of the police say last night," Joe said, yawning wide and stretching before continuing, "the vandals probably began in the file room and had the door shut. You can't hear anything with that heavy door closed. From there, they more than likely worked their way down the hallway just tossing files and papers. The cops think they were looking for something."

"Looking for what?" I asked in astonishment.

Woobie's practice was comprised of mostly corporate and real estate law, some estate planning, and the dull end of civil litigation; nothing glamorous and dangerous by a long shot. For a fleeting moment, it crossed my mind that this involved the Holy Pail, but then I dismissed it as ludicrous. Besides, I had nothing to do with the missing lunchbox.

"And I still don't understand how they got this far without Steele hearing them," I said again to Joe.

Joe grinned sheepishly but said nothing more.

"What?" I asked, taking notice of his amusement.

"You won't believe it," he said, starting to laugh. It was just a titter at first, but threatened to erupt into full-blown belly bouncing.

"Try me," I said, putting my hands on my full hips and giving him a threatening look. He only laughed more.

Joe looked up and down the hallway. Even though no one was in sight, he quickly stepped down the hall and into Steele's office, motioning for me to follow, which I did. Once we were inside, Joe closed the door.

"I really don't want anyone hearing me tell you this," he told me, keeping his voice down in spite of the closed door. My ears went immediately on alert. "Apparently, Mike Steele wasn't alone."

Well, that I had already surmised. "You know who was here?" I asked Joe, wondering how much he knew.

"It was Trudie, his new secretary," Joe whispered. "Surprise, surprise."

I leaned against Steele's expensive, modern desk for support. "Go on," I said, encouraging Joe, knowing he knew a lot more than Tina was planning to tell me.

"I heard Trudie tell the police before they ushered her into a conference room." Joe's boyish face lit up as he spoke. He was clearly enjoying the moment, in spite of the long night and extra work. "She told the police that she and Steele were working late in his office—yeah, right," he interjected sarcastically into his narrative, "when Steele heard a noise in the hall. He went out to check on it and *whack*," he said, emphasizing the word with a karate chop in the air with one hand.

Joe was really starting to ham it up, and I was simultaneously horrified and entertained by his telling of Steele's fate. As much as I dislike Mike Steele as a person, I certainly did not wish him ill and was very thankful he was not hurt worse than he was.

"Now we get to the good part," Joe said with relish. He was grinning so broadly his small eyes were almost hidden in his plump face. "Seems the intruders didn't know Trudie was here 'cause Steele's door was shut while he investigated the noise. So Trudie hid in here until she felt it was safe to come out. She's not even sure how long it was from the time Steele left his office until she finally came out, but she thinks the creeps left shortly after clubbing Steele."

I thought more about this. "Not sure I wouldn't do the same," I confessed. "But I still don't understand how Steele didn't hear all the noise and why he didn't call the police immediately."

Joe grinned again, pleased with himself. I was impatient to hear the whole story, and his coyness was getting on my last nerve. He had no clue how dangerously close he was to doing an imitation of a chicken leg in a Shake 'n Bake bag. He licked his lips before continuing, savoring what he was about to say.

"It's not like Steele didn't hear the vandals," Joe began slowly, letting the words sink into my thick skull. "He just wasn't in a position to do anything about it."

My brain whirred as it tried to piece together what Joe wasn't saying with what he was saying. The result was sure to damage my psyche forever. I turned my head away from Joe and gazed out the window at the morning sky. I felt a sly smile cross my face. "He couldn't let them see him nekkid," I said out loud to myself, still not looking at Joe.

"Huh?" Joe said.

"Nothing, Joe." I turned to face him. "It's not difficult from this point," I said, "to assume that Steele heard the intruders and probably thought it was someone from the firm. It simply took him time to get dressed."

"Bingo, Odelia," he said, laughing really hard as he spoke. He moved to the door and listened for the stirrings of life within the firm. "At least that's what I heard Trudie say to the police. Scream hysterically at them is more like it." Joe turned from the door and back to me. "You should've heard her, Odelia. She was petrified her husband would find out."

"As well she should be," I said. The outrage of having our office torn apart mixed delicately with the hysterically funny thought of Steele almost getting caught with his drawers off. I felt bad for Trudie, but, hey, she was an adult, a married adult, who should have known better. "Where's Trudie now?" I asked Joe.

"Divorce court, most likely," he quipped. Then he shrugged. "Dunno. Home probably. Tina got her out of here as soon as the police were through questioning her. Tina also told me not to speak to anyone about it."

"I'm sure she did." I smiled.

"She said later today the firm would send out a memo."

I nodded, knowing that the memo would be a sanitized account of the vandalism and a mostly fictionalized account of Trudie and Steele's part in it.

Out of curiosity, I moved around to the back of Steele's desk and looked into his trash can. Whatever Steele and Trudie had been up to, it had commenced after the daily cleaning staff had emptied the trash. Steele's standard office issue black plastic trash can was empty except for its liner, a few crumpled papers, two condom wrappers, and two plump clumps of wadded tissue. I plucked the trash can liner out of the can and brought it over to Joe.

"Get rid of this, Joe," I told him. "Just in case someone other than us gets curious and blows the story Tina, no doubt, has been fretting over all night." I smiled at him when I spoke, and he smiled back knowingly.

He took the plastic bag, peeked inside, and smirked. "Nice to know Steele practices safe sex, of a sort," he said. "Just not safe enough."

I placed an index finger on the side of my nose and gently pushed it to one side. "Make sure it sleeps with the fishes. Know what I mean?"

Joe chuckled and nodded.

"By the way," he began, "you said last night you were going to call me. What's up?"

In all the hoopla of last night and this morning, I had almost forgotten. "Yes, I was. I was going through all that information on Chappy Wheeler. Great stuff. I really appreciate your friend loaning it out."

Joe grinned broadly. "Yeah, he's got a cool collection."

I took a deep breath and decided to take the plunge. Last night something had caught my attention among the articles provided by Joe's friend. I had not noticed the same pattern with the articles I knew had come directly from Joe. Venturing a guess about the origin of the other articles, I decided to broach Joe with my conclusion. However, a bit of trickery was in order if I was to confirm my suspicions, as I did not believe Joe would willingly tell me his friend's name. I watched as Joe pressed his ear to the door again, and then took my best shot, knowing I would only get one chance.

"Please tell Lester thanks for letting me borrow the stuff," I said with as much innocence as I could fake.

"Sure, no problem," he said casually with a wave of his hand, his ear still tuned to the door. Then he stopped short and turned.

His look was wary. "What? Huh?" he asked. "I'm sorry, I didn't hear you."

"Busted!" I said to him.

"What are you talking about?" Joe said. He was doing a good acting job, but his flushed face gave him away.

"Lester Miles is your friend with the Chappy memorabilia. Admit it," I said, moving toward him with a smug smile and a pointing finger.

"Who's Lester Miles?" he asked. His small eyes widened in mock ignorance. He was overacting now.

"Lester Miles, former cast member of *The Chappy Wheeler Show*," I said with know-it-all sarcasm. "Lester Miles, former well-known character actor who appeared not just in *The Chappy Wheeler Show*, but in numerous other TV shows and feature films. Lester Miles, the most famous post-*Wizard of Oz* little person of his generation, second only to Billy Barty."

"Oh, *that* Lester Miles," Joe said with exaggerated understanding. He moved away from the door and slumped into one of the visitor's chairs across from Steele's desk. "How'd you know?"

Propping myself up against the desk again, I crossed my arms in front of me. I was pleased with myself for having done my homework last night. After Tina's call, I had trouble sleeping and did some detailed online research into Lester Miles. That information, combined with my suspicions about the Chappy papers, led me to conclude that Lester Miles was still alive, still acting, and was the owner and collector of the stacks of articles Joe had given me. Still, I felt bad for having tricked a friend—but not that bad.

"The possibility first crossed my mind," I said to Joe, "when I noticed that included in the stacks were a lot of articles focusing solely on Lester Miles, and not only about his time on *Chappy Wheeler*. It was a long shot, I admit. This was either the personal collection of Mr. Miles, a family member, or some really big-time fan. But I felt that there was something personal about the articles and their content." I relaxed my arms and leaned toward Joe. "I'm really sorry I tricked you like that, but I didn't think you'd confirm it willingly."

Joe looked at me and smiled. "You're right, I wouldn't have. I met Lester at a collectors' convention several years ago. He's very private and asked me not to tell you." He shook his head and chuckled. "But he'll appreciate your deductive talents."

"I'll explain that you didn't squeal," I said, putting a hand on his forearm. "So, how about setting up a meeting for me with Lester Miles? I promise I won't bite."

Joe shot me a dubious look.

SHORTLY AFTER THE DOORS of Woobie officially opened for the day, Tina Swanson called me in for our meeting. Jolene McHugh, the other attorney assigned to Trudie, also took part in it. She was visibly upset by Tina's announcement that Trudie had decided not to come back to work at the firm. This would be the third secretary Jolene had lost in less than two years through no fault of her own. This turn of events prompted Tina to admit to Jolene and me about Steele's indiscretion with Trudie, saying that Trudie decided it best never to see Mike Steele again. Wise choice, I thought. Tina went on to assure us that Trudie's job would be left open for a week or two in case she changed her mind after the trauma wore off, and that a temporary secretary would be called in beginning Monday.

As for the rest of the firm, Jolene and I were given a preview of the memorandum that would be circulated just before lunch. It explained how Trudie and Steele had been working late and had surprised the intruders, thought to be two in number, whose motives were yet unknown. In the memo, Steele was applauded for his courage and for preventing further damage to the office. Everyone would know better, but with the launching of the official memorandum the issue would be dropped from open discussion like the proverbial hot potato. I knew, though, that discussions over lunches and happy hours outside the office would be lively and creative for both the staff and attorneys for weeks to come.

On the way back to my office, Joyce, the receptionist, gave me a message. It was from Dev Frye. He wanted me to call him as soon as possible. Earlier, I had been questioned by the police. Two uniformed cops, a man and a woman, had efficiently taken my statement and asked if I had noticed anything missing. They also asked about the cases I was currently working on, and I was thankful for the guidance of one of our partners, Carl Yates, during the questioning. Outside of the file room, my office was the only office demolished. It was looking more and more like the intruders were looking for something specific, but I could not, for the life of me, think of what it could be. The possibility of it being the Holy Pail kept popping up in my brain, but I swept it away like a bothersome fly. It was just a coincidence. And besides, I didn't have the lunchbox, and never had.

I called Dev Frye back as soon as I returned to Steele's office. Until mine was back in shape, I had taken up residence at the small conference table in one corner of his office. The police were still picking over my office, looking for prints and clues.

The number on Dev's message was his cell phone. When he answered, I said a chirpy hello, hoping to mask my stress from recent events. After asking how I was doing and saying he had heard about the vandalism at the firm, Dev cut right to the chase.

"Odelia, are you sure Sterling Price didn't give you the Holy Pail?"

It was the same question Stella Hughes had asked me yesterday.

"Uh-huh. I'm positive," I answered. "You think this business at the office is connected to Sterling Price's murder, don't you?"

My question was met with deep silence.

I groaned. My mind was a disturbed pool of muddy water. When it cleared, I wasn't sure I liked the reflection it offered up. This time the pesky fly wouldn't go away. It demanded my attention.

"The police think the vandals were looking for something. You think it might be the Holy Pail, don't you?" I paused. Dev's breathing was the only sound from the other end of the line. "My office was the only one trashed," I continued, vocalizing the facts for my own personal review. "Nothing was stolen from the firm or otherwise damaged."

"Odelia," Dev started to say, but I cut him off.

"What is the big deal about that damn lunchbox?"

Dev chuckled softly before answering. "I'd like to know that myself, Odelia. But honestly, I'm not even sure if the disappearance of the box and the murder are connected. And I'm not sure that's what your intruders were looking for, but I am concerned about the coincidences. Are you sure you're okay?"

Coincidence. There was that word again. I smiled at his concern.

"Yes, I'm fine, thanks. And no, I don't have the Holy Pail. You know, Stella Hughes, Price's fiancée—well, ex-fiancée—asked me that yesterday after the funeral."

"Thanks for letting me know that. We've questioned just about everyone connected with Sterling Price but nothing concrete has come up. We'll talk to her again."

I wondered how much to tell Dev about what I had overheard yesterday in the study. Reluctantly, I acknowledged to myself that Zee was probably right. I should let Dev handle this. I wasn't a detective and could be sitting on pertinent information that could help him.

"Also," I began, wanting instead to clam up and claim the information for my very own, "Kyle Price and Jackson Blake are both involved with Stella Hughes. And you might question Kyle about his father's gift to him of the house and the acquisition of the Good Life Center. I think he might have either blackmailed his father or brokered some information to obtain them, something like that. Something involving his sister, I think." Then, I added a disclaimer. "Of course, I could be wrong."

"We knew about Stella Hughes and Kyle Price," Dev said. "But this other information's new." There was a pause. "By the way, how—"

"Don't ask, Dev. Please, don't ask."

He paused again. Once more I heard breathing, life going in and out of that massive body.

"I know this is going to fall on deaf ears, but please be careful, Odelia."

123

"Thanks, but I'm—"

Now it was his turn to cut me off. "Sterling Price was poisoned, Odelia. It was in his coffee," Dev said bluntly. "Someone put poison into the ground coffee Price kept in his office. Do you understand that?" he asked, giving each word weight.

Dev's words hit me like a bucket of ice water. My eyes widened as I remembered Price and I having a cup of coffee together. He had said it was a special blend. Suddenly I felt woozy.

"What kind of poison?" I asked, the words gurgling out with effort.

"Oleander," Dev said flatly. "Someone laced his personal coffee stash with ground oleander."

I bent over, putting my head between my knees while still clutching the phone to my ear. "Oh," I groaned weakly.

"Odelia, are you all right?" I heard Dev ask anxiously.

"I had a cup of coffee with Sterling Price that morning," I told him in a faint voice from my bent position. There was a long pause on Dev's side. A very long pause. Then he cleared his throat. It sounded like a short blast from a garbage disposal. "He made it himself, but only had enough for a half pot," I continued.

In a voice straining to be positive, Dev finally responded, "The poisoned coffee was brewed in the afternoon. It was made from a newly opened bag. We found that bag and another that had been tampered with. There was an empty bag in the wastepaper basket, probably from the morning, with no trace of the poison."

There followed more throat clearing from Dev and a sound from me that was curiously similar to the mooing of a wounded cow. How blindly close had I come to death? I mooed again. Just last year, I had been chased and shot, but at least I knew I was in danger and did my damnedest to make it as difficult to kill me as possible.

After lunch on Monday, Sterling Price had cheerfully made himself a pot of his beloved French Roast and Sumatra blend—coffee to die for. He never had a chance.

"Is Greg back yet?" Dev asked, interrupting my emotional retreat into the womb.

I pulled my torso back up and looked at the photo of Greg and me that I had rescued from the rubble of my office. It resided now on Steele's conference room table. The glass had been cracked and the wood frame scratched during the night's activities, but the photo was untouched. I traced Greg's handsome face with a fingertip.

"No, he's not," I answered. "There was a death in his family. I'm not sure when he'll be back."

"You are to call me immediately if anything else happens," Dev said gruffly. It was a tone he had never used with me before. "I mean it."

I saluted feebly at the phone.

THIRTEEN

SOUTHERN CALIFORNIA IS LOUSY with oleander bushes. They line freeways, farmland, and back yards, and are often used as natural fences and windbreaks. It is a colorful and hearty plant that blends into the landscape without much notice and is accessible to anyone anytime. Because of its copious availability, as a weapon it is almost impossible to trace back to an individual.

I remember being cautioned at an early age about the poisonous nature of oleander. From time to time, there would be reports of children and animals falling ill after chewing on the leaves. I had even heard that using a branch of oleander to roast hot dogs or marshmallows over a campfire could prove toxic. It had just never occurred to me that parts of the oleander bush could be ground up and brewed into a deadly cup of coffee. I wonder if Starbucks knows about this yet.

At Woobie, the morning had dragged on. The police were still going through my office and asking questions of both attorneys and staff, making it impossible for me to work. It would be at least until after lunch when I would be able to start cleaning up my office, so when Carmen Sepulveda called and asked me to meet her for lunch at twelve thirty, I didn't hesitate. We agreed that I would pick her up, and together we would go to a nearby restaurant. So for the third time in less than a week, I found myself on the road to Sterling Homes, eyeing suspiciously the cheerful and bountiful oleanders I passed along the way.

I must confess that my acceptance of the lunch date was twofold. One, I wanted to pump Carmen for more information, particularly about Stella and the Price clan. And, two, I wanted to meet Amy Chow, the young woman who initially found Mr. Price's body. Since recovering from Dev's revelation about the poisoned coffee, I was like a pit bull in my determination to find out more.

Rosemary had said that Amy covered the front desk from eleven thirty until twelve thirty. Carmen had advised me that she would be in a meeting until almost twelve thirty. It was my plan to ignore that bit of information and arrive early for our lunch date.

So far, so good, I thought to myself when I entered the main door of Sterling Homes and found Rosemary gone. Sitting at the receptionist desk was a young Asian woman. She seemed about the same age as Rosemary, maybe even a little younger, but gave off an air of seriousness and maturity, as if she alone bore the weight of the world. She had straight, blue-black, shoulder-length hair and blunt-cut bangs down to her brow. She was as slim as a reed, with a delicate face of flawless skin and a rosy mouth. Her makeup was sparse, but artfully applied. Without it, she would have looked twelve.

After scribbling my signature and time of arrival into the guest book, I gave my name and purpose to the fill-in receptionist, letting her know that I was early and happy to wait. I plopped my weary body down into the visitor's chair nearest the receptionist desk. The phones were quiet and the young woman was preoccupied with reading a paperback novel. Not wanting to appear too eager, I waited a few moments before shelling her with questions.

"Excuse me," I said to her quietly. She looked up from her book and gave me a small, shy smile. "I'm sorry to bother you, but aren't you Amy Chow, the one who found Mr. Price?"

Instantly, the corners of her pretty mouth turned down and she cloaked herself in wariness.

"Carmen told me," I quickly explained. "It must have been just awful." The girl nodded, but still said nothing. "It must have been quite a shock. I hope you're feeling better now."

"I am, thank you," she murmured in a very tiny voice before going back to her book. I wondered if she was hesitant because the memory was still painful or because she was afraid to talk about it.

I was stumped about how to proceed, afraid that if I pushed, Amy would freeze up. She was obviously much more reserved than Rosemary.

"It's all so horrible," I said.

Her face took on the color and fragility of ecru lace. "It was horrible," she said in a shaky voice.

I tried to be comforting. "I'm sorry you had to be the one to find him. I understand you were just filling in for Carmen."

Her head went up and down slightly. The phone rang and Amy answered it expertly. Once finished, she came back to our conversation. "Yes, I was there in case he needed anything while Mrs. Sepulveda was gone," she told me, still speaking very softly. "But Mr. Price didn't want to be disturbed. Maybe . . . ," she continued, her voice drifting off, trailing guilt like a frothy wake behind a speed-boat.

I waited while a small group of people crossed through the reception area. They lingered only long enough to tell Amy they were going to lunch. She wrote something down. Once they were out the door, I stood up and moved slowly closer to my prey, not wanting to spook her. It was obvious she was carrying some of the burden of Price's death on her small, sensitive shoulders.

"From what Carmen told me," I said to the girl kindly, "there was nothing you could have done. Mr. Price didn't want to be disturbed and you followed his wishes." I looked down at her and she slowly raised her face to mine. "Believe me, Amy, none of this is your fault. And I'm sure you did everything you could to help the police."

The phone rang again just as I saw her face change from the earlier beige to the stark white of correction fluid. She definitely looked rattled, but once more handled the incoming call deftly and with a steady voice. After the call, she did not look up, but instead fiddled with the pages of her novel, dog-earring the corners nervously.

"Mr. Price was a very nice man," she stated simply as she watched her fingers mutilate the edges of the book's pages.

"Yes, he was," I commented softly. I paused briefly before continuing my cautious dance around the uneasy girl. "Amy, after you found Mr. Price, what did you do? Did you scream? Run out of the room? You must have been very frightened."

She twisted her small face into a thinking position, but I knew she would not have to work hard to remember the event. It was only four days ago and that type of thing had a talent for permanent scarring. She was probably wondering if she should tell me or not. She was probably wishing Rosemary would swallow her lunch whole and return early.

Amy's onyx eyes studied me from behind their slanted lids. I smiled slightly, willing her to decide in my favor. Pulling the guest book to her, she turned it around so she could read it. I watched as one of her fingers traced along the last entry—my name, my place of business, and who I was there to see.

Quickly, she flipped her head up. "You're from Mr. Price's law firm, aren't you? The one that was here that morning."

I nodded. "Yes, that was me. I had an eight o'clock meeting with Mr. Price."

She looked hard at me, and I hoped she was arriving at a verdict about my credibility. Her lined brow and small shoulders relaxed some. Inside I breathed easier, sure she had decided to talk.

"I screamed first. Then I ran out to get help," Amy told me in almost a whisper. "Then it was sort of a jumble."

"Who responded to your scream first?" I asked.

"I think it was Mr. Blake," she said. "At least that's what I told the police. His face is the first one I can remember." She pondered her answer a little more. "Yes, I'm pretty sure Mr. Blake ran into Mr. Price's office first."

Jackson Blake. Hmm. "Do you remember what Mr. Blake did as soon as he entered the office?"

She shook her head, the dark curtain of her hair swaying. "No, I never went back in. I couldn't."

"I guess Mr. Blake's office is close to Mr. Price's."

"No, his office is at the other end of the building, next to Mrs. Blake's. Same floor, though. Only Mr. Price's office is at that end of the hallway, and the boardroom."

"Did Mrs. Blake come in when you screamed?" I asked.

Amy hesitated. I noticed that her fingers worked the edges of her book a little faster. "No, I don't think she did. She came after that."

"But I bet both Mr. and Mrs. Blake spent a lot of time with Mr. Price? In his office, in meetings and such?"

Like a threatened turtle, Amy seemed to shrink inward, drawing herself into her torso. She looked around to make sure no one was listening. Seems like everyone I spoke to today was looking over their shoulder.

"No, at least not the times I was there," she said, her voice barely audible. She seemed eager to unburden herself, but still kept herself in cautious check. I leaned in, all ears, my hefty boobs half draped on the high counter in front of her. "In fact, Mr. Price specifically told me not to let Mr. or Mrs. Blake disturb him that day."

"Do you know why?" I asked, keeping the volume on my own voice down.

"No, just that it seemed like Mr. Price was angry with them."

"And what happened next? After Mr. Blake went into Mr. Price's office?"

"After I screamed, lots of people came running. Mr. Blake's secretary took me into the boardroom and stayed with me because I was so upset. Then the ambulance and police came. But just after—" she started to say before stopping short.

I heard footsteps on the staircase behind me and turned to see Karla Blake descending. She approached Amy and announced that she was leaving for an appointment and would return in two hours. Amy dutifully noted it on a sheet.

Karla turned her ice blue eyes to me. She was dressed in a cream-colored silk pantsuit, perfectly tailored to her small and shapely figure. Suddenly, I became self-conscious about my casual attire.

"You were at my father's funeral, weren't you?" she asked with a tight smile.

"Yes, Mrs. Blake. I'm Odelia Grey, a paralegal from Wallace, Boer."

"Of course, Uncle Dell's firm. You're the one who handles our corporate records." Her voice was even and she seemed less brittle than the day before. She reached out a slim hand with long fingers in my direction. "I want to thank you for being there," she continued.

Her politeness held all the warmth of a shark circling an ill-fated life raft. I accepted the offered hand for a short, well-mannered shake.

"You're welcome, Mrs. Blake," I told her, my eyes meeting hers, hoping for an opportunity to read what was behind them. "Your father was one of my favorite clients."

"Seems he was everyone's favorite something," she replied, never dropping her smile for a second. "Is there something I can do for you, Odelia?"

"No, but thank you, Mrs. Blake. I'm waiting for Carmen Sepulveda. We're going to lunch today."

She looked me up and down just by moving her eyes. "Very well. Nice to see you again."

Before I could respond, she stepped through the door into the August heat.

The phone rang just as Karla left and Amy answered it. I noted as she reached out to punch the buttons on the console that her hand trembled slightly. Something was up, something she was not talking about; maybe something to do with Karla Blake.

"That was Mrs. Sepulveda," Amy told me after disconnecting the call. "She'll be down in about ten minutes."

"Thank you, Amy," I said and went back to my abandoned chair where I picked my tote bag up from the floor.

I continued standing while I waited for Carmen and eyed the girl peripherally. Amy was now pretending to be fascinated by her book, but her hands were tense and white knuckled as they gripped the sides of the paperback novel. The unfortunate book would be in a state of disintegration before Rosemary returned from lunch.

"And thank you for being so helpful," I told her, keeping us connected conversationally.

She glanced up at me, nodded quickly and shyly, and dropped her eyes back to the words in front of her. It was clear that seeing Karla had put a cork in Amy's need to talk. The information about Sterling being angry with his daughter and her husband the day he died was interesting, but Amy's complexion and edginess in Karla's presence spoke volumes. But volumes of what?

"Amy, forgive me, but I have one more question."

She glanced up from her book with a worried look that frankly said please go away. There was no doubt in my mind that she was suffering from an attack of chatterer's remorse and wished she had not opened her mouth in the first place. I almost felt ashamed of myself for putting her in such a state. She straightened her shoulders, steeling herself for more of my nosiness. I gave silent thanks that she was too polite to say buzz off.

"During the day," I began, saying the words precisely and slowly, "before he died, did anyone go in and out of Mr. Price's office?"

Amy shrugged before answering. "Not really. Like I said, Mr. Price gave orders not to be disturbed."

She started to say something else, but stopped short and thought about it. I waited, hoping she would get it out before Carmen showed up. Once again, Amy looked around to make sure no one was listening.

"Our mailroom guy came up to get a box that Mr. Price wanted delivered."

"Just the one box that day?" I asked.

She eyed me carefully. "No, actually there were two boxes—a large one and a smaller one. Going to his lawyers, I think. In fact, they went to you, didn't they? I remember typing the address labels."

"Yes," I said to her, "those boxes were delivered to me."

Before I could say anything further, I heard the elevator ding. Turning, I saw Carmen Sepulveda walking toward me, her posture perfect. Like everyone else these days, she seemed exceptionally nervous and I caught her glancing about as she moved forward. Without saying hello, she took me by the elbow and steered me out of the building.

FOURTEEN

"THEY THINK I KILLED Sterling," Carmen announced as she sat in the passenger seat of my car. We were heading for a restaurant known for its salad bar and soup. She talked nonstop, emotions running between disbelief and outrage. I wanted to say something to her, but thought better of it. Instead, I let her talk uninterrupted. Her usual professional composure had been laid to waste, crumpled around her feet like baggy hose.

We each ordered the salad bar and iced tea. Well, I ordered the salad bar and iced tea. Carmen merely nodded in grim silence at the waitress and handed her the closed menu. She was even silent when we walked to the buffet table laden with fresh vegetables, hot soup, and pre-made salads like potato, macaroni, and tuna tarragon. It wasn't until we were reseated that she started up again about being a suspect.

Concentrating first on a cup of soup, I let Carmen continue spilling the events of the past two days. According to her, she'd spent much of yesterday evening and early this morning being grilled by my pal, Detective Devin Frye. Most of the questions were about her whereabouts over the weekend and on Monday, and the poisoned coffee. Of course, she did not know that I was acquainted with Frye outside this case, and I thought it best not to volunteer the information. She picked at her food, eating tiny bites every now and then.

"Carmen," I finally said, putting my spoon down and resting my hands in my lap. She looked up at me, eyes wild, face splotchy, and interrupted me.

"They suspect me of killing him," she repeated for the umpteenth time.

I remained silent. The same possibility had crossed my mind in the past few days. An assistant killing her boss seemed like a natural flow of events to me. If Steele ever ended up dead, I'm sure his secretary *du jour* would be the first suspect, with me running a close second.

"My fingerprints were on the coffee bags, they said." She was repeating the story again, getting more distraught as she spoke. I glanced around the restaurant, glad we were in a corner booth away from most of the foot traffic.

"They came to my house last night after I got home from the funeral. They questioned me for hours," she stammered between nibbles of salad. "They even had a search warrant." She paused to take a deep breath and drink some tea. "But, of course, my fingerprints would be on the coffee bags. I bought the coffee for him! I always did."

She finally sat still, a mixed bag of devastation and indignation. Her face was flushed and her thin lips pressed tight, sharp as a straight pin.

"Carmen, where did the coffee come from? What store? And did it come pre-ground?"

She looked at me with hollow eyes. Her fork started moving robotically from plate to mouth, shoveling in bits of lettuce. A pearl of ranch dressing clung to her bottom lip. She put her fork down and pushed her plate away. Immediately, a busboy came to clear it.

Carmen turned to stare out the window at the parking lot. It was a blistering hot August day and waves of heat shimmered above the blacktop like ripples of fine silk.

Taking a deep breath, she answered. "As I told the police, I ordered it from a specialty store in San Francisco every two weeks. It came in whole beans … a bag of French Roast and a bag of Sumatra. We ground it in the office, mixing the two equally, and refilled the bags. Actually, I ground it and refilled the bags." She said these last words with a distasteful turn of her lip. "There's an electric grinder in the kitchenette by my desk." Her nose was slightly running. She wiped it with a paper napkin before going on. "But they found no oleander traces in the grinder."

"But that's a good thing, isn't it?" I asked.

She nodded. "When they searched my home, they found nothing, of course. I don't even own a coffee grinder. I never drink the stuff, only tea." Carmen started to sniffle a little and her shoulders showed signs of a slight tremble. "Just someone thinking I could do that to Sterling Price makes me ill."

I nodded sympathetically and rotated my head to focus on the heat patterns just beyond the insulated window pane. Turning around again, I looked at Carmen. "When did you last grind coffee for Sterling?" I asked.

"Friday," she responded, "just before I left for my long weekend. To make sure it was fresh, I never ground it too far ahead. I knew he was low on coffee in his office and wouldn't have enough until I got back on Tuesday."

"So you blended and ground the beans, refilled the bags, and put them in his office?"

Carmen gave me a very odd look. Then her eyes widened like saucers and the long, bony fingers of one hand popped up to her thin lips in surprise.

"No, not this time," she said, almost in wonder. "Usually, I did put it in his office, in the cupboard above his little sink, but not Friday. I remember now. He was in a private meeting in his office when I had to leave. I left right after lunch. I was driving to Henderson, Nevada, to visit my sister, and I wanted to leave straight from the office to miss the bulk of the weekend Vegas traffic. So I left the two full bags on my desk with a note for Amy to make sure she put them in his office on Monday morning." She stopped talking, and astonishment wandered across her face. "Oh my, I forgot to tell the police that."

I tried not to show my own surprise at the mention of Amy. So Amy may have put the poisoned coffee in Price's office. No wonder she seemed so burdened. New possibilities reared up like wild horses. Was the coffee poisoned before or after Amy stored it in Price's office? Amy said no one went into the office except for the person picking up the boxes being delivered to me. But what about lunchtime? Amy couldn't have been there the whole time. And besides lunch, she would take breaks.

"Did anyone fill in for you on Friday afternoon?" I asked.

"No," Carmen said, shaking her head slightly. "Friday afternoons are usually quiet, and often Sterling went home early."

"When you get back to the office," I told her, "be sure to call Detective Frye. Make sure he knows that you left the coffee bags out on your desk Friday."

She nodded slowly. "I'll do that right away. How could I have forgotten that?"

"You were in shock, Carmen," I said. "It would be easy to forget things, considering the stress you've been under. Think hard before calling the police; you might remember something else, too."

"Yes, I'll do that. Thank you, Odelia. You've been such a comfort." She sighed deeply and cast her eyes around the table. "That vegetable soup you have looks delicious."

"It is."

While Carmen went in search of vegetable soup, I re-examined the coffee issue. Whoever poisoned Sterling Price probably worked at Sterling Homes, or was close enough to someone in the office to know about his coffee preferences and how they were administered. Since the bags containing the poisoned coffee had Carmen's prints on them, it seemed obvious either that someone had ordered the same coffee, doctored it with oleander, and substituted it for the coffee in the bags Carmen prepared, or they had simply mixed pre-ground oleander into the already ground coffee. The switcheroo apparently was done sometime between Friday afternoon and Monday morning. It had to be someone in the office. Someone who would not raise suspicion if they were seen in the executive wing on the second floor or at the office on the weekend. Jackson and Karla Blake came to mind first. Perhaps even Kyle, if he visited his father from time to time. I wasn't sure if Stella could get by with that. It was common knowledge that Sterling had broken off the engagement. Her appearance in his office just prior to his death would seem too suspicious.

And what about Amy? What part did the young woman play, if any, in this drama of death? Damn tootin' she knew something, but was it about the murder or about one of the players? Specifically, what made her nervous about Karla?

When Carmen returned with her soup and a large blueberry muffin, I was ready with fresh questions.

"Did Sterling drink the same coffee at home?" I asked.

"Why yes, he did on occasion, but not often," she answered, her voice back to her normal efficient tone. "But as I told that huge, nasty detective, Sterling's doctor had insisted that he cut down. He used to drink coffee all day and night—it's a wonder he ever got any sleep. He absolutely refused to switch to decaf. Finally, he cut out his evening coffee. One pot in the morning, one in the afternoon during the week at the office. I believe he only drank it in the morning on weekends."

"Did you grind the beans for his home coffee, too?" I asked, smiling at her description of Dev Frye. Huge, maybe, but nasty?

"Yes, I did," Carmen said. She fiddled with her iced tea glass, smearing the condensation on the outside with an index finger. "Every now and then he'd tell me he was getting low, and I'd order and grind extra for him to take home. The police checked out the coffee at his house and it was fine, no tampering."

Sterling had been poisoned at the office, not at home. I thought about Stella Hughes. It did not seem likely that she would be able to do the poisoning at the office. More than ever, I was sure it had to be someone with unquestioned access to the Sterling Homes corporate offices.

"Why did Sterling break off his engagement to Stella Hughes?" I asked, leaning forward eagerly for the answer.

Carmen sliced her muffin in half, lightly buttered it, and took a healthy bite before answering. She seemed in total control of herself now. I studied her as she relished the taste of the fresh-baked pastry. She seemed a different person from the one sitting before me just a few moments ago. Muffins never did that for me. But hey, everyone has their own personal comfort foods. Still, I found it hard to believe that someone recently questioned as a murder suspect could turn off the concern and distress as easily as buttering a muffin. Innocent or not, I'd be peeing my pants if the police had my name on a short list of suspects, especially if my fingerprints had been found on the murder weapon. But there's no accounting for the human psyche. Maybe Carmen just needed to get it off her chest, and now that she had vented, she could comfortably go back to her lunch.

Devouring the half of muffin in short order, Carmen dabbed at her mouth with her napkin and settled in to do damage to her soup. I began to wonder if she intended on answering my question or if she was simply going to ignore it. But I needn't have worried. After two sips of soup, she was eager to spill the beans on Stella Hughes.

"Plain and simple," Carmen said as she picked up a salt shaker and applied it liberally over her bowl, "Stella Hughes is a tramp."

This wasn't exactly news to me, but I kept quiet and started in on my tuna tarragon pasta salad, which I had piled atop a bed of mixed greens. It was plain to see that Carmen was not going to need the nudging I had thought. I guess once your boss dies, discretion dies, too. Not that I was complaining.

Carmen swallowed more soup before continuing. "I saw that plain as day the first time I saw her. She sashayed into Sterling's life all dolled up and ready for action. It was shameful how he followed her around like a lovesick puppy. His first wife, Millie, must have rolled over in her grave, bless her soul.

"Anyway, in no time at all they were engaged," Carmen snapped her fingers for emphasis. "Of course, his kids were upset, especially Karla. I don't think Kyle liked it much either, but he never was one for rocking the boat. That was more his sister's style."

No, I thought to myself, *Kyle's style was more rocking the desk.* I smirked, then scolded myself silently and plastered on a facial expression more suitable for sympathetic listening.

"As soon as they were engaged," Carmen continued, "Stella moved into that big house and was spending Sterling's money like it was Monopoly cash. Everything was top of the line. Only the best for her."

I thought about my first meeting with Carmen. "The day I brought over the flowers," I said, "you mentioned something about the family always having money problems. That's why they were so anxious to find the Holy Pail."

She looked at me briefly before starting up with her soup again, not stopping until the bowl was empty. Apparently, I had hit a sensitive topic or something she didn't recollect. But I could have sworn a comment of that type had passed between us that day.

Finally, Carmen pushed the bowl away and wiped her mouth. "Yes, both children went through money pretty quickly, but in different ways. Kyle was always broke, always trying some new venture to make money. Poor boy, he never seemed to find his place in the world. A few years back, his father put him through school to learn to be a massage therapist, and he got a job at the Good Life Center. He finally seemed to find his niche, and now he's the manager.

"Karla spent money on investments and research. She's the brains of the two," she said, and I thought I caught a morsel of distaste in the words, like she had suddenly encountered a bit of eggshell in her food. "Karla is never broke like Kyle, but she tends to tie her money up in business ventures and the like."

"You worked a long time for Sterling Price," I noted. "Did you get along with his family?"

"Millie Price and I were especially close over the years. And Kyle has always been very respectful and sweet to me."

"And Karla?"

Carmen started in on the second half of her muffin, using the chewing time to think about her answer. "Karla. Well, Karla can be difficult."

"In what way?"

"For starters, she has no respect for me, never did. And she badgered her father a lot, especially about the business. As soon as she finished her MBA and started working at the company, nothing was good enough for her."

Carmen took a deep breath and pushed it out before continuing. "She and her father often argued about the management of the company. Sometimes I think he wished he'd never put her on the board. She always stirred up the meetings and they took forever when she was there. She was never satisfied, always wanted to change the way things were done." Carmen laughed. "Her daddy was a successful businessman long before she arrived on the scene, I can tell you that."

The brittle, petite blond in the cream silk suit came to my mind. Somehow, I could see Karla Blake being a mover and a shaker, and difficult. But I could also sympathize. Change in business is good and necessary to survive in our modern economy. And being a woman struggling to be heard in a staid company was sure to be tricky and frustrating. I saw it all the time in law, even at Woobie. Female lawyers often had to work harder to prove their competency, and those who were assertive and opinionated were labeled as bitchy.

An energy surge flooded my thoughts, and I remembered something Steele had said the night I called him. "What about Jackson Blake?" I asked Carmen.

She smiled before answering. It was an affectionate and motherly smile. "Jackson's a lamb. He's always a gentleman, very sweet, and extremely smart. He's done wonders for the company." She paused. "Besides being beautiful, I don't know what he sees in Karla. She treats him terribly."

A possibility was expanding in my brain like yeast dough rising in a toasty kitchen. Karla wanted changes in the company, but no one would listen to her. Steele said she didn't get along with the board of directors. Suddenly Jackson is on the scene, married to Karla and rising meteorically to senior vice president from field engineer. Steele had also said that Jackson was good for the company, saving it from stagnation and instigating positive changes.

Was Jackson a shill for his wife? Was he the promoter of Karla's progressive ideas, getting them heard and approved by a gender-prejudiced board? And did Sterling Price discover that he was being duped by his daughter and pay for it with his life? Amy had said that Sterling seemed angry with both Blakes that morning and had given orders that neither was allowed in to see him.

But what about Jackson and Stella? And Kyle and Stella? And Sterling and Stella? It was looking like a con game, with the men the shells and Stella the little ball. Keep your eye on the ball, ladies and gentlemen. Which one will she be under next?

And what about the Holy Pail? Where did that fit in? I knew for sure that Stella and Jackson were both interested in it, but Stella didn't mention it to Kyle at all during their time in the study. Was Karla searching for it, too? And if the vandals of last night were looking for it, who were they or who sent them?

A dull throb was making itself known behind my eyes. Reaching into my tote bag, I extracted a small container of Tylenol caplets and popped two, downing them with iced tea.

"Headache?" Carmen asked.

"Mmm, just starting," I said, "gonna be a doozy." The waitress came over with more tea and I thanked her.

"So," I said to Carmen, getting back on track, "exactly why did Sterling break off his engagement to Stella? Did she fool around on him?"

I already knew the answer to the last part, but wanted to hear what Carmen had to say on the subject.

"Actually, he broke it off with her because of the baby."

"Baby? You mean Stella's pregnant?" I asked curiously, remembering what Kyle had told Stella.

Carmen gave me a wicked grin. "That's what she claims. Personally, I think she wanted to make sure he married her. Of course, the little fool either didn't know or didn't remember that Sterling

145

couldn't have children." She stopped when she saw the surprise on my face. "That's right, all his children were adopted, even Eldon, his first. Several years after Eldon died, Millie and Sterling adopted the twins.

"Of course, once she made that little announcement, Sterling knew she was sleeping with someone else. He just didn't realize it was his own son until the week before he died."

All this new data was making my headache worse. "If Kyle slept with Stella, why did Sterling buy the Center for him and make him a joint tenant in the house in Newport Coast? Why would you give such gifts to someone who betrayed you?" I asked with the fingers of one hand gently massaging my right temple.

Carmen looked surprised, but collected herself quickly. "But of course," she said with a smile, "you were the notary on the documents. They were on my desk with a note from Sterling when I returned."

She waved the waitress over and asked for our check before continuing.

"Kyle came by the office one day early last week. He and his father were behind closed doors a long time. I think that's when he confessed to the baby being his. Sterling had just broken up with Stella the day before, and she was supposed to be all moved out that day by the time he got home."

The check came, and Carmen and I each plunked down our share of money.

"I know this because Sterling asked me to send one of our private security guards to the house that morning to make sure she was packing and not taking anything of his. I think if she'd had any family, he would have thrown her out of the house the minute she told him about the baby. Anyway, Kyle came by, told his father about the two of them and that the baby was his. Immediately, Sterling gave her a reprieve until the end of the month. Even had me call off the security guards."

"So Sterling bought Kyle a business and gave him half the house, just like that?" I asked incredulously. "Was it a wedding present or a baby gift?"

Carmen, noting the sarcasm in my voice, shot me a displeased look.

"I see you find it bizarre," she said. "But that was Sterling for you. He never could stay mad at the kids, no matter what. And you have to understand that Sterling always felt that he had failed Kyle somehow. It bothered him that his son was aimless and unmotivated, while his daughter had the backbone of a Hun."

"Does Karla know about the house and the Center?" I asked.

"Oh yes, and was she ever upset about it." Carmen looked out the window, then back to me, her mood turned thoughtful. "Karla pitched a nasty fit about it right after the funeral. Kyle picked that time, right after everyone left, when it was just the family, Stella, and me at the house, to announce that he and Stella were getting married and moving permanently into the house.

"But in Karla's defense," she said, "I don't think she was upset about Sterling giving the Center and the house to her brother. In fact, I think she would have been okay with it had Stella not been in the picture."

Carmen gathered up her purse and stood to leave. I followed suit. We both had jobs to return to, which gave me another thought.

On the way to the car, Carmen continued talking. "You see, Odelia, I think Sterling gave the Center and the house to Kyle in the hope that Kyle and Stella did, just by coincidence, fall in love. All fathers want their sons to have a solid foundation to support a family. That was how Sterling Price operated. He was always an optimist."

I mulled this over as we got into the car and buckled up. It was obvious to me that Carmen didn't know about Stella and Jackson. Once on the road, I voiced another question.

"Carmen, what's going to happen to you now that Sterling's gone? I imagine the office will need you more than ever, but how will your position change?"

She looked at me and smiled grimly. I glanced over a few times to take in her expression.

"Who knows, Odelia?" she said flatly, like a person giving up. "I'll just have to wait and see. I'm close to retirement age but hadn't planned on it just yet."

I dropped Carmen off in front of Sterling Homes. Just before she shut the car door, she leaned her head inside. "I almost forgot," she said. After digging around in her purse, she produced a slip of paper and held it out to me. "One of those kooks called about the Holy Pail. He's phoned several times. Here's his number, if you still want to pass it along to your friend."

"Sure, no problem," I replied as I took the phone message. "They can have a good chat about metal boxes with rusty hinges."

We laughed and exchanged waves as I drove off. Almost out of the parking lot, I glanced back through my rear-view mirror.

Carmen Sepulveda was still standing in front of the entrance, staring after me. With her gray hair and dull, conservative suit, she reminded me of an old armchair discarded by the side of the road.

FIFTEEN

THE SURLY RENT-A-GUARD WAS still at his post in the lobby of Woobie when I returned, but this time, I didn't have to undergo inspection. I simply held my ID aloft, and he waved me through the doors. If possible, he looked even crankier than this morning.

As soon as I entered the reception area, Joyce handed me two handwritten messages. One was from Tina, saying I was free to begin the cleanup in my office. The second was from Joe, saying that Lester Miles had invited me to lunch Saturday afternoon at twelve thirty at his home. Attached to the note was the address, somewhere in a city called Glendora, and a phone number. Also with Joe's note was a copy of a newspaper clipping. It was the recent article about lunchboxes Joe had mentioned at the Reality Check meeting. I folded it and stuffed it into my tote bag to be read later. There were also two messages on my voice mail. One was from Greg, letting me know he would be home Sunday afternoon and would call tonight. My heart did a pirouette like one of those dancing hippos in *Fantasia*.

My brows knitted together as I listened to the second message. It was from Mike Steele, saying he could not reach Trudie, and demanding that I call him. He sounded weak but fussy. And obviously he did not have a clue about his secretary's flight from the firm.

Mumbling under my breath, I looked up the hospital's phone number and dialed. The phone in his room only rang once before someone snatched it up.

"Steele," the familiar voice answered as if he were sitting in his squeaky chair here at Woobie.

"Hey, Steele," I said, "how are you feeling?"

"Grey?"

"The one and only," I answered, feeling rather spunky in his absence.

"Where's Trudie? I've been trying to reach her all day." He sounded testy but foggy, like a junkyard dog on Percodan.

"Didn't Tina tell you?" I asked. "Trudie quit. Guess all that working late got to her."

"Quit?" he asked with a half-hearted growl. "Now what the hell am I supposed to do?"

I shrugged as if he could see me and answered. "A temp is starting on Monday."

There was a big sigh on the other end. "I don't know why Tina can't find good help," Steele said.

I gave the phone a you-gotta-be-kidding look.

"Grey, I need you to bring the Westchester and Build-Rite files to the hospital. They're keeping me here another night at least, and I have to get some work done. Bring my recorder, too. And don't forget a box of tapes. And a couple of legal pads and some good pens. You know the kind I like. And don't forget my BlackBerry. It's in my suit coat, which should still be hanging behind my door," he demanded without stopping for a breath.

Hesitating only slightly, I plunged forward with my answer, which I knew would be met with the same excitement as news of an emergency root canal. After all, I was not his secretary. His secretary was long gone, thanks to him.

"I'll arrange to have it all sent over," I offered simply.

The silence was deafening. I tapped my foot and waited for a response. Nothing. I started wondering if maybe the drugs had kicked in and he was snoozing on the other end, phone held limp in his hand, drool escaping from the corner of his drug-slack mouth. I was about to gently hang up and let him sleep it off when I heard a throat being cleared. Uh-oh. I moved to shut the office door just in case he inspired me to scream and quit, joining Trudie in the unemployment line.

"Grey, may I remind you," Steele said with a superior tone more like his old self, "that I wouldn't be in here if it weren't for you."

"How do you figure that?" I asked incredulously.

"The police think those hoodlums were looking for something, Grey," Steele said, starting to raise his voice. "Something they obviously think you have, like that damn lunchbox."

"But I don't have the damn lunchbox," I responded, my own voice going up an octave. "I told the police that today. And, come on, you don't know that's what they were looking for. I mean, just because my office got the worst of it. If you hadn't stopped them, who knows what they would have done? Maybe even trashed *your* precious office."

I took a deep breath to calm myself down a bit before continuing. "And besides, you wouldn't have been there in the first place if you and Trudie hadn't been up to monkey business. Court filing, my foot, Steele. This is me you're talking to. I'm the one who deep-sixed the evidence."

"Evidence? Of what?" His tone was really snotty now. The drugs must be wearing off instead of kicking in. Leave it to me to catch him coming down instead of flying high.

"The evidence, Steele. The little wrappers left behind in your trash can."

Another round of silence, longer this time. I took the time to collect myself. I held steady, refusing to be the one to back down.

Finally Steele spoke. "Have the messenger get that stuff to me ASAP, Grey." Then he hung up.

While I had the phone in my hand, I placed a call to the number Carmen Sepulveda had given me. It was an Orange County number. The name Willie Porter was written on the message slip, but the date and time of the call had been left blank. The phone on the other end rang several times before an answering machine picked up. It gave no introduction, just a mechanical prompt to leave a message at the tone, which I did, leaving both my work and home numbers.

Once the messenger was on his way to the hospital with the items Steele had requested, I got down to the business of straightening my office. It was surprising how fast I was able to tidy up once I applied myself. Joe and one of the male paralegals righted my file cabinet for me and replaced it in its original corner. I cleaned up everything else, using the opportunity to rearrange my desk and file drawers. I was about done when the phone rang. Looking at the display, I recognized Zee's number.

"Hey, you," I answered cheerfully, happy for the break.

"Hey back," she said. "So when were you going to tell me about your office being trashed?"

"How'd you find out?" I asked in surprise. "Is it on the news?"

She laughed. "It's news, all right. Seth heard it from Doug." Zee was referring to Doug Hemming, Seth's law partner. "Doug heard it from an attorney he had lunch with today, who heard it from his secretary, who heard it from a court reporter, who heard it from his girlfriend, who is a word processor at a law firm where the husband of one of your firm's attorneys works."

Ah, yes, the legal circle of life. We're so caught up in confidentiality when it comes to our clients that we can never resist gossiping about ourselves. All that pent-up chatter had to vent somehow.

"I was going to tell you tonight. I'm cleaning up my office as we speak," I said.

"You mean they actually trashed your office? Not just the office in general?"

"Doug didn't tell Seth that?" I asked with a slight chuckle. "He's falling down on the job."

"Apparently not," she told me. "And I'm sure Seth wouldn't have left that out. All I got was that the firm had been vandalized and Mike Steele was in the hospital. I figured it was a disgruntled employee. Lots of Steele's ex-secretaries floating about. Not to mentioned disgruntled husbands of ex-secretaries."

She had no idea how close she was to the truth. It was here at Woobie years ago that I had first met Zee. She was a young mother with only one child then, and Seth was starting to build his own practice. Though she was long gone before Mike Steele came onboard, she had heard the stories, and not just from me.

"Zee," I said into the phone quietly, still not believing it myself, "my office and the file room were the most seriously damaged. The police, and even Steele, think the guys last night were looking for something that might have been in my office. Like maybe the Holy Pail."

"You're joking," she said, her voice getting tense. "But you told me you don't have it."

"I don't," I insisted yet again. "I only have the Zorro box and that they left behind. I found it on the floor under my desk without so much as a scratch. As far as I can tell, they took nothing or else didn't find what they were looking for."

"Mercy," Zee whispered into the phone. "This is just too strange."

We hung together silently on the phone, clutching each other over the phone lines, guarding against the possibility of danger, unseen but very real. We didn't need to speak.

"Oh, I heard from Greg," I finally said. "He's coming home Sunday afternoon."

"Good," Zee said, sounding relieved to change the subject. "Any decision yet?"

"Uh-uh." Quickly, I changed the subject back to the Holy Pail, finding that easier to think about than Greg and his proposal. "Tomorrow, I have an appointment with one of the actors from the old *Chappy Wheeler Show*. Maybe I'll learn something from him. His name is Lester Miles."

"Lester Miles," Zee said, musing. "Is he a midget or dwarf or something like that?"

"Yes, a dwarf," I answered. "You know him?"

155

"I know of him. He used to be in lots of movies and TV shows." She was quiet for a second. "And I think he was in a made-for-TV movie just a couple of weeks ago. In fact, I'm sure of it. Something about a grandfather who raises his grandchildren in spite of everyone's objections. You know, the usual three-hankie stuff."

"He lives in Glendora, according to Joe Bays. Do you have any idea where that is?" I asked.

"Somewhere near San Dimas, I believe. I only know because it's near the waterpark the kids like."

I looked down at my hands. My nails, bad a few days ago, were truly shameful now after the cleanup.

"I think I'm going to see if I can get a nail appointment around ten or ten thirty and leave from there." I picked up a pad of Post-It Notes and jotted down NAILS on the top sheet so I would remember to call for an appointment when I finished talking with Zee.

"By the way," I said into the phone, "do you know anything about the Good Life Center? It's a day spa or massage place or something like that?"

"Sure I do," Zee answered.

Why was I not surprised? Sometimes I wondered why I ever wasted my time doing research when all I had to do was call my best friend. She was a bottomless well of information, a virtual fount of minutia.

"Remember earlier this year, when I won that spa visit for high sales from Golden Rose?" she asked. "Well, that's where my gift certificate was for. It was wonderful. It's over off of Jamboree Road, in the same shopping center as Houston's."

"I found out that it's owned by Sterling Price's son, Kyle," I told her. "His father signed the final papers the day he died."

"Nice gift."

"I'll say. Price also deeded over the house in Newport Coast to Kyle the same day. Seems the whole thing caused a big ruckus in the family the day of the funeral."

"He signed the papers and a few hours later he's dead?" Zee asked. "Well, that's about as fishy as an open can of tuna."

I could almost see her standing by the phone with one hand on her bulky hip. It was her intimidating stance, a posture that said she wasn't having any of it.

"I agree," I told her. "But did someone kill Sterling Price because of the gift to Kyle or to stop it? Or did someone kill him to steal the Holy Pail?"

"I'm leaning toward the theory that the theft of the lunchbox and the murder had nothing to do with each other," Zee threw in. "What better time to steal something valuable? I mean, think of the chaos after he was found."

"That seems to be the consensus," I said. "But if that's the case, why would someone search our law firm for it, if that's what their motive was last night? And who were they? Steele thinks there were only two men, and he said they wore ski masks."

"Which matches the description of almost every burglar in history," Zee said with a frustrated sigh. "I just don't like the idea that they searched your office."

That made two of us. I was trying to decide if I should tell her about the poison, but knew she would worry needlessly. It also occurred to me that we may all be off base. Maybe the murder had nothing to do with either the Holy Pail or the gift to Kyle. Maybe there was still a missing motive, something eluding me in all the hubbub.

"I have to run," Zee said in a hurry. "Seth and I are having dinner tonight in Laguna Beach with the Carroltons. I still need to get some things done before I start getting ready. What are you doing tonight?"

I groaned audibly. "Going to my dad's. A belated birthday dinner."

I could hear a soft chuckle from the other end of the phone. "I'd tell you to have fun, but I know better," she said. "So just have as good a time as possible."

I mumbled something that I hoped passed for a human sound.

"It may be your birthday dinner, but tonight is really for your father," she added.

I tapped my nails on my desk in impatience. She was right, of course. Tonight was more for Dad. My occasional visits brightened his dreary existence among the evil mole people more commonly known as my stepfamily. Under my breath, I cursed Greg for not being here to go with me. Then I thought about his Uncle Stu and his sweet Aunt Esther, now a widow, and immediately felt guilty and cheap for my selfishness. Greg was where he needed to be at this moment, and I could weather the visit to my father's solo. I'd done it for years already.

"You be careful tomorrow, Odelia," Zee said before saying goodbye and hanging up.

Hmm. Tomorrow didn't worry me. It was getting through dinner tonight without being charged with homicide. *That* would be the real challenge.

SIXTEEN

PARKED CURBSIDE, I STUDIED my father and stepmother's house. From the outside, it looks like any normal three-bedroom bungalow found in a Southern California working-class neighborhood. Painted the color of a honeydew melon and sporting white shutters, it sits in the middle of a no-frills lawn consisting only of well-tended grass and low-maintenance shrubs. There wasn't a flower in sight and, unlike a lot of their neighbors, not an RV in sight either. My father, Horten Grey, still does the lawn work himself, even though he's in his early eighties. Once in a while, he hires a neighbor boy to cut the grass when the summer heat gets to him. The outside of the house, as simple and as uncluttered as a shoebox, is much like my father.

They bought the house over thirty years ago when they first married. I had been thirteen when my parents divorced, fourteen when my father married Gigi, and sixteen when I came home from high school to find my mother gone. Against everyone's wishes but my father's, I moved in with my father and Gigi, striking out on my own almost before the candles on my eighteenth birthday cake were blown out.

It's not like anyone within the walls of this house ever beat me. In fact, my father never laid a hand on me in anger my entire life. But I can only take my stepmother and her family in very small doses, like arsenic. Let me put it this way: holidays and family dinners resemble a casting call for *The Jerry Springer Show*.

My own mother had been no picnic either. A sullen alcoholic, when we lived alone together after the divorce, she would go days without speaking to me. She was emotionally devoid and unavailable, as if her insides had been beamed up by aliens, leaving behind a shell. It was the middle of May, just weeks before the end of my junior year of high school, when I came home from school and found her gone. She took only her personal items and left the rest of the apartment intact, as if she thought I would live there alone after she left, like a discarded roommate instead of an abandoned offspring. She left no final note, and I have not heard a word from her since. Looking back at things now with an adult perspective, I'm surprised she didn't leave earlier.

The main reason I was still sitting in my car in front of my father's was that I wanted to mull over the disturbing call I received shortly before leaving the office tonight. It was my return call from Willie Porter.

The call did not go the way I had expected, although I am not sure what I did expect. Still, it rattled me from the ground up and left me shaken and thrilled at the same time—like riding out a fair-to-middlin' earthquake.

Willie Porter was very articulate, with a confident, cultured voice. In short order, I had pegged him as another wealthy business tycoon hoping to land the prized lunchbox.

I was wrong.

Once he established my identity and place in the Holy Pail saga, he announced himself satisfied and got down to business. I could tell that this was a man used to being in control and calling the shots. In a firm voice, he informed me he had information, important information, about Price's murder and the curse of the Holy Pail.

Quickly, I had changed my idea of Willie Porter as a wealthy collector to just a kook looking for attention—well-spoken or not. I advised him to call the police if he had a lead on the murder. Before I could recite the final numbers of Dev's cell phone, Porter dropped a bomb.

"My real name is William Proctor," he had said evenly.

I half expected him to follow up with " … and I've got a secret." On this, I would not have been wrong.

"I owned the Holy Pail before Sterling Price."

I thought carefully about Porter's claim before answering him. This could easily be someone who read the magazine article and knew the order of ownership.

"But you can't be," I said firmly into the phone. "William Proctor is dead."

"Only on paper, Ms. Grey, only on paper." When I failed to respond, he continued. "Meet me tomorrow, Saturday. First thing in the morning." It had not been an invitation, but a gentle demand.

"I … uh … I can't," I said, stuttering. "I have appointments most of the day."

"You have an appointment at six A.M.?" he asked in a mocking tone.

"Ahh … no," I said, a bit spooked. The urge to hang up on him had been strong. Talking to dead people wasn't my thing. "I think you should call the police. Really, I do."

He chuckled. "Can't, Ms. Grey. A little matter of fraud. And besides, I am dead."

I sat stunned and speechless. A bump on a log was more mobile.

"Then six it is," he said with confidence. He rattled off an address in Santa Ana. I mechanically jotted it down, telling myself the whole time there was no way in hell I was going to meet this man. "And Ms. Grey," he added, "don't bring the police, bring coffee. Good, strong coffee. I prefer Ethiopian."

The call had been just over an hour ago. I had thought of little else since. Rummaging in my purse, I located Dev's card and my cell phone. Before I could switch on the phone, a bark sounded in my ear, followed by a squeal shooting out of my mouth.

It was Wainwright. I had been so lost in my thoughts about Porter, I had forgotten that the dog was in the back seat. Greg took Wainwright almost everywhere with him. Since coming to my house, the poor animal had developed a bad case of cabin fever. Tonight when I stopped home to give him a quick walk, I crumbled before his sad, imploring eyes. Besides, Dad loved the animal and treated him like one of the family whenever Greg and I visited.

Wainwright barked again, this time louder. Turning, I saw JJ, my stepbrother, standing on the sidewalk a few feet from the car. He had his eyes on the dog, nervous even though he'd been around the animal before.

"You gonna sit in there all night?" JJ yelled at me.

I reached across and rolled down the window halfway, swearing that my next car would have power windows. Wainwright poked part of his big yellow head out the window and whined. No matter what I thought of JJ, Wainwright, at least, recognized him as extended family.

"I'll be right in, JJ," I told him. "I need to make a personal call." I was thinking I should contact Dev Frye, in spite of what Porter had said.

"Jesus, Odelia, I wanna eat," JJ whined. "Horten won't let us eat until you get your fat ass in there."

JJ is in his early sixties. He was actually married once, decades ago. He has children who cannot stand to be near him, which is not hard to believe. Most of the time, he survives by sponging off Dad and Gigi. Tonight, he was dressed in khaki shorts—period. Seeing the dog was friendly, he approached a few feet, but still kept his distance.

"Whaddya so fat now you can't get out from behind the wheel?" He snickered at what he thought was a brilliant remark.

Ignore him, I told myself. *He isn't worth the effort.*

With a deep sigh, I stashed the phone back in my purse and jerked open my car door. JJ was already heading for his place at the dinner table when I extracted the dog from the back seat.

However simple and bare the outside of the house was, the inside was its opposite. Gigi believed that more was more, and the more from yard sales and flea markets, the better. Greg, following his first visit to my family, announced that Gigi redefined the word *kitsch* and lowered it to a new level. Personally, I think he was too kind.

Entering the house, I smelled glazed baked ham. My mouth started to water. Wainwright licked his chops and gave off a little moan. He was no fool. My dad was a soft touch when it came to begging, and Greg wasn't around. Tonight, table scraps would flow like cheap beer. Just to make sure, the dog sidled up to my dad, nudged his leg, and wagged his tail. I had to laugh. He reminded me of Greg when he wanted to have sex.

As soon as I set foot into the kitchen, JJ started piling a plate up with ham, green beans flecked with bacon grease, and mashed potatoes made from instant flakes. Without a word, he carried it into the living room to watch TV.

My father was standing beside his chair at the table, waiting for me. One gnarled hand stroked the dog's head. Dad beamed, his wide, fleshy face breaking into a genuine glow when he saw me. He was of average height and slightly stooped, like punctuation that can't make up its mind if it's a question mark or a parenthesis. Like many men his age, he had a pot belly but no butt and had to use suspenders to keep his pants up. I hugged him tightly and he kissed my forehead.

"Happy birthday, little lady," he said. "You look like a million bucks."

"Thanks, Daddy," I answered, locking my eyes onto his. They were green like mine. The way he smiled told me he had his hearing aid turned on for the occasion.

Gigi shuffled in from the kitchen with a salad of iceberg lettuce and tomatoes smothered in Thousand Island dressing. Her usual bouffant hairdo looked freshly done and had a pinkish glow to it, like it had been rinsed in Pepto-Bismol. She was spindly, the sharpness of her structure emphasized by tight turquoise knit pants and a clingy synthetic top. Over the years her features had taken a downward turn, as if molded out of melting wax. I looked behind her and was pleased to see that my stepsister, Dee, was nowhere in sight. Dee was in her mid-sixties with a family of her own. She lived only a few miles away, but seldom visited.

I said hello to Gigi and thanked her politely for having me over for dinner. Zee would have been proud of my civility. But the politeness was shaky at best. I knew it was just a matter of time before my stepmother opened her mouth and I'd be fighting for control. It didn't take long.

"Where's that cripple boyfriend of yours?" she asked, eyeing the dog with disfavor. She put the salad bowl down on the table with a thud.

My stepmother believes that Betty Crocker is a real person, and that Martha Stewart is her illegitimate daughter. She also thinks Aunt Jemima and Uncle Ben are real, too. Married to each other, of course, and running a diner outside of Birmingham, Alabama.

I swear to you, she told me so.

I took a deep breath. Dad glanced at me and I saw caution flash in his eyes as clearly as a flare at a highway accident. We took our seats and started passing the food.

"Greg is in Minneapolis," I explained. "His uncle died."

"Was he a cripple, too?" Gigi asked.

"Hate to disappoint you, Gigi," I said, flashing a polyester smile, "but accidents resulting in spinal injuries aren't genetic."

"I like that Greg," my father said with a nod to the ham he was placing on his plate.

"Me, too, Daddy." I hesitated, wondering if I should say anything about the proposal.

Gigi pointed her fork at me. "For a minute, I thought that cripple dumped you and stuck you with the damn dog."

"Figures," JJ added, coming into the kitchen to load up his plate again, "she couldn't even hang on to a cripple. Shit, he was probably afraid she'd squash him in the sack."

"JJ, that's enough," I said through clenched teeth. "As a matter of fact, Greg asked me to marry him."

My father looked up and smiled. Instantly, he looked younger and happier than I had seen him in years. It made me glad I had said something, even if the circumstances were not exactly prime for such news.

"Cripples can't screw, can they?" Gigi asked. She looked to my father. "Horten, can cripples screw?"

Dad looked at Gigi in undisguised horror. For a minute, I actually thought he would lose his temper. But he didn't. I love my father dearly, but he has no backbone.

Turning to Gigi, I announced, "Since you're interested, Greg and I have a perfectly wonderful sex life."

"Didn't know you were into kinky stuff, Odelia," JJ said with a leer. "I hear lots of girls line up for guys like that. Kind of a freak thing."

I started to rise, but felt my father's hand reach under the table and gently squeeze my knee. *Follow my lead,* he was telling me. His head was bent over his plate and his face was slightly flushed. His other hand was busy shoveling food into his mouth.

Gigi lifted a can of generic beer halfway to her lips and stared at my father. "Well, I guess half a man's better'n none." My father flinched, but kept eating.

"Don't worry, Ma," JJ said, "it'll work out. Greg's half a man and Odelia's double a woman."

I slammed down my fork.

My father's hand left my knee. Out of the corner of my eye, I saw it move to his hearing aid and turn it off.

I counted to ten. Then to twenty. On twenty-one, I turned to my father and coaxed him into turning his hearing aid back on. I did my best to ignore Gigi and JJ, but I didn't have the luxury of a hearing aid to shut off at will.

I asked my father about Chappy Wheeler. Did he remember the show? Surprisingly, he did remember it, telling me that he and my mother had watched it faithfully.

"I remember that show," Gigi chimed in. She was through eating and was now smoking at the kitchen table while the rest of us ate. "That Chappy Wheeler was real handsome. Tall and blond, and very serious."

Even JJ got into the act. "Hey, isn't that the guy who was murdered?"

"Yep," his mother said, taking another puff.

"Yeah, I remember," JJ said. He scratched the stubble on his chin. It sounded like sandpaper. "He was a real big fag. Probably got himself killed by another fag."

Gigi turned on her son. "Chappy Wheeler was not a homo," she snapped.

"He was so, Ma. Everyone knew it." JJ picked at the ham, stuffing a small piece into his mouth. "Hell," he said, speaking with his mouth full, "I was just a kid when he was killed, but I remember. Everyone talked about it for months."

"Chappy Wheeler was not a homo," Gigi insisted. "He was married to that cute girl on the show. The one who played the schoolteacher. Oh, what was her name?" Gigi snapped her bony fingers as she tried to think.

"Catherine Matthews," I said, filling in the blank.

"Huh?" Gigi asked, looking at me vacantly.

"Catherine Matthews," I explained, "was the actress who played Lorna Love on the show."

Gigi pointed a finger at me like she was accusing me of stealing her dentures. "That's right, that's right. Pretty little thing, blond and tiny. They were married in real life. That proves he wasn't a homo. Had a little girl, too. Poor thing was born after her daddy was murdered."

I was in shock, though I don't know why. Celebrity scandal was exactly the type of stuff Gigi and her family thrived on. I should have realized that the murder of a television star would be something they would remember. War, famine, Nobel Prizes—no. But Hollywood murders—absolutely. Gigi once made a pilgrimage to Bundy Drive, to the site where the Simpson murders occurred, and complained to the police because she couldn't see a chalk outline of the two bodies.

I looked over at her. Gigi's eyes were closed, and she was mumbling to herself, no doubt trying to conjure up sleazy details she had read in the tabloids fifty years earlier. Grudgingly, I had to admit that I was impressed by her recall faculties.

My father watched the whole thing like a favorite TV drama while he fed bits of ham to the dog. I looked at him and he shrugged. Beyond watching *The Chappy Wheeler Show* weekly, he was in the dark.

"Now I remember," Gigi said, slapping her hand down on the table. The green beans gave a little hop in their serving bowl. "Yes, I remember. It was that midget."

"Midget?" I asked.

"Yes," my father said, "there was a midget. He played Chappy's friend." He smiled at me, happy to assist in any way he could.

"The midget did it," Gigi said with enthusiasm.

"You mean the midget—I mean, Lester Miles, the actor –killed Wheeler?" I asked. "But I thought the murder was never solved."

"No, no, no," Gigi said, waving her hand impatiently in the air. "The midget married Lorna. I mean—not Lorna—oh, now I've forgotten. You're confusing me."

I rewound and replayed what Gigi just said in the depths of my mind until it clicked.

"You mean," I said slowly to my stepmother, "that in real life Chappy Wheeler was married to Catherine Matthews?" Gigi nodded, her pink hair bobbing. "Then after Wheeler died, Lester Miles, the actor who played Hi on the show, married Catherine?"

"Isn't that what I just said?" Gigi snapped. "And not too long after poor Chappy's murder either. Always thought that was a bit suspicious."

For once, I didn't doubt my stepmother. Odd, though, none of this was mentioned in the memorabilia I received through Joe.

"You know what else?" Gigi asked, tapping my arm with a finger. "That Lester fella wasn't a real midget."

"He wasn't?" I asked.

"No, not a real midget at all. I read somewhere that he just played one on TV. In real life, he's really six feet tall."

SEVENTEEN

THE HAM AND GREASY green beans rolled around in my stomach like a roller derby. We had sat down to dinner about six. Looking at my watch, I saw that it was almost eight and I was halfway home. On the seat beside me was a pink bottle of Pepto-Bismol. I had picked it up at the mini mart when I stopped for gas. I took periodic swigs from it and tried not to think about Gigi's hair. The dog was sprawled on the back seat, snoring.

It was my intention to take a hot, scented bath as soon as I got home. It would be as good a place as any to think about the new information Gigi and JJ had provided. I could take the portable phone into the bathroom with me in case Greg called while I was soaking. I giggled, knowing that it would turn Greg on to tell him I was in the bath while we talked.

Half a man, my big behind.

Pulling up in front of my townhouse, my hot, soapy indulgence dissolved into a symphony of popped bubbles. Sitting on the low step to my front door was a woman—Stella Hughes, to be precise.

A very unladylike belch escaped my lips as I thought about driving by and going somewhere—anywhere. For all I cared, Stella could just sit there and ponder the mystery of my intelligence until her butt ached from the cold concrete. Unfortunately, she spotted me and waved. Crap. I waved back, gave her a slight smile, and hit the automatic door opener to my attached garage. While she watched, I pulled in. There was a door leading from the garage into my townhouse, and I wanted desperately to escape through it and pretend she wasn't there. I took another swig from the pink bottle instead.

"I'm sorry I just popped in on you like this, Odelia," Stella said in her low, sexy voice as I unlocked my front door.

Wainwright seemed eager to get inside. Surprisingly, I didn't hear Seamus on the other side of the door raising a fuss as usual. As soon as the door opened a sliver, the big dog pushed his way in and started sniffing the premises. No cat in sight.

"That's odd," I said to Stella. "Usually my cat is waiting for me."

"Maybe it's the dog."

I shook my head. "No way, they're pals."

Wainwright circled and sniffed, covering every inch of the downstairs like a Hoover vacuum. Still no Seamus.

"Seamus," I called out. "Seamus, come on out. Here, kitty, kitty." I turned to Wainwright. "Find Seamus, boy. Find Seamus." The dog took off upstairs.

"Please have a seat, Stella," I told her. "I'll be with you in a minute."

Upstairs, in my bedroom, I found Wainwright flattened on my bedroom floor, his long snout buried under the bed. I crouched down and peered under the bed next to him. Two glowing eyes peered back at us.

"Seamus," I said to the cat. "Come on out. We have company, nothing to be afraid of."

The cat stayed put and gave off a pathetic whine.

I stood up. "Oh well, come down when you're ready."

Stella was looking at the items in my curio cabinet when I returned. Wainwright came back downstairs with me.

"Cat's under the bed," I explained.

"You collect nativity scenes?" Stella asked, indicating the pieces in the cabinet. "How extraordinary." There was a touch of amusement in her voice.

"Not really. More people than you realize collect them. I have just over fifty different ones now. They're scattered about the house."

"Uh-huh," she murmured and continued scanning my collection, moving to those displayed on my bookshelves.

I didn't like the way she was scrutinizing my things. Unfortunately, nervousness makes me gabby.

"I like to see how different people express their faith through this common theme," I explained. "It's amazing how many ways the birth of Jesus is depicted around the world, from true art pieces," I pointed to a simple but elegant pen and ink drawing, "to what some would consider sacrilegious." I moved my hand to indicate a beer bottle with a label showing a manger scene and the words "Savior Suds" hanging on the staircase wall.

Stella turned to me. "No lunchbox?" she asked with one eyebrow cocked.

"Haven't come across one yet," I answered. "But I do have a nativity cookie jar. Bought it recently from someone on eBay."

I made a gesture inviting her to sit. "Would you like something to drink? A Coke, coffee, iced tea?"

"Iced tea would be nice, if it's no trouble," Stella said, taking a seat on the sofa.

I returned a few minutes later with a tray of two tall glasses of iced tea, wedges of lemon, sugar, sugar substitute, and spoons. There was also a small plate of Thin Mint cookies, fresh from the freezer.

While I was in the kitchen, Seamus had ventured downstairs. I found Stella trying to coax him out from under the rocking chair.

"He's not user friendly," I said, putting the tray down on the coffee table and sitting across from her. "A few years ago, he was living wild, and he's adopted me but still isn't comfortable around many people."

Wainwright moved in closer. Usually mellow, the dog seemed edgy and obviously did not like a stranger making advances on Seamus.

"Wainwright, down," I commanded gently. The big golden dog dropped to the floor, but not before putting his snout in the path between Stella and Seamus.

Stella laughed nervously. "Very protective, isn't he?" She took her tea, added sweetener, and stirred before sipping.

"Yes, they really are quite close. Wasn't that way at first, though." I added only a lemon slice to my tea before taking my first sip. "Wainwright is actually my boyfriend's dog. I'm keeping him while he's out of town."

I thought about reaching for a cookie, but changed my mind. I was nervous, and nerves made me eat. Buzzing through the cookies like a woodchuck would hardly add to an appearance of calmness, and I did not want this woman knowing I was anything but cool and calm.

"How did you find out where I live?" I asked.

"The phone book," she answered quickly.

"But I'm not in the phone book."

"The online phone book." Stella hesitated when she caught my skeptical glance and looked embarrassed. "Actually," she confessed, "I used People Search."

"Oh?"

I took another sip of tea. I didn't like the fact that someone who hardly knew me could find me that easily. In my opinion, lack of privacy was one of the potholes on the information highway. And People Search charged for their searches. I studied Stella and not shyly. This woman had paid money to find me. She must have had a good reason and I was dying to know what.

The cookies were calling my name.

Stella was dressed in jeans, tight and fitted to her curvy hips and thighs. Her top was knit, worn off the shoulder, with the cleavage of her large breasts mounded slightly at the neckline. On her feet were sexy high-heeled sandals. Good-size hoops of gold hung from her ears and a thin gold chain caressed her neck. All were of excellent quality, even her designer handbag and fancy watch. Her hair was curled today, worn fluffy around her face. She looked like a lot of women in Newport Beach: like an aging, expensive tart, except that she didn't look half-starved. She was also very tan. Somewhere between the funeral yesterday afternoon and today, Stella had found time to sunbathe. I took a guess that she probably hung around the pool this morning at Price's. After all, she no longer had to spend her time moving.

"Why did you pay for People Search when you could have reached me at my office?" I asked.

"I called, but you were already gone," she explained. "I'm sorry if it bothers you, but I really needed to see you." Her deep voice was beginning to sound strained. "I couldn't wait until Monday."

In less than twenty-four hours, my office had been vandalized and I had had to deal with Carmen, Willie Porter, my family, and now this—not to mention a wounded Mike Steele. Couldn't someone have waited until Monday? Was everyone into instant gratification at my expense?

"What's so important?" I asked.

She hesitated. "May I smoke?" she asked, pulling a package of Virginia Slims out of her purse.

"Sorry, not in here. But you're welcome to go out on the patio."

She put the package back. "No, that's okay. I really don't smoke much, just when I'm nervous." She picked up a cookie instead and bit it in half.

Wait a minute. Smoking? And she was supposedly pregnant? I looked at her and waited. When she didn't say anything more, I rephrased my earlier question. "So why are you here tonight?"

"They think I killed Sterling," she said matter-of-factly while dabbing cookie crumbs from her lips with a painted fingertip.

Geez, where had I heard this before? I looked at her with what I hoped was a blank expression.

"Of course," she continued, "why shouldn't they? I'd even suspect me." She gave a gravelly laugh and popped the rest of the cookie into her mouth. "I love these things frozen," she said when she was finished chewing. She reached for another.

"Did you poison him?" I asked directly. A mutual taste in cookies did not make us friends, or her innocent.

"Of course not."

"Convince me," I challenged her. "You had motive and opportunity. You lived with him, could have easily added ground oleander to a bag of his favorite coffee. How you slipped it into his office is still a mystery. I imagine after the breakup you weren't welcome there."

She gave a short snort of laughter. "Hardly. Between Karla and Carmen, I wasn't welcome there even when we were together." She narrowed her eyes at me. "You seem to know a lot about the case."

It was my turn to snort. "For some reason, people can't seem to leave me alone about it. And for some reason, people seem to think I have the Holy Pail. My office was even vandalized last night. Not to mention, I was one-half pot of coffee away from being poisoned along with Sterling Price. Believe me, my interest in this matter has gone way beyond mild curiosity."

"But you don't, right? Have the lunchbox, I mean?"

The fact that I was almost poisoned went right over Stella's well-coiffed blond head like a summer breeze. I twitched my nose in annoyance. I was doing that a lot lately, I noticed—twitching my nose when something bothered me. Maybe I should cut carrots out of my diet.

"I don't, I assure you," I told her firmly. Finally giving in, I picked up a cookie, took a bite, and washed it down with iced tea. "And I still don't understand why that lunchbox is so important to you. To anyone."

"Odelia, that lunchbox is worth a great deal of money."

"I know, thirty thousand." I reached for another cookie. I loved them frozen, too.

"Try one hundred thousand."

I dropped the cookie and barely had time to swoop it up before Wainwright came in for the kill.

"One hundred thousand dollars!" I said, turning my attention back to Stella. "Who in the world would pay that for a lunchbox? Obviously," I said, immediately answering my own question, "someone with more money than brains."

Stella smiled. Pushing the hair on the left side of her head back behind her ear, she leaned forward across the coffee table in my direction. Her posture encouraged her brown 'n serve boobs to say howdy. Too bad Greg wasn't here. He would have loved the view.

"Let's just say," she said in a conspiratorial whisper, like the dog and cat might overhear something they shouldn't, "that there's someone who's been trying to get his hands on that box for a long time."

This tidbit of information struck me as odd. If another collector had been willing to buy the box for one hundred thousand dollars, how did Sterling Price get away with only paying thirty thousand? Talk about a blue-light special.

Listen to me, *only* thirty thousand! I was starting to worry about my perspective on cash.

"A long time, you say?" I asked, still half lost in my thoughts.

"Yes, several years. Just before Sterling bought it the price jumped to one hundred grand."

I put down the cookie and slouched in my upholstered chair. I looked up at the ceiling while thoughts and questions sloshed around in my brain like laundry in a washer. I only hoped the right thoughts matched up with the right questions like pairs of socks.

"Okay," I began, sitting up straight and resting my hands on the arms of the chair. "So tell me, if this person was offering one hundred thousand dollars, why was Sterling Price able to buy the box for thirty thousand dollars? Why didn't the previous owner—a Mr. Proctor, I believe—sell it to this mystery collector?"

She sat back up and looked at me in amusement, her dark eyes locking onto my green ones. "Mr. Proctor? My, my, Odelia, seems you're not the lunchbox novice you'd like us to think."

"Occupational hazard, Stella," I told her, staring back. "I'm trained to do research. The history of the Holy Pail was the first thing I looked into after Sterling's death."

"I'm impressed," she said, turning her eyes away from mine.

My question still had not been answered. I asked it again. "But why didn't William Proctor sell the box to this other collector when he could have gotten a lot more money?"

Stella looked away nervously, pretending to study the cookies. My last question had hit a nerve. Something to do with the last sale of the Holy Pail had made her balk internally.

Stella looked at me again, her third cookie in hand. Secrets were definitely lurking just beyond her brown irises like predators in a swamp. Then it occurred to me that she seemed to know an awful lot about the Holy Pail's history herself. I straightened up even more and scrutinized her unspoken words and body language while waiting for an answer.

"Sterling got the box by sheer default, Odelia. Or maybe it was luck." She spoke evenly, without emotion. Only her eyes told me she was cautiously editing the information as she went. "From what I understand, Proctor didn't like the person offering the hundred thousand. You see, Proctor didn't sell it through an auction. He simply put the word out and decided himself who would get it. It was more like a popularity contest. Sterling won."

"He sold it before he disappeared?"

"Apparently so," she said, forcing a casual tone. "From what I understand, it was sold but not yet delivered to Sterling when Proctor and his wife were killed. Boating accident, wasn't it?"

"Lost at sea is what I read," I told her simply, sure her question was a test to see how much I knew on the subject. "I saw no mention of whether their bodies were ever recovered."

She seemed to settle momentarily on my last remark; her hesitation short but still noticeable. "Sterling told me he received it from the estate after the paperwork on the sale was verified," she told me, moving along with no further mention of Proctor.

Hmm, this was interesting. I was getting excited about my morning appointment and thinking I should definitely keep it. If Porter was, in fact, Proctor, I had a lot of questions for him. Stella's sudden appearance on my doorstep wasn't annoying me as much anymore.

"Tell me, Stella," I began, watching her carefully, hoping she'd squirm a bit, "did you know about the Holy Pail before you met Sterling?"

A slow, hesitant smile crossed her face, but her eyes moved rapidly. "Yes, I did," she said. She put the cookie down on a napkin and wiped her fingertips. "It was one of the things that brought us together. When we met, he was impressed that I knew so much about it. You see, my late father was interested in it."

I dug through my tired brain for the Holy Pail information filed deep in my gray matter. Who were the men who owned it before Price? Proctor, of course. Kellogg and Fisher, those were the names—Jasper Kellogg and Ivan Fisher. But I couldn't remember their personal details. Was one of them Stella's father? Proctor wasn't old enough. He would be a bit younger or about the same age as Stella. Of course, there could have been other owners of the Holy Pail besides those. Also, Stella never said her father owned the box, just that he was interested.

I didn't think she was lying outright, but she continued to be cautious, choosing words and details carefully as she dished them out for my consumption. Not lying maybe, but definitely playing fast and loose with the truth.

Many possibilities crossed my mind. Was she marrying Sterling for the lunchbox? Was she marrying Kyle for it? What about Jackson? Added to the pile now was this nagging suspicion that she might have contacted Proctor about the box when he owned it. Maybe her father was the mystery shopper.

"Did your father own the Holy Pail at one time?" I asked her.

She laughed. "No. But it was a big dream of his."

"'Was' as in he's no longer around, or that he's given up?"

She cast her eyes toward the carpet briefly, then brought them back up to connect with mine. "My father died a long time ago," she said, simply and quietly.

The dutiful daughter fulfilling daddy's dreams? Nah. Looking at Stella, I couldn't make that leap. This had to be about the money. What else could it be? I decided to bring out the claws.

"You've cut a wide swath through the Price family," I said bluntly. "Sterling, Kyle, even Jackson." At the mention of Jackson, Stella's head snapped to attention and her eyes blazed into mine, but she said nothing. "I understand you're now engaged to Kyle—that you're going to have his baby. Or is it Jackson's baby?"

She sat ramrod straight on the sofa across from me, defiant and challenging, every muscle and ligament tense and taut, about to snap. Out of the corner of my eye, I saw Wainwright sniff the air and go on alert. Stella noticed the dog's slight change, too. She willed her shoulders to relax. Her posture eased up, along with her facial features. She looked tired, as well as edgy.

"How do you know so much?" she asked with annoyance. "What are you doing, spying on me?" Her deep voice was strained, like her vocal cords were wrapped tight with a rubber band.

I said nothing. Inside I burned with embarrassment, remembering the two of them on the desk. I hoped my face wasn't flushed to match.

"Must've been that bitch Carmen who told you," she said. "She's like a spook the way she knows all, sees all—sneaking around silently on orthopedic shoes."

Stella measured me with her eyes, and I could tell she was deciding something. Finally she sighed. "Want to know the ugly truth?" she asked.

"The truth would be nice," I said, giving her a half smile. "I'll take it ugly, pretty, or just pretty ugly."

Stella gave me a wry half smile. It made me wonder if I should get out a shovel just in case.

"I'll admit it. I got close to Sterling to get my hands on the Holy Pail. I knew about the standing hundred-grand offer. It was common knowledge among the collectors. And I thought I could convince Sterling to sell it."

"What was in it for you?"

"If I could get Sterling to sell it to this particular buyer, I would get a bonus—a sort of broker's fee—a big one." She took a sip of tea and fiddled once again with her cigarette package. "But after Sterling asked me to marry him, I changed my mind. After all, he was offering me a lifetime of security, something that doesn't come along every day at my age.

"I really liked Sterling. Honest, I did. But, well, he was old, and Jackson's a very sexy man and much more exciting. We had an affair." She sighed again. "The thing with Kyle just sort of happened. I went to him for a massage and next thing we were involved."

"And after Sterling died, you thought you could use Kyle to keep a roof over your head?" I asked, looking straight at her. She matched my gaze, eye for eye.

"Ouch, that's cold, Odelia," she said with a mean-looking smile. "After Sterling broke off his engagement to me, Jackson and I planned to run off together. We were going to steal the Holy Pail and cash it in for the entire one hundred thousand dollars. But someone beat us to it."

"And the baby?"

She got up and started pacing. Wainwright lifted his head and she looked from the animal to me. "Is it okay to move?"

"Yes," I answered. "Just don't make any sudden moves in my direction." The warning sounded good to my ears. I knew Wainwright was trained to protect Greg, and I knew he was somewhat loyal to me, but to what extent he'd protect me, I had no idea. But if the potential threat worked to keep danger at bay, I felt no guilt in using it.

Stella nodded and continued. "When I first found out I was pregnant, I was going to get an abortion. After all, why would someone my age want a baby?"

My mind flashed for an instant to my dilemma with Greg. As if reading my mind, Stella picked up a large photo from a table. It was an action shot of Greg. He was in his wheelchair, naked from the waist up, in the midst of a basketball shot. Another man in a wheelchair, a powerfully built black amputee named Isaac, was attempting to block it. Isaac had failed and Greg's basket had won the game for his team. After the game, Isaac and his wife had taken us to dinner. I loved the photo.

"Your brother?" Stella asked, holding up the photo for my inspection.

"My boyfriend," I answered.

She cocked an eye my way and re-measured me. After replacing the photo, she returned to the sofa and continued her story.

"Then I thought the baby might hurry the wedding to Sterling along. We were engaged, but he seemed happy to leave it at that indefinitely. There's no security in just being engaged. Nothing was in my name. Everything was his. But I knew he would never turn his back on a child." She laughed ruefully. "How stupid could I have been? Not to have at least looked into whether or not Sterling could father a child. After all, I knew his kids were adopted. But no, I just went ahead with my plan and got the boot."

"Whose is it?" I asked.

"Honestly, I have no idea. I didn't even think I could get pregnant anymore." She laughed to herself. It was a low, ugly, sad cackle. "When my periods stopped, I thought it was menopause."

She had no idea? Three men and any of them could have fathered her child? And what about health issues? Had this woman never heard of safe sex?

Stella rested her elbows on her knees and held her head in her hands, covering her face. "Oh, Odelia, I've really screwed up." Her voice sounded strained, almost crying. "Here I am in my mid-fifties, pregnant, broke, and alone. Even if Sterling were alive, he wouldn't have me. Jackson will only leave Karla if we can get the money for the Holy Pail. And Kyle...," she looked up at me. Her face was splotchy and mottled in spite of her new tan. "Kyle's an idiot."

I tried my best to feel sympathy for Stella. I really did. But it just wasn't in me. The best I could offer in the way of comfort was a box of tissues produced from the downstairs bathroom and a plate of thawed cookies.

While she pulled herself together, I retreated to the kitchen to refresh our iced teas. When I returned, I settled back down into my chair, ready for more. This was one drama I didn't want to miss.

"Stella, are you and Jackson the only ones looking for the Holy Pail? Or are Karla and Kyle also looking for it?"

She shrugged and turned to me. I could tell she was giving it some thought.

"I'm not sure Karla cares about it one way or the other, except as an inheritable asset. And I did mention it to Kyle before Sterling was killed, but he was so caught up in the purchase of the Center, I don't think it registered. Believe me, he's not the brightest bulb on the tree."

No, I thought, but he was bright enough to pull something over on his father, or at least to think he did.

"Stella," I began, wondering how much she knew about the purchase of the Center beyond what Kyle had told her that day in the study. "Exactly why did Sterling deed over a joint interest in the house to Kyle? And why did he buy the Center for him? Especially after finding out about the two of you."

She looked at me in undisguised shock. "Is there anything you don't know?" she asked, her temper rising again.

I gave her a smile and batted my lashes just slightly for affect. "I was the notary on the documents," I told her.

Stella was traveling between playing the victim and being the bitch, and I was enjoying throwing a bit of the bitchiness back.

"You know what I think?" I said to her, leaning forward in my chair. "I think Kyle found out something important, something about his sister, like maybe her using Jackson as a cover while she manipulated the company. And I think Kyle traded that information for the house and the Center."

"Boy," she said, her eyes wide and bright with anger, "you're up to your ears in this shit, same as the rest of us. Maybe I should ask you, Ms. Odelia Grey, did *you* murder Sterling Price?"

EIGHTEEN

SATURDAY MORNINGS WERE USUALLY reserved for sleeping in, cuddling with Greg, a leisurely breakfast—not so today. It was five minutes after six when I finally located the address Porter had given me. It was a rundown six-unit two-story apartment building, three up, three down. The building was two-toned; originally mud brown with wide slashes of turquoise where some industrious soul had started painting, then changed his mind. The structure was wedged behind a strip mall that housed a liquor store, a beauty supply store, a travel agent, and a small boutique of cheap women's clothing. Except for the liquor store, none of the businesses looked prosperous. I parked my old Toyota Camry between a dumpster and a Chevy up on blocks. As soon as I opened the car door, my nose snorted the odor of urine and decay.

Porter's place turned out to be the last apartment downstairs. I held a cardboard tray in one hand. Balanced on it were an extra large cup of Ethiopian-blend coffee for Porter and a medium cup of hazelnut coffee for me. I also brought along packets of sugar and creamer and a couple of cranberry scones. Dressed in strappy sandals festooned with beads that matched my khaki skirt and blouse, I felt incredibly overdressed and silly. Obviously, I had no idea what to wear when meeting a dead man in a shabby part of town.

I knocked and waited.

Almost immediately, I heard movement on the other side of the scuffed door. The drapes covering the window next to the door moved slightly. About the same time, I heard a noise by the fence that separated the building from the strip mall. Turning, I saw a rat. A big rat. One that could have given Seamus a run for his money. I knocked on the door again, my rap harder and more insistent than the first. Warily, I watched the rat bustle around the bottom of the fence. Every now and then he looked my way, nose in the air, whiskers moving rapidly. I was sure he was smelling breakfast.

I began counting to myself. On ten, the plan was to throw the coffee and scones at the rat and run. At seven and a half the door opened. A man's head popped out. He looked up and down the deserted street before beckoning me to enter. Solemnly, like a death row inmate heading for the chair, I started across the threshold.

Zee's right, I am out of my mind.

The apartment was dark, cool, and orderly. Based on the outside of the building, I had expected squalor. But once my eyes adjusted to the dim light, I found instead a very clean and freshly painted apartment. The sparse furnishings were fairly new and reminded me of an IKEA catalogue.

The man motioned for me to sit down. He was a young, trim Latino, not quite six feet tall, dressed in clean jeans, a white T-shirt, and expensive running shoes. His shiny black hair was pulled back into a tidy ponytail and his upper lip played host to a wispy, dark moustache. The arms poking out from the short sleeves of his shirt were sporadically tattooed. When he turned to look back out the door, I noticed a gun wedged in the waistband of his jeans at the small of his back.

Stifling a tiny whimper, I took a seat on the futon-style sofa, knees demurely pressed together, ankles crossed, and perched the coffee on my lap.

"Mr. Porter in?" I asked him. No response. "How about Mr. Proctor?"

Remaining silent, he positioned himself in front of the closed front door, legs apart, arms folded across his firm chest. I stared at him. He was cute, in spite of the thin white scar running down the left side of his smooth, brown face. He stared back, regarding me with no visible emotion.

Nervously, I looked at my watch. "I'm sorry I'm late," I said, helpless in the grip of an urge to babble. "Then I couldn't find the address." I held up the tray of coffee. "The big one is for Mr. Por-ter … umm … Proctor. Ethiopian, like he asked." The gangster kid said nothing. "Would you like the other? It's hazelnut. My personal favorite, although I also like Kona." More nothing.

I picked up the white bakery bag and waved it gently in the air. "How about a cranberry scone?"

This time, the young man lowered his head slightly and wid-ened his coal black eyes at me. I think it meant if I kept talking, he was going to shoot me.

"Odelia Grey?"

I jumped at the words, nearly spilling the coffee. It was the same confident voice I had heard on the phone. I turned toward it.

Standing in the doorway that I assumed led to the bedroom area was another man, this one about my age. He was pale with freckled skin, bony, and no more than five foot eight or nine. More skin than hair adorned his head. Black horn-rimmed glasses and the large nose upon which they rested took up most of his angular face. He was dressed in designer jeans and a Polo shirt and resembled several professors I had in college. However, I reminded myself, most professors do not hide out in slums with bodyguards.

I sat frozen in fear. A bullet list of cold facts listed themselves vertically in my head:

- There were two of them, one of me.
- At least one of them had a gun.
- A forty-seven-year-old woman should know better.
- Greg will kill me if he finds out.
- He'll have to get in line behind Seth and Zee.
- Everyone will have to get in line behind Dev Frye.
- Who'll take custody of Seamus?

"Is that for me?" the man asked, pointing at the coffee.

"You Willie Porter?" I asked in return, trying not to shake too visibly.

He smiled. His teeth were straight and white behind thin, colorless lips. He held out his right hand to me. "Willie Porter, aka William Proctor. But I haven't used Proctor for a long time, so just call me Willie."

He didn't look like a Willie to me, but I took his hand anyway and shook it uneasily. He again eyed the coffee and I held out the tray to him.

"The large one's yours," I said, then added, "I brought scones, too." Immediately my fear was overcome with foolishness. This was hardly a tea party.

He laughed lightly, taking both the large cup of coffee and the pastry bag. "Thanks. Good to see you know how to follow instructions." He looked inside the bag. "The scones are a nice touch." He closed the bag and placed it on the coffee table.

He turned to the young man by the door and said something in Spanish. The kid said something back and they both laughed. The young man grinned at me, displaying crooked teeth. I felt my face grow hot. He and Willie exchanged a few more words in Spanish. Some I understood, most I didn't. Occasionally, they looked my way, studying me.

"I asked Enrique if he searched you," Willie told me. "But he said no, it would be too much like frisking his own mother."

I offered Enrique a weak, red-faced smile, not sure if I should be offended or flattered. He chuckled and said something else to Willie, who laughed hard enough to slightly slosh his coffee.

"Enrique thinks you're cute," Willie translated, "big and soft like his mama, but much more *loco* ... crazy."

After studying the young man for a moment, I leaned toward Willie and asked softly, "How do you say 'bite me' in Spanish?"

The roar of laughter that came from Enrique let me know that no translation would be needed.

After further words from Willie, Enrique covered up his gun with a loose shirt grabbed from a nearby chair and slipped out the front door, leaving us alone.

Willie sat down on the sofa at the opposite end. He crossed one leg casually, ankle resting on knee, and took a big swig of his coffee. Like Enrique, he wore running shoes, but his were well worn.

"Very nice," he commented, indicating the coffee.

"Do you know how Sterling Price died?" I asked him.

"I heard poison." Willie took another big drink.

"Yep, oleander. In his coffee."

Willie froze, cup to his lips. He peered at me over the rim, made a decision, and swallowed.

"Let's just hope you're not the one who did it," he said to me with a smile.

I smiled back. "No, not me. Not my style." Though I had no doubt that there were thousands of people willing to line up to poison this man's java.

As soon as Stella Hughes left last night, I jumped on the Internet to see if there was anything on William Proctor that I should know about. Much to my surprise, there was quite a bit. There were a few photographs online of Proctor as well. All resembled the man in front of me.

In his former life, Willie had been William Proctor, founder and chairman of Investanet, a dot-com company specializing in retirement plans and investments. Actually, Investanet specialized in fleecing honest citizens out of their hard-earned nest eggs with cooked books and double talk. William Proctor had disappeared just ahead of a federal raid, but not before embezzling about twenty-five million dollars in other people's money. He left his executives holding the bag and his employees high and dry without jobs. I remembered reading about the scandal at the time, but failed to connect it to the man mentioned in the *American Executive* article about the Holy Pail. It surprised me that the magazine itself didn't bring the connection to light. But maybe they didn't want to remind readers that some American executives were sleaze balls.

"Except for the connection to the Holy Pail, I didn't know who William Proctor was when you called yesterday, but I do now."

Scared as I was, I tried to appear casual about the whole thing. I doubted if the felon sipping coffee across from me would tell me anything of value if I appeared on the brink of emotional collapse, so I shed my nervousness as much as possible. Shifting around to face him, I curled one leg up under me and smoothed my skirt modestly over my legs. Anyone watching us would think we were old friends catching up over coffee.

"I'm curious. Why did you contact Price's office?" I asked. "Kind of risky, wasn't it? I mean, I assume there's a price on your head."

"Hmm, yes, there is—a big one. You going to turn me in, Odelia?" He appeared laid-back, not at all what you'd expect for a fugitive on the run.

I gave thought to what I should say and what I wanted to say, and decided on averaging them out. "I'd love to," I answered honestly. "But I'm sure I'd never get the chance. Either you'd stop me cold, one way or another, or you'd disappear like smoke in the wind."

Willie looked me over thoughtfully. "I like you, Odelia. You're smart and straightforward."

He tilted his head back and took another big swallow of coffee. I could see his throat muscles working in his neck. Frisked or not, he obviously didn't consider me a threat to his personal safety. Too bad I didn't have the same sense of security.

"I liked Sterling Price," he said, putting the paper cup down on the coffee table in front of us. "I only met him once, just before I sold him the Holy Pail. Decent sort, good businessman. I'm very sorry about his death."

He got up and went into the kitchen, returning with a pack of cigarettes, a cheap lighter, and a small ashtray. He offered me a cigarette. I declined. He lit up, took a long drag, and made an effort to blow it away from where I sat.

"Nasty habit," he said, before taking another puff. "Wife always wanted me to quit."

"You and your wife living in Mexico now? Where your boat was found?"

"You just never mind where my wife and I live these days, little mama." He chuckled and took another puff, considering me through the cloud of his exhale. "I asked you here, Odelia, because I want to help you find Price's murderer."

"Why?" I asked, looking directly at him with interest. "Just because he was a nice man and you once sold him a lunchbox?"

"Really," he answered with a chuckle, "you give me too much credit. I'm not that nice."

Somehow I knew that.

"This is about revenge, plain and simple. You see, the feds were tipped off about my company, hence my hasty disappearance. I had planned on running Investanet a few months longer, selling it lock, stock, and scandal to some sucker, and fading into the sunset. The whole thing about the boat was last minute."

"A whistleblower in your midst? How does that connect with Sterling Price?"

"Worse than a whistleblower, Odelia, a vicious, jealous woman." He winked at me, then continued. "There's an unknown collector trying to get his hands on the Holy Pail. Someone outside the usual lunchbox network, which can be very tight-knit. He's offering big money for it. I have no idea why."

I nodded. "Yes, I've heard that. It's up to one hundred thousand now." Pausing, I scrutinized Willie. "You sure you don't know who the collector is?"

He shook his head. "No, sorry. He never contacted me directly. But there is a woman hunting the box down on his behalf. Kind of a bounty hunter, if you will. I think you've met her."

I thought about Stella Hughes. "A flashy blond, mid-fifties, with a Marilyn Monroe figure?" I asked.

He gave me a big smile and stubbed out his cigarette. "That's Stella."

So Stella did know William Proctor, or at least he knew of her. "She contacted you, didn't she?"

"You could say that." He pulled back the drape slightly and looked outside as he spoke. The gesture seemed more something to do than out of nervousness.

"I hired Stella to work for me at Investanet. It was shortly after I obtained the Holy Pail. She had recently moved to California from the Chicago area. Unfortunately," he said, giving my hefty chest a quick glance, "I have an appetite for endowed women, especially blonds who throw themselves at me."

Okay, I thought, squirming a bit under this gaze, *this fits the Stella Hughes I know.*

"Don't tell me," I said, holding up one hand. "She wanted you to leave your wife and marry her, or run away with her—with the Holy Pail, of course."

"Of course," he said dryly. "Now, I may not be a Boy Scout, but I loved my wife and had no intention of trading her in for a chippie. When Stella started making a stink, I offered her money to disappear."

"But all she wanted was the Holy Pail, right?"

"Right. There's something about that lunchbox, something important, but damned if I know what it is. I think Stella knew, although she said she didn't."

"So you think Stella killed Sterling?"

He shook his head. "It's possible, but I doubt it. She's vicious and manipulative, but I never pegged her for being a killer. But I could be wrong. I was wrong about her before. Never dawned on me she'd do what she did.

"She finally threatened to go to my wife if I didn't give her the lunchbox. I flatly refused, mostly on principle. My wife already knew I had a mistress, so Stella's threat was no big deal. But I wasn't about to be threatened with blackmail for any reason, so I sold the box to Sterling Price just to teach her a lesson." He grunted. The sound came from deep inside his scrawny chest. "I should have just given her the damn thing and saved myself a lot of trouble."

And maybe Sterling's life, I mused silently, wishing Willie had done just that.

"She turned you in when you wouldn't cooperate, didn't she?" I asked.

"Oh, yes," he said in amusement, coming back to sit on the sofa. "I don't know how or exactly when, but fortunately I had a friend inside the Securities and Exchange Commission. I found out just in time." He picked up his coffee and took another swig.

"Right after I relocated," he said, grinning as he said the last word, "I started looking closer into Stella's background. At first I was sure I'd find some business competitor behind her manipulations, or maybe even some disenchanted investor with his own plans for revenge. Instead, I discovered something much more intriguing." He looked at me expectantly, like he was waiting for applause.

I shrugged, clueless.

"Do you know who owned the Holy Pail prior to me?"

I nodded. "Someone named Kellogg or Fisher, I believe."

"Fisher," Willie said, "Ivan Fisher, out of Chicago."

I thought a minute. "Chicago? But you said that's where she was from."

"That's right. And guess who she was involved with while she lived there?"

Dread settled in the pit of my stomach like a bad taco. "Ivan Fisher?"

Willie's head went up and down. "He even married her."

I sucked in my breath. "He died in a car accident, didn't he?"

"Yes, but it's not what you think. Shortly before they were married, he sold the Holy Pail to me. The price then was a mere ten thousand dollars. Fisher was comfortable, but not wealthy like Price or me. He'd bought the box for less than a thousand a few years before."

Wow, I thought, *that's what I call a good return on an investment.*

Willie put his coffee cup back on the table, stretched his legs out in front of him and laced his hands behind his head. He chuckled again, as if reminiscing about the good ol' days.

"Now comes the best part," he said, throwing me a big grin. "Poor Mr. Fisher was in his fifties and had never been married before, so he wanted to do it proper. Right after they were married, he took his new bride on a big trip to Europe. Three weeks—Paris, London, Rome—all paid for by the sale of his extensive lunchbox collection."

"Including the Holy Pail?" I asked without needing to.

"Uh-huh," he replied with relish.

"And she didn't know?"

Willie shook his head. "Not until they got back. By then, the lunchbox was already in my collection in California."

"What about Mr. Kellogg?"

"That, I'm happy to say, was not Stella's doing. Kellogg died of a heart attack, plain and simple; had heart disease for years. Fisher bought the Holy Pail from Kellogg's son, Jasper, Jr."

I still didn't understand. "But you said she didn't have anything to do with Fisher's death."

"Not directly." He sat back up and rotated his head. I could hear the joints in his neck and shoulders pop with the movement. "According to my investigator, who interviewed Fisher's elderly mother, after Stella found out about the sale of the pail," he said, grinning over his little rhyme, "she tried to get him to buy it back, but poor Fisher refused. He had spent the money on his honeymoon and wasn't about to go into debt for a lunchbox. When Stella couldn't get her way, she walked out on him and moved to California, following the trail of the pail." He grinned again.

"So the car accident was just an accident," I said. I thought about the *American Executive* article. Two of the four owned the lunchbox at the time of their deaths. Two sold it just before their deaths, or disappearance in Proctor's case. "So there is no stupid curse."

Willie shrugged. "Depends on your definition of curse, little mama."

I twitched my nose at my apparent new nickname.

"Fisher didn't have a car accident," Willie continued. "He was despondent over his bride's departure. Two days after she left, he drove his car into a tree at seventy miles an hour."

My whole body shuddered at the news. During the story, I had been clutching my nearly empty coffee cup so tightly it had almost caved in. I leaned over and placed it on the coffee table. Thinking about Fisher, I wrapped my arms around myself and tucked inward in a poor imitation of a pill bug.

"This is insane," I finally said when I could talk. "Why don't you just send an anonymous letter to the police?"

"Boy, Odelia, you really do live the straight and narrow. Probably don't watch much TV either." He shook his head at my naiveté. "Letters can be traced right down to where the paper was manufactured and who licked the flap. Besides, legally, what has she done wrong? She didn't kill Fisher, I doubt if she killed Price, and she sure as hell didn't kill me."

He picked up his coffee again and took another sip.

I leaned back against the sofa to mull over a few things. Willie seemed to understand my need to cogitate. He picked up the white bag, pulled out a scone, and took a big bite.

"Nice," he said to no one in particular.

NINETEEN

"You know, Willie, I may be a bit thick-headed, and heaven knows I've been accused of such, but I still don't get it," I said. "If you want revenge on Stella, but don't think she's the one who killed Sterling Price, why do you want me to find Sterling's murderer?"

He finished chewing before he spoke. "Think of it as a business deal. You want to solve the murder. I want the lunchbox. By my giving you the background on the Holy Pail, you may be able to sort out the murder."

"So you think the murderer took the box?"

"Not necessarily, but I do think they're connected." He sipped more coffee between bites of scone. "I also did a quick background on Sterling Price. He was a nice guy, no hidden agenda, no skeletons in his closet. Just an elderly businessman with an established company. Even his corporate competitors liked him. Whoever poisoned him did it for personal reasons and personal gain."

"Poison is a very personal weapon," I said.

"Exactly."

"But why do you want the box?" I asked. "You owned it once, and if you stole all that money, you surely don't need the hundred thousand."

"What I want, Odelia," he began, wiping his mouth with one of the napkins the bakery had tucked inside the bag, "is to deal with Stella once and for all. To make her pay for what she did to me."

A horrible thought crossed my mind. "Whoa," I said in horror, both hands held up, palms out to him. "I don't care one whit about getting revenge on anyone. And if you think I'm going to lead you to Stella so you can kill her, you've got another thought coming."

Willie let me rant. He was about to say something when Enrique opened the front door and slipped in. He said something to Willie I didn't understand. Willie nodded back at him.

"Now, Odelia, back to business," Willie said, taking one of my hands in both of his. He moved closer to me and looked into my eyes.

"I have a lot of friends among the collectors. And, unfortunately, due to my unique situation, I can't contact them and warn them. But I do know that as long as the Holy Pail and Stella both exist, no owner will be safe." He smiled broadly at me. "I may have relieved some dim-witted folks of their money, but I do have some loyalties.

"Now, Stella may not have killed Sterling, but I'm damn sure she's connected somehow. I want her nervous. I want her to suffer. I want her to know the Holy Pail can never be hers. Ever. I want her to know she can't screw with my life and get away with it."

I jerked my hand away from him. "I told you, I won't help you kill her."

I started to get up, but Willie grabbed me by my shoulders and forced me back down. His face was inches away from my own. His breath smelled of coffee and tobacco. Enrique didn't move a muscle.

"I am not going to kill her!" Willie yelled at me. "I'm a thief, not a killer."

I looked at him, jutting out my chin in stubbornness. "Then what do you want?" I yelled back.

Willie let my shoulders go and sat back against the futon. He took off his glasses and rubbed his eyes. I remained seated, but shifted away from him. We sat still for a minute, like two boxers sent to their corners.

"All I'm asking you, Odelia," he said, returning to a calm voice, "is to give me the box so I can destroy it, preferably right in front of her bitchy little nose. Once ruined, no one will want it and she won't see a dime. Everything she's planned and done and given up in the past several years will be down the drain."

Willie ran a hand over his thinning hair. "That's what I should have done. Should have taken the damn box to the parking lot of Investanet and driven my car over it. Better yet, I should have left it behind one of the tires on her car."

His last scenario appealed to my sense of drama.

"But I don't have the Holy Pail," I told him. My voice walked the tightrope of hysterics. "And I don't know where it is."

Willie put his glasses on and looked hard at me. "You sure you don't have it tucked away somewhere? Someplace no one would ever look?"

"No," I said in frustration, "though everyone seems to think I do."

I looked at Willie, then at Enrique. My brain buzzed fluorescent with insight.

"Oh my gawd," I cried out, "you're the two guys who broke into my office two days ago, aren't you?"

Neither said anything. Willie looked at Enrique; Enrique at Willie. Eyes communicated silently, speaking this time a language I could understand.

I jumped to my feet. This time Willie didn't make a move to stop me. He didn't have to. Enrique's young, strong body blocked the door. If I left without permission, I was going to have to go through him. I remembered the gun, but he made no move for it.

The fear I had when I first arrived returned in full force. I could feel it bubbling and boiling inside me, tainting the blood in my veins with foolish bravado.

"You almost killed one of our attorneys!" I screamed up into Enrique's face. "I thought you weren't killers!"

I steeled my shoulders, ready to do whatever I needed to get out of the apartment. Briefly, I thought about running the other way, toward the bedroom or bathroom. The idea of putting a door between me and them was appealing. But who was I kidding? Even if I were wearing sturdy sneakers instead of sandals, I'd never be able to outrun either of them, especially Enrique. And even if I could manage to outrun them, then what? Even if the door had a lock, it wouldn't take much for them to break it down.

I thought about screaming, but in this neighborhood, I didn't think anyone would pay it any mind.

My mind flipped quickly to the women's self-defense course I had taken shortly after I had been shot. I looked up, directly into the large, dark eyes of my target. Automatically, my knee jerked up, fast and furious, between his legs, the force of my entire two-hundred-plus pounds thrown behind it.

Trust me, when I fantasize about a young, hunky man being on top, this is not it.

I coughed and sputtered as air re-entered my lungs. The room spun slightly. I was on the floor, flat on my back, with Enrique on top of me, straddling my hips. My arms and hands were at my side, trapped by his strong legs. A cold metal cylinder pressed hard against my temple. I closed my eyes tight. My stomach lurched dangerously.

It wasn't that I was a bad aim with the trusty old knee, just that Enrique was a mind reader with the reflexes of a jungle cat. He had anticipated my not-too-original move and grabbed my moving thigh the instant my foot left the floor. Memories of mama or not, he had lifted my thick leg and yanked, dumping me hard onto my back. He followed through with his own body, knocking the wind out of me.

"Get off me," I ordered in a half-choking, squeaky voice.

I opened my eyes and studied Enrique. His face was impassive, but his arms and neck were taut with corded muscle. He continued to push the gun barrel into the side of my head.

"Please," I added, trying to keep tears out of my voice.

"Odelia," I heard Willie say from somewhere above me. He moved into my line of vision. "You have to listen to me." He crouched down next to Enrique. "What happened to that attorney was an accident, I assure you."

I looked at him briefly before turning my head away. The gun barrel stayed at my temple and followed along.

"I want to get even with Stella," Willie said, "not kill her." He placed a couple of fingers on my chin and moved my face toward him, forcing me to look at him. "I want to destroy the Holy Pail—for everyone's sake."

"But I don't have it," I told him through tight lips.

Willie smiled down at me. His fingers lightly stroked my chin. "I want to believe you, Odelia. God knows, we've searched everywhere—your office, car, even your home."

My eyes popped until they hurt. "You've been to my house?" I asked through dry lips.

Willie smiled and nodded. "Last night. It was convenient that you took your dog with you. Enrique here just finished going through your car. Nothing. Big zero."

I closed my eyes tight. No wonder Seamus was hiding under the bed. No wonder Wainwright sniffed the dust mites out of the carpet. Both of them knew my home had been invaded. Stupid me.

Willie gave a little snort. "We were searching your place while Stella sat on your front doorstep waiting for you. She didn't have a clue. Too bad we didn't find it. Could have taken care of business right then and there."

I mumbled something.

He bent down closer to me. "What? I'm sorry, I didn't hear you."

I cleared my throat. "I said, thanks."

Both men looked at me oddly. "Thanks for what?" Willie asked.

"Thanks for not making a mess."

Willie Porter laughed heartily and stood up. He said something to Enrique. The young man grinned, moved the gun from my temple, and slowly raised himself off me. My skirt was bunched up high around my thighs, but I didn't care. I stayed on the floor, unmoving.

The two men stood above me. I made no move to get up. Enrique tucked his gun back in its place and held out a hand to help me. I refused it. Willie said something again in Spanish and both men moved away from me, giving me space and watching. Finally, I rolled partially to my side and onto my knees. I took it a little at a time, giving the remaining dizziness time to subside. From there it was a short haul to set one foot flat on the floor. I followed with the other foot and raised myself erect. I faced the men as I unfolded my bruised body. My eyes burned into theirs—first Willie's, then Enrique's.

"Shame on you," I said to Enrique in a quiet voice. Sheepishness flickered in his eyes like a sputtering candle, and just as quickly, they returned to their previous unemotional condition.

Once I was standing, I allowed Willie to steer me back toward the sofa. I clutched my gurgling middle with one arm. Enrique softly said something in Spanish. I caught the word *cojones* somewhere in the mix.

Willie seated himself on the coffee table directly in front of me. He took my hands. I looked down at them, but didn't jerk away. I still was not sure what was expected of me—not sure what I wanted to do or believe.

Willie and Enrique were the men who had vandalized Woobie and clubbed Steele into unconsciousness. They had violated my home and broken into my car. They were looking for the Holy Pail. They thought I had it.

I wanted to go home, lock the door, and not come out until Greg returned and coaxed me out with a cookie, like I sometimes entice Seamus out from under the bed with a tuna-flavored treat.

"Odelia, look at me," Willie said softly. Obediently, I raised my face to his. "I promise you, we didn't mean to hurt that attorney. We thought the place was empty. He took us by surprise and, well, things happened. We also don't want to hurt you."

I lifted a finger to the spot where the gun had been and rubbed it thoughtfully. I was looking into the eyes of a criminal and wanted to believe he wasn't a thug or a killer. A person should have some redeeming qualities, shouldn't he?

"It's true," he continued, "we are looking for the lunchbox. We were told you or someone in your office had it."

"By who?" I asked, totally bewildered. "Who did you talk to? Who would say such a thing? Was it Carmen? The woman you spoke to when you left your number?"

"No," he said, shaking his head. "That old biddy didn't say a thing. Just took my number and said someone would call. When it was you who called, I was sure our informant was correct."

My eyes bore into his.

"We paid someone for the information," he confessed. "When I first heard about Sterling's murder, I contacted one of the employees there, someone mentioned in the newspaper, and pumped her. When I asked her who she thought had the box, she gave your name right off. Said Sterling gave it to you the day he was murdered."

"Sterling did send me a lunchbox that day," I told him. "A Zorro box."

"We found that in your office."

Willie stood up and got himself another cigarette.

"Originally, I thought she might have it—the one who gave us your name. And maybe she does. She was one of the few people who had an opportunity to grab the box between your visit and Sterling's death. But I offered her a great deal of money for it. She said she didn't have it, didn't know anything about it. My personal opinion is that if she did have it, she would have handed it off like a hot potato instead of trying to contact another buyer. She seems a nervous sort, and that box isn't going to be easy to sell."

"Unless she'd already sold it," I said.

He shrugged. "Could be, but I don't think so. I think she would have confessed if she had, if only to get Enrique here off her back."

I looked at Enrique. He stood immobile in front of the door, like an Aztec god guarding a temple.

"Good point," I said.

I turned to look Willie straight in the eye. "So, just how much did you pay Amy Chow?"

Willie winked at me. "Like I said, Odelia, smart and straight-forward."

TWENTY

A SCATHING HEADACHE CAUSED me to squint my eyes as I drove from Santa Ana to Tustin. I was on my way to Amy Chow's place. Willie had given me the address. According to him, she lived alone with her widowed mother.

I still had almost two hours until my manicure appointment. After that, I was heading to Glendora for my visit with Lester Miles. It was just after eight in the morning; a little early to go calling, but a good time to catch someone at home. I found the house easily. It was a small white bungalow set behind a larger house on a quiet middle-class residential street.

The front door behind the screen door was open. I felt better knowing the household was already awake. Peering through the mesh, I saw an immaculate and nicely furnished living room with a huge TV as the focal point. Sounds of movement drifted to me from other parts of the house. I knocked on the screen door gently.

"Yes?" a woman asked as she made her way to the door. She was a middle-aged Asian woman, very thin and under five feet tall.

"What you want?" she asked, stopping in front of the door. Her English was choppy and accented, but easy to understand. She looked me up and down suspiciously. Before I could say anything, she started in on me. "We don't want to buy nothing. We don't want your religion." She started to shut the front door. "Go away. Leave people alone."

"But I'm here to see Amy," I said quickly, before the door closed completely.

The woman reopened the door slightly. "You want Amy?"

"Yes," I told her. "I know her from work. Is she home?"

The woman shook her head. Her hair was black like Amy's, but worn pulled back tight into a bun. She was dressed simply in cotton trousers and a sleeveless shirt. "Not right now, sorry," she said in a friendlier tone. "Later. She'll be back later."

"How much later?"

"Not long. She left early, say she had to pick up something. Say she'd be home by nine. Then we go to my sister in Phoenix."

Phoenix? Phoenix, Arizona, was hardly a day trip. Was Amy leaving town for a reason?

"How nice," I said. "Going for a little visit?"

"Yes," the woman answered, smiling. "Amy say if we like, we move there. She go to college ASU next semester maybe."

When I hesitated, she said, "You wait, okay? I have to pack. Very busy."

I said thank you and headed back to wait in my car. Fortunately, it was still cool enough not to melt inside a vehicle.

From where I parked, I had a great view of the drive and walk-way leading to the Chow house. Amy would have to hurdle a back fence to avoid me. I checked my watch. It was almost eight thirty. My nail appointment was for ten thirty. I put my sunglasses on, scrunched down in the seat, and waited. Fortunately, I had used the facilities at Willie's place.

The face of the young woman came to mind. I found it hard to think of her as a cold killer, but as an accomplice, maybe. For sure, Amy was in the middle of this somehow. She had access to the bags of poisoned coffee before they were put in Sterling's office. She had access to the Holy Pail before its disappearance. And she had been the one to find Sterling's body. Added to that was her strange be-havior around Karla. And let's not forget that she sold my name to Willie and Enrique. She may not have the Holy Pail, but I'd bet one of Seamus's lives she knew where it was.

A little before nine, a silver Honda Accord pulled up and parked in the Chow driveway. Amy got out and occupied herself with something in the trunk. She had her long hair pulled back in a ponytail and wore black shorts and a blue tank top. I quietly left my car and slowly approached. Amy didn't hear me until I spoke.

"Hi, Amy, going somewhere?"

She jumped out of her skin and whipped around, turning pale at the sight of me.

"What are you doing here?" she asked in a whisper, looking back over at the house. "How did you find me?"

"I just came from seeing mutual friends—Willie Porter and his muscle boy, Enrique. Know them?"

Quickly, she looked behind me, clearly frightened. She dropped her head and I heard big gulps.

"Where's the lunchbox, Amy?"

"I don't know," she said in a stifled voice, her head still bowed.

"I don't believe you," I responded sarcastically. "Wonder why? Could it be maybe because you lied about my having it?"

She looked up at me. Her cheeks were splotchy. "Please," she begged, "my mother knows nothing. I need to get her out of here to someplace safe. Please, Odelia." She voiced my name in supplication, like a prayer.

"Amy," a voice from the house called. "Is that you?"

Amy flashed me a pleading look before turning her head to the house. "Yes, Mom, it's me."

"You see your friend?" her mother called out.

"Yes, Mom, I did."

Amy looked at me again and bit her bottom lip. She was clearly terrified. Of me? What a laugh. Was it Willie and Enrique? Did they threaten Amy and her family? Or was it someone or something else?

"I'm going for a walk with my friend, Mom. I'll be back soon. Then we can go. Okay?"

"Not long, Amy," her mother called back. "Must leave before too hot."

"I'll be right back."

Amy lifted a small gardening spade from a pile of pots and plants at the side of the house and started walking down the driveway. I followed. About a half block down the street was a small park. It was deserted.

She walked to a small cluster of trees by a utility shed and knelt down. The ground at the base of one tree looked as if it had been recently disturbed. Using the spade, she began digging, scooping out small clumps of the soft, churned dirt. Just a few inches below the surface, she hit something hard and started digging around it. A moment later, she put the spade down and worked with her hands to free the item. It was the Holy Pail, wrapped tight in protective plastic. She handed it to me.

"There," she said with soft finality. "You take it. I don't want any part of it."

While I opened the plastic and checked out the box, Amy started walking away with double-time steps.

"Not so fast," I called after her. Trotting, I caught up and grabbed her arm. "You have a lot of explaining to do, starting with who killed Sterling Price."

She stared down at her feet, clad in sturdy sandals. Her shoulders shook with her tears. "I don't know. That wasn't part of the plan."

"The plan?" I firmly guided her over to a bench and plunked her down, hard. "Out with it," I demanded.

She cried harder. "I didn't know the coffee was poisoned, honest." She wiped her eyes with the back of her hand. "I was just supposed to steal the lunchbox."

"Who were you working for, Amy? Stella Hughes?"

She nodded. "Yes. She said she'd give me twenty-five thousand dollars if I'd get it for her." She looked up at me. "I was going to take the money and move my mother to Arizona. I was going to finish college with it."

She sniffed and coughed slightly to clear her throat. "It seemed easy enough. Carmen was gone. I planned on never going back there again. I would have been long gone before they noticed it missing the next day."

"But someone poisoned Sterling?"

She started crying again.

"When did Stella contact you about this?"

"That Friday, just before … just before he died. She was waiting by my car in the parking lot. I knew who she was. She asked me if I wanted to make some money. But all she wanted was for me to take the lunchbox. She never said anything about killing Mr. Price."

"Do you think she did it?" I asked her. Amy hesitated a long while. I waited patiently.

"I don't know," she finally responded. Her nose was running. Before she could use her hand again, I grabbed a tissue from my bag and handed it to her. "Thanks."

I waited while she blew her nose before continuing. "Amy," I said quietly, "what you did was wrong, you know that." She nodded. "But I get the feeling you know something much more important that you're not telling anyone." She looked at me like a bunny caught in a trap. "Do you know who killed Mr. Price?"

There was another long pause while she stared out at the open park. A young mother with a baby in a stroller and a toddler in tow arrived. The toddler made a run for the colorful plastic climbing structures embedded in a sand pit.

"The coffee was sitting on Carmen's desk when I got to Mr. Price's office that morning," Amy recited in a nearly dead voice. "There was a note from Carmen to make sure I put it in the cupboard over the sink as soon as I got in. Which I did."

"But you didn't know it was poisoned or who poisoned him?"

We both watched the child, a small boy, gleefully climb the lower blocks and shimmy through the tubes while his mother cautioned him to be careful. Amy never looked at me while she spoke.

"Not really, but I did overhear something that day. It was early in the morning. I was working on the other side of the building. I often came in early and worked for Mrs. Blake on the side, on her personal business that she didn't want anyone knowing about. She paid me quite well to keep my mouth shut. Said she'd get me a good promotion in the company, too."

Secret personal business. This could be what Kyle dished to his father in return for the property. Thinking back to the day Sterling died, I remembered hearing the sound of a keyboard that morning coming from another office on the second floor.

"Were you working that morning around eight?" I asked her.

"Yes, I was there. Mrs. Blake had me come in around seven and leave her area by eight thirty so her secretary wouldn't see me. The executive staff always began at nine. I would leave by the back stairs. I had been doing this for several months."

"What were you working on, Amy?"

She sighed. "Mr. and Mrs. Blake were working with another company, feeding them information, setting up separate agreements on their own. I overheard Mrs. Blake tell Mr. Blake that morning that as soon as her father was gone, things were going to change."

The box of documents in my car came to mind. The documents I was supposed to review for irregularities and loopholes. It was one of the assignments given to Woobie that came to a halt as soon as Sterling died, supposedly on Jackson's orders.

"Was that other company Howser Development?"

"Yes." Her voice remained small and resigned.

This still didn't prove that Karla or Jackson poisoned Sterling, but it showed they had motive.

"Did Kyle Price know about this plan?" I asked Amy.

Finally, she turned and looked at me. Her bottom lip was bleeding where she had chewed it.

"I don't know. But he did come in one morning about two weeks ago for a meeting with Mr. and Mrs. Blake."

"Really?" I asked with greater interest. "I didn't think he was involved with the company."

"He wasn't, but Mr. and Mrs. Blake asked him to be on the board of directors."

"But there wasn't an opening until Mr. Price died. Mr. Blake filled the last opening. Are you sure this was two weeks ago?"

Amy nodded and started crying again. "They had me type up minutes showing Kyle Price taking Mr. Price's place. They had me leave the date blank."

The crying turned to sobs. I put my arm around the young woman and drew her close to me. She buried her head in my shoulder and sobbed harder, her small, delicate body shivering in my arms like a child's.

Directors were usually elected by the shareholders of a company. Normally, in the event of the death or resignation of a director, the remaining directors appoint someone to fill the vacancy. But even without the other directors' approval, it would be a slam dunk. Sterling Homes is a privately held corporation with the majority of stock owned by the family. Banded together, they could pretty much put anyone on the board.

Wow, I thought. Sterling Price wasn't even gone yet and they were filling the vacancy. Now that's pretty darn cold and calculating, and a vote in favor of possible premeditated murder.

All cried out, Amy straightened herself up. "Thanks, Odelia. But I've got to get back."

I stopped her. "Not quite yet, Amy. I need to know what you were planning on doing with this lunchbox. How were you supposed to get it to Stella?"

Amy pulled away from me like she'd seen a monster. Or at least one standing behind me.

"When I first took it, everything was so crazy, I changed my mind. I mean, I didn't want to be involved with a murder. So I hid the box here in the park and told Stella I didn't get the chance to grab it. I told her that it wasn't there when I found Mr. Price."

"But you told Willie Porter that I had it."

She nodded, her head down. "I knew that Mr. Price had sent documents to you that day and that he had included one of the lunchboxes, so when Willie Porter offered me money for information, I gave him your name. Sorry.

"Late last night, I changed my mind and called Stella. I told her I had the box and would sell it to her for the twenty-five thousand dollars. I ... I ... I was supposed to go by her place early this morning with it," she stammered, "and she'd give me the money." She hesitated again, shook herself slightly and said, "I did, but she wasn't home."

"But you just dug it up for me, so you couldn't have had it with you when you went to see her."

She looked down at the ground and her cheeks reddened. "I didn't trust Stella to pay me like she promised. I thought she might pull something. I planned on giving her a map of where to find it in return for the money."

Smart girl.

Amy dug into the back pocket of her shorts and produced a piece of paper. On it was a map from Newport Beach to the park in Tustin and the exact place where the box had been buried.

She started back to the house. I followed.

"So you're leaving for Phoenix without the money?"

"Yes," she said resolutely and walked faster.

"Why?"

She came to a stop in the driveway just behind her car. She had turned pale again. In spite of it being almost eighty degrees out, Amy shivered and wrapped her arms around herself. She started to say something, but just then Mrs. Chow came out of the house with a couple of suitcases. She ran to help her mother.

"Mom, don't worry, I'll put those in the car for you."

"I'll be back," Mrs. Chow said. "I have more things. Lunch, too."

"Amy, what are you running from?" I asked as I helped her put the bags into the trunk of her car.

Looking first to make sure her mother was nowhere around, Amy looked me square in the eyes. "Death, Odelia. I'm running from death."

She started to tap the lunchbox, but restrained herself, afraid to touch it. "That thing really is cursed." She took a deep breath. "I should have left it in the ground to rot."

TWENTY-ONE

Eyes closed, I leaned back in the comfy chair and tried to connect the dots to and from the players in the Sterling Homes drama, and finally to the missing lunchbox that was no longer missing.

William Proctor had pulled a Lazarus and wanted revenge on Stella Hughes. Stella hired Amy Chow to steal the Holy Pail. Amy was running for her life, leaving behind the twenty-five thousand dollars promised her by Stella. Jackson and Karla were in bed with Howser, plotting changes in management after Sterling's death, but while he was still vital and healthy. Kyle, after accepting the offer to join the board of directors, had pulled a double-cross on his sister and brother-in-law and told his father of his sister's plans. And Stella was romantically involved with both Jackson and Kyle. Stella Hughes seemed to be the most common denominator.

Stella had told me last night, after being pressed, that Kyle had uncovered a plan of his sister's to take over Sterling Homes and that Karla was working in cahoots with another company to pull the rug out from under her father. Stella claimed not to know any more, only that, in gratitude, Price had bought the Center for Kyle and given him the house. According to what Kyle told Stella, Price was going to oust his own daughter and son-in-law from the company the very next week—the week following his death.

This information jelled pretty much with what Amy had divulged before setting off for Phoenix, although Amy had no way of knowing that Kyle had pulled a fast one and that the plug was about to be yanked on the Blakes.

Geez, it wasn't even eleven thirty and I was already on overload.

At least part of the puzzle was solved. The Holy Pail was found and safe, although I was still dying of curiosity about its background. I had stashed the lunchbox in the box of Howser documents in the trunk of my car and taken the box back to my office at Woobie. After all, my office had already been ransacked once. What safer place could there be for it?

Somewhere on the road from Amy's house and the office, it briefly crossed my mind to turn the Holy Pail over to Dev, but I decided not to until the entire puzzle was solved. After all, I wasn't positive that the murder and the theft weren't connected. And even if the box wasn't a part of the murder, it might be useful as a bargaining tool.

In the middle of all this contemplation, I tried not to think about the fact that I was in possession of stolen property.

A woman at my feet had just finished applying a final coat of lacquer to my toenails and another was starting to do the same to my fingertips. The color I had chosen was called Bleeding Heart, a dark, sexy red, a color that would go well with the slinky black lace negligee I intended to wear on Greg's first night back.

Greg would be home tomorrow mid-afternoon. After picking him up at the John Wayne Airport, we would grab Wainwright and head to Greg's home in Seal Beach for a cozy evening. I started dwelling on just how cozy the evening would get, using it to push the craziness of the morning out of my mind, when I heard a familiar voice.

"Hey there, almost ready to go?"

I opened one eye, knowing full well who I would see standing there.

"Go where?" I asked Zee, who stood a foot away from my chair dressed in a long floral summer dress.

She looked fresh as a daisy, something I was long past, even though I did make a quick pit stop home to freshen up and let the dog out for a fast pee. Still, I'd bet a thousand dollars Zee didn't spend the morning with a famous felon and his bodyguard, or digging up lunchboxes in a city park, for that matter. She smiled at my manicurist and said hello. It was the same woman who did her nails.

"To Glendora," she said cheerfully. "To see Lester Miles."

"I didn't know you were invited," I said.

Both of my eyes were open now and I watched as the manicurist applied the fast-drying top coat to my newly done nails. I didn't want to look at Zee. I knew she'd be standing there with one hand on her hip, as solid and immovable as a mountain. I concentrated on watching my nails dry and hummed low like a refrigerator.

Zee cracked first. "Come on," she said with just a hint of a whine. "I really want to meet Lester Miles."

"It will be boring talk about lunchboxes and old TV shows," I told her, still not looking at her.

"I'll be quiet as a mouse," she promised.

Wiggling my fingers in front of the fan to dry, I thought about it. It would be nice to have some company. According to the Yahoo! map I had downloaded, Glendora was about a fifty-minute drive.

No, no, no, I scolded myself in silence. I could not get Zee involved in this.

"It's a lunch meeting," I said, "at his house. Kind of rude to just bring someone along, don't ya think?"

Zee moved in closer. "All the more reason to take me along," she reasoned. "You certainly don't want to show up at a strange man's house all alone."

Something akin to a knife stabbed through my gut from the inside out. I covered my discomfort with a nervous giggle.

"Zee, Lester Miles is an old geezer about four feet tall. Don't you think I'd be able to handle him myself?"

Her big brown eyes rolled around in her head, reminding me of a TV with a broken horizontal hold. She was standing in her heavy-duty posture now, one plump hand on each hip, like an ill-tempered nightclub bouncer challenging someone to take him on. I had seen her use this stance whenever one of her kids crossed the line big time. It still worked on them, but just barely. Those who loved her knew Zee was just a big marshmallow. I wondered how she'd do against Enrique.

I tried to discourage her further. "Besides, I have another appointment right after that. Someone else interested in the Holy Pail. You'd be bored into next week."

What I had in mind was a trip to Newport Coast to see Stella. I was hoping that Lester Miles could shed some light on the unknown collector and his obsessive interest in the Holy Pail. Using that new information, I intended to put further pressure on Stella. Before this day was out, I wanted to know as much as possible about that damn lunchbox.

"Oh, come on," Zee tried again. "What do I have to do, hold a gun to your head?"

Sweat broke out on my upper lip, and I felt the blood drain from my face like water from a tub.

"You okay?" Zee asked. "You just went white as a sheet."

Bleeding Heart nails waved away her concern. "Fine," I said slowly, "probably just an early hot flash."

She watched me closely, but continued to stand her ground, totally unfazed by the people in the nail salon having to walk around her. It was fast becoming apparent that it was my turn to give. I made one last attempt, playing my trump card.

"Zee, you can't go," I said firmly, after regaining my composure. "If there's any danger, Seth will skin me alive if I drag you into it. After all, this may be connected to Price's murder."

She laughed and leaned in close to my ear. She smelled of jasmine. "Odie, honey, if there's any danger, my darling husband will skin you alive just for getting yourself involved in it."

It was hard to argue with logic like that. Then Zee made an offer I couldn't refuse.

"We can take my car," she announced.

"I'll call Lester Miles and let him know there'll be two of us," I said as I slipped my newly pampered feet into my sandals.

Moaning with unabashed delight, I settled into the buttery leather seats of Zee's Mercedes as we whizzed up the 55 Freeway and made the connection to Interstate 5. Christian pop music floated out from the CD player. The car was so quiet and smooth, if I closed my eyes, it felt like sitting in someone's posh living room. The vehicle was less than six months old, a present from Seth on their last anniversary, their twentieth, and it still had that new car smell. Sometimes, I have the car wash place spritz my car with new car smell and pretend.

Before heading on our way, we dropped my car off at Zee's house and left Seth a note saying we'd be back around dinner time. Zee said he was off playing golf. Jacob was still on his camping trip.

We took the connecting ramp from Interstate 5 to the 57 Freeway. Just beyond the junction, the freeway is flanked on the left by Angel Stadium, home of the Angels baseball team, and on the right by the Arrowhead Pond, where the Mighty Ducks hockey team resides. Greg loves hockey and has season tickets. Seeing the Pond reminded me of him and the fact that in just over twenty-four hours we would be together again. I tingled at the thought in spite of my lingering dilemma about the proposal.

Zee seemed happy to hum along with the music, so I took the time to re-evaluate the continuing lunchbox saga. I started by mentally sorting out what I knew for sure from what was still an unknown.

Known: The Holy Pail was in my possession, and Stella and Willie Porter seemed to be the only ones who cared about finding it. Jackson expressed an interest that day after the funeral, but only in connection to Stella.

Known: Karla and Jackson were up to no good at Sterling Homes, and Kyle was playing both sides of the fence. Considering that he had been boinking his father's fiancée on the side, why should that surprise me?

Known: Unless the Blakes and/or Kyle killed Sterling, they got everything they wanted. Kyle now owned the Center and the house. And Karla had free rein over Sterling Homes.

Known: Amy Chow had worked in secret for both the Blakes and Stella. This seemed to me to be just a young woman who saw opportunities to make some quick cash and take care of her mother and her education. Something told me Amy Chow would not be back to Southern California unless dragged back.

Unknown: Why was Stella working so hard to get her hands on the Holy Pail? Was it just for a hundred grand? Or was there something more going on with that tin crate?

Unknown: Who killed Sterling Price? Kyle, Karla, Jackson, and Stella all had motives of one kind or another. But who was desperate enough to kill?

Unknown: Carmen Sepulveda. Did she know about the corporate manipulations? Did she have an unknown motive to bump off her boss? It seemed unlikely, but you never know.

It was all so confusing. I felt like a white rat scrambling in a maze, looking for cheese.

The big question in my mind was still if the Holy Pail and the corporate takeover were linked or two separate agendas with two separate casts of villains. Willie Porter had made no mention of Sterling Homes, only of the lunchbox and his desire to see it destroyed, supposedly to get back at Stella. Something told me he was telling the truth about this. I don't think he cared one way or another about Sterling Homes, only about watching Stella wither.

I leaned back in the comfort of the luxury car and thought about what Willie had said. If he was to be believed, then Stella was hunting down the Holy Pail, going from owner to owner in her quest. There did not seem to be any corporate intrigue connected with her past behavior, only a single-minded pursuit of the lunchbox. Only Kellogg had escaped her plotting. I wondered where Kellogg got the box? Willie had said that Fisher bought it from Kellogg's son.

Before hitting the road, I had transferred the box of Chappy documents belonging to Lester Miles to the trunk of Zee's car. In my tote bag was Joe's copy of *American Executive*. Even though Willie had said that Jasper Kellogg had never met Stella and had died of heart problems, I still wanted to talk to someone about him. The article gave the name of the small town in which Jasper Kellogg had lived in upstate New York. Jasper wasn't that common a name, and Willie said that Fisher had purchased the lunchbox from Jasper, Jr. I powered up my cell phone, glad I had remembered to recharge it last night.

Zee glanced over at me, but said nothing. Reaching forward, she turned down the music and went back to driving.

Long-distance information had nothing on a Jasper Kellogg in that particular town, but there were three other Kellogg listings, including one for a J. David Kellogg in another town in the area. I jotted them all down on the back of an envelope I found in my purse.

The first Kellogg listing was a Michael Kellogg. No answer. I dialed the next one for a James Kellogg. On the third ring, someone answered. It was a boy's voice, maybe around eleven or twelve. I told him I was trying to reach Jasper Kellogg, Jr.

The boy hesitated, then said, "You mean Uncle Dave?"

J. David Kellogg—why not?

"Maybe," I told the boy. "Is your Uncle Dave Jasper David Kellogg, Jr.?"

"Yeah, but he hates the name Jasper. That was Grandpa's name."

"Does your Uncle Dave live in . . . ," I paused to look at the name of the town Information had given me, "Bentwood?"

"Yeah, that's him."

"Thanks, I have his number, I'll try him there."

I was about to hang up when the boy stopped me. "But Uncle Dave's here." I paused. Could I be that lucky? "He and my dad are working out back. Want to talk to him?"

"Why yes, thank you."

There was a clunk on the other end of the line and the thumping of fast footsteps retreating from the phone. I could hear his young voice calling out for his uncle, announcing a phone call—"some lady." More footsteps—slower and heavier—getting louder as they approached the phone.

"Hello?" said an adult male voice. He sounded laid-back, but not lazy. There was spring in the tone.

I took a deep breath. "I'm looking for Jasper Kellogg, Jr.," I told him.

"You found him."

"Mr. Kellogg, my name's Odelia Grey. I'm sorry to bother you."

"Then just cut to the chase, miss. Got a truck in pieces in the driveway." I pictured Kellogg in a mechanic's jumpsuit covered with grease.

"I'd like to ask you some questions about the Holy Pail, Mr. Kellogg."

"You mean that damn lunchbox of Dad's?"

"Yes, sir. If this is a bad time, I can call back."

There was a pause. Then I heard him call out to someone. "Kenny, get me a beer like a good boy. And take one out to your daddy. Tell him I'll be a few minutes." Then I heard a deep sigh.

"Can I ask you something first, Della?" David Kellogg said into the phone.

"Odelia," I corrected him.

"Odelia, got it." I heard him thank someone. A pop-top sounded, followed by a long pause and audible swallow.

"First, Odelia, I want you to tell me why all of a sudden people want to know about that damn beat-up lunchbox. Last week, someone saying he was a cop called from some beach town in California."

"Was it Detective Devin Frye of Newport Beach?" I asked.

"Yes, I believe that was the fellow. Earlier, some slick PI showed up at my house, and now you're calling, all asking about some hunk of junk my dad kept in the garage for nearly forty years. Something I sold years ago." A slurp of beer. "Tell you what," he said, giving off a short laugh, "I'm beginning to think I should have sold it for more money than I did."

Dave Kellogg would probably throw himself under his disassembled truck if he knew how much was currently on the table.

"Mr. Kellogg, I know Detective Frye. He's a good man and investigating a murder."

"That's what the man said."

"I don't know how much Frye told you, but the present owner was killed a week ago, and the lunchbox went missing. As for the private investigator, I spoke this morning with the man who sent him."

Zee shot a wide-eyed look my way.

"As for me, I knew Sterling Price, the man who was killed, and I have a few questions of my own. Seems a lot of people are looking for that lunchbox, and I want to know why. I was hoping that knowing more about its background will help me figure some things out."

"So it's true, the last owner of the lunchbox was murdered?"

"Yes, Mr. Kellogg, he was poisoned."

"Over a kid's damn lunchbox?" Another big chug-a-lug.

"Honestly, no one knows yet. The police are looking into it." I stared out the windshield. The freeway was winding through some low hills. "Mr. Kellogg, I'm calling on a cell phone from a moving car. If we get cut off, stay put and I'll call right back. Okay? It's important."

"Sure. No problem."

"You said your father had the box for forty years. Do you know where he got it?"

"Sure. My dad used to live in California. Worked on some of the very first TV shows, mostly on the sets, building them. A real pioneer."

"Did he work on *The Chappy Wheeler Show?*"

"That's the one on the lunchbox, isn't it? The one where the star got killed?" he asked.

"Yes, that's right."

"I believe that show was the last one he worked on. After the show closed down, he and my mother came back East. This is where they both grew up. He worked in New York City for a long time, building sets for shows, before retiring."

"Do you know how he got the box?"

Kellogg called for another beer before answering. "I remember Dad saying he found it in the garbage at the studio. This was shortly after the show closed down. He took it as a souvenir."

A souvenir? "Are you sure?"

"Hey, Jimmy," I heard Kellogg shout to someone. "Didn't Dad say he found that old lunchbox in the trash?" I heard a voice respond, but couldn't make out the words.

"My brother remembers the same thing." More mumbling. "Yeah, I should tell her that, huh?"

"Tell me what?" I asked, growing excited.

The connection grew weak. I heard Kellogg talking through static and then he was gone. I gave the car time to ease along the highway before hitting redial. Kellogg picked it up on the first ring. Zee had turned off the music completely and was engrossed in my half of the conversation.

"Tell me what?" I asked Kellogg again.

"Something my brother and I remembered after the investigator was here. Something strange." He paused to drink, gave a mild belch, and excused himself before moving along with his story.

"Shortly before our dad died, he was going through all the old stuff in the garage. He had read somewhere that old lunchboxes were becoming popular and valuable. So he got out the lunchbox from that Western show and started cleaning it up.

"I remember he was having trouble fixing the handle because of his arthritis, and asked me to help. There was a big dent, too, on one corner of the box. We fixed the metal ring that held the handle."

Another slurp of beer. I was beginning to crave one myself.

"But before I could start working on the dent," Kellogg continued, "Dad stopped me. After that, he wouldn't let anyone touch it. Kept it wrapped in plastic. Said he read something about it being more valuable as is. About a week later, he told us he thought he had a buyer. Claimed he was going to get top dollar for the thing. 'Big money' was how he put it."

I remembered seeing the dent on one corner of the box the day I was at Sterling Homes.

"Do you know who the buyer was?"

"He said someone from the show," Kellogg said. "That's right, isn't it, Jimmy?" Kellogg asked someone on his end. "Yeah, that's right, Odelia," he confirmed, speaking to me once again. "One of the actors from the show. That's all he said about it."

Hmm. Lester Miles, a known collector of memorabilia, came instantly to mind. I watched the road. We were almost to Glendora.

"Do you remember seeing anything strange or unusual about the lunchbox?" I asked Kellogg.

"Well, it really wasn't a kid's lunchbox, just a model or mock-up of one. But outside of that, not really. Once Jimmy caught Dad going over it with a magnifying glass, but he never let on what he was looking for. After Dad died, I had no idea how to get in touch with that buyer he always talked about. Ended up taking out an ad in a newsletter for people who collect stuff. Sold it to the first one who contacted me, some guy in Chicago, for nine hundred dollars."

"Nine hundred dollars?"

"Yeah, I had no idea what it was worth, so I left the price open and waited to see what would happen. The guy offered five hundred. I asked for twelve, we compromised on nine." He chuckled.

"Truth be told, I about shit when he offered the five hundred. Just said twelve to see what the fool would do. We split the money between the four grandkids. Said it was from their granddad."

His last comment made me smile. "Your father died from a heart attack, correct?"

"That's right. He had a bad ticker and emphysema. Smoked like a chimney. He was a walking time bomb."

"Mr. Kellogg," I said to him, "thank you for being so helpful and answering my questions. I only have one more."

"No problem. Shoot."

"Before your father died, did a woman call him about the lunchbox? Or has a woman called you about it since his death? A woman with a very low voice, almost like a man's?"

"Funny, that investigator asked the same thing. The cop just asked where Dad got it from." A pause. I waited. "As I told the PI, I don't recall Dad getting a call before he died, but he might not have told anyone if he did. But right after I sold the box to that man from Chicago, I did get a call from a woman. She was mighty upset about it already being sold and offered me a lot of money to get it back for her. I told her no, but gave her the name of the guy who bought it. Told her she could buy it from him herself."

Geez, Kellogg set up Fisher and didn't have a clue. *Better he didn't*, I thought.

"Thank you again for your time, Mr. Kellogg. You've been most helpful."

"No problem. But I've got one last question for you, Odelia."

"Sure, go for it. Seems the least I can do," I told him.

"Do you have any idea what that old lunchbox is really worth?"

I hesitated, not sure if I should tell him.

TWENTY-TWO

"WHAT A CUTE LITTLE city," Zee remarked as we exited the freeway and wound our way through the city of Glendora. Following the map, we headed north, toward the foothills of the San Gabriel Mountains.

The city was almost Norman Rockwellish. A few turns here and there and we found ourselves driving through a small downtown area, passing under large banners that advertised a weekly farmers' market and an upcoming choir concert. Seconds earlier, we had passed the post office, police station, library, and city hall. I craned my neck to get a good look around. The fire station could not be far.

"Look at all the craft and antique shops," Zee said with glee. She glanced at me with hope. "Think we could stop on the way home and check out some of the stores?"

With all the stuff I had just learned from Kellogg, the last thing on my mind was shopping. But Zee did drive us here, and shopping was a favorite hobby. "Sure, as long as it's not too late." An idea dribbled into my mind and out of my mouth. "Hey, why don't you go shopping after lunch while I chat up Lester Miles?"

She shot me a frown. "I don't think so."

I told her to take a right at the next stop sign, a street called Sierra Madre. She followed my instructions.

"So, you going to tell me what Mr. Kellogg said?" she asked.

I ignored her and told her to turn left at the next street. After making the turn, she pulled over to the side of the road and put the car in park. She turned in the leather seat and looked at me. Her dark, round face said she could wait all day. A glance at my watch told me it was twelve fifteen. According to the map, we weren't very far from our destination. I could walk it if I had to. I tapped my freshly done nails on the armrest.

"Oh, all right," I said in a peevish tone. "You win." I undid the seat belt and turned to face her. "I just don't want you mixed up in anything that might be dangerous. I'm already up to my neck—no sense both of us getting mired down."

"I'm an adult, Odelia," she said patiently. "I've given birth twice, had one miscarriage, and buried both a parent and a brother. Trust me. I can handle anything the good Lord brings my way."

I shook my head at her well-intentioned but misplaced spunk. "Something tells me it's not the good Lord who's behind this."

Quickly, I filled Zee in on the other side of my cell phone conversation with Kellogg, including my suspicion that Lester Miles was the person Jasper Kellogg had contacted about buying the Holy Pail. She listened intently.

"What do you think Jasper saw in the box?" she asked.

I shrugged. "Who knows, but whatever it was, he didn't want it disturbed. That's why he wouldn't let his son finish fixing the box.

And I have absolutely no doubt that Stella Hughes was the woman who called Kellogg, Jr. after he sold the box to Ivan Fisher."

I also told Zee what I knew about Fisher and Stella's part in his death. Conspicuously absent was how I came by such knowledge. Zee started to ask, but changed her mind. Guess she figured she could only pry so much out of me before I balked like a mule, and she was right.

Deciding in for a penny, in for a pound, I told her everything about Karla's plans for the corporation, her brother's double-cross, and even my speculation about Jackson being a front for his ambitious wife.

Lastly, for good measure, I added the gossip from Gigi about Lester Miles marrying Chappy Wheeler's widow.

"You think Gigi's right?" Zee asked.

"Normally, I'd say she's off her rocker. But this is tabloid stuff. Gigi has a PhD in this crap."

"Well, we'll know soon enough, won't we?"

Only a teeny-weeny tidbit was missing from my account of the Sterling Price murder to date—the current location of the lunchbox. Zee cannot lie to save her life. If Lester Miles asks us if we know its whereabouts, her expressive face will give it away. I, fortunately or unfortunately, depending on one's viewpoint, don't suffer from such scruples.

"Sure you wouldn't rather go shopping?" I asked her when I had finished bringing her up-to-date. "You could drop me off and come back in an hour or so. Or I could call you on the cell to pick me up."

She put the car in gear and pulled away from the curb. "Not on your life, girlfriend."

Lester Miles lived on a cul-de-sac just where the road began to climb into the hills. There were only four homes on his short street. The lawns were manicured, the landscaping carefully planned. All the structures smacked of custom treatments. The Mileses' abode was a ranch-style house the color of fresh peaches. It rambled for half the short block and backed up to the base of the hill. Most of the open property was to the left and fenced behind a brick wall painted white, with an iron gate. The gate was open. We parked on the street, and I retrieved the articles from the trunk. We made our way through the gate and up the few steps to the heavy, carved door. It opened just as we reached it.

"Come on in, ladies," said a Santa Claus in miniature. Not an elfin figure, mind you, but a perfect diminutive Santa, complete with white hair, white beard, and bushy eyebrows. Only his eyes were dark, sitting in his jolly face like the coal eyes of a snowman. "I'm Lester Miles."

I introduced us both. He took my offered right hand within his two pudgy ones and pressed it warmly. He did the same with Zee's hand.

"Please call me Les," he told us.

I handed him the box of memorabilia and thanked him for the use of the information. He smiled, took the box from me, and set it down on a table by the door.

Lester Miles was but a hiccup over four feet in height. For once I actually felt tall. He was robust and rounded, especially through the middle, and walked with a mild bowlegged gait. He looked a lot younger than I expected. Based on his photos during the Chappy Wheeler days, I had calculated Lester Miles to currently be in his late eighties. But research on the International Movie Data Base website advised me that his real age was seventy-six. He had been only twenty-six when he played Hi Miller on TV, although he had looked much older.

He guided us through the lovely house filled with tasteful furnishings and personal mementos until we emerged through a sliding glass door onto a covered patio. Just beyond the patio was a small, sparkling swimming pool. Along one side of the white brick fence, roses climbed trellises. Along two other sides were healthy bougainvilleas and even some oleanders. Other flowers of every imaginable color flourished everywhere else, traveling along the ground, standing in terra-cotta pots, and hanging in vessels from eaves, posts, and trees. The hot August air was redolent with earthy smells, both sweet and spicy. It was magical.

At the center of the patio was a white wrought-iron dining table with cushioned chairs, perfectly set for a summer luncheon. Counting four place settings, I hoped the fourth was for Catherine Matthews. Of course, I reminded myself, Lester Miles might not still be married to her. My online research did not produce much on Catherine Matthews following *The Chappy Wheeler Show*, only small parts in two B movies produced shortly after the show was canceled—unlike Les, who had been acting continuously for the past fifty years.

"It's cooler today, so we thought we'd have lunch out here," Les said, showing us to our seats. Much of the furniture was slightly scaled down.

"Your property is beautiful," Zee remarked.

"Thank you, Zee," Les said. He offered us a choice of iced tea or lemonade. I took tea, Zee the lemonade. "My wife and I love to putter in the garden. Each plant is like a child to us."

Zee, an ardent gardener, continued the chitchat. It was becoming clear to me that her presence might be advantageous. "And it's much warmer here than in Newport Beach," she said to Les. "The plants must require a lot of water."

"Yes, we can easily hit over one hundred degrees up here in the foothills," he informed her with a bright smile. "And in the winter it can get quite cold—very different from your beach cities. But we look for species that are drought and heat resistant."

Les turned to me. "Do you garden, Odelia?" Zee let out a snort that she tried to hide with a polite cough. Les looked at me, slightly puzzled. "Is she trying to tell me something, Odelia?"

I pointed to a couple of the hanging baskets festooned with healthy blooms. "I have those same plants hanging on my patio," I told him, "but they're silk."

Les chuckled, took a good look in my direction, and stopped short. "Oh my, you're not teasing, are you? You really potted fake plants outside?"

I nodded slightly, not one bit embarrassed, as Zee giggled from behind her napkin. Her chubby cheeks puffed and her eyes squished in laughter. She lowered the napkin.

"Believe me, Les, Odelia's many other talents more than make up for it." I kicked Zee lightly under the table. She giggled again. Sipping my iced tea, I re-evaluated her worth as a snoop buddy.

"Will your wife be joining us?" I asked, changing the subject.

"Yes, she's in the kitchen finishing up with the preparations." At that moment, another sliding door opened and an attractive elderly woman joined us. Behind her followed a thin, uniform-clad young woman pushing a service trolley laden with food. Through the door behind them, I could see into the kitchen. "Ah," Les said, "here's Catherine now." He introduced us.

In the past fifty years, she had thickened slightly through the hips and waist, and shallow, fine lines outlined her eyes and mouth. But except for those few trophies of aging, Catherine Matthews was still a beauty. She was barely over five feet tall, with fine, short hair that reminded me of silver cellophane. Her eyes were blue and penetrating, her nose aristocratic. She wore a cotton skirt and matching blouse in lilac. Pearls adorned her neck and ears. Her smile was courteous but stilted and could have been generated by either shyness or annoyance.

"I hope you both like chicken salad and cold asparagus with lemon," she said.

"Sounds wonderful," Zee answered. I knew Zee despised asparagus. Good, payback for the silk plants.

The four of us ate companionably and talked about the weather and recent movies—safe topics. Not sure how to broach the subject of the Holy Pail, I was thrilled when Les brought it up first.

"So, I understand you're looking for the Holy Pail, Odelia?" he asked me as he reached for a third piece of Catherine's incredible homemade date bread. I was working on a second slice myself.

I used the excuse of chewing to weigh my words carefully. "I'm not really looking for it, Les," I told him truthfully. "It's odd, but for some reason several people seem to think I already have it. My office was even burglarized the other evening."

"Joe told me about your law firm when he called to ask if I'd see you. Pretty nasty business." Les paused. "But are you sure that was about the lunchbox?"

"Not a hundred percent sure," I lied, all the while picturing Willie and Enrique in ski masks. "But even the police are thinking along those lines." I hesitated, aware of Zee sitting next to me happily munching on gourmet chicken salad with almonds. I decided not to mention that even my home had been searched. "And people keep calling and asking me if I have it."

Les nodded. "It certainly sounds odd. And you say this started after the Holy Pail went missing from its present owner?"

"Missing after Mr. Price was murdered," I added.

"Hmm, yes, Joe told me that, too. Very tragic." He stroked his beard in contemplation. "I understand that supposedly the lunchbox is cursed. Provided, of course, you believe in such things. I also understand Mr. Price makes the fourth owner in a row who has died."

I nodded. "From what I've been able to find out, there have only been these four owners."

"Really?" Les seemed surprised. "In fifty years, only four? My, someone held tight to it, didn't they?"

"A man named Jasper Kellogg had it for about forty years. He worked on the show with the two of you. A set builder, I believe, or something like that. Do you recall him?"

Both seemed to think about it for a moment.

"I'm sorry, but no," answered Catherine evenly, with a slight shake of her head. In spite of her answer, there was a slight jump in her eyes, like an unexpected touch to a hot stove.

Les's face contorted in contemplation. "I'm not sure, but I think I do. After all, the name Jasper is not a common name." He finally shrugged. "The name sounds familiar, but I can't put a face to it.

There were so many people connected with the show and it was so long ago."

I looked into the jolly, intelligent face of Les and the reserved, closed face of his wife. The glimmer in Catherine's eyes was gone, replaced again by—what, detachment? Wariness? Fear? She was a hard read. *Remember, Odelia,* I told myself, *these folks are actors, particularly Les.*

"When was the last time either one of you saw the lunchbox? Or did you ever see it?"

Catherine looked to her husband, her eyes questioning, thin lips tight. "Fifty years ago?" she asked him. Before he could answer, she turned back to us. "Yes, I'm sure," she said in a light monotone voice. "It was back then, fifty years ago. We all—meaning all of us on the show—saw it after it was designed. It was unveiled at a cast party. We were all so excited." She turned to Les. "Remember that, dear?" He nodded. She turned to gaze out at the roses, her classic profile lost in remembering. "But I don't recall seeing it at all after that."

"Same here," Les agreed. "After Chappy was killed, I don't think it was ever even mentioned. I heard about it again just a few years ago. I was at a collectors' show, a convention for fans of old television shows held at the Convention Center. In fact, I believe that's where I first met your friend Joe Bays." He looked thoughtful, as if trying to conjure up the day clearly. "I remember I was signing autographs when someone asked me about it. Rather took me by surprise. Guess I always figured it was destroyed after the show was canceled." He took a sip of tea. "You say this man Kellogg had it?"

Nodding slightly, I studied the warm, friendly man across from me. It struck me as odd that someone who collected stacks of old articles about Chappy Wheeler would not know that the box was in play among collectors. But maybe it wasn't. After all, Kellogg owned it for over forty years, and no one even knew he took it in the first place. And to my knowledge, it had passed from hand to hand privately after that, not through public auction. But it still had to be advertised somewhere, somehow, each time someone put it up for sale, and not just by Kellogg's family. Fisher had to find a buyer, and so did Proctor. Joe knew all about it, and he didn't even collect lunchboxes. As soon as Kellogg's family placed the first ad, the box's existence would have become common knowledge among those who followed such things.

"So Jasper Kellogg never contacted you about buying the lunchbox from him? Maybe five or six years ago?"

"No, not ever. Why should he?" Les asked.

"Just a guess. Seems he contacted someone from the show about then, but no one knows who."

Les looked puzzled. "Like I said, a lot of people worked on the show."

He was right, it could have been anyone.

The table grew quiet as we all finished our meal and settled down. I decided to focus on another aspect of *The Chappy Wheeler Show*, the personal angle. It made me uncomfortable, but there were things I wanted to know. If Catherine and Les didn't want to answer my questions, that was their prerogative.

"I'm sorry to pry," I told the couple, "but I understand that you, Catherine, were married to Chappy Wheeler—I mean Charles Borden—at the time of his death."

Her eyes faded to old bleached denim. Catherine Matthews Miles had a poker face, but emotional eyes. "Yes, that's correct," she answered.

She looked over at Les. Her facial expression was one of composed affection, but this time her eyes clearly looked like a runaway's—vacant and scared. He reached a chubby, thick-fingered hand over, placed it on her arm, and gave her a slight nod. Catherine sighed.

"It was a marriage in name only," she finally said. "A publicity stunt thought up by the studio. We were married partway through the first season."

"You married him for publicity?" Zee asked incredulously.

"Yes," Catherine answered, mild defensiveness creeping into her voice, "and it wasn't that unusual, especially in those days. An actor and actress were often paired romantically for ratings' sake. Mostly, they lived private, separate lives; only publicly were they married. When the show ended, you got a divorce or annulment and moved on. If you didn't agree, you could find yourself without a career." It was the most she had said since our arrival. It seemed to tire her. "Remember," she continued, "that was fifty years ago. People didn't go from partner to partner then, at least not publicly. The studio insisted that everything appear to be wholesome and moral."

"Did you and Chappy Wheeler get along?" Zee asked. One of my top questions also.

Catherine cast her eyes down into her lap. "Not really. He could be very difficult, both on and off the set."

"A real ass, if you'll pardon my language," Les added tightly. "Fortunately, they only saw each other when necessary."

I gave them both a pleasant smile, hoping to break the building tension. "And you two got married after Catherine was free?"

Catherine blushed and Les smiled at her with love. They did make a lovely couple.

"Yes," he said. "Two months later. As soon as we were released from our contracts for the show." He turned to look at us. "You see, Catherine and I were dating before her marriage to Chappy."

"We wanted to get married," Catherine added quickly, "but the studio wouldn't allow it." She looked at Les and reddened again. "They said it would be bad publicity if I married Les."

"Bad publicity?" I asked.

"What they said exactly," Les said, with a deep frown across his snowy brow, "was that the public wouldn't like it if the pretty schoolteacher married the freak."

I gasped at the hideous statement. Next to me, I heard Zee say in a low voice wrought with scorn, "Uh-huh, sounds about right."

"When we did finally marry, one tabloid referred to us as beauty and the beast." Les's voice was bitter. "Other reports were that Catherine was so grief stricken, she didn't know what she was doing. That I had drugged her. Had even killed Chappy for her. You wouldn't believe the hate mail I got."

Catherine laid a hand over his. "Now, dear, don't get yourself worked up over it." She smiled at us, but her eyes were cold and angry. "That was fifty years, two children, four grandchildren, and one great-grandchild ago," she announced proudly. I half expected her to tack on "so there!"

Zee and I both congratulated them.

I thought about Greg's proposal. These people had made it work for fifty years and under a shroud of negativity. Did I have the right stuff to attempt the same under good circumstances?

"Do either of you have any idea why someone would be so obsessed about that lunchbox?" I asked, returning to my main topic.

Both shook their heads.

"And what about Chappy Wheeler's murder? I understand it was never solved."

"Unfortunately," Les said, "that's true. We were all questioned, especially Catherine and me." He glanced at her briefly and squeezed the hand resting on her arm. "Everyone at the studio knew how we felt about each other. And everyone knew she was having a tough time with Chappy. He was abusive, verbally and physically."

"Physically?" I asked. "You mean he beat you, Catherine?"

Catherine got that cold, unfocused look again. She looked beyond us, once more at the roses. "Not really, just pushed me around. Especially if he'd been drinking."

"He hit her," Les said firmly. Looking at his wife, he added, "I'm sorry, sweetheart, but let's be honest about it. The bastard's been gone more than fifty years. No need to protect him now."

Catherine gave no indication that she heard him, just continued to stare at the roses.

Les sighed and patted her arm. "The studio made them share a house and a bungalow on the lot," he told us. "Said it wouldn't look right if they were seen separately. Chappy was an unhappy man and an angry drunk. Sometimes, if the shoot didn't go well or he didn't like an episode, he'd tie one on and smack her around. It was the same if the studio bigwigs gave him a hard time. By the start of the second season, anything and everything gave Chappy an excuse to drink and beat on her."

Catherine got up abruptly and started to clear the table. The maid popped up magically and assisted.

"I'll help you, Catherine," Zee said, rising and picking up our plates. She gave me a solemn, wide-eyed look.

I wanted to help, too. Anything would be better than sitting here, listening to the details of violence. But this was part of the history of the Holy Pail, part of *The Chappy Wheeler Show* background. My butt stayed in my chair, though I squirmed a bit.

"Did it happen often?" I asked Les.

"Once is too often, Odelia."

"I agree, Les." I sipped my tea, lost in thought. I despised men who beat on women emotionally and physically. Actually, I despised bullies of any kind, of any age or gender. "But why didn't the studio step in? They put Catherine in that situation."

Les tugged on his beard. "There was a lot of stress on the set, on all of us. TV was still in its infancy. *The Chappy Wheeler Show* was a pioneer. People had invested big in Chappy and the show and were banking on its success.

"And viewers were more naive than they are today, less tolerant. In those days, a star with a publicized penchant for assaults on women would have been shunned by the viewers. The studio did its best to keep Chappy under control and people from talking. Stories in fan magazines were carefully edited, people paid to keep their mouths shut. I'm sure it's still the same today, but to a lesser degree. Actors today flaunt their bad behavior, like they're proud of it."

"How did you cope? I can't imagine how you must have felt. And not just about the violence."

His dark eyes grew shiny. "As much as possible, I tried to make sure Catherine was never alone with him. I became the third wheel. But I couldn't be with her all the time."

Thinking back about the articles about the show and its cast members, I did recall seeing a lot of photographs with the three of them—Catherine, Chappy, and Lester.

"But what about the baby?" I asked. "Didn't Catherine have a child by Chappy Wheeler?"

Les' cheerful countenance drooped considerably. "Yes, she did. The pregnancy happened during one of his drunken rages."

"You mean he raped her?"

"Our eldest child, Charles Borden's daughter, doesn't know anything about his drunken violence. She thinks he was a prince—a famous TV personality loved by everyone. She's very sensitive and, well, often given to instability. We feel it best she not know about that side of him. I'm sure you understand."

"Fifty years is a long time to keep a secret," I said to him.

"Like I said, people were paid to keep their mouths shut."

"But aren't you afraid she'll find out her father was gay and start asking questions?"

Les looked at me in astonishment, as if I had kicked the chair out from under him.

He said nothing, just looked at me like a frozen garden gnome. A bee buzzed nearby.

"Les, I just heard that yesterday, from a reliable source." I groaned inwardly, never imagining I'd ever think of JJ as a reliable anything.

"Like I said," he finally answered, breaking his silence, "times were different." He took a sip of his beverage. "It's true. Chappy's drinking and brutality weren't the only things the studio was hiding. They were also covering up the fact that he was a homosexual.

"That was probably one of the reasons for his uncontrollable anger and self-abuse. He wasn't allowed to be himself and live his life openly, any more than Catherine and I were. In fact, the marriage to Catherine was planned to quell surfacing rumors about Chappy."

I closed my eyes and leaned back in the chair. Even under the shade of the patio cover, I could feel the afternoon sun baking my body like an oatmeal cookie. It felt good, reassuring. All this new information made my brain feel like a locomotive about to jump the tracks. I got up and stretched my legs by wandering around the yard and enjoying the flowers. Les accompanied me. We walked toward the back of the property. After a few minutes, he cleared his throat. It roused me from my attempt to re-center my thoughts.

"Personally," he said, once he had my attention again, "I always believed Charles was murdered by a gay lover. And that the studio knew it and covered it up."

"But a murder?"

"Why not?" he asked with a shrug. "They certainly covered up a lot of other things."

I thought about this while I watched a bird nibble at a nearby feeder. A possibility had occurred to me over lunch—just a fleeting thought that was now insisting on a closer look. Maybe the studio wasn't the only one covering up. I decided to take a shot and see if I hit a bull's-eye, or at least a nerve.

"The child is yours, isn't she, Les?"

At first, he looked at me in astonishment. That was followed by offended sputtering. Eventually, Les melted into resignation, ending with a big sigh. I had definitely hit on something important.

"You and Catherine were dating before her marriage to Chappy Wheeler, and I'll bet you continued after the marriage. You married quickly once he was gone." I bent my head down to look at Les. His eyes were sad, but his chin was held high.

"Things were different then, Odelia." He looked at the patio area, where Zee and Catherine were busy setting out dessert and coffee. "I couldn't very well have the world thinking Catherine was an adulteress, a common tramp, could I?" he whispered. "Chappy did get drunk and beat her. But that was his only interest in her. He never had any sort of physical relationship with her outside of the beatings."

"So you adopted your own child?"

"Yes. And the birth certificate says that she is the natural child of Charles Borden."

I started back to the patio, but Les put a hand on my arm to stop me.

"God forgive me, Odelia," he said in a husky whisper, "but although I understood Chappy's frustration, more than he probably realized, I'm not sorry someone killed him. If he hadn't died when he did, who knows what would have happened to Catherine or to the child. I feared he would beat it out of her if he ever found out."

Before sitting down to dessert, I asked for the location of the powder room. Catherine gave me directions and off I went to freshen up. Along the way, I passed a table loaded with framed photographs. I glanced at them briefly. There were pictures of children of all ages and sizes, including several older photographs of a boy and girl in various stages of growth, from toddler right up to college age. Must be their two children, I thought, and the rest the grandchildren. I picked up one of the photos and studied it. Stunned, I picked up another framed photo, and another. Holding my breath, I hurriedly ran my eyes over them all.

Looking over my shoulder, I made sure I was alone. Secure in my privacy, I plucked the smallest of the photos from the table and stashed it in my tote bag.

TWENTY-THREE

"You did what?" Zee yelled at me as we sped down the freeway back to Newport Beach.

After our lunch with Catherine and Les, we stopped briefly in the downtown area of Glendora. Zee bought some hand-painted glassware in one shop and a silk floral wreath in another. Being eager to get on our way, I bought nothing and tried not to let Zee see my foot tapping while she shopped.

Once we put some distance between us and Glendora, I filled Zee in on Chappy Wheeler's lifestyle and told her about the photo I pinched. I ignored her inquiry into my sanity, but she wasn't to be deterred.

"Did you just tell me that you stole something from those nice people?"

"I'll give it back," I assured her.

"This I want to see," she said with mild sarcasm. "What are you going to do, Odelia? Mail it back with a note that says 'oops, look what jumped into my purse'?"

Had to admit it, she had a point.

"Stealing and peeping. Good Lord, what's next?" she ranted.

"Zee, the photo is important. I think the girl in the picture is Stella Hughes."

Zee shot me a side glance. "You mean Price's gold digger?"

"Yes. I'm not entirely sure, but pretty sure. I think she's their daughter. And if so, Stella thinks she's Chappy Wheeler's daughter, not Les's."

"Providing it is her," Zee added.

I didn't share Zee's skepticism. After all, I knew Stella, and I was almost one-hundred-percent positive the girl in the photo was her. "Why else would they have photos of her growing up?"

Zee just shrugged and continued driving.

"I was thinking about talking to Stella this afternoon after we got back," I told Zee. "Now I'm definitely heading over there."

"What about dinner?" Zee asked. "Seth's doing chicken on the grill tonight."

"I'll be back in time," I assured her. "The Price house is in Newport Coast, not far from you. I just want to ask Stella some questions."

My plan was to simply drop in on her, like she did me, and catch her off-guard. Maybe Kyle would be there, too. I wanted to talk to him as well. It being a Saturday evening, I was afraid if I didn't get there soon, they might be off for dinner or something.

"Something about Catherine and Lester didn't sit right with me," I told Zee after a while. "But I can't quite put my finger on it. One thing, I think they did know who Jasper Kellogg was, but I'm not sure they knew he had the lunchbox the whole time. They don't even seem to care about the lunchbox, which surprises me, because Les is a big collector of Chappy Wheeler and other TV Western memorabilia. If he found out about the lunchbox's existence, even a few years ago, it would be natural for him to try to track it down. I can't help but think he's the cast member Kellogg contacted prior to his death."

"But, if that's true, why didn't Les come forward and contact the Kelloggs later," Zee added, "after Jasper's death? If he had agreed to buy the box, wouldn't he have followed up on it?"

"You'd think so. But Kellogg's son said they didn't know who the potential buyer was. Otherwise, they would have sold it to that person instead of running the ad that Fisher answered."

I tilted my head back against the leather headrest and closed my eyes as I spoke.

"And I still don't know if the lunchbox is tied in with Sterling Price's murder. But the more I learn about the Holy Pail, the more convinced I am that there's something sinister about it; something that only a few people know or knew, like maybe Lester and Stella, or even Jasper Kellogg."

Something Stella said to me the night before suddenly came to mind like a photo flash.

"You know what, Zee?" I turned halfway on the seat to look at her. "Stella said that her father's dream was the Holy Pail. That he was very interested in it, and that he's dead. If Stella believes Chappy Wheeler was her father, it could explain why she's so obsessed with it. What do you want to bet Stella is the mystery buyer with the hundred grand?"

Zee twisted her mouth around as she chewed on my theory. "I thought you said she was a gold digger. That she wanted to marry

Mr. Price for security, and that's why she has her hooks into his son now."

"She could be lying. And it sure wouldn't be the first time, either. And just because she's offering a hundred thousand dollars doesn't mean she actually has it or plans to fork it over."

I thought about the deal Stella made with Amy. It was for twenty-five thousand. And once again I wondered what scared Amy off from collecting it.

"You know, Zee, she could be doing both. Stella could be marrying for security and be hunting the box down on her own behalf." I thought about her initial hesitancy with Kyle that afternoon in the study. "She also could be stringing Kyle along to get to the box. After all, it would be part of his and his sister's inheritance once it's found."

"I wonder where that silly box is," Zee said almost absently.

"Probably closer than we think," I said as casually as throwing away a used tissue.

Zee laughed. "Wouldn't surprise me."

We continued our drive home, passing between the two sports venues once again as they stood like sentries on either side of the freeway. Rummaging through my tote bag for some breath mints, I discovered the newspaper article Joe had given me. I pulled it out, unfolded it, and read it. It was just a couple of short paragraphs in a question and answer column on collectibles, and it gave a very brief history of children's lunchboxes. I read it several times. It contained nothing I hadn't seen recently in my research, but one sentence did catch my eye. I was mulling it over and exploring new possibilities when Zee cleared her throat.

"Odelia," Zee began in a serious tone, "I want to ask you something, but I don't want you to get mad."

Uh-oh. Whenever someone starts off like that, I just know I am not going to like what follows. After I refolded the newspaper and tucked it back into my bag, I closed one eye as if in pain, scrunched up my mouth, and looked at her. With any luck my evil stare would discourage her from going further. It didn't.

"I've been thinking that maybe your obsession with this lunchbox thing is pure avoidance." She talked while she drove, every once in a while casting a look my way. "Maybe you're using Mr. Price's murder to avoid making a decision about Greg."

Who? Me?

"Zee, did you not notice that my office was broken into?"

"I didn't say that this matter didn't involve you in some way. I just made an observation that maybe you're getting so involved because you don't want to think about Greg's proposal. After all, the Newport Beach police and Detective Frye are more than capable of handling this."

She concentrated on changing lanes before continuing. "In fact, are you even communicating with Detective Frye? Are you telling him any of what you're finding out?"

I looked out the passenger's window, my lips compressed in a pout. Sterling Price had been killed less than a week ago. Looking back, I pinpointed the funeral as the starting block for the frenetic race I was running, a treadmill of crazy and bizarre events all packed into three days—technically two, if you're counting true twenty-four-hour increments.

During this time, I had communicated very little with Dev. But, I told myself, it was only two days, and most of the action had taken place last night and this morning. When was I supposed to call him? Let's face it—in choosing between a manicure and pedicure or making a call to a cop you know will nag you, it's a no-brainer. And I didn't want to bother him when I had nothing concrete to offer. *Although,* my little voice nagged, *you do have the lunchbox.*

As for avoiding my answer to Greg, Zee was wrong. In spite of appearances of avoidance, it was very close to the front of my crowded mind. Not an hour went by without my thinking of him and our possible life together, for better or for worse.

"Actually, Zee, I *have* made up my mind about Greg."

She glanced at me, her saucer eyes bugged in anticipation. "And?"

"How do you feel about wearing a taffeta banana yellow matron of honor dress with huge mutton sleeves and a bustle?"

"Something's wrong," I told Zee as we stood on the doorstep of the Price home.

We had rung the bell several times and followed up with raps to the front door. Two cars were in evidence. A Jeep sat parked in the semicircular driveway and a Lexus was in the garage, which was open. We had pulled in behind the Jeep.

"Maybe they're out back and can't hear us," Zee offered.

"Could be," I said, but I didn't feel it in my gut. My nervous stomach, which had settled somewhat following lunch, was threatening to gear up again. A rancid taste oozed into my dry mouth. Most people in Southern California did not leave their garage doors wide open, not even in good neighborhoods.

Zee had insisted on coming with me. Nothing I said, promised, or threatened could change her mind. Oh well, why not? She knew most of the story anyway, and maybe that menacing stance of hers would work on Stella.

Leaving Zee posted at the front door in case someone did answer, I walked around to the side of the house, looking in windows as I went. Nothing. No sign of life anywhere. I came across a gate in the high fence, but it was locked and there was no place for me to get a foothold to climb up and look over. Not that I was any good at climbing anything anyway.

I walked back to the front of the house, thinking about my next move. Walking over to the Jeep, I touched the hood. It was cold. Chances are the other car's engine would be also.

Zee came up to me. "Where'd you learn that?" she asked.

"On TV," I replied. "They always check the hood of the car." She nodded solemnly at my wisdom.

"I'm going to check the garage," I told her. "See if the door connected to the house is locked."

I walked slowly into the garage, all the while hoping someone would answer the front door—maybe Stella wrapped in a towel, fresh from the shower. That would make me feel foolish, but better. Zee shadowed me. At the same time, both of us touched the hood of the Lexus—stone cold.

I was about to grab the doorknob of the connector door to the house when Zee touched my shoulder, stopping me. She pulled a linen hankie from her purse and offered it to me. *Like on TV,* I thought with a smile. Taking the hankie, I used it to cover the doorknob while I turned it. It opened easily. On the other side was a service room that led to the extra-large kitchen I had seen on Thursday.

"Helloooooo," I called in a raised voice. "Stella? Anyone home?" Nothing, only Zee's breathing close behind me.

I entered the kitchen and called out again. Still nothing. Looking out the large windows facing the back yard, I scanned the pool area.

"Call 9-1-1!" I yelled to Zee. "Call 9-1-1!"

Dropping my bag, I started running for one of the French doors leading to the back. Someone was face down in the pool. I yanked open the door and dashed outside, kicking off my sandals and undoing my skirt as I went. At the pool's edge, I dropped my heavy cotton skirt to the ground and plunged into the water.

I turned the body over. It was Jackson Blake. Looping an arm under one of his, I started making for the shallow end and the stairs leading to the deck. He was naked, the heavy, dark hair on his head and body matted. I had almost reached the stairs when a piercing scream came from the house.

Zee. My heart almost stopped.

A quick look at Jackson's face told me he was already dead. I let go of the body. Frantically, I swam to the nearest edge and hoisted my bulk up out of the water. My thick legs pumped in the direction of the house and my wet feet almost skidded out from under me. Zee met me by the door and collapsed into my arms in a dead faint.

"Zee! Zee!" I yelled loudly. I patted her face firmly, increasing it to slight slaps. She moved and groaned but didn't come to. Lifting my soggy blouse, I wrung out a section over her face. The cold water roused her. She looked up at me, her dark face the color of cigarette ash.

"Body... kitchen," she forced out. Sirens could be heard in the distance.

"Shhhhh," I told her, cradling her head in my lap and rocking gently. "Shhhhh. It's going to be okay."

TWENTY-FOUR

I WATCHED AS THE coroner's office took charge of the lifeless body of Jackson Blake. Officers and other officials were taking photos and going over and tagging every inch of the grounds. Just like on TV.

Devin Frye was sitting with Zee and Seth at one of the several patio tables, asking her questions. Seth's arms were wrapped protectively around his wife. I had called them both as soon as the paramedics arrived.

Sitting on a patio chair, I shivered under the blanket the paramedics had given me. I had retrieved and slipped on my dry skirt, but my other clothes were still wet. Not far from me, Dev's partner, Detective Zarrabi, was talking to several police officers. I could hear him giving instructions on questioning neighbors. Then they disbursed.

The other body, the one that caused Zee to scream, wasn't a corpse at all, but the barely living form of Karla Blake. She had been stabbed numerous times and left to die in the archway between the kitchen and family room. Zee had literally stumbled across her after making the emergency call. Unlike her wayward husband, Karla had been fully clothed. An ambulance spirited her away minutes after arriving.

Dev walked over to me. Behind him were Seth and Zee. Zee was bundled under a blanket of her own. She smiled weakly at me. Her color was better, but she still looked shaky.

Seth spoke first. "I'm going to run Zee home, Odelia, then come back. I want to be here when Detective Frye questions you."

"I don't need a lawyer, Seth," I told him. "Go home, take care of Zee. This is my fault anyway."

Zee started to say something, but Seth stopped her with a look. He knelt in front of me. From his face, I knew he was angry, but he was keeping it under control. Barely. Dev excused himself and went over to talk to Zarrabi.

"Zenobia told me that you didn't want her to go with you today; that you didn't want her to come here either, but she insisted. That's her own doing." His voice was deep and soothing, but stern. "But what in the hell, girl, were you doing mixed up in this in the first place?"

"But Seth," I argued feebly, "they kept mixing *me* up in it."

"Uh-huh. And they, whoever *they* are, kept you from calling the police, too, I suppose?"

I looked at Seth, but said nothing. I wanted to cry. I was cold, tired, and wet. And I wished I had never talked to Sterling Price about lunchboxes.

I wanted Greg.

I had a lot to tell Dev Frye. A lot of it Zee didn't know. But I still didn't think I needed a lawyer, especially one who'd kill me once he found out about my escapade with Willie and Enrique.

"Seth, I'll be fine. You need to be with Zee." He started to say something, but I stopped him. "I didn't do anything wrong, and I promise I'll spill my guts to Detective Frye." Almost magically, Dev showed up next to us. "If I feel I need a lawyer, I'll call you," I told Seth.

I thought about something else, letting my mind dwell on practical matters for a moment. It felt like a mini vacation from the topic of murder. "My car's at your place," I told Seth. "I'll drive Zee's car back to your house and pick up mine as soon as I'm done."

"I'd prefer you stayed with us tonight," Seth told me, standing up to his full height.

"I'll be fine. And besides, Wainwright's there. He's a great watchdog." I paused. "Oh, geez, I forgot about the dog, he'll be busting his bladder if I don't get home soon."

"Don't worry, Zee and I will swing by and let him out for a minute. Should we feed him, too?"

I shook my head. "No, he eats in the morning, like Seamus. But you might toss them both a couple of treats. They're in the pantry. And tell them I'll be home soon."

Seth shook his head in resignation and looked to Dev, who responded with a shrug.

Before leaving, Seth bent down and kissed my forehead like the good surrogate brother he was. "Do yourself and me a favor," he said in a low voice slightly tinged with humor. "Marry Greg and move to Seal Beach."

After the Washingtons left, Dev moved me into the living room and deposited me on one of the hunter green sofas. He sat on the other.

"You and Greg getting married?" he asked as he got out his trusty notepad and pen.

"He asked me," I answered.

"Congratulations," he said in return, not looking at me. "Greg's a fine man."

"I know."

Dev glanced up at me. His eyes held mine for a moment before he looked back down at his notebook. "Now, let's talk about this Sterling Price mess and what you know about it."

I told him everything I knew, unloading all the information given me by the various players like unwanted Christmas gifts. I even told Dev about the day of the funeral when I witnessed Stella playing both Jackson and Kyle, and about her visit to my house. I told him how Sterling Price had given Kyle the house and the Center in return for information on Karla's plan to take over Sterling Homes, and how I had witnessed some of the documents on those transactions the day Sterling was killed.

Much of this, he told me, he already knew or suspected from talking to each of the parties in the murder investigation. People had motives, but so far there was no evidence pointing to anyone in particular.

Finally, I told him about Amy Chow and the Holy Pail buried in the park in Tustin.

"So you have the lunchbox?" he asked.

"Now I do," I told him. "Amy gave it to me this morning, before she left town. I stashed it in my office at the firm."

"And she told you she was going to get twenty-five thousand dollars for it from Stella Hughes."

I nodded. "Yes, but she said she stopped by here this morning to collect and Stella wasn't home." Amy's frightened face swept across my consciousness. "Dev, Amy Chow was scared spitless this morning. Do you think she came by here and saw something, like Jackson and Karla?"

"Maybe she saw Jackson's body," he said. "The coroner's early estimate is that Jackson Blake has been dead and floating in the pool a while—maybe since late last night or early this morning. Karla's wounds were fairly recent, fortunately for her, or she would have bled to death."

"Like maybe she came by and surprised the killer late this afternoon?"

"It's a possibility. Could be she was looking for her husband." Dev looked at his notes. "You said he was having an affair with Stella Hughes, correct?" I nodded in confirmation. "And Stella lives here."

"Was he stabbed, too?" I asked.

"Yes, he was. From what we can determine so far, he was stabbed while laying on a lounge chair and then rolled into the pool, probably while still alive."

Dev studied me while he took a pack of gum out of the breast pocket of his jacket and offered me a piece. I took one and together we unwrapped them and stuck them in our mouths.

We chewed in peace. Dev was a big gum chewer and now I knew why. It was relaxing. The spearmint filtered through my mouth, bringing freshness and comfort, much like a Thin Mint but without the calories. Murder was melting away momentarily, even if it was only as long as the flavor lasted.

"Okay," Dev said, "we know where the lunchbox is, but what did you find out about it?" He shot me a look that demanded an answer. "I know you, you've been busy."

"Well, since you've asked," I began, and I told him the history of the cursed Chappy Wheeler lunchbox, including my visit with Lester and Catherine.

Pulling the photograph out of my bag, I showed it to him. "I think Stella Hughes is the daughter of Lester Miles and Catherine Matthews, two of the actors from *The Chappy Wheeler Show*. But if that's true, she doesn't know it. She thinks she's Chappy Wheeler's daughter by Catherine; that Lester Miles is her adoptive father."

Dev took the photo and looked at it. He shook his head slowly. "Seems you stole a photograph the last time I worked a murder case involving you. This becoming a habit?"

I started to smile, but it faded to black when I saw he wasn't trying to be amusing. With a big sigh, I squared my damp shoulders and spilled the beans about my morning with Willie Porter and about his wanting revenge on Stella. Of course, I told it with some careful editing.

"Wait a minute," Dev said, stopping me. "You actually met William Proctor, the Investanet guy?"

I nodded. "Yes, this morning in Santa Ana."

He looked at me in disbelief. "And you didn't think that was significant enough to call me?" Dev stood up abruptly. "Damn it, Odelia," he said angrily. "He might be tied to what happened here."

"I don't think so, Dev," I said, keeping my cool. "Willie told me he was a thief, not a killer, and I believe him."

"Willie?" Dev asked, towering over me, scowling down at me. He ran a big hand over his weary face. "Odelia, I know you're not a stupid person, so why would you believe someone like Proctor? Just because he said so? He's a criminal, Odelia. A big-time criminal who made millions lying to people."

I looked away, anywhere but at Dev.

"Please, Odelia, *please* don't tell me you feel it in your heart." He said it with his right hand placed over his heart for emphasis, his tone laced with sarcasm. It was something I hadn't seen in him before.

"So where's Proctor now?" he asked, trying to get a grip on himself.

"I have no idea."

Dev sat down next to me on the sofa, his face inches from mine. "Okay, Odelia, out with it. The whole story again on Proctor, from start to finish, no omissions, and I want the address and phone number you have for him."

I told him everything, minute by minute of my morning, no delicate exclusions this time. When I got to the part about rolling around on the ground with Enrique and the gun, I thought Dev was going to have a seizure. I even told him about Willie admitting to searching my home and how he and Enrique were the two men who vandalized Woobie.

When we were through, Dev walked me to Zee's car. One of his beefy hands gripped my upper arm firmly, like I was a criminal he was afraid would escape.

"You are to go straight home after you go to the Washingtons," he demanded. "Got it?"

I nodded.

"I'm going to call you later to make sure. Got it?"

I nodded.

"You are not to go out or let anyone in—no one. Got it?"

Nod.

"You still have a security alarm at your place?"

"Yes."

"You are to set the alarm and keep that dog with you at all times."

"Got it."

He gave me a grin, in spite of himself.

"But what about the lunchbox?" I asked Dev.

He let loose his grip on my arm and I felt the circulation return to it. He sucked in a deep breath and blew it out while he thought about what to do.

"Anyone else know you have it?"

"Only Amy Chow, and she's probably hiding in the desert by now."

"Keep it where it is. It's probably safe there and we don't need it right now for anything. I'll stop by on Monday to pick it up."

"Okay."

Dev started to turn away, to go back into the house, but stopped. "Have any weapons?" he asked.

"A purse-size pepper spray and a baseball bat. My dad gave them to me after I was shot last year."

"Get them out and keep them with you. Got it?"

TWENTY-FIVE

THE PHONE RANG. I opened one eye and cocked it at the digital clock. Six A.M. on the nose. Groan.

True to his word, Dev had called me the night before. He called late, around eleven. Said he had just finished up at the Price house for the day, but would have to go back the next. Karla was out of surgery but still clung to life. There had been no sighting yet of either Stella or Kyle.

After assuring him that the hatches were battened down and the pepper spray, dog, and bat were close by, Dev said he would call again in the morning.

Greg, too, had called late last night. Suffice it to say, he was not a happy camper. Not able to reach me early yesterday evening, he had called Zee and Seth looking for me. Seth brought him up to date. Once Greg did reach me, he was sick with worry and ranted for a half hour.

I could have killed Seth. I didn't see why Greg had to know any of this until he got home. It wasn't like he could do anything about it from Minnesota but stew. Before hanging up, Greg had insisted that I give him Dev's number.

The phone rang a second time. The dog was stretched out next to me. He yawned, slightly lifted his large head, and dropped it back down. The cat, curled at the foot of the bed, didn't even make that effort. The three of us were in total agreement.

It had been a hard night. After accidentally setting off the house alarm when I let the dog out on the back patio, I paced the floor, dragging the bat along as a walking stick. Each crunch of tires on the street or scratch of shrubs on the windows set my hair on end like straight pins in a tomato-shaped pincushion.

On the third ring, I reached for the phone and said a sleepy hello into the receiver.

"What's going on over at Stella's place?"

I shot straight up into a sitting position. "Willie?"

"Yes, it's me."

"Where are you?"

"Never mind where I am. Enrique saw you at Price's house yesterday. The news last night said that someone had been killed there?"

"Umm, yes, that's true. Jackson Blake, Sterling's son-in-law, was stabbed to death and thrown into the pool." I swallowed hard. "I found him. And Sterling's daughter has been critically stabbed."

Wait a minute. I rubbed sleep from my eyes. "Enrique was there?" I asked with surprise.

"Of course," Willie said casually. "But he never saw Stella. Where is she?"

"I don't know. Sterling's son, Kyle, is also missing. The police are looking for them both."

There was a long pause. I thought the line had gone dead. "Willie, you still there?"

"Hmm," he mumbled. "You okay?"

"Yes, I'm fine, just rattled."

"Stay put," he ordered. "Don't go anywhere unless you absolutely have to. There's a real sick screwball on the loose."

"The police pretty much told me the same thing."

Willie chuckled into the receiver. "For once, I'm on their side." He paused. "You want me to send Enrique over to keep you company?"

Oh boy, a cute young bodyguard with a gun. How lucky could a girl get?

"Thanks, but no thanks," I said. "Not that I don't find him competent."

Willie laughed lightly. "I'll tell him that."

"I have to pick my boyfriend up at the airport later. I don't think he'd be too thrilled to see Enrique standing next to me when he got off the plane. He's already pretty upset over this." Now it was my turn to pause. "Umm, Willie, you and Enrique had nothing to do with this, right?"

"No, Odelia, we didn't." His voice was heavy with impatience. "I have no beef with the Price family, only with Stella."

The phone went dead. I tried punching in star-six-nine to call back the number, but a recording advised me that the feature was not available at this time. Weary, I flopped back in bed.

The phone rang. I opened one eye and cocked it at the clock: 7:43 A.M. Groan. I picked it up.

"What?" I mumbled into it.

"You decent?" a man asked. It sounded like Dev Frye.

"Unfortunately, always these days," I replied.

He laughed. It sounded like short spurts from a mower.

"I'm on my way over," he said cheerfully. "If you've got coffee, I've got donuts."

"Mmm, a man bearing donuts. How could I refuse?"

Quickly, I washed up and tossed on a caftan. The coffee had just started dripping when he rang my bell.

The first thing I did was ask about Karla Blake. According to Dev, she was still in critical condition. It might be as much as a day or two before she could answer any questions. Still no sign of Kyle or Stella, but they did find blood streaks on the sheets of the bed in the master bedroom. But not enough blood, according to Dev, to have come from stab wounds.

"What about the cars, Dev," I asked. "Did they belong to the Blakes?"

"The Jeep belongs to Kyle. The Lexus to Karla."

"That's odd."

"Maybe, maybe not. If the Blakes arrived together, they might have only brought one car."

I couldn't see Jackson and Karla dropping in for a friendly family visit with Kyle and Stella. If Jackson was there and naked, he had come on his own.

"And you were right about Stella, Odelia," Dev said, taking a bite out of a maple bar. We were sitting at my kitchen table. The animals were lounging on the patio in the morning sun. "Stella Hughes is the daughter of Lester Miles and Catherine Matthews. Her real name is Dixie Miles."

He took another bite and washed it down with coffee. "This is interesting. Stella Hughes was the name of Charles Borden's

271

mother. Stella took it as a stage name in her early twenties. She is, or was, an actress."

"Did you talk to Les and Catherine?" I asked after swallowing a piece of a buttermilk bar.

"Yes, last night. I called them shortly after I saw you. They say they haven't seen Stella in quite a while, that she comes and goes. Said last they knew she was working in Chicago, a play or something."

"Do you believe them?"

He gave a noncommittal shrug. "Hard to say. They sounded upset. Kami and I are driving up there this afternoon to question them."

The phone rang. The clock on the microwave said eight thirty. I excused myself from the table and answered it. It was Zee.

"You okay?" she asked.

"Hanging in there. How about you?"

"I'll be better after church, which is why I called. Why don't you go to services with us today? It'll be good for you."

"Thanks, Zee, but not today."

"Why not? Greg's not due back until late this afternoon." She sighed softly. "Seth will take us out for lunch someplace nice after."

I heard an extension being picked up, followed by Seth's deep voice. "Odelia, come on to church with us."

Sometimes I did go to church with the Washingtons. Sometimes Greg went, too. But today wouldn't be one of those days. I wanted to relax until Greg got home. I needed to detox from murder mania and lunchbox lunacy.

"Thanks anyway, guys. But Detective Frye is here right now and we're going over some stuff. Then I just want to forget about all of this."

They said they understood and told me to call if I needed anything this afternoon.

Dev and I continued to hash over details of the case. He pressed me to remember anything I might have missed. I briefly considered telling him about Willie's call, but decided not to. My gut told me Willie and Enrique had nothing to do with Jackson and Karla, and telling Dev about the call would just net me more lectures. Quite frankly, I'd had a bellyfull of that.

Around ten, after having been fortified by a half pot of coffee and a couple of donuts, he took his leave and headed back to Sterling Price's house.

I promised him to lock up the house good and tight as soon as he left.

The phone rang again as I was putting our coffee cups into the dishwasher. It was Greg.

"Hi, sweetheart," he said when I answered. He sounded better than he had the evening before, much calmer.

"Hi, honey," I cooed back.

We hung there, not saying anything, just enjoying the tones of each other's hello. Finally, he broke the lovely silence.

"Odelia, I'm really sorry I yelled at you last night. I was so upset and worried about you, and felt so helpless being so far away."

"I know, Greg. And I love you for it, but everything's fine now."

"You sure everything's okay?"

"Yep, just dandy. Dev Frye just left. He plied me with donuts while he interrogated me."

"Smart man."

More silence. This time I sensed it wasn't a pleasant one.

"I have some bad news, sweetheart. Not terrible, just not great."

My lower lip quivered. Something else had happened and he wasn't coming home today, I just knew it.

"You're not coming home today, right?"

"Oh no, baby, I'll be home today. Just that they canceled my flight and put me on a later one."

"Oh, thank God," I whimpered like a baby. "I really need to see you today."

He laughed. "If I had a pair of ruby slippers and two good legs, I could click my heels together and be there in a flash."

I sniffed back the urge to blubber and pulled myself together. *He would be home soon,* I assured myself.

"Greg, if you owned a pair of ruby slippers, we wouldn't be having this conversation." He laughed. "And Greg?"

"Yeah?"

"If you owned a pair of ruby slippers, I wouldn't be saying yes."
Silence.

"Did you just say yes, Odelia?"

"Ask me again, like you did on my birthday."

A pause, then a deep intake of air. "Odelia Patience Grey, will you be my wife?"

"Yes, Gregory William Stevens, I will."

Wow, I thought to myself, *I did it. I said yes.* And it had felt as natural as the air going in and out of my lungs. There's something about death that makes you realize the clock is ticking away for all of us. Whatever time I had left on this earth, I wanted to spend it with Greg. For better or for worse, he was going to be stuck with me like a barnacle on the hull of a ship.

Another pause and deep breath. "Odelia, you have the ring there?"

"Hang on," I said. Opening the fridge, I rummaged around in the vegetable bin until I located the small velvet jeweler's box. It was tucked safely inside a small plastic bag and inserted into another plastic bag holding prewashed salad mix. I pulled it out, blew hot breath on it, and polished it with a nearby dishtowel. The large diamond shined, blinking like a star lassoed and dragged to earth.

"Got it," I said into the phone.

"Slip it on for me, sweetheart."

"Wouldn't you rather do it yourself tonight?"

"No, I want you wearing it when I see you at the airport."

TWENTY-SIX

HUMMING, I BUSTLED AROUND the house picking things up and tidying. It was busywork, really. I had a twice-monthly cleaning lady who kept my place spotless, so outside of putting away my own clutter, there was little for me to do in the way of housework.

I packed an overnight bag to take to Greg's, including the black lace negligee I was saving for a special occasion. The last thing I pulled from the closet was a dress to wear to work tomorrow. Looking at it, I mentally kicked myself for not asking for Monday off so I could spend an extra day with Greg.

Thinking about work put Steele on my mind. I had meant to call him yesterday, to see how he was doing and find out when he'd be able to go home. But, well, things got out of hand starting at six in the morning and went downhill from there.

With the idea that there's no time like the present, I called the hospital. When I asked to be connected to Steele's room, I was told he had been released yesterday afternoon. I tried his home, but there was no answer, just a machine. I left a message letting him know I hoped he felt better and asking when he'd be back in the office.

I felt restless. I could see that Wainwright was picking up on it. He eyed me with anticipation. He'd been cooped up all week, except for the trip to my folks' house.

"You want to go for a walk, boy?" I asked the animal.

In response to the word *walk*, Wainwright started doing a little doggy jig.

Why not? I'd be safe enough with Wainwright by my side. We could take the Reality Check route around the Back Bay. The trail should have lots of people on it on a Sunday—safety in numbers.

Quickly, I changed into capri pants, a knit shirt, and a sturdy pair of sneakers.

THE WALK HAD BEEN invigorating, both mentally and physically. After a brisk turn around the Back Bay, Wainwright and I ran some errands and stopped by the car wash. Feeling generous, I opted for the works: wash, hot wax, tire trim, and fragrance—new car smell, of course. Following that, I picked up some lunch at a favorite fast food joint and took Wainwright to the Bark Park, a park specially made for dogs and their owners. Between bites from my grilled chicken sandwich, a few fries, and the company of the other canines, Wainwright was in doggy heaven. It made me happy to see him so excited. It was almost like having a kid. Had it been Christmastime, I would have dragged the animal off to have his photo taken with Santa.

Back at home, I could hear the phone ringing as I slipped my key into the lock of the front door. Thinking it might be Greg with an update on his flight, I hurriedly turned the key and pushed the door open. The big dog rushed in, almost tripping me in the process.

Déjà vu.

Still as a marble statue, I stood just inside the doorway to my townhouse and watched as Wainwright anxiously picked his way through the rubble. The phone stopped.

Bookshelves had been emptied and furniture overturned. Even the doors to my curio cabinet stood ajar, and pieces of nativity groups lay scattered across the carpet.

Wainwright sniffed feverishly, his nose to the floor.

The kitchen was worse. Every cupboard was open, the lower ones emptied of pots and pans and baking equipment. Cutlery and utensils were strewn everywhere. Counters were cleared of cookbooks and appliances. Flour, pasta, and canned goods spilled from the pantry. On the floor in front of the refrigerator, a milk carton lay on its side, the milk long since gurgled out like blood from a wound. I opened the fridge and freezer and found they, too, had been ransacked. In fact, all my Girl Scout cookies were gone from the freezer. The creeps had taken my five remaining boxes of Thin Mints.

Immediately, my right hand grasped the large diamond on my left hand, and I said a prayer of thanks that Greg had insisted I start wearing the ring right away.

Leaning against a wall, I slowly slid down it until my butt hit the floor with a heavy thud. Shock ran through me like an electrical current. I had been gone about three hours, long enough for someone to render my home a wasteland. It made me wonder if they had been watching me, seizing the opportunity when I left with the dog. I should have listened to both Dev and Willie and stayed put. I should have at least left Wainwright behind and in charge. From my perch on the floor, I watched the dog casually lap up the spilled milk.

I started to my feet. "Seamus," I called excitedly. "Here kitty, kitty." I made little coaxing and kissing noises as I started moving slowly through the rooms. "Come here, baby. Here kitty, kitty." Wainwright followed me with great interest and put his nose back in service.

"Wainwright," I commanded. "Find Seamus." The dog looked at me keenly and wagged his tail. "Go on, boy, find Seamus."

Four legs flying, the animal crossed the room and flew up the stairs. I followed, stumbling up the stairs in mounting panic.

The upstairs, too, was in total disarray. Clothes had been pulled from closets and drawers, even from the hamper. The bed had been stripped and the mattress overturned. The guest bedroom that doubled as a home office was also trashed.

This time, Wainwright didn't stick his nose under the bed, entreating Seamus to come out. Instead, he went in and out of the bathroom and bedrooms hunting his friend down. I looked under the bed myself. Emptiness looked back. I searched each closet, under every pile of discarded clothing, even behind the toilet and under the sink. No Seamus.

"Find Seamus, Wainwright," I ordered the dog again, my voice rising along with my fear for the cat's safety.

The dog barreled downstairs. Once again I followed.

It wasn't until we searched the kitchen a second time that I spotted the note. It was stuck to the front of the refrigerator, under a magnet advertising the Pike Place Fish Market in Seattle, Washington. Hastily written in red ink in a tight scrawl on the back of a large envelope, it gave me instructions for the return of my pet.

> *The lunchbox for the cat. Paramount Ranch,*
> *7:00 P.M. tonight. No cops. This is not a joke.*

The last two sentences had been underlined three times each.

I had to call Dev. *No, no,* I told myself. *They might hurt Seamus.* A horrible thought occurred to me. They might have already harmed him. I started crying and ordered myself sharply to stop it this instant. I had to think rationally. I had a bigger issue to think about. Namely, where in the hell was Paramount Ranch?

Could Willie and Enrique have done this? I didn't think so. Willie claimed they had already searched my place. But Dev was right; Willie had parlayed lying into a multi-million-dollar heist. I shouldn't trust him. Although, I remembered, he did offer to send Enrique over to guard me. Looking around my destroyed home, I wished now that I had taken him up on the offer. Dev could scoff all he wanted; in my heart, I knew Willie and Enrique did not do this.

Stella had tried to make friends with Seamus when she was here. Wainwright had been suspicious from the start on that deal. And Stella was missing. Did she come back and kidnap my cat? I scanned my environment again. This vandalism had taken time and effort. If Stella did this, she did not do it alone. Dollars to donuts, if Stella was involved in this, Kyle or another of her sexual victims provided the muscle.

I jumped a foot when the phone rang. It took me a minute, but I finally located it under the dining table.

"Hello," I answered warily. Silence. I thought I could make out breathing and a lot of static. My guess was the call was coming in via a cell phone on the move.

"Hello," I said again, my voice rising.

"You get the message?" a muffled voice asked.

My heart pounded in my ears. "Yes," I answered. "Do you have my cat?"

"I got the sucker. Nasty little bastard, isn't he?"

"Hope he clawed your eyes out," I snapped into the phone. Try as I might, I couldn't recognize the voice. In addition to the static, it sounded like the caller was speaking through a handkerchief or some other filter. In any event, it sounded male. I thought of Stella with her low, husky voice and decided with a stretch it could be her, but I didn't think so.

"Now, now, be nice."

"What do you want?"

"You know what I want, Odelia." The caller had fun with my name, stretching it out and pronouncing it O-deeeeeeel-ya.

"How do I know you really have Seamus?" I swallowed a chunk of fear the size of a chicken breast. "How do I know you won't hurt him or haven't already?"

"Gotta be more trusting, I guess," he said.

"No dice," I told him. "Prove to me now you have my cat."

"How do you expect me to do that?"

"Let me talk to him."

"What? Are you nuts?" A long pause. "You want to talk to your kitty cat, lady?"

"Yes," I answered. "Hold the phone by his head. If you do have him and he's okay, he'll respond to me."

I heard whispered swearing from the other end.

"I'm not going anywhere," I told the caller, "unless I know Seamus is okay. And I'd better get him back alive and in one piece or I'll destroy the Holy Pail. It means nothing to me."

I hoped the caller couldn't hear my chubby knees knocking.

There was another long pause.

"Okay, hang on," the caller finally said.

There was shuffling and some thrashing, during which I heard a vicious yowl and hiss, followed by a human screech of pain. I breathed a sigh of relief. My baby was alive and well and being his usual charming self.

"Okay," the caller said. "Talk to the little shit."

"Seamus," I said, forcing an upbeat tone. "Hi baby, mommy's here." No response. "Hi, kitty, kitty. How's my Seamus?"

Finally, I heard a low meow, followed by another. I spoke some more words of comfort and was rewarded with more communication. I definitely felt better.

"Okay," the caller said, returning to the phone. "You've had your fun. When you get to the ranch, park and walk into the town. Act like a tourist."

"But—" I started.

"Just walk around, close to the buildings. Pretend you find them fascinating. Don't worry, I'll find you. You can bet on it."

"But—" I started again, growing hysterical.

"See you at seven." The line went dead.

"But," I screamed into the phone, "where am I going?"

THE HALLWAYS OF WOOBIE were deserted as I made my way toward my office. The rent-a-guard was gone, having only been hired for Friday.

It was almost four now. I had three hours to get the box, stash the dog, and find someone to pick up Greg at the airport. I had called Zee about handling the last two jobs, but she and Seth weren't home. They probably decided to visit Zee's mother after church or go to a movie or something. Actually, I was rather glad they weren't home. I didn't want to answer any questions.

I also had to figure out what Paramount Ranch was and where it was located. I prayed it wasn't too far of a drive. It sounded vaguely familiar, but I couldn't place it, no matter how hard I tried. Since the intruder had pulled apart my home computer, I was going to have to use my office computer to see if I could find any reference or directions to Paramount Ranch.

Also, as soon as I got the box and directions, I was going to call Boomer, Greg's assistant. I had both his cell and pager numbers for emergencies, and this was definitely an emergency. Greg was going to be livid when he found out what was going on, but that wasn't a reason to leave him stranded at the airport.

My head was occupied with my to-do list for the next hour, so I didn't hear the noise until I was almost on top of it. I stopped dead in my tracks and listened. The hair on my arms stood at attention. Sure enough, there it was again. It wasn't my imagination. There was definitely a noise and it definitely had a regular rhythm to it—squeak, squeak. I let go of the breath I was holding.

The door to Steele's office was slightly ajar. I knocked lightly before slowly pushing it open. Steele looked up just as I poked my head in.

"Got nothing better to do on a Sunday, Grey?" he asked casually. Except for the cast on his left forearm, you'd never know that he'd been assaulted just three days prior.

"I—um—I forgot something," I lied. "Couldn't wait until tomorrow."

"You mean this?" He reached down behind his desk with his healthy arm and raised up the Holy Pail. It was no longer wrapped in the protective plastic Amy had put around it.

Stunned, I said nothing.

"I found it in the box of documents Sterling sent over the day he died." He looked at me with disgust. "I can't believe you had this all along and didn't tell anyone."

"But I didn't have it," I tried explaining.

He banged the box down on his desk. "Grey, I almost got killed over this!" he shouted.

"Honest, Steele," I shouted back, "I didn't have the lunchbox until yesterday morning. I hid it in the box of documents to keep it safe. Detective Frye even knows it's here. I told him yesterday afternoon."

Steele started to say something, but thought better of it. With his good hand, he motioned for me to come in and park myself in a chair across from him. I did just that and noticed that the closer I got, the paler he looked. There were shadows creeping around his eyes and he looked road weary. He was dressed very casually in a white T-shirt and navy blue warm-up pants. A ball cap emblazoned with the Lakers logo was perched on his head. It was a sporty look I'd seldom seen him wear.

"You okay, Steele?" I asked. He seemed to be far away.

"Yeah, I'll be fine."

He squinted at me like he had a headache, and I remembered that he'd received quite a bash to his head.

"How's your head?" I asked. "Can I get you something? Advil maybe?"

He shook his head. "No, I've already taken plenty." He took off the ball cap and carefully felt the top of his head. "These damn stitches hurt like hell."

Gingerly, he replaced the cap. He looked at me expectantly. It was my cue to begin my opening remarks to the judge.

"Like I said, Steele. I just got the box yesterday. The person who stole it had it buried in a park in Tustin."

"And that person dug it up and gave it to you, just like that?"

"Well, not exactly."

I gave Steele a summarized version of the past few days, including my visits with Stella Hughes, Carmen Sepulveda, Willie Porter, Lester Miles, and Amy Chow. I also told him about the stabbed body of Karla Blake and the dead body of Jackson Blake, finishing off with the ransacking of my home and my abducted cat.

"And all this happened just since Thursday night?"

"You could say I've been busy."

He shot me a sardonic smile. "Too bad we can't bill the time to Sterling Homes."

He lost himself in thought again. I was getting antsy, feeling each minute tick by like the setting on a time bomb.

"And you really met William Proctor?" he finally asked in awe.

"Yes. In fact, he's the one who clobbered you. Or it was his body-guard." I shrugged. "One or the other."

Steele leaned back in his chair and studied me a long while. Squeak... squeak... squeak. I studied him in return, waiting for his next comment.

"You have the note with you?" he finally asked.

I handed Steele the note the cat-nappers left. He read it slowly, thinking as he did so.

"So," he said, looking me square in the eyes. "Now you're going to take the box, drive all the way to Paramount Ranch, and bargain for your cat's life. Is that the plan?"

"That pretty well sums it up," I said with a nod. "Except for one small hitch: I have no idea where Paramount Ranch is."

Picking up the Holy Pail, he stood up and came around the desk to stand in front of me. He handed me the box.

"I do know where it is," he said to me. "Come on, I'll drive."

"You'll *what?*" I said, not believing my ears.

"I'm coming with you."

What was it about people wanting to tag along with me on dangerous outings?

"Absolutely not," I told him, standing up to face him. "Besides, you can't drive. Your arm is in a sling and a cast, if you haven't noticed."

"Not to worry, Grey, it's not my shifting arm."

"They told me to come alone," I argued, pointing at the note Steele still held in his hand.

"No, they didn't," he said, heading for the door. "They said no cops. Not the same thing at all."

I sighed in defeat. Only a lawyer could slant a ransom note to read in his favor.

TWENTY-SEVEN

PARAMOUNT RANCH, IT TURNED out, was up near Malibu Lake in the Santa Monica Mountains. According to Steele, it was, and sometimes still is, used as a town for movies and TV shows. It finally dawned on me where I had read about it. It had been mentioned briefly in some of the Chappy articles. Paramount Ranch was where much of *The Chappy Wheeler Show* had been filmed.

Before leaving the office, I called Boomer. Fortunately, he was home and happy to take charge of both the dog and picking up his boss. He lived in Huntington Beach, not far from Greg's shop. It was on our way.

I needn't have worried. Steele's car was a Porsche and he drove like a bat out of hell. We made it to Huntington Beach in record time, dumped off the dog, and gave Boomer Greg's flight instructions. I also handed him a note to give to Greg explaining everything.

"Is that a rock on your hand, Grey?" Steele asked as we sped up the 405 Freeway.

Steele moved in and out of traffic deftly, but it would take a few more miles before I released the death grip I had on the armrest.

"Yes, Greg and I just got engaged." I looked over at him. Steele's attention was fixed on the road, his eyes hidden behind expensive sunglasses. He weaved and bobbed like a boxer through the Sunday early evening traffic.

"Go ahead," I said with annoyance, "take your best shot. Tell me how Greg must be out of his mind. Tell me how I should grab him before he comes to his senses."

Only then did Steele's head turn momentarily my way. "Actually, Grey, I'm thinking he's a lucky man."

I whipped my head in Steele's direction, but his eyes were riveted back on the road, his face unreadable.

"Excuse me," I said, "but did that knock you got on the head cause a personality change?"

"I'm trying to be nice to you, Grey. Don't get used to it."

We rode in silence until we reached the 101 interchange. We were making good time. Barring a traffic snarl, we might even be early.

"Know what I was working on at the office?" Steele asked once we were heading north on the Ventura Freeway.

Looking straight ahead, I answered dryly, "Résumés from Hooters for your next secretary?"

A sound came from his throat that sounded like a chuckle, but his lips never moved. I wondered if he was practicing ventriloquism.

"Good one, Grey. And well deserved." He cleared his throat.

"I was going over those documents Price sent over the day he died. I saw them when I went to drop something off in your office.

That's how I found the lunchbox. Did you get a chance to look any of it over?"

"No, never even opened the box until yesterday when I hid the lunchbox in there."

"Odd thing is, they aren't Sterling Homes documents on Howser, but look like Howser internal documents. In many cases, originals."

"You think Kyle gave them to his father?"

"Could be," Steele said as he sped up and passed a truck. "Some of those documents mention Karla Blake by name. Others were generated by her. They were probably lifted from her office. Seems she was working with Howser, which supports what you were told by that girl."

"You mean Amy Chow?"

"Uh-huh. Price told me several times in the past six months or so that his kids, including Kyle, were trying to get him to retire. From the documents, I'd say Karla had positioned everything and was just waiting for the day.

"Once Price was out of the way," Steele continued, "and with the board stacked with her own people, she could pretty much run it any way she wanted."

"You mean a merger with Howser?"

He shook his head. "I don't think that was her plan. Although there were confidential memos in those files talking about it as a possibility, but they originated with the Howser people." Steele cast a brief glance my way. "But there did seem to be a lot of side dealing going on and promises of big contracts in the near future.

"No, I think Karla Blake wanted to be the queen of her own castle, not a lady-in-waiting at Howser—not even a well-compensated one. She was too independent to be folded into a big company like Howser."

"Was Sterling Price thinking of retiring?" I asked.

"Thinking about it, yes. He talked about retiring and traveling with Stella. But no decision had been made on his end. He started thinking seriously about it after his pal Wallace retired. And he might have done so right after that, had Karla not pushed him."

I thought about that a moment. "You mean, if she'd left her father alone, he probably would have retired on his own and handed her the company?"

"Pretty much." Steele glanced at me again. For a fleeting moment, I could see my reflection in his sunglasses. "Want another news flash?" He looked back at the road.

"I contacted the attorney for that touchy-feely Center this morning. He's a law school buddy of mine. Price had the purchase of the place in the works for his son long before Kyle supposedly told him anything about Karla."

"This is all so confusing," I said without enthusiasm. All I wanted was my cat back. Then I could marry Greg and forget about Sterling Homes and the nut jobs that populated its annual company picnic.

I thought about what Steele just told me. In my head, I shifted facts around, seeing where each might fit. It was a lot like shopping for shoes. I slipped the information on, checked for comfort level, discarding and moving to another until it clicked.

"I stand corrected," I said to Steele. "When you think about it, it's actually pretty simple. If Sterling was already toying with the idea of retiring, he probably would have left the company to his daughter, especially since his son had no desire to be involved. And being the fair man that he was, he might have bought the Center and given the house to his son to equal things out. But instead of letting things move along naturally, someone got antsy and jumped the gun. If Kyle told Sterling about Karla's plan, Sterling might have decided not to retire and to boot her from the company for being so cheeky. And with Stella's indiscretions, his plans for leisurely travel with a companion would have been disrupted."

Steele looked straight at the road and nodded his agreement. Michael Steele was thirty-six, just a year younger than Greg. I took in his profile—a straight nose and chiseled jaw; strong, angular lines and an inviting mouth. Thick, dark hair, stylishly cut, peeked out from under the Lakers cap. Behind the glasses, his eyes were dark and perfectly spaced and brimmed with intelligence. With features rugged enough not to be considered pretty, he really was a looker. His body, too, was about perfect. I knew he worked out daily, and it showed, especially today when not covered by a suit coat. It was plain to see why women fell to his seductions so easily.

"Why haven't you ever married, Steele?" I asked.

A smile crept across his lips. "Who says I haven't?"

I felt my eyes pop in his direction. "You have?"

"A long time ago. Ancient history."

"But who was she? Do you have any children?" Michael Steele had been married. Now this was truly a news bulletin.

"It was during law school. No kids, thankfully. Only lasted three years."

Steele looked over at me briefly, the smile still on his lips. "You're getting off track, Grey. Not good. Not even for an amateur detective."

He turned his attention back to the road. "Who do you think killed Jackson and attacked Karla?"

"My vote is either Kyle or Stella, or maybe both together. Strange thing is, Detective Frye said Jackson had been killed and dumped into the pool much earlier than his wife's stabbing. They think he was killed sometime in the night or early morning out on a chaise by the pool. And he was naked. She was not."

"Naked by the pool on a lounge? Hmm," Steele said, thinking out loud. "My guess is that he'd had sex with someone just prior and had taken a dip. Or else they had been skinny-dipping together. Jackson was probably dozing on the chair when it happened."

"And he had been stabbed, too," I added. "Someone got close enough to stab him. Either he didn't hear them, especially if he'd been sleeping, or he had no reason to be alarmed."

"Probably sleeping," Steele decided with a quick nod of decision. "Jackson Blake was a strong guy. If he saw a knife coming, he could have easily fought off either Kyle or Stella, with only cuts for his trouble."

"True," I added, "and he certainly would have been wary of Kyle. After all, he was sleeping with Kyle's girlfriend. I don't think Kyle knew about Stella and Jackson—although I think Karla suspected something."

Then I remembered something about Stella and Jackson that might help make sense of Jackson's murder.

"Stella was supposed to get the Holy Pail from Amy that morning. She told me that she and Jackson had planned on going away together once they had it. That was before Sterling Price was killed, but maybe they renewed their plans. Maybe Jackson came over to spend the night. Kyle wasn't living there yet. Or maybe he came over very early in the morning. He and Stella got it on, and Kyle caught them in a post-coital nap."

"So where's Stella? Don't you think Kyle would have stabbed her, too?"

"Maybe," I said. "Unless she fast-talked her way out of it. She always said Kyle wasn't that bright."

Steele laughed. "He isn't. Always seems a bit off-center to me."

As the local landscape sped past my window, I pictured the Price house and people playing in the pool. A couple happily coming together under the sky until they passed out for a refreshing snooze. I turned to Steele.

"To my thinking, the most likely scenario is that Stella killed Jackson. Maybe he came by to give her one last boink before giving her the heave-ho. Maybe she went berserk and killed him. Later, when Karla came by looking for her straying husband, Stella was waiting for her."

"Except for the word *boink*, Grey, that theory could work."

"And Amy could have seen the body, or even seen Stella kill him, and ran like a rabbit."

Steele nodded. "This definitely has possibilities."

"But what about the blood upstairs on the bed?" I asked. "They don't know yet if it's Jackson's, or whose it is."

"Try this on for size, Grey. After boinking Jackson," Steele said with a grin, "Stella killed him. Like a black widow spider. Then, instead of eating him, she went upstairs and napped like a baby."

"Could be." I had to admit, it was a good theory. "If Stella stabbed Jackson, she probably would have gotten blood on herself. She could have been in shock and went upstairs to sleep it off.

Later, when Karla came over, she was waiting for her." I nodded and said to myself out loud, "I like it."

"And Price's murderer?" Steele asked.

"On that I'm clueless," I told him. "The police have questioned everyone and have come up with nothing. Anyone who had access to Sterling Homes that weekend could have put poison into the coffee bags. Nothing points to anyone in particular. And the only one with an alibi and without motive is Carmen Sepulveda."

"Not so fast on that assumption, Grey."

"Why?"

"If Karla was trying to prematurely retire her father, what do you think would happen to Carmen?"

I thought about that a bit. "Well, I do know that there's no love lost between Karla and Carmen, but that's more old school versus new ideas, I think."

I considered life at Sterling Homes without Sterling Price at the helm.

"But I doubt, now that her father's gone, that Karla would keep Carmen on."

"Exactly. Carmen was Sterling's right hand, but has no allegiance to Karla. I saw that clearly whenever I was there for meetings."

"Carmen killing Sterling doesn't make sense. She needed him around to keep her job."

"True. If Sterling retired, Carmen would have had to retire, too." Steele tossed his head toward the back of the car. "See that file I brought with us? It's tucked behind my seat. Get it."

I did. It was Sterling's will.

"Read the pages I have flagged," Steele said.

I did as I was told, my eyes widening. When I was through, I tucked the file back where I'd found it.

According the will, Carmen was to receive a very large cash bequest, including company stock, if she was still in the employ of Sterling Homes when Sterling Price died. If he retired before her, she received a smaller sum. If she was not in his employ at the time of his death or retirement, she received nothing. It was clearly an inducement to keep her on board as long as he needed her.

"Okay, so now Carmen has a motive, but the police questioned her and searched her place."

"I didn't say she did it, Grey, just that she had a motive like everyone else, especially if she got wind that he was thinking about retiring."

He glanced at me. "So, Grey, who do you think has your cat?"

I shook my head in dismay. "I have no idea. Could be Stella and Kyle. Could be Willie. Maybe it's a third party I haven't considered before."

"Willie? You mean Proctor?"

"Yes, but honestly, I don't think Willie would have trashed my place. He said he'd already searched it.

"And you know what, Steele?" I asked, remembering the strangest thing about the ransacking of my house. "They took my Thin Mints!"

Steele jerked his head in my direction. "They took what?" he asked in disbelief.

"Thin Mints. You know, those chocolate mint cookies from the Girl Scouts."

"Who in the hell but you, Grey, would have Girl Scout cookies in August," he said, laughing hard.

"I'm glad you find that so amusing," I said in a huff, crossing my arms in front of me.

Steele was still laughing. "Well, it certainly makes this easier. Just smell everyone's breath. Or check to see who stopped to buy a gallon of milk between Newport Beach and Paramount Ranch."

TWENTY-EIGHT

WE HAD BEEN DRIVING in silence for quite a while, each of us lost in personal reverie, when Steele turned off the freeway. I looked up in time to read a sign for Kanan Road. I had no idea where we were. To me, this area is just a patch of road I zoomed through when driving north to places like Morro Bay or Santa Barbara. Looking at my watch, I saw that it was only five forty-five. If Paramount Ranch was close, we were very early.

After turning onto Kanan Road, Steele made a right turn into the parking lot of a small cluster of businesses and restaurants. He pulled in to a space near an Islands restaurant.

"You hungry, Grey?" he asked as he turned off the engine and unbuckled his seat belt.

"Hungry?" I asked back. "At a time like this?"

Steele looked out the windshield and smiled slightly. He took off his sunglasses and turned back to look at me. His usual smart-ass smirk was gone. There was actually concern in his eyes.

"Paramount Ranch is just down the road. We're pretty early and it's dinner time." He turned to open the car door. "We have no idea what's facing us, Grey. Better to do it on a full stomach."

Like the drive, we spent most of our meal in silence and ate quickly. Steele devoured his China Coast Chicken Salad—no fried noodles, dressing on the side, please—while I nibbled the edges of my Hula Burger and slurped iced tea. After eating, we both visited the bathroom. By six forty-five, we were back on the road with my heart in my throat.

As Steele said, Paramount Ranch was just down the road from the restaurant. It was also situated in a state park. From Kanan Road, Steele turned onto Mulholland. We took the windy road until coming to the entrance of the park and Paramount Ranch. He pulled in to the large dirt lot where a couple of cars were already parked. Two women on horseback rode past us. Behind us, I noted an official-looking building with utility vehicles stationed near it.

"That's the park ranger's office," Steele said, noticing my study of the building. "Recognize any of these cars?"

I scanned the other parked cars. "No."

To the right of the ranger's office, across the exit road, was a building that looked like a large garage. In front of that stood a very small structure that had carved wooden signs announcing public restrooms. On the side of the parking lot in front of the car was a bridge leading to what appeared to be an Old West town. I could make out a few of the buildings through the trees. There were a few people milling about here and there, mostly returning to their cars from the direction of the town. The sign at the entrance to the park had said the park closed at sunset. But since it was summer, it wouldn't be dark for a while yet.

"It seems odd," I said, "that whoever took Seamus would want to meet in such a public place and so close to where police are stationed."

"I wondered about that, too," Steele said. He reached into the glove box and pulled out a flashlight. "Unless he was so caught up in the atmosphere of the place that he didn't care or realize there were rangers posted here."

"You may be right. On the drive up, I remembered reading somewhere that *The Chappy Wheeler Show* was filmed here. If that's true, I can see why this place was chosen."

"What's that for?" I indicated the flashlight.

"Just in case we have to go inside some of those buildings. I doubt seriously if movie backdrops have electricity." Steele climbed out of the car. "Now what?"

I slid my bag under the seat to be less encumbered and got out of the car, clutching only the Holy Pail. With an aim of his key fob, Steele locked the car and set the alarm.

"I'm not sure," I said. "The cat-napper told me to walk through the town like a tourist. He said he'd find me." I walked around the car to where Steele stood. "I don't think you should go with me. He might think you're the police."

"I'm not letting you go in there alone," he said firmly. "He's probably watching us right now. And he might not be alone."

Steele was right. I scanned the area as carefully as I could, but there were so many trees and bushes. The creep could be just a few feet away and I would never notice.

Steele handed me the flashlight and moved away from the car, out into the open. He held out his good arm in airplane fashion and started slowly rotating three hundred sixty degrees. The arm with the cast was cradled in its sling next to his body.

"What are you doing?" I asked in amazement.

"Showing them I'm not armed."

"Duh, you could have something in the sling or stashed under a pant leg."

Deciding I had a point, Steele clumsily undid the sling and stripped it off. With more difficulty, he rolled up both legs of his warm-up pants almost to the knee. Then he went into his airplane thing again, this time with both arms outstretched, the arm in the cast banking slightly.

"You're as nuts as I am," I told him, shaking my head. "Forget the cat-napper, let's just hope the park ranger isn't watching."

I waited for Steele to reassemble his sling and roll down his pants before starting toward the bridge. Although it was nearly seven o'clock, the heat accrued from the hot August day had not diminished one whit. It was much hotter here than in Newport Beach. After just a few steps, I felt sweat build on my upper lip and under my arms.

While crossing the bridge, I noted it spanned a creek. Lots of brush and vegetation crowded both banks. Great, more potential hiding spots. On the other side of the bridge, there was a wide dirt road that branched in several directions from the main road. To the left was an open meadow with a gully near the road. Across the gully were two different-style bridges going nowhere—no doubt props for TV and movie shoots.

To the right of the main road, where the smaller roads branched out, was the town—several clusters of old wooden buildings, a stable, wooden sidewalks, a miscellaneous wagon here and there. It might have been a Hollywood set, but it looked every bit like a real town from the Wild West that had been abandoned by its occupants and left to the dust of time.

Steele and I stood in the road and looked down one of the smaller roads. On both sides were more old, weatherworn buildings, some more rustic than others. The windows on them all were shuttered. Slowly, we started walking down the middle of the first road. On the left was one building I was sure would have been used as a jail. A two-story building near it had a balcony across the second floor, and with just a little imagination I could imagine it as a hotel. Directly in front of us, where the road forked, was another two-story building, this one painted in a terra-cotta hue with green doors. It wasn't as weather-beaten as the others, making me wonder if it had been used recently for filming.

At the fork in the road, we looked up and down in both directions. The smell of fresh horse droppings hung in the hot, still air. Except for the huge, annoying flies that attacked me like kamikaze pilots, the make-believe town seemed deserted. I surveyed the area. All the buildings and spaces between them offered numerous hiding spots. The cat-napper could be anywhere, waiting for us. Waiting to ambush us.

The right fork in the road was much shorter than the left. With a nod of his capped head, Steele motioned that he would check out the couple of buildings on that side. For a brief moment, he disappeared behind the terra-cotta building. I gave a sigh of relief when he reappeared.

"Nothing," he said, returning to my side. "Behind this building there's a riding arena, not much else."

We slowly walked down the middle of the left road. On either side were more Western buildings, including one decked out like a blacksmith shop on the left. It was attached to a long line of closed stables that extended back toward the meadow area. On the right, at the end of the street, was a building bearing a weathered sign that said GROCERIES. Another dirt road intersected the one we were on, and across the road was a structure that could only have been used as a train depot.

As I checked out the buildings, I had an eerie sense of déjà vu, like I had seen all of this before, many times—and probably had in numerous television shows like *Little House on the Prairie* or *Dr. Quinn, Medicine Woman*. I could almost picture the various characters going about their rustic lives, moving in and out of the buildings, dressed in bonnets and heavy skirts that swept the dusty ground.

Behind the depot and off by itself was a shack that looked like a small, dilapidated log cabin.

"Should we check that out?" Steele asked, pointing to the shack.

"I don't think so. He was very specific about walking through the town. 'Like a tourist' is how he put it."

"Then let's walk the town again, Grey. Maybe try some of the buildings. See if any are open." Steele winced.

"You okay?"

"Yeah, just a headache."

We started back through town again, but this time we walked along the raised wooden sidewalk. The first building we checked was the grocery store, but the door was locked tight. The same with the building next to it.

"Careful, Grey," Steele said. "These floorboards are not in the best shape."

I looked down and saw that I was about to step on a severely splintered plank in the sidewalk. I sidestepped it and kept moving. We were about to cross a small alley from the last building and approach the terra-cotta building when I had an idea.

"Maybe we should each take a side of the street," I suggested. "It'll go faster that way."

I didn't want to leave Steele's side. Though he would never admit it, the heat and physical activity were clearly taking a toll on his recently battered body. But I wanted Seamus back. Maybe if I were alone, the cat-napper would come out of hiding.

Steele started to say something, but was cut short by someone stepping from the shadows of the alley. It was Kyle Price, holding a gun. Behind him was Stella Hughes. Using the gun, Kyle motioned us into the alley. In a small, tight group, we walked through the short, small area between the two buildings until we came out the other side to the horse arena Steele had discovered earlier.

"You bitch," Stella growled at me in her deep voice, "I knew you had the box the whole time."

I held the box close to my chest. Except for Kyle's gun, both were empty handed.

"Where's my cat?"

"Your what?" Kyle asked.

"My cat." They looked at me like I was crazy. "You said you'd trade me the lunchbox for my cat," I said, starting to get upset. "What have you done with him?"

They stole glances at each other.

"I don't know anything about your mangy cat, Odelia," Stella said. "We followed you up here. We've been following you since you left your house this afternoon."

Kyle pointed the gun in my direction. "Come on, lady, give us the box so we can get out of here." He looked nervous and edgy. Perspiration clung to his high forehead like raindrops.

I clutched the box tighter. "No cat, no lunchbox."

"Grey," Steele said through tight lips, "they have a gun. Give them the lunchbox."

"No," I said to Steele. "It's all I have to bargain with."

"Grey," Steele said, leaning closer to me. "If you don't give them the damn box, they might kill us. They're probably the ones who killed Jackson."

"Jackson?" Stella stepped closer. "What about Jackson?"

Both Steele and I turned to look at her with curiosity. She either didn't know about Jackson Blake or was resurrecting her acting career.

"Jackson was found murdered yesterday at your place," I told her matter-of-factly.

"But he couldn't have been." Stella's face reflected horror.

"Why not?" I asked. "Were you there?"

She stammered. "Yes, I was. All morning. I had an appointment, but she didn't show."

"Amy Chow?"

Now Stella looked exasperated, her shock about Jackson disappearing as quickly as a photo flash. "How do you find out these things?" she asked me.

"I never had the Holy Pail until yesterday morning," I explained. "Amy gave it to me after she stopped by your place and you weren't home."

"But I was home. She was supposed to come by around eight. Kyle and I were both there." She turned to Kyle with a questioning look.

"We never saw her," he said, backing up Stella with the whiney voice I remembered from the study. "We left around ten and went to Ojai for the day."

I glanced over at Steele. He looked rather pale and pasty. He held his bad arm with his good and his eyes were partially closed. With a light touch, I guided him to a nearby bench and sat him down. He didn't resist.

"You haven't been back to your father's house yet?" I asked as I got Steele settled.

"No," Kyle said curtly. "We went to my apartment, then to your place."

"Yes, I wanted to talk to you again," Stella added quickly. "But we got there just as you were leaving. We followed you to your office. When you came out with him," she indicated Steele, "I saw that you had the Holy Pail, so we kept following you."

Stella looked at me. Once again she adopted a look of horror and disbelief. "Are you sure Jackson's dead?"

Steele stirred himself enough to answer. "She should be. She's the one who found him."

"He'd been stabbed to death and dumped into the pool. And Karla had been stabbed, too." I said, watching her closely.

"Karla! What in the world was Karla doing there?" Stella cried.

Kyle interrupted. "Stella, grab the damn lunchbox and let's get going."

I backed away from Stella and held the box tighter. The news of Jackson's death appeared to rattle her. But Kyle didn't seem surprised at all about his brother-in-law and twin sister.

The time to make a move was now. I only hoped it was the right move, not a clumsy misstep that would land Steele and me in Boot Hill.

"I know about you, Stella," I told her as she approached me. "I know that you've been hunting this box down all over the nation. That you married Ivan Fisher to get it, and because of you, he killed himself."

Stella stopped in her tracks and went gray. I continued.

"I know you tried to get it out of William Proctor, and when you failed, you turned him in to the government on his Investanet scheme. The only reason you went after Sterling Price was to get the Holy Pail. And you're only with Kyle now in order to get it."

She looked at Kyle, her eyes angry slits. "That's not true, Kyle. Don't listen to her. She's just trying to keep the box for herself."

"Get it and let's get out of here!" he shouted at her, his voice cracking.

"I know you think you're Chappy Wheeler's daughter," I said to Stella in a calm, quiet voice.

"I am Chappy Wheeler's daughter," she said with conviction, turning on me.

"No," I told her. "You're Catherine Matthews' daughter by Lester Miles. Les told me himself that he and your mother were dating while she was married to Chappy Wheeler. Their marriage was a sham, Stella. The studio made them marry for publicity and to cover the fact that Chappy was gay. Your real father is Lester Miles."

"You're lying," she screamed at me. "That freak couldn't be my father. My father was Chappy Wheeler, the famous cowboy star." Stella's face was crimson.

Steele stirred. He was looking at her, watching her carefully. He had shaken off the pain of earlier and was fully alert. Not standing, but alert.

"I'll tell you about Lester Miles," Stella spat. "He's the one who murdered my father. He killed Chappy Wheeler."

"By hitting him on the head with the Holy Pail?" I asked.

I held up the box so that the dented corner was visible and recalled what I'd read in the *Los Angeles Times* article.

"These boxes have reinforced corners. In the early seventies states started outlawing them for use by children because the kids were bashing each other with them. Chappy Wheeler was killed by several heavy blows to the head—probably with this lunchbox."

I looked Stella in the eyes. "That's why you want this box so bad, isn't it? You want to solve Chappy Wheeler's murder. The murder of the man you think was your father."

"You're wrong," Stella cried, her husky voice growing deeper with each word. "He is my father. But you're right about the murder. Chappy Wheeler was killed with this lunchbox. Jasper Kellogg found out and called Les, trying to blackmail him. That's when I found out. I overheard him tell my mother that Kellogg knew. When Kellogg died, Les thought that was the end of it. But he was wrong. I intend to make sure he pays for what he's done."

I noted from the corner of my eye that Kyle was getting restless. I was pretty sure he didn't know about Stella's true reasons for wanting the Holy Pail until now. He probably just chalked it up to greed. Any stability he had was waning with each passing minute. Even the hand that held the gun shook slightly.

I continued to work on Stella. "Are you sure Les is the killer? Maybe he's protecting someone, someone he loves more than life itself? Someone like your mother?"

"No, no, no," Stella said, bordering on hysterics. She clutched her face in her hands. "My mother married him because she was afraid. She knew he killed my real father. He forced her to marry him. He took advantage of her."

Geez, what a couple, I thought. Both Stella and Kyle were looney-tunes. Looney-tunes and armed—a combo that made my teeth chatter.

"Stella, they've been together fifty years. If Catherine didn't love Les, why would she have stayed all this time? Think about it."

"No, you're wrong. She loved my father. She loved Chappy Wheeler." Stella leaned against one of the arena railings and began crying.

"But you didn't go after Jackson for the lunchbox, did you?" I said, moving slightly closer but still clinging to the lunchbox. "No, you fell in love with Jackson Blake. You were going to go away with him, weren't you?"

Sobbing into her hands, she wailed, "Oh, Jackson!"

"Did Jackson spend the night with you Friday? Did he come over after you left me?"

She nodded. "Yes." She looked up. "But he left around four or so. He decided to go for a swim first. He often did ... after. He enjoyed the exercise. When I woke up, his car and clothes were gone. I just assumed ..." Her voice trailed off.

"You didn't go out into the back yard that morning?"

"No. When Amy didn't show up, Kyle suggested we drive to Ojai for the day. We left right after breakfast."

I looked at Kyle. His eyes were darting wildly from me to Stella to Steele.

"Stella, what time did Kyle get to your house? Was it after you woke up or before?"

"Jesus, Grey," Steele said softly. I saw that he was looking at Kyle when he said it.

"Enough, bitch," Kyle snapped. "Stella, get the damn box now or forget about it. We've gotta get out of here."

Stella looked at Kyle a long time. "You killed Jackson, didn't you?" she asked him with wide eyes. Kyle said nothing. His eyes moved with the madness of a trapped animal. "But why?"

"Why?" Kyle repeated. He paused to think. Sweat matted his hair. "Because I found him naked and asleep by the pool." Kyle's words gained confidence as he watched Stella. "You must have worn him out, babe. He was dead to the world."

He tried to sneer at Stella, but came across like a schoolboy mimicking a cartoon villain. "He woke up just as I drove the knife home. Didn't say a word, just wheezed. I threw him in the pool. Bye-bye, Jackson."

Stella was sobbing again.

"But what about your sister?" I asked.

For a brief moment, Kyle's eyes went blank and he seemed to struggle inside, searching for something.

"That was … it was unfortunate," he started to explain, reaching for the right words. "She dropped by looking for Jackson just before we left." He hesitated. "Stella was still upstairs. Karla saw Jackson in the pool. She screamed."

"So you stabbed her," I said, finishing the story for him, "there in the utility room off the garage."

"Yeah, that's right." He hesitated again. More thinking. "But you said she's still alive."

"Barely."

I could have sworn I saw relief on his face.

"Tell me, Stella, when you left for Ojai, didn't you find it odd that Karla's Lexus was in the garage?"

"Her Lexus?"

"Yes, her Lexus. You would have seen it when you backed your car out of the garage. Kyle's Jeep was in the driveway. Karla's car was in the garage."

"What are you suggesting, Odelia?" asked Stella. Her sobbing suddenly halted, like a spigot turned off with a quick jerk of a wrist. She stood up straight, away from the railing.

"I don't think Kyle killed Jackson or tried to kill his sister. I think you did it."

Steele rose unsteadily to his feet. "Careful, Grey," he warned again.

Steele was right. I was on shaky ground and needed to be careful about my course.

"Me?" Stella asked in surprise. "Why would I kill them? Or try to kill them?"

"Because, unlike the other men you've manipulated, you fell in love with Jackson. And he did come over Friday night. But when you told him that you finally found the Holy Pail, he backed out on your plan to go away together, didn't he? So you killed him."

"You're out of your mind," she said, her mouth open in disbelief.

"Am I? You told me Friday that Jackson wouldn't go away with you unless you had the Holy Pail or the money from it. Friday night, when Amy called you to say she had the box, you called Jackson to let him know. He came over, not to celebrate, but to tell you it was over, that he decided to stay with Karla. After all, she was now in charge of her father's company. Why would he leave when things were looking up for them?"

I shot a quick glance at Kyle to measure his agitation. It was gaining momentum like a brewing storm.

"How'd you do it, Stella?" I continued. "Did you convince him to have one last roll in the hay, then caught him off guard in the afterglow?"

"No, you have it all wrong," Kyle shouted at me. "It was self-defense. She tried to break it off with him, but he got angry and starting beating her."

Looking at Kyle, I realized Stella was right about one thing—he wasn't too bright.

"Is that what she told you, Kyle?" I asked. He said nothing.

"And Karla? What about her?" Steele chimed in.

I looked at the two of them. On the outside, Stella seemed in control, but her eyes darted about nervously. Kyle was fidgeting noticeably. His thin arms twitched, especially the one with the gun. I put my money on Stella doing the cutting on Karla.

"I told you what happened," Kyle said, trying to sound like a tough guy.

"Karla did come by looking for her husband, that much is probably true," I said, keeping my eyes on both of them. "And she probably did scream when she caught sight of Jackson through the French doors. But your sister wasn't attacked in the utility room, Kyle. She was stabbed in the kitchen, near the family room, next to the phone. She was probably calling for help."

I turned to Stella. "Isn't that right, Stella?"

Stella looked at me with steely hatred before turning to Kyle. For his benefit, she turned on the waterworks again. She was going for an Oscar.

"You've got it all wrong," Kyle said to me. He looked at Steele for support. "She's wrong. Stella killed Jackson in self-defense. He fell into the pool. He was already dead when I got there. There was nothing we could do. Stella was beside herself."

"And Karla?" Steele asked.

"Shut up, Kyle!" Stella demanded. "Don't tell them anything. They just want to hurt us—to hurt me." She started crying again.

"Karla was an accident," Kyle tried to explain, his gun hand wavering slightly. "Wasn't she, Stella?"

Stella was livid. She watched her control over Kyle disintegrate and felt the noose close around her neck. I was thrilled she didn't have the gun.

"Karla was calling the police," Kyle continued. "Stella just tried to scare her, to give us time to get away. But Karla went after her and got cut in the struggle."

Cut in the struggle? Karla Blake came to mind as I last saw her, laying in a pool of blood with multiple stab wounds. An accident that happened over and over?

"So why didn't you call the police?" Steele asked with great interest.

"We needed to sort things out," Kyle said as if the answer was obvious. "We didn't think anyone would find them while we were gone."

"You stupid bastard!" Stella screamed as she lunged for Kyle.

Steele leapt to his feet as Stella moved in. "Run, Grey," he shouted.

Instead, I stood transfixed as Stella's hands and nails reached for Kyle's face and found their mark. He raised the hand with the gun and struck her hard across the face. She fell in a clump at his feet, like a bag of dirty laundry. Blood gushed from her nose.

Steele threw the flashlight at Kyle, then made a run at him. With his good shoulder down, he tackled him hard. They hit the railing together and fell to the ground. The gun fired. The bullet hit the building behind me just a few feet from my head. I almost collapsed from fright.

The two men struggled, but Steele was no match with his injured arm. They rolled around until Kyle was on top, pinning Steele to the earth. Steele's hands clutched Kyle's gun hand, forcing it away, but I could tell he was losing strength.

Running into the melee, I raised the Holy Pail and started bashing Kyle's blond head with it. He howled in pain, but still struggled as if possessed. On the last blow, he dropped the gun and fell on top of Steele, not unconscious but dazed enough to render him temporarily helpless.

As Kyle clutched his head and moaned deeply, I rolled him off Steele and helped the wounded attorney to his feet. Blood trickled from his mouth and he struggled to walk. His broken arm hung limp and heavy in its cast.

Quickly retrieving the lunchbox from where I dropped it, I threw Steele's good arm around my shoulders and force-marched him out of the arena area and through the alley. We had to get to the ranger's station for help. With any luck, someone heard the gunshot and was already on their way to investigate. Steele moaned as we moved, and I realized he couldn't make the trip in his condition, at least not quickly. If the park rangers weren't on their way, Stella and Kyle would catch us before we got too far. The town was still deserted.

"Quick," I whispered to Steele. "Before they come."

Steele gathered his resources and moved as quickly as he could, but I could see from his ashen face he wouldn't be able to keep it up for long. He'd lost his Lakers cap in the fracas and his previous head wound was seeping blood, matting his dark hair at the back of his head. I'd have to stash Steele and go for help alone.

I half carried, half dragged Steele to the other side of the road. Facing us was a small, shabby building. Between it and the black-smith shop was a wide area with tufts of scrub grass and a few trees. The area ran between the stables and the backs of the buildings in the first part of the town. We ducked into the area. Looking quickly around, I spotted a wooden wagon partially hidden under a large tree and steered Steele toward it. The wagon was open, but it was deep enough to hide him if he kept his head down.

"Hurry," I whispered as I helped him up into the wagon. "Get in here and stay down. And be quiet. I'll go get help."

As soon as Steele was safely hidden, I moved between two of the buildings and peeked around the corner to see if Stella and Kyle were coming. They weren't. Everything was still and quiet. Maybe they left the town by another way. Maybe they were hiking out through the vegetation that bordered the riding arena. But maybe they weren't. Maybe they were hiding in the dusky shadows of the alley, waiting for me to offer myself up as a big, fat target.

I tiptoed back to the wagon and did a quick check on Steele. He was out cold. Keeping close to the backs of the buildings bordering the scrub area, I started quickly making my way toward the meadow and the main road. Once there, I would make a run for the bridge and the ranger station.

Just as I was about to break out into the open, I took a last look around for Stella and Kyle. Immediately, I took cover again back behind one of the buildings. Someone was coming. But it wasn't Stella and Kyle, and it wasn't the park ranger either.

Two men were walking slowly up the road from the direction of the bridge. If I didn't move, they would see me when they made the turn into the town. I crept quietly back to the wagon and hid as best I could behind it. It was getting late and the growing shadows gave me good coverage while I decided what to do.

After a minute or two, I moved from my hiding place. One side of the small, rundown building faced the back of the hotel. The area between them was very small, barely the width of my shoulders. There was a door in the back of the hotel. But like the others Steele and I had tried, it was locked. I turned sideways and hugged the boards of the hotel as I slowly made my way toward the end of the building. Once there, I scrunched down until I was almost ground level and peeked out to where the road forked in front of the terra-cotta building. From here, I could see the entire intersection.

I waited and watched.

TWENTY-NINE

THE NEW ARRIVALS WERE none other than Willie and Enrique. Both had guns drawn but kept them close to their bodies. They stopped in the crossroads and looked around. They couldn't have been more than twenty feet away.

I almost came out of hiding until I noticed that Willie was holding a cloth bag in one hand. I recognized it as one of my pillowcases. The bag wiggled and squirmed and emitted familiar low animal moans.

My heart sang at the realization that Seamus was alive and well, yet sank at the knowledge that it was Willie and Enrique who trashed my place and took Seamus. I didn't want to believe it, but there it was—the proof wiggling in a cotton sack.

Holding the battered lunchbox in one hand, I wondered if I should go out and make the exchange. The box was truly damaged now. The dent left by the Wheeler assault was nothing in comparison with the damage I had done to it. Would Willie still want it?

Was he telling the truth about wanting to see it destroyed? If so, it was well on its way.

Just as I was about to make myself known, a commotion came from the alley across the road, the one that led to the arena. Willie and Enrique each took cover between nearby buildings, weapons ready. Shortly, Stella emerged from the alley with Kyle close on her heels.

"You let them get away, you moron," Stella snapped at Kyle over her shoulder. She was wearing a long, loose blouse and was wiping her bloody nose with the hem of her shirt. In her other hand she held Kyle's gun.

Damn. I should have picked up the gun.

"You go around that way and I'll take the main road," she ordered. "Find them."

While Kyle took off toward the depot, Stella started slowly moving down the main road, her back to Willie and Enrique.

With great stealth, Willie came out of his hiding place. He put the pillowcase down against a wall and moved into the open.

"So we meet again, Stella," Willie said. His voice was light, even playful.

Stella was almost, but not quite, out of my field of vision. I saw just a sliver of her spin around, but her shriek was clear enough. Stella and Willie had their guns drawn on each other.

"It can't be you," she said. "You're dead."

"Yes, my dear, I am dead," he told her. I could see that Willie was smiling. "And I see you are up to your old tricks again. Time to put a stop to them, don't you agree?"

Just as Stella was about to say something, she let out another shriek. She spun around again and backed up just in time for me to see Enrique sneak up behind her and kick the gun out of her hand. In a flash, he had her on her back with his gun to her head. She squirmed and bellowed. I knew how she felt.

Willie motioned to Enrique. He unpinned her and got to his feet, leaving her to fend for herself.

Stella sat up in the dirt road sputtering, her nose swollen and bloodied from earlier, and looked up at Willie. She blinked through her disheveled hair and pushed it away from her eyes with one hand. As though she'd seen a ghost, she began scooting away from Willie like a crab doing the backstroke.

I heard running.

"Hey," I heard Kyle yell. "Leave her alone."

Willie pointed his gun in Kyle's direction. Enrique moved closer to Stella and aimed his gun at her head.

I felt like I was watching a scary movie from the front row of an IMAX theater.

"Okay, sport," Willie said to Kyle. "I want you to walk slowly over to your girlfriend and take a seat in the dirt next to her."

I watched as Kyle entered my field of vision and did what he was told.

"What are you doing here?" Stella asked Willie, her words half hidden in a mucus squeak of fright.

"The same as you. Following the trail of the pail." Willie chuckled at his tired joke. "Knowing it would eventually lead to you."

Stella cowered closer to the dirt, desperately trying to find a hole to fall into.

The pillowcase squirmed and yowled. Willie walked over to retrieve it while Enrique continued to cover Stella and Kyle. Holding it up, he said something in a low voice to Seamus that I didn't hear.

"So you have that bitch's cat," Stella said, her voice thick and nasally. "She tried to blame us."

Willie indicated the bag. "Poor thing misses his mama." He clucked a bit. "Little guy has one nasty temper."

He looked down at Stella. "So where is Odelia?"

Stella said nothing.

Willie approached and squatted in front of her. "Where's Odelia Grey?"

When she remained silent, Willie cocked his arm back and smacked her hard with the hand holding the gun. Stella went sprawling in the dirt.

"She's someplace around here," Kyle gushed with his familiar whine. "And she's not alone. There's a guy with her. An attorney from her office. My father's attorney. He's injured, so they couldn't have gotten far."

"And she has the Holy Pail," Stella chimed in with a snivel.

"Good," Willie said, his voice light and casual, "I was hoping she would."

Willie stood up and looked around. "Odelia, come on out," he called loudly. "It's safe now." He put the pillowcase on the ground, cupped his free hand to his mouth, and called again. "Odie, Odie, Oxen Free. Come out, come out, wherever you are."

I wanted to believe him. I needed to get help for Steele.

Trying to make up my mind, I watched as Willie hovered over the two on the ground. "She'd better be okay," he told them. "Enrique here has grown rather fond of her."

As if in reply, Enrique moved a step closer with his gun.

"Why did you come back, William?" Stella asked, finally getting up her courage.

"Why, for you, baby," Willie cooed at her. "Why else? We have a little debt to settle, don't you think?"

Stella shrank from him. "I ... I don't know what you're talking about."

"Oh, sure you do. I'm sure you remember the little matter of squealing on me to the feds and my hasty departure. And I know you remember Ivan Fisher and your latest conquest, Sterling Price. Oh, and don't forget my wife. You do remember my wife, don't you?"

He leaned in closer to her. "Well, Stella, darling, I'm here to make sure you don't hurt anyone ever again."

I watched in horror as Willie gave a sign to Enrique, who obeyed by jerking Stella up and onto her knees. Then he put the barrel of his gun to the back of her head, execution-style.

Kyle started blubbering. Willie turned to him with a look of disgust.

"You're Sterling's son, aren't you?"

Kyle nodded as he sobbed.

Willie considered him for a long moment. "Too bad you don't have even a modicum of your father's decency." He looked at Enrique. "Maybe we should do him first, seeing he's so pathetic and all."

Wordlessly, Enrique moved a step sideways and placed the gun to the back of Kyle's head. I thought Kyle was going to wet himself, he went so white. Stella slumped to the ground, crying.

"You have no reason to kill me," Kyle moaned.

"Give me a good reason not to," Willie said.

"No, don't!" I screamed. I quickly stood up and edged out from between the buildings. My hands were above my head in surrender. The battered Holy Pail dangled from one hand.

Willie turned toward me, but Enrique never moved. The gun stayed at the back of Kyle Price's head.

"Please don't kill them," I said again in a weak voice, trying to sound strong. "I'll give you the lunchbox. Just don't kill them."

"Odelia!" Willie cried in what seemed like delight. "We have a good friend of yours here." He nudged the bulging pillowcase with his foot and received a hiss in return.

Willie's exuberance made me nervous. He might be as insane as Stella and Kyle, only more dangerous. I walked slowly up to Willie, my hands still up in the air.

He laughed. "Put your hands down, woman. You look ridiculous."

My arms fell to my side. "Willie, please don't kill them."

He leaned close to whisper. "I told you I was a thief, not a killer, Odelia. This little dog-and-pony show is to put the fear of God in Stella."

"Well, it worked on me," I whispered back, not enjoying his little joke at all. If it was a joke.

I held out the Holy Pail to him. "Trade you," I said, "the box for my cat, like you promised."

Willie looked puzzled. "Like I promised?" Then he smiled. "I think you have me confused with someone else."

"You didn't trash my place and hold my cat ransom?"

"Of course not, little mama. We'd already searched your place. But there is someone you might be interested in meeting a little later."

He looked at the lunchbox in my hand and frowned. "You didn't have it all along, did you?"

I shook my head. "Amy Chow took it. Like you first suspected."

A loud kitty growl came from the wiggling bundle near Willie's feet. I handed him the Holy Pail and bent down to check on Seamus. For my loving efforts, I received a nasty hiss and sharp claws aimed in my direction, fabric or not. Instead of opening the sack, I picked it up by the top and held it at arm's length.

"I think I'd better open this little package at home."

Willie lifted up the lunchbox and turned it around, inspecting it. "Looks like you kept up your end of the bargain and destroyed the Holy Pail like I asked." He grinned at me.

Turning his attention back to the scum on the ground, he asked, "So which of you killed Sterling Price?"

Neither answered. Enrique pressed the gun hard against Kyle's head. He started whimpering.

"I don't know who killed my father." He pointed feebly at Stella, careful not to appear to be making a fast move. "But Stella attacked my sister and brother-in-law. I had nothing to do with it. Nothing." He dissolved into tears. But unlike Stella's earlier performance, his were real.

"Shut up, you idiot," Stella screamed at him.

Willie squatted in front of her again and held his gun in her face. "Did you kill your sugar daddy?"

"No, I didn't."

"Why do I not believe you?"

"I swear I didn't." Stella cleared her throat. "It was Amy Chow. She poisoned the coffee that morning. But it was a mistake."

"Seems there are lots of mistakes being made," I said, wondering if she was using young Amy as a scapegoat.

"Well, that one was a doozy," Stella said with a sick grin. "Amy was supposed to put something in the coffee just to make him a little sick, enough for him to go home early so she could steal the lunchbox. But she had no idea how poisonous oleander is or how much to use."

That wasn't the plan. That's what Amy had said to me.

A murderer had driven off into the desert, and I had helped her load her luggage.

THIRTY

"WHAT ARE YOU GOING to do with them?" I asked Willie.

He was still squatting in front of Stella, eyeing her miserable, battered face, lost in thought.

"Leave them with you," he said. "Enrique and I will tie them up. Then you can call the cops." He looked up at me. "Hope you understand if we don't stick around."

I gave him a tired, small smile. "I'll have to talk to the police about you. You know that."

Willie stood up and faced me. "Little mama, I wouldn't expect anything less out of you."

He said something to Enrique in Spanish. Enrique stored his gun behind him and from his pocket pulled something that looked like thin cord. He yanked the sniveling Kyle to his feet and dragged him over to a post attached to one of the buildings, where he dumped him back on the ground. He made quick work out of tying Kyle up to one of the posts. Once done, he moved on to Stella.

Just as Enrique was trying to get Stella up and on her feet, we heard a loud noise coming from behind the buildings.

"Steele," I said. I placed the bundled cat back on the ground and rushed to where the scrub area joined with the road.

Sure enough, it was Steele. He was hanging out of the wagon, trying to get out. Panic filled his face.

He waved his good arm and shouted at me. "Run, Grey, run!" Then he lost what little balance he had and keeled over the end, onto the ground.

"Steele!" I yelled.

Taking advantage of the distraction, Stella struck like a cobra. She kicked at Willie's legs, sending him tumbling and his gun sliding. At the same time, her head rammed back and caught the usually diligent Enrique square in his face. A sickening crunch echoed when her skull hit his nose. He slumped to the ground.

Buoyed by the change of events, Kyle yelled, "The gun, Stella, go for the gun!"

Willie and Stella both dived for Willie's gun, wrestling in the dirt together as they crawled toward it. The air was populated with grunts and curses.

I looked in the direction of the wagon. Steele lay motionless on the ground next to it. Torn between helping Steele and helping Willie and Enrique, I stood, momentarily cemented to the ground. But if Stella reached the gun before anyone else, there might not be anyone left to help.

Decision made, I dashed to help Willie, taking a shortcut across the rickety wooden sidewalk of the small, beat-up building. I had only gone a couple of steps when I felt pain in my ankle and one of my moving legs go taut. I fell sprawling onto the sidewalk, scraping my face on the wood. Something had grabbed my foot, and that something was a hole in the dilapidated planks. I struggled to free my foot, but only succeeded in tangling it further. I tried to slip out of my sneaker, but the hole had swallowed my foot to above the ankle bone. I watched with wide-eyed helplessness at the struggle going on, and cheered on Willie in response to Kyle's shouts.

The gun was within reach of their fingers. If Stella was the one to reach it first, I was toast, served up hot and fresh on a platter. I had no doubt that she'd kill me and everyone else in her bid to make a getaway. I continued to struggle to free my foot.

When I saw Stella's fingers touch the gun barrel ahead of Willie's, I started stomping at the hole in the splintered plank like a madwoman, hoping to break it down further and free the trapped foot. I stomped and stomped, using all my weight to work at the already weakened boards. It worked. The old wood gave way. With a desperate yank, I managed to pull my foot out, leaving the sneaker behind. Ignoring the searing pain in my ankle, I flew in the direction of the scuffle. But my ankle wouldn't hold, and I collapsed in the dirt just beyond the sidewalk.

Willie and Stella both had their hands on the gun. Stella was surprisingly strong. Kyle continued to encourage her. He was screaming for her to look out, letting her know I was free. Enrique was moving slowly, trying to shake off his daze. On my hands and knees, I tried crawling to the scuffle. But it was too late.

Only one hand had possession of the gun now—a woman's hand. Raising it, she clubbed Willie in the head and untangled herself from his clutches. After struggling to her feet, she put some distance between herself and us and held the gun steady, sweeping between us, looking for a reason to shoot.

I sat up, breathing heavy, and felt something hard under one of my buttocks. Hoping not to attract attention, I slowly moved one hand under me. It was Stella's gun—the one that went flying when Enrique kicked it. It was the first time in my life I had ever felt the cold and fearsome sensation of gunmetal.

Willie was sitting up now. About ten feet away in another direction, Enrique, too, was sitting. He seemed to be alert, but the front of his handsome face was bloodied.

"Way to go, babe," said Kyle happily. "Now come untie me."

"Seems the tables have turned, Stella," Willie said. "But you can't cover us all. So, who you gonna shoot first?" He gave an ugly chuckle.

Stella's nervous ball-bearing eyes darted about, taking in each of us in quick succession, weighing who was her biggest threat. Out of the corner of my eye, I saw Enrique go for the gun at the small of his back.

Scared spitless, I braced myself for a gunfight at the OK Corral.

"Look out," shouted Kyle.

A shot rang like thunder. Enrique grabbed his right shoulder and fell back in the dirt. Stella aimed the gun again at the young man. Another shot rang out. This time it was Stella who staggered.

I clutched the gun so hard with both hands, I felt my bones mold themselves to the grip. Stella looked at me. On her face was complete and honest shock, her mouth poised in a silent Oh. With one hand, she clutched her middle, as if trying to staunch the blood that was beginning to flow. The other still held the gun. She aimed it at me and screeched like a banshee.

Another shot.

This time she fell, motionless.

Silence fell so hard it was deafening. We sat there, too shocked to move, until Kyle sent up a shrill shriek of grief like a coyote over its dead mate. It sent shivers up my spine and released me from my trance. Only then did I realize I was holding a fired gun in my hands.

Willie reached me first and worked to release my fingers from the gun. "Come on, little mama," he cooed. "You can let go of that now." Silently, I let Willie take the gun from me.

I stared at the fallen body of Stella Hughes and listened to the continued wails of Kyle. A strong hand gripped me under an upper arm and gently encouraged me to my feet. It was Willie. My right ankle couldn't support me, so he put an arm around me and helped me hobble to some steps.

Once he had me settled, he kissed the top of my head and said, "Be good, little mama."

THIRTY-ONE

SITTING ON THE SOFA in the dark, I raised the crystal goblet to my lips and drank deeply of the rich red wine. Merlot—my favorite. The TV was on, the sound off. It didn't matter. Playing onscreen was *Robin Hood, Prince of Thieves*. I knew the dialogue by heart. It was the end of the movie—the part where Morgan Freeman kills the witch and Kevin Costner puts an end to Alan Rickman. Good conquering evil, Hollywood style.

I wonder. Did Robin Hood feel bad about killing the Sheriff of Nottingham? If he was real, I'd pick up the phone and ask him.

It will be exactly two months tomorrow since I shot and killed Stella Hughes. Technically, I would have killed two people—a woman and a fetus—but the autopsy showed that Stella wasn't pregnant after all. It was little comfort to me, but it was some comfort. I tipped the goblet again and drained the glass.

The park rangers may not have heard the first shot fired by Kyle, but they sure heard the last three shots. After depositing me on the steps, Willie grabbed Enrique and the two of them disappeared in the direction of the horse arena. They were hardly gone before two armed rangers came roaring onto the main road in an official vehicle.

Kyle, still tied to the post, finally stopped wailing and stared at Stella's fallen body in docile silence.

Kyle, Steele, and I were taken to the local hospital; Stella to the morgue. For hours we answered questions. But mostly it was me they questioned. I told the police everything. About Sterling Price. About the lunchbox and its history. About Willie and Enrique. About my trashed home and Seamus, who I insisted be allowed to come to the hospital with me.

I was sitting in the emergency room, waiting to have my badly sprained ankle wrapped, when Dev Frye and his partner showed up. After more questions, Dev drove Seamus and me to Greg's house, where Greg waited in a state of anger, frustration, and relief. I wanted to go home, but the doctor said because of the shock and my ankle, I shouldn't be alone. Also, as Dev reminded me, my home was not in a habitable state. Detective Zarrabi drove Steele's Porsche back to Newport Beach. Steele had to remain behind a few days for observation.

But there's more.

While the police were combing the area and processing the crime scene, they came across something interesting. Left gagged and tied up in the men's public restroom near the entrance to the park was Joe Bays. Across his white T-shirt, in ink, was scrawled *Cat Napper*.

This was the person Willie had said I would be interested in meeting—Joe Bays.

Before I left for the hospital, the police brought him to me and asked if I knew him.

My friend Joe had vandalized my home and stole my beloved pet in exchange for the Holy Pail. I wanted to vomit at the sight of him.

With a puffy, flushed face, he told me and the police that he wanted it to look like the job had been done by the same people who'd trashed Woobie. He said he'd seen an ad on a collector's Internet bulletin board asking for the Holy Pail's whereabouts and offering one hundred thousand dollars for it. Sure I had the lunchbox, he'd turned my home upside down. When he came up empty-handed, he decided to take Seamus and ransom the animal for the lunchbox. He'd made a date with the person who posted the ad to meet him here at seven thirty. At seven, he would give me the cat and take the lunchbox, then turn the Holy Pail over for quick cash.

The problem was, it was Willie who had posted the ad. And Willie and Enrique showed up early. When they saw what Joe had in the sack, they sacked him and left him hogtied.

"I'm sorry, Odelia," Joe said to me over and over, with tears in his eyes. "I didn't mean to hurt anyone. I just wanted the money. A hundred grand is a fortune to someone like me. It could change my life." He sniffed deep. "I would never have hurt you, Odelia. You gotta believe me."

I was tempted to ask the police to gag him again. Better yet, stuff his mouth with Thin Mints, *then* gag him.

In the end, I didn't press charges against Joe. But he did have to pay for damages, including the replacement of two rare and expensive nativity pieces that were broken, and a thorough cleaning of the townhouse, top to bottom. Steele brokered the settlement deal between us and wanted to throw in pain and suffering, but I said no. I knew Joe didn't have much money, and once Woobie got through with him, he was also unemployed. Joe found wrecking my place very costly.

Karla Blake survived the knifing and is still recuperating. She asked me to visit her in the hospital a few days after the shooting, which I did, seeing that she was a client. She thanked me for saving her life and told me that she planned on taking charge of her father's company as soon as she was well. In parting, she said she looked forward to working with me in the future. I billed Sterling Homes for the time I spent at the hospital, including mileage. Steele told me last week that Woobie is considering dropping them as a client. They'll get no argument from me.

After the incident at Paramount Ranch, Kyle Price suffered a real honest-to-goodness nervous breakdown. He now resides in the psychiatric ward of the jail pending trial, though Steele doesn't think he'll go to trial, considering his mental condition.

Steele broke his leg in the fall from the wagon. Now he hobbles around the office with his left arm and right leg in casts, looking like a war veteran. Injured, he's even more insufferable. Which, in a weird way, is comforting.

Willie and Enrique disappeared like mist on a hot day.

Dev dropped by tonight, just as he did on the first month's anniversary of my killing of Stella Hughes. He's concerned about me. Says I need to move on. Says it could not have been helped—that I was a hero for what I did. I don't feel like a hero.

Dev also told me tonight that they finally found Amy Chow, who, after depositing her mother in Phoenix, tried to disappear into the Northwest. He said that she confessed to putting the oleander into the coffee, but claimed Stella Hughes had given it to her, saying it would just make Sterling Price a little sick. Amy also told the police that she saw Jackson's body in the pool. Like me, she had gone inside after getting no response to her knocks and saw the body. She never saw Stella that morning.

As for Catherine and Les, there wasn't any evidence to link either of them to Chappy Wheeler's murder. The Holy Pail, the supposed murder weapon, disappeared the night of the shooting. No matter what happened all those years ago, I was glad they were cleared. I liked the two of them and they were going through a lot, with the death of their daughter and her connection with the two murders. As I told the police, my theory about Chappy Wheeler being killed with the lunchbox bearing his likeness was just that, a theory. An idea I got after reading the article in the *L.A. Times*. Personally, I think it's true, but no one seems eager to pursue it, especially me.

When I think about Carmen Sepulveda, a smile creeps across my face. Who says good guys always finish last? Carmen Sepulveda, the only one who didn't act upon a selfish motive, inherited the money and stock due her pursuant to Sterling's will. She retired, moved to Henderson to be near her sister, and travels extensively. I just received a postcard from her from Greece.

I look down at the bare ring finger on my left hand. The day after the shooting, I gave Greg back his ring.

Reaching for the bottle of wine on the coffee table, I refill my glass. Seamus is curled up on the sofa beside me. He stretches and yawns. I rub him behind his raggedy half ear and he purrs like an electric toothbrush, his time as a hostage apparently forgotten. Lucky cat.

Do I still love Greg Stevens? Yes. But I also know I'm not the same person I was two months ago. I became someone else the moment I pulled that trigger. But it's not my love for Greg that's changed. It's my capacity for love that seems to have taken a hike.

He fussed at first, of course. Said we could get counseling, together and separately. He pleaded with me to stick it out, to let him help me through whatever struggle was taking place within my soul.

Part of me wants to lay my head in Greg's lap and beg him to love me forever.

Another part of me wants to throw dirt clods at him for his own good, until he goes away and forgets about me.

He used to call every day. Then it was a few times a week. Then once a week. This week he didn't call at all. Maybe the dirt clods of silence are working.

I look up at the TV. Robin Hood was marrying Maid Marian. He had killed the Sheriff of Nottingham and now was celebrating his marriage to the cousin of the king. The movie never said, but I wanted to know just how much time had lapsed between the killing and the marriage. Were there rules of etiquette for such things? Would I wake up one morning and have a craving to wear white? Would it be similar to a craving for a waffle?

The phone rang. I didn't answer it. It would be Zee. Last month, on the one-month anniversary of Stella's death, I laid flowers on her grave in the morning, before going to work. I plan on doing it again tomorrow. I'm not sure if it's penance or guilt that drives me, or how long I will continue, but it's something I need to do.

Zee would be calling to make a last-ditch plea for me not to go. It would end in her crying. I let the phone ring until my voice mail picked it up.

With the movie over, I drained the wineglass again and headed upstairs to bed. I had been having trouble sleeping and the wine helped. I'd also lost twenty-five pounds in the last two months. Guess every cloud has a silver lining.

Shoot someone and lose weight. Wonder if I could host an info-mercial?

I don't know how long I had been asleep when I woke with a start. A hand clamped down hard on my mouth and a body strad-dled mine, pinning me to the bed. The bedside light snapped on, and I squinted as it assaulted my eyes.

On top of me was Enrique. Standing next to him, with his hand on the light, was Willie. I rolled my eyes at them both, and Enrique uncovered my mouth.

"Miss me?" I asked Enrique. He grinned and climbed off of me.

"Of course we did, little mama," Willie answered for them both.

"How's your shoulder?" I asked Enrique. He rotated it freely in response and smiled.

"Thank you," the young man said in excellent English, "for sav-ing my life." He grinned. "My mother thanks you, too. She says prayers for you every day."

I smiled back, even though I wanted to cry. Why? I had no idea, but I could feel the flood surging against the dike I had built over the past two months.

Willie moved his head slightly and Enrique took his leave. I heard him bounce down the stairs with vigor.

Willie looked around. "Where's that ill-tempered cat of yours?"

"Probably hiding under the bed."

Willie chuckled. "Sorry about the bump-in-the-night approach, but I needed to see you again."

He walked around the bed and climbed up on it, stretching out beside me on top of the covers. I made no protest. Oddly, I didn't feel insecure about being in bed with Willie. Thief or not, I liked the man and trusted him. Well, maybe not with my money, but I trusted him with my safety.

Supporting his head on one hand, he looked at me a long time. "Like Enrique, I came here to thank you."

"Why?" I asked with sarcasm. "Did I save your life, too?"

"In a way, you did."

I turned to look at him. He was serious.

"I have a confession to make, Odelia. You were right. I did want to kill Stella Hughes. And probably would have."

"Glad I could be of help."

Willie grabbed one of my arms roughly and shook me. If we'd been standing, my teeth would have rattled.

"Stop it, Odelia. Stop it right now," he demanded. "You had no choice in what you did."

I stared at the ceiling. "I know that, Willie. In my mind, I know that. In my heart, it's different." I turned on my side to face him. "Have you ever killed anyone?"

"No, not yet. Thanks to you."

"Willie, I feel like I died with her."

"But you didn't, Odelia. You survived. You need to get on with your life. You have great things ahead of you." He laughed lightly. "Esmeralda, that's Enrique's mother, believes you were spared for a reason. More importantly, she believes you're her son's guardian angel."

"I do think Enrique could do better," I said, turning again onto my back to stare at the ceiling. "Hmm, and how does Esmeralda feel about her baby boy being your hired thug?"

"Hired thug?" Willie asked, giving a short laugh. "I'll have you know that Enrique is in the middle of getting his master's degree in global economics. And he speaks four languages."

I turned my head to look at him and felt my face pull in surprise.

"It's true." He grinned at my frozen stare. "Hey, it pays better than bussing tables through school."

Willie also turned to stare at the ceiling, lacing his hands behind his head. You would have thought we were laying in a meadow, staring at the stars. We stayed that way a while.

"When my wife and I escaped to Mexico with the money," he said, breaking the silence, his voice somber, "we didn't have it planned out. Thanks to Stella, we had to leave quickly, without proper preparations. But something happened off the coast. A storm came up and our boat was severely damaged."

I turned onto my side and watched his face as he spoke.

"My wife was struck in the head by debris," he continued, forcing his voice to stay even. "She fell overboard and drowned. I've always blamed Stella for that. I've always blamed myself for it, too."

I reached over and stroked his face. He put a hand over mine and moved it to his lips, kissing my fingers tenderly.

"I didn't come here to kill Stella. Honest. But when I saw Enrique's gun at her head, I wanted so badly to do it. You don't know how close I came to thrusting my own gun in her face and pulling the trigger." He closed his eyes and swallowed hard.

"But when I saw you coming out of hiding with your hands up, begging for Stella and Kyle's lives—putting your own life on the line for their miserable existence—I just couldn't do it."

"It wasn't because of me," I whispered. "It's because you're not a killer."

"And neither are you."

He turned to me. One arm went around my thick middle. I felt his hand, hot and eager, against the satin of my nightshirt. He drew me close, nose to nose, mouth to mouth. Our lips played footsies with each other, barely touching, breath mingling with breath. When they came together finally in a kiss, they welded passionately, fusing us in our individual grief and need.

We kissed a long time. Over and over, our mouths locked, sometimes softly, sometimes with fervor, until our lips were chapped and tears ran down our faces, turning our kisses salty.

After a long time, Willie pulled back and looked into my eyes. "Come with me," he said.

"Go with you?" I asked with surprise.

"Yes, tonight, Odelia. Pack a few things and let's go away. I have plenty of money. I want to take care of you. I want to make you happy."

But I am happy, I thought, *or at least I was.*

Rolling away from him, I plucked two tissues from the box on the nightstand and handed him one. After blowing my nose, I sat up in bed.

"You want *me* to go away with *you?*"

"Yes, I do." He also sat up. "I know you didn't expect this, so let's make a deal. Come away with me for a short while. If you don't like it, I'll send you home. Anytime you like, you can come back."

Confused, I ran a hand through my hair and tucked it behind one ear. Go away with Willie. Live on the run, awash in ill-gotten wealth. On many levels, it was appealing.

THIRTY-TWO

When I woke, I was alone. Seamus was back at his usual spot at the foot of the bed, curled into a ball.

I had cried myself to sleep in Willie's arms after turning him down. He didn't ask why, and I didn't offer an explanation. But it wasn't for the reasons he probably thought. The truth is, my heart wasn't mine to give. It wasn't even mine to loan, not even for a short while.

After showering, dressing, and grabbing some breakfast, I picked up some flowers at the grocery store and drove to Forest Lawn in Covina Hills. The cemetery was near Glendora, and it took about an hour to get there in weekday traffic. I would arrive when it opened, pay my respects, and drive back to Newport Beach. I had let Tina know the day before that I would be in around ten.

I didn't dawdle at the grave. I didn't need to. I knew today would be the last time I'd be back. Setting the flowers on top of the headstone, I said my final goodbye.

Turning to go, I spotted him. His van was parked a few yards behind my car. He had driven all the way here early this morning. I hadn't even noticed anyone drive up. But there he was.

I studied him, taking note of the firm chest and strong arms. The way his hair curled around the tops of his ears and collar. The set of his sensual mouth. I noticed the strength of character in his eyes; how they looked at me with confidence and love grounded in maturity.

He sat in his wheelchair at the edge of the curb, watching me. He made no gesture of salutation. No overture of encouragement. Wainwright stood sentry next to him. Seeing me, the dog whined with excitement. He gave a quiet order and the animal stilled.

For a long time we simply watched each other, my Greg and I.

Read on for a sneak peek at
Mother Mayhem
by
Sue Ann Jaffarian
IN STORES FEBRUARY 2008

EXCERPT

"WHY AM I NOT surprised?"

The question, phrased more like a long-suffering supplication to a supreme being, was accompanied by a copy of this morning's *Orange County Register* being tossed onto my small, cluttered desk like an under-thrown Frisbee.

When it slid to a stop, just short of smacking my almost-full coffee mug, I saw that the paper was open to the front page of the local news section and folded in such a way as to show off a photo of me—yes, *moi*, Odelia Patience Grey. The caption above the photo blazed: *Food Fight Erupts at Local Market.*

A resigned sigh escaped my lips. I had hoped that no one would recognize me. After all, in the caption under the grainy photo, I was merely referred to as an unidentified woman.

The question had come from Mike Steele, my boss. He stood in front of me, waiting for an answer to what I felt was not a question deserving of a response. In my opinion, it had sounded purely rhetorical in nature. I continued to stare down at the fuzzy photo in the paper, my lips tighter than a pair of size 6 shoes on size 9 feet.

Michael Steele is a partner at Wallace, Boer, Brown and Yates, the law firm in Orange County, California, at which I am employed as a paralegal. I've been with the firm for about eighteen years, and I would be looking forward to the next eighteen years, if it were not for the man standing in front of me.

I didn't need to raise my face to know that Steele would be immaculately groomed from his *GQ*-handsome, close-shaven face, right down to his fingertips, which would be professionally buffed and shining like dew in the morning sun. And I didn't need to glance in his direction to know that he was wearing an expensive and beautifully tailored suit. It was also unnecessary to look up to know that he was peeved at me. The sarcasm in his voice hung in the air, waiting to be admired, round and bright, like ornaments on a Christmas tree.

A few years ago, when my old boss, Wendell Wallace, retired, I somehow fell within Steele's grasp. Steele had requested that I be assigned to him, and the firm agreed. They had even sweetened the pot for me with a nice raise and a private office.

They assigned me to him with an apology, claiming they trusted me to keep Steele and his law practice in line. In other words, I became his professional keeper so the firm's founding partners could sleep at night. The firm also gives me a special bonus at the end of each year for this added responsibility. It is money that I earn many times over and which can only be classified as combat pay.

Now, don't get me wrong—Mike Steele is an incredible lawyer. He's brilliant, focused, and ethical, which in this day and age is an accomplishment all on its own. He brings in a ton of new business and is the firm's top attorney in generating billable hours. He's Midas with a law degree.

It's just that sometimes he needs to be beaten about the head with the people-skills bat.

Without raising my face to look at Steele, I gave in and broke my silence. I pushed the newspaper back in his direction. "Not exactly my best side, is it?"

In the photo, my two-hundred-plus-pound bulk was being squeezed from either side by two angry women. I looked like a pesky pimple ready to pop. The young woman on my right was cute, twenty-something and, like me, plus size. The other woman, who turned out to be her aunt, was trim and looked a lot like her niece, just older. Both women towered over my five foot one inch frame.

Steele cleared his throat. Peeking up through the hair that slightly hid my face, I saw him cross his arms in front of his chest. He wanted an explanation and would wait all day for one, if necessary. I didn't owe him any details, and I could be just as stubborn. However, today I decided to go for bonus points with shock value.

Lifting my chin in his direction, I shook my head and tossed my almost-shoulder-length medium brown hair away from my face.

"Jesus, Grey!" In a flash, Steele's arms uncrossed and he was leaning toward me, with both hands flat on my desk. He angled his head to get a better view. "What the hell happened to you?"

"I was slugged by a leg of lamb," I explained, trying to be nonchalant about it—pretending that assaults by butchered meat happened every day.

At that moment, Kelsey Cavendish, the firm's librarian, strolled into my small office. With three people, it now reached capacity under the local fire code.

"Hey, Odelia, any plans for lun—." She stopped mid-sentence, then exclaimed in a folksy accent, "Damn, that's one helluva shiner!"

Kelsey immediately pointed an accusatory finger at Steele. "Did he give you that?"

"What?" Steele half shouted, turning an indignant, flushed face her way.

"Well, Greg certainly didn't give it to her," Kelsey shot back.

"Actually," I said, interrupting, "I believe my assailant came from New Zealand."

"Cavendish," Steele snarled in Kelsey's direction, "you don't really believe that I'd strike Grey, do you?" He glanced at me. "No matter how tempting."

Kelsey coolly looked him up and down. She was one of the few people at Woobie who didn't shrink in his presence. My guess is that if I ever left the firm, she'd be next in line for the keeper position.

"Nah, Steele, I don't."

A woman in her mid-thirties, Kelsey Cavendish was tall, slim, and angular, with a plain, friendly face. She was Olive Oyl in the flesh, but with a bigger clothing budget. She gave Steele a wide grin, slipped past him, and plopped herself down in the small chair across from my desk.

"Though I'll bet you lunch at Morton's, Odelia's thought about clobbering you a few times."

I couldn't help myself. Like a rude belch, a short, loud guffaw escaped my lips. Kelsey was right, I *had* thought about clobbering him, and on more than just a few occasions. In fact, I know dozens of people who would like to gather in the parking lot and beat the living crap out of him, starting with his last twenty secretaries.

Michael Steele went through secretaries like I buzzed through Thin Mint Girl Scout cookies. Our office manager, Tina Swanson, had given up on keeping the secretarial bay outside his office filled and now the placement job fell to yours truly. Lucky me. Currently, we were trying out a very talented temp named Rachel Keyo. She had just completed her third week with us and so far, so good. At least she didn't show signs of bolting—yet. And even though Rachel was a drop-dead gorgeous woman with long, sculpted legs and the face of a Nubian princess, Steele didn't show signs of seducing her—yet. Of course, Rachel was also in a very advanced state of pregnancy. This latter situation seemed to have a good, yet strange, effect on Steele. Instead of his usual behavior toward secretaries, which could swing between charming, sexual scamp and overbearing, demanding ass, Steele treated Rachel with uncharacteristic tenderness, even reverence. Kelsey, who never misses a trick, referred to it as his Madonna fixation. Personally, I don't care what it's called, as long as he keeps treating Rachel with respect and the work keeps flowing out the door.

Jolene McHugh, another attorney at Woobie who shares secretarial services with Steele and me, loves working with Rachel. No wonder. Rachel's legal skills extend far beyond typing and dictation. Her last job had been in the legal department of a large corporation, but several months ago she was laid off when that company downsized. If Rachel's temp assignment continued smoothly, Jolene and I would recommend that Tina hire the woman permanently after her maternity leave—providing, of course, Rachel was equally excited about the idea. But Jolene had already expressed her concern to me that somehow Steele would screw things up for everyone.

Kelsey looked down at the newspaper still on my desk and her smile grew wider. "Is that really you?" she asked.

I nodded slowly, suddenly wishing I had called in sick.

Kelsey leaned in closer. "So, just how did you get that shiner?"

Steele, who was now leaning against the door jamb, also moved in closer. You would have thought no one had work to do.

With a deep sigh that swelled my hefty bosom like a rolling wave, I began the saga of the leg of lamb, only to be interrupted by my phone ringing. A look at the display told me that the caller was Zenobia Washington, my best friend. No doubt she had also seen the morning newspaper. I ignored the phone. I would call Zee back later. I returned my attention to Kelsey and Steele and sighed again.

"It's nothing, really," I began. "I was simply in the market last night—just popped in to pick up some food for Seamus and dinner for myself—when these two women started arguing next to me at the meat counter. Rose, the older one, who turned out to be the younger one's aunt, began chiding her niece about her weight. In fact, she was being kind of mean about it."

"Oh, no," Steele groaned, shaking his head. "Odelia Grey, champion of chubbettes, to the rescue."

Steele was sarcastically referring to Reality Check, a local support group started several years ago by my late friend Sophie London. Now I lead it, together with Zee Washington. Originally, Reality Check was formed to help large people emotionally cope in a weight-obsessed society. Now it included others facing similar bigotry over other issues, such as physical disabilities.

I curled my lip at Steele before continuing. "Anyway, the niece—her name's Manuela—started crying and snapping at Rose, and pretty soon the scene escalated into a full-blown family feud."

"And you couldn't keep your freckled nose out of it, could you, Grey?" Steele gave another shake of his perfect head. "You couldn't just walk away? Maybe head to the frozen section and grab a carton of Ben and Jerry's?"

"Steele!" Kelsey snapped. Turning to me, she said, "Go ahead, Odelia, clobber him. I won't tell."

"You want to hear this or not?" I asked with annoyance. "If not, I have work to do."

"Sure, Grey," Steele said, supporting himself once more against the door jamb, hands casually shoved into his pants pockets. "Sing us a stanza of 'Odelia Had a Little Lamb.'"

Rolling my eyes, I continued. "By the time I tried to break Manuela and Rose apart, it had turned quite nasty and a crowd had gathered, including, I later found out, a photographer from the *Register* who just happened to be in the store and had his camera bag with him." I stopped to take a drink of lukewarm coffee from the mug on my desk.

"Anyway, Manuela was calling her aunt some pretty colorful names and Rose was getting in some good, sound slaps. I had almost succeeded in pulling them apart when, out of nowhere,

Manuela picked up that darn leg of lamb and swung it like Babe Ruth, hitting a homer with my left eye."

I looked from Kelsey to Steele. "Satisfied?"

Kelsey looked at me, then at Steele, then back to me. "Did you at least get to keep the leg of lamb?" Both of them cracked up with laughter.

"Just for that," I said to Kelsey, "you're buying lunch."

It was then we noticed Carol Evans, a senior associate, standing just outside my door. She was tall and willowy, with a long mane of thick, blond hair and a very attractive face that would be downright stunning if she smiled more. As usual, she was all business and wore an air of disdain like a heavy fragrance. Around the firm, she was getting the reputation of being the female counterpart of Mike Steele. Once she had our attention, Carol indicated she needed to speak to Steele.

Steele told her he'd be with her shortly. She paused, looking unsure of whether to wait or go. When Steele didn't make a move, Carol tossed her hair and took her leave. Once she was gone, he pulled his hands out of his pockets, stood straight, and looked me in the eye.

"I repeat myself, Grey. Why am I not surprised?" He shook his head yet again. "You're the only person I know for whom it seems perfectly natural to go into a market for cat food and end up being KO'd by a roast." He laughed. "Only you, Grey."

"Too bad about the shiner, Odelia," Kelsey told me, ignoring him, "especially with your big reunion this weekend. But maybe it won't be that bad. Might change from plum purple to puke yellow by then; much easier to cover with makeup."

Steele raised an eyebrow in curiosity. "Reunion?"

Crap, I thought, *something else for him to bug me about. He'll probably come up with a weekend full of work just to spite me.*

"Odelia's thirtieth high-school reunion is this Saturday," Kelsey cheerfully informed Steele.

"Damn, Grey, didn't know you were that old." Steele appeared to be calculating something. I almost suggested he remove his shoes if he needed help. He finally said, "I was . . . what . . . about eight years old then." He paused for what I'm sure he thought was dramatic effect. "Were you an actual flower child? Did you trip the light fantastic to Joplin and Morrison? Do any streakin'? Heh, heh, heh."

My future with Woobie was looking more like being sentenced to death row.

When he didn't get a rise out of me, due to an amazing amount of self-control on my part, Steele gave a *humph* and started to leave. Partway out the door, he stopped and turned back around. "Don't forget, Grey, I'll be out of town the beginning of next week."

"Where ya goin'?" Kelsey asked eagerly. "And how long can we count on you being gone?"

Steele gave her a chilly smile. "If you're a good girl, Cavendish, maybe I won't come back." Then he strode down the hall to join Carol.

"Why," I asked Kelsey, as I retrieved my purse from a file drawer in preparation for lunch, "do men always make promises they never intend to keep?"

WHOA! WAS MY IMMEDIATE reaction as I walked into my thirtieth high-school reunion. My palms grew clammy. My legs threatened to buckle. *Please, please, please, tell me I'm hallucinating.*

As soon as we entered the hotel ballroom, my eyes were assaulted by an explosion of soft blue and sea foam green crepe paper. The ballroom was decked out in an exact replica of our senior prom—20,000 Leagues Under the Sea—right down to the real fish tanks positioned throughout the room and the *blub-blub-blubbing* of waterlogged air bubbles piped in over the sound system. I didn't know which would happen to me first—passing out from shock or wetting myself; maybe the two would happen simultaneously. Talk about multi-tasking.

The invitation to the reunion had only said that the reunion committee was cooking up a big surprise. Some surprise. My heart rate increased notably. If I had known in advance that one of the worst nights of my life was going to be revisited, I would not have come. Needless to say, my prom night had not been warm, fuzzy, or romantic. Although I must admit, it could have been worse. After all, I hadn't been doused in pig's blood like Stephen King's Carrie. Yet it was definitely not one of those evenings I discussed wistfully with middle-aged girlfriends over a glass of wine. Nor was there any decaying corsage lovingly pressed into a scrapbook anywhere in my house. I had attended the prom, true, but it was one of those memories I've spent thirty years trying to erase, like a magnet continuously passed over a hard drive.

My thoughts of bolting were disrupted by a commotion near the entrance. I turned toward the noise to see Donny Oliver entering the ballroom on the shoulders of several former members of the football team. He was waving and cheering, making his way through the fake sea creatures and his former classmates like a conquering hero returning from war.

I couldn't move. My feet felt encased in cement blocks instead of my new black suede pumps. Donny Oliver was the very worst of my high school memories—the bogeyman in a quarterback uniform. I watched warily as he slid to the floor from the shoulders of his high-school comrades and started shaking hands. Someone handed him a beer. Someone else gave him a cigar. I half expected Donny to announce he was running for public office.

I prayed for early senility.

"Odelia?" I heard a female voice tentatively ask. "Odelia Grey, is that really you?"

I turned toward the melodic and kind-sounding voice to find a woman looking at me with happy curiosity. She was medium height, with bobbed dark hair and a long, lean face with deep crow's feet nestled around the eyes. She beamed at me, displaying a mouth of slightly crowded teeth.

"Johnette? Johnette Spencer?" I inquired, answering her question with a question. She nodded enthusiastically and we hugged.

Johnette Spencer had been in most of my classes during our four years in high school. She had been tragically shy, painfully thin, and sported thick, black-rimmed glasses. Over the years, we had eaten lunch together often. Like me, she had been a loner, not belonging to any specific clique.

The glasses had been replaced by contacts, or maybe laser surgery—who knew, these days. But Johnette was still thin and bony. She had not succumbed over the years to middle-age spread and a losing battle with the bulge. Glancing around at many of our former classmates, I comforted myself with the knowledge that I hadn't really been the fattest kid in my class, but merely a woman ahead of her time.

Johnette continued beaming her high-watt smile. "Well, it's Johnette Morales now. Has been for quite some time. Twenty-seven years, to be exact."

Johnette tugged on the shirtsleeve of the man standing behind her, urging him to come forward. He looked vaguely familiar. I tried to subtract three decades. He was bald, just under six feet tall, and built like a weightlifter gone slightly to seed. Football and the name Victor Morales came to mind.

"Of course," I said to Johnette, still trying to shake off the initial shock of the reunion theme and Donny's entrance. "You married Victor. I remember hearing about that."

"Funny how things work out," she said. "Victor and I hardly knew each other in high school. It wasn't until college that we became friends and eventually fell in love." Johnette blushed. Victor smiled broadly.

Victor Morales had been on the football team. He had been a quiet boy, not given to rowdiness like so many of the guys on the various sports teams. He had been popular, but not stuck-up. His only flaw, I recalled as I stood looking at him and his wife, had been his friendship with Donny Oliver, big man on campus and school bully. Nice boys like Victor had circled around Donny like moths to a flame because of Donny's prowess on the football field. Under Donny's influence in high school, Victor would never have dated a wallflower like Johnette. Yes, funny how things work out.

"Isn't this amazing?" Johnette said, sweeping her hand in an expansive gesture as if spreading pixie dust over the room.

"Swell," I responded in a voice cold enough to keep the ice caps from melting.

"But it's just like our senior prom, Odelia," she said with enthusiasm. "Remember?" Suddenly, it was Johnette who remembered. Her smile vanished and she reddened. Victor studied the wall behind me.

Remembering my manners and eager to change the subject, I indicated my date and introduced him. "Johnette, Victor, this is Dev Frye."

Devin Frye is a homicide detective in Newport Beach. I met him when he was assigned to the murder investigation of my friend Sophie London several years ago. He has curly blond hair flecked with gray and compelling blue eyes. He also stands well over six feet tall and is built like a moose on steroids. Dev is a football team all by himself and makes me feel downright petite in spite of my size 20 body. The two men shook hands amiably.

Johnette quickly surveyed Dev, then looked to me with an eager smile. "So, is it Odelia Frye now?"

Taken aback, I shot a glance at Dev. He was blushing and studying, or pretending to study, a five-foot-long cardboard seahorse that dangled near his head. A thought came to mind and I glanced down at Dev's left hand. Sure enough. Dev, a widower of just a couple years, still wore his wedding band. Johnette had made a natural assumption.

"No" I answered with a slight chuckle. "Dev and I are just good friends."

Johnette looked at the two of us with suspicion and her face lost some of its friendliness. Victor, on the other hand, looked at us with renewed interest.

"Oh look, there's Sally Kipman," Johnette said with forced cheer. She tugged at Victor. "Let's go say hello." And with a slight nod, they were gone.

"That went well," I said to Dev.

Dev bent down so his mouth was near my ear. "So what happened at your prom?"

"Nothing."

"Give me a break, Odelia. I'm a cop. Nothing doesn't make people that uncomfortable."

"Nothing, Dev, really. Just childish pranks long forgotten." I aimed my eyes at Dev's wedding ring and shamelessly used it to get his attention off my senior prom. "I think Johnette thinks you're married . . . and I'm not."

I scanned the crowd in the direction Johnette and Victor had headed. Sure enough, there was Sally Kipman, another personal annoyance from my past. This was turning out to be a reunion of my worst nightmares. A glance at my watch told me we had only been here seventeen minutes. That was long enough to bond with old schoolmates, wasn't it? After all, the fiftieth reunion was just twenty years away. Why do it all in one night?

I turned to Dev. He had stopped scrutinizing the seahorse and was now staring sheepishly down at his shoes, no doubt wishing he had worn sneakers so he could make a quick getaway should the need arise. I sighed and gave him a small, warm smile. Hard to believe this very same man could make a hardened criminal shake in his socks.

He shook his head slowly. "I should have told them I was a widower. Or at least taken off my ring."

"Why?" I asked. "It's no one's business who you are." I guided him over to the registration table, where more former classmates waited to hand us our name tags. "Besides," I told him with a grin, "I always wanted a bad rep. Maybe I'll finally get one."

My official boyfriend, Greg Stevens, was supposed to accompany me to the reunion. But a few days ago, he woke up with a cold that turned nastier with each day. Greg's illness gave me mixed feelings. On one hand, I was worried about him being ill. But on the other, it gave me an excuse not to attend the reunion. Why he had to be his usual gallant self and insist on my going anyway, I'll never know. He had suggested that I take Zee, but instead, at the last moment, I changed my mind and had asked Dev Frye to be my escort. There was no way in hell I was going to go to this clambake alone or without a proper date.

Dev and I made our way into the main seating area and snagged ourselves a couple of chairs at one of the tables set for ten. Several chairs had been tilted so that their backs rested on the table, letting all newcomers know they were already taken. After tilting our own chairs, Dev disappeared into the crowd to wrangle us a couple of drinks while I blazed a trail to the ladies' room.

I had checked my black eye—not a bad cover-up job, if I do say so—and was reapplying a fresh coat of lipstick when Johnette Spencer, now Morales, came into the large restroom. She looked quickly down when she saw me and started for a stall, but stopped short before entering. She just stood there, frozen. I watched her slim back reflected in the mirror in front of me. It seemed like she wanted to say something, but wasn't sure how to go about it.

As teenagers, we had been good friends, and I had spent a lot of time with her. Many afternoons after school we had studied together at her house while her mother, in true June Cleaver form, plied us with Cokes and snacks. When I was sixteen, my own mother abandoned me and disappeared, and I went to live with my father and stepmother. Johnette and I had become especially close during that turbulent time in my life. It bothered me now that a possible misunderstanding had tainted what should have been a happy renewal of friendship. It bothered me that she had been so quick to judge. And it bothered me that I had been so quick to cut her off about the prom. After all, our senior prom had been a happy night for many people. I just wasn't one of them.

Without preamble, I explained Dev. "Dev's a recent widower. His wife died of cancer."

Johnette glanced quickly over her shoulder, catching my eye in the mirror. "Oh," she said softly. "I'm sorry. About his wife, I mean."

She turned her face back to the stall, but instead of entering, abruptly turned on her heel like a soldier doing an about-face.

"Odelia," she began, still speaking softly. "I'm also sorry that I was so rude out there. And I'm very sorry I brought up the prom." She took a couple of steps toward me. I glanced down and noticed that she was wringing her hands slightly. "I really am so very glad to see you."

"It's okay, Johnette," I told her. "I'm very happy to see you, too. And the prom is ancient history. Really." Before another heartbeat passed, I took a step toward her and reached out my arms for a hug. Not so much because I wanted to, but because instinct told me she needed a hug—badly. And she did. She fell into my arms, burying her small frame into my ample bulk. I could feel her shoulders slightly shaking. When we parted, I saw that she was weeping.

"It's okay, Johnette," I told her again. "Really. No harm done."

"It's not that, Odelia," she said before starting to cry in earnest.

There was a small sitting area just inside the ladies' room door with a small padded bench. Grabbing some tissues from a dispenser, I handed them to Johnette and steered her toward the bench.

"What's the matter, Johnette?"

She looked down at the tissue that was quickly being mangled in her grasp. I had one arm around her shoulders and could feel her take a deep, lung-expanding breath before answering.

"Victor's having an affair."

Now it was my turn to give a soft "Oh."

"That's why I was so upset when I saw you with that man. I thought he was married and you were cheating with him." She looked up at me. "Stupid, isn't it? You having a fling with a married man?"

Her remark confused me. I didn't know whether she thought that highly of my ethics or if she thought I couldn't find a man with whom to have an affair. But this wasn't about me.

I gave her shoulder a squeeze. "Are you sure Victor's having an affair?"

She nodded. "I followed him one afternoon. He was supposed to be playing golf, but instead he went to some woman's house." She started weeping again. "Oh, Odelia, she was very young. And very pretty." She blew her nose. "I saw them embrace."

I found myself speechless, not a natural state for me. I continued to squeeze my arm around her shoulders and pulled her close. Occasionally, a woman would come into the restroom, glance our way, and keep going toward the stall area. In due time, Johnette stopped crying, blew her nose, and straightened her shoulders.

"You go ahead, Odelia," she told me, taking one of my hands and giving it a little squeeze. "You go on out there and keep that nice man company. I'll be along very shortly."

"You sure?" I asked skeptically.

She nodded. "I'm just going to freshen up before going out myself."

Still not convinced she should be left alone, I did as she asked and started to leave the bathroom, only to be stopped by bony fingers clutching my arm.

"Please don't tell anyone about this, Odelia. I don't want anyone's pity."

Assuring her of my discretion, I said, "I'm sure you and Victor can work this out. You've been together a long time."

"Yes," Johnette said, contorting her thin lips into a forced smile. "I'm sure it'll be all right in time. Lots of men have a mid-life crisis and return to the nest once it's out of their system." She looked to me to validate the statement.

"So I've heard," I responded automatically, all the while thinking that if Greg ever cheated on me, he'd be going from paraplegic to quadriplegic in no time flat.

Back again in the main ballroom, I made my way to our table to find Dev and Victor deep in sports talk. The Moraleses were going to join us at our table, Dev informed me. I smiled tightly at the alleged cheater as I took the seat Dev offered. A much younger woman, huh? The cheating would have been bad enough, but as a middle-aged woman, I took it somewhat personally that he might be straying with a newer and shinier model.

I was telling the men that Johnette would be along shortly when movement caught my eye. Approaching our table was Donny Oliver. Grr.

"Hey, Vic, great to see you," Donny boomed as he made his way to Victor's side. The two men shook hands as Victor beamed with delight. He looked ready to abandon everything and follow Donny into the jaws of hell. With Donny was another former football player whose face was familiar but remained nameless to me. Victor shook his hand, too.

Then Donny saw me.

"What?" he said, looking at me in exaggerated surprise. "This can't be Odelia—Odelia Grey."

In high school, Donny Oliver had been a commanding sight. Ruggedly handsome with wavy brown hair, a dimpled chin, and deep-set, dark eyes, he stood just over six feet tall with a trim, hard body and wide shoulders. He didn't look all that different now, except that his dark hair was laced with gray at the temples and his face was marked with slight lines around his eyes and mouth. A boozy smell emanated from him. Yep, just like in high school.

Memories as rancid as week-old tuna invaded my brain and anger gurgled inside me. I felt ready to blow, like a shaken soft drink. *Let it go, Odelia,* I cautioned myself. *Control. Control. Control. You can do it.*

"Hello, Donny," I said through teeth clenched hard enough to worry me about cracking a crown.

Donny looked at me with amusement, then opened his arms wide. "Ah, come on, Odelia. Give your old friend a hug."

I glanced at Victor, who was looking embarrassed, then at Dev, who was looking both puzzled and concerned. I searched my brain for something glib and funny to say, something that would ease my tension and put Donny in his place.

"Eat shit and die, Donny." The comment may not have been original, but it was heartfelt.

He laughed. So did the guy with him. They were the only two amused. On my other side, I felt Dev start to rise.

"Is Tommy Bledsoe with you tonight?" Donny asked as he looked around. He turned to the guy with him. "How about it, Steve? Wouldn't that be perfect? Odelia, Bledsoe, and this damn sea hunt shit, together again. Now *that* would be a reunion." They both laughed.

I said nothing. Dev stood up, but Donny took no notice.

"Come on, Odelia," Donny said, still with his arms spread. "Give me some of that heavyweight lovin' like you used to."

"Leave her alone, Donny."

It was a woman's voice. I turned to see Sally Kipman standing near the table with her hands on her hips, looking rather formidable. Johnette stood behind her, doing a great imitation of a frightened rabbit. I could have sworn I even saw her long, bony nose twitch. Geez, could this get any worse?

I continued my quest for the very elusive self-control. My jaw, still clenched, was starting to ache. What I really wanted to do was to push Donny's head into one of the nearby fish tanks until it became one of the bubbling tank ornaments alongside the toy pirate ship. Without much effort, I could picture little multi-colored fish swimming in and out of his nose. Entertaining this thought, I could feel control within my grasp.

"Yes, leave the lady alone." This command came from Dev as he moved to stand by my chair in front of Donny.

"Who the hell are you?" Donny asked Dev. I was pleased to see Donny flinch at Dev's size. My jaw relaxed a tad at the sight.

"Detective Devin Frye of the Newport Beach Police. And this lady's date."

"Let's get out of here, Donny," his buddy said, putting a hand on his arm. Suddenly, I remembered his name—Steve Davis.

Donny looked down at me, then up at Dev, seeming to make up his mind about something. He turned to Victor. "Come on, Vic, let's go get a beer."

Victor looked at the people gathered around the table, including his wife. "Sorry, Donny, have to pass."

Donny looked surprised at Victor's insubordination.

"Leave it alone, Donny," Steve said, trying to steer him away from the table.

After glancing once more at me, then at Dev, Donny Oliver strode away. In seconds, he was shaking hands and slapping backs in another crowd of people.

"Some people just never grow up," Johnette said. She moved to Victor's side. Her husband slipped a protective arm around her waist.

Dev sat back down in his chair and looked at me. "Okay, *now* are you going to tell me what this is all about?"

I didn't look at him when I answered. "Maybe someday."

"Sally's going to join us," chirped Johnette, trying to move the mood of the table along to happier thoughts.

Oh boy, I thought. Although, I reminded myself quickly, Sally did just come to my assistance with Donny.

"Hello, Odelia," Sally said as she took a chair across from me and Dev. "Nice to see you again." Her voice was clear but clipped.

In high school, Sally Kipman and I got on each other's nerves on a daily basis. Thinking back, I can't remember why. Maybe it was because our personalities mixed like oil and water. Or maybe it was because we were too much alike.

Sally Kipman transferred to our school after her mother and father divorced and her mother relocated the two of them to Southern California from New Jersey. Sally wasn't happy to be in California and even less happy to find herself from a broken home, a status that was still fairly new in the late 1960s.

Until Sally came on the scene in our sophomore year, I was one of the only kids in school whose parents were divorced. While I retreated into boxes of cookies, Sally took a different approach in expressing her emotions. She was surly and belligerent to everyone, including teachers, and quick to start a fight. She quickly embraced youthful rebelliousness and her right to freedom of speech, no matter what was said or who got hurt by her machine-gun tongue. Like Johnette and me, Sally was a loner. At first, we invited her to have lunch with us. But she responded to our invitations with such verbal abuse, we finally stopped asking.

For reasons unknown, Sally's hackles would rise whenever she saw me. And, I must admit, the feeling was mutual. In our junior year, she told everyone I was fat because I was pregnant. I retaliated by telling everyone Sally was a lesbian. Shortly after that, after two weeks of detention and an order from Mrs. Zolnekoff, the school principal, we called an uneasy truce and made it to graduation without assaulting each other.

I looked across the table at Sally Kipman. Like Donny, she still looked very much as she had thirty years ago. Maybe mean people don't age. Maybe all their natural vileness acts like embalming fluid. It seemed like a plausible explanation to me.

As in high school, Sally's body was tall, slim, and athletic. Her hair was dark blond and cropped short in a becoming, tousled cut. She wore no makeup that I could see, and never did that I could remember. She was tan and fit and very attractive in a no-frills way. She no longer had an air of pent-up anger, but still definitely one of no-nonsense. Seeing me looking at her, she flashed me a non-hostile lukewarm smile and I returned it. It looked like the truce would hold.

With Donny staying on the other side of the room, no doubt avoiding Dev like he was my personal junkyard dog, the reunion turned out to be much better than I had expected. Meaning, I actually had fun once my jaw unlocked. During a lovely dinner, the people around the table caught up on each other's lives and passed around photos of children and grandchildren. I was the only one at the table who didn't have either. Even Sally Kipman had a grown daughter and one young grandson. I showed a photo of Greg and one of Seamus, my ill-tempered, antisocial, champagne-colored cat.

During dessert, the DJ started playing dance music, and Dev coaxed me onto the floor.

"I'm glad to see you're finally having a good time," he said to me as we awkwardly danced to a slow tune. Dev Frye is way over six feet tall and I top out at five foot one. He had to almost bend in half to whisper in my ear.

"Yes," I answered, "I am. Thanks for coming with me."

"You're welcome. Thank you for asking." He smiled down at me and pulled me closer to him. My nose hit somewhere in the middle of his chest. Suddenly, I was overcome with guilt.

I have always known that Dev Frye likes me a lot, and the feeling is mutual. I also know that he would be actively pursuing me if not for Greg Stevens. And, if not for my love for Greg, I would be encouraging this mountain of a man in his pursuit. When I called Dev about escorting me tonight, I had made it clear that it was a friendship date—that he would be filling in for an ill Greg. Dev had said no problem, but questions peppered my mind. Was I leading this kind, decent man on with my selfish need to prove something to someone? To whom? To Donny Oliver? If that was true, I wasn't playing fair with Dev's feelings.

Greg. Therein lay the bulk of the guilt. Greg was at home right now suffering with a head cold and thinking I was with Zee. He had no idea that I had changed my mind and asked Dev instead. I know that if he knew I was dancing in the arms of Devin Frye, he would be upset. Although Greg likes Dev, he's not in the dark about Dev's feelings for me. In fact, it was Greg who first brought them to my attention shortly after we met the man. And Dev is always there, ready to lend a hand or look out for me whenever I manage to get myself into a jam. Or stumble upon a body. Which are really one and the same since I never seem to be in a jam that doesn't involve a dead body in the mix.

Simply put, Dev, Greg, and I are engaged in an emotional yet polite ménage à trois.

Thanks to me, Greg and I are not engaged, though he has asked and even has a gorgeous ring waiting for when I'm ready. We were engaged for a whole day just over a year ago, but I gave the ring back until I could sort out some personal issues.

I giggled. Dev looked down. I shrugged, not wanting to share my secret. I had decided that on Thanksgiving, just over four weeks away, I would ask Greg to marry me. I would let him know that I'm ready to accept his ring, to be his wife, to formally begin our life together. No one knew of my decision yet, not even Zee.

I shook myself out of my girlish daydreams. Here I was, forty-eight years old, dancing with one man among cheesy, fake sea creatures and make-believe waves while being dreamy-eyed about another. He loves me, he loves me not. All I need is a bunch of daisies to pluck, petal by petal. But I really don't need the daisies; I know without a doubt that Greg Stevens loves me.

By the way, I'm blaming this thirty-year regression on crepe paper fumes. That's all there is to it.

Another slow song started and Dev showed no sign of loosening his grip. We continued swaying and gently moving to the music. I closed my eyes and lost myself in thoughts of a white gown and altar flowers. Greg sitting in his wheelchair dressed to kill in a tux; Zee in a gawd-awful taffeta bridesmaid's dress; people screaming...

What? People screaming? At my wedding?

My eyes popped open, returning me to a room of blue and green chaos.

Dev stopped dancing and stood stock-still, as if sniffing the air for the direction of the trouble. More screams. Dev and I turned to face the doorway just as the crowd parted and a man staggered in, his shirt front soaked with blood. Dev made a dash in his direction just as he collapsed to the floor.

It was Donny Oliver.

An Interview with Sue Ann Jaffarian

by Julia Buckley,
author of *The Dark Backward* and the forthcoming
Madeline Mann Mysteries. For more of Julia's interviews
with mystery authors, go to http://juliabuckley.blogspot.com/

Your protagonist, Odelia Gray, is "middle aged and plus-sized." Do you hear from a lot of readers who are glad to see a heroine who is, let's say, more realistic than most?

Absolutely! I get lots of e-mail from women (and even some from men) of all ages and sizes saying they find it refreshing to see a not-so-young, not-so-thin heroine—someone they can relate to very well and who faces many of the same issues in her life.

Jaffarian is a neat name. What ethnicity is it?

It is Armenian—I am half, obviously on my father's side.

Speaking of names, how did you come up with "Odelia"?

I found it in a baby name book. I don't know why, but I was determined to have a character whose name began with an O. She was Olivia in the very early stages, but it never seemed to fit, so I bought a baby book and studied the names until I found one that suited the character.

You've got some amazing blurbs. Not to sound envious, Sue Ann, but how did you make all of these big-time writer friends?

Meeting these wonderful folks came naturally during my involvement in both Mystery Writers of America and Sisters In Crime. I also have attended a lot of mystery conferences, where I have met many writers who live outside of Southern California. One of the fabulous perks of being a writer is meeting and getting to know the people you've been reading for years.

You list Jon Stewart's *Daily Show* as one of your favorite shows. Do you and Jon have similar political leanings, or are you both just fans of good satire? Or both?

It's definitely both. I love his dry wit and irreverence, and do indeed share many, if not most, of my political leanings. Absolutely no one can mimic George W's laugh like Jon Stewart, although Wanda Sykes does an admirable job. (BTW, I'm impressed. You had to comb my website to get this info.)

Your character, Odelia Gray, has a green, one-eyed cat. Does this continue your theme that people shouldn't judge by appearances, or were you just trying to create a really memorable pet?

The odd thing is, I was just trying to give Odelia a funny pet, an animal quirky like her, but after *Too Big To Miss* was done I realized what a connection Seamus makes to the underlying theme of the book. It was totally something that happened on an unconscious level, but not while I was actually unconscious.

Good distinction. Your website doesn't have too much biographical information. Are you a mysterious woman?

Nah, boring maybe—I go to work; I come home; I write. I'm single and live with two cats and have dinner most nights with Jon Stewart.

The Holy Pail is a lunchbox and an important clue. What came first, the clue or the title?

The lunchbox came before the title. I was kicking around the idea of centering a plot on a lunchbox and an old TV cowboy and during my research came across a collectible lunchbox actually nicknamed "the holy pail." It was a perfect fit for the story and a perfect lead into the title.

Odelia often has very emotional attachments to food. I can relate to this, because my mom was a very food-is-love sort of nurturer. Did you grow up with this sort of family dynamic?

Not really. My mother was not a good cook and had very bad eating habits, which, of course, I picked up. Eating is emotional for me also, but not in a food-is-love way; it's more of a food-is-legal-dope way. I think Odelia is more like me in that regard.

Greg, Odelia's boyfriend, is wheelchair-bound, and her best friends are black. Does Odelia sometimes seek out people who she feels might be stereotyped for one reason or another?

I don't know if Odelia sought out Greg and the Washingtons for that purpose, but I sure did. (Actually, Zee is patterned after a good friend of mine in real life.) But I like bringing real people into my books, and I want readers to see real people within the pages. For me it brings more realism to the stories. I strive to make every book a slice of life in Southern California and that includes the disabled, Asians, blacks, Latinos, even dwarfs, as well as wealthy matrons, *GQ*-handsome bosses, and criminals.

Odelia says, at one point, that she never felt young, even when she was young. Did you ever feel this way?

Absolutely, that thought came straight out of my own life. I remember being 16 going on 32. I think this often happens to people forced to take on a lot of responsibility at a young age.

Odelia, after book one, has an interesting bullet wound. How did you decide to write this into your plot?

Again, it was something that came about naturally. She was shot; she'd have a wound from that and the wound would now be part of her physical being. It also helped me weave some background from the first book into the second one without giving too much away.

Who are your mystery inspirations?

It there is one author who has given me a vision for my own writing it would be the late Anne George, author of the Southern Sisters mysteries. I remember reading one of her books and knowing immediately I wanted to write mysteries that made people laugh about everyday events and everyday people.

Odelia loves food, and I'm guessing Sue Ann has her favorite foods, too. What's the best restaurant in the world, in your opinion? If I were in town, would you take me there? What should I order?

I don't really have a favorite restaurant—I have restaurants that serve favorite items. But if you were visiting me in West Los Angeles on a weekend I would take you to the Overland Café for the best brunch in LA, and it's walking distance from my home. You dropping by anytime soon?

Hey, you never know. I wouldn't rule it out. Odelia, at the beginning of *Holy Pail*, talks about how many commandments she has broken. Are you willing to confess? What's the most recent commandment Sue Ann has broken?

Boy, I wish I could say it was something horribly shocking. Let's see, I just ate half a carton of Ben & Jerry's Brownie Batter and swore at myself for doing so. I guess it would be taking God's name in vain. Told you I was boring.

Odelia has a boss she really loves to hate. Not to make constant Odelia/Sue Ann comparisons, but have you ever had a boss like that?

I have worked in the legal field for over thirty years, so the answer would have to be yes. But I have never had a boss exactly like Michael Steele. He is a compilation of all the stereotype bad traits of an attorney, except that he is ethical. He had to be ethical or Odelia would never work for him.

What's the most rewarding piece of fan mail you've received for your plus-sized mysteries?

I received one recently from a reader who said that after reading *Too Big To Miss* she was loving herself more and thanked me for that. I've had several along those lines over time and each one warms my heart like you wouldn't believe. But the most triumphant was an e-mail I received from a man who said he'd read my book because his wife had enjoyed it so much. She didn't write, but he did—to tell me he'd never look at fat women quite the same again and would think twice about how he treated them in the future.

That is indeed an accomplishment to be proud of. Is it difficult to maintain a day job and a writing career?

Absolutely—there's not much down time for just relaxing. I have to schedule everything, even cleaning the house. When I'm not at my day job, all my focus seems to be on writing, promoting my books, or attending writers' events. It can be exhausting. I don't know how people do it with day jobs *and* families.

How many Odelia mysteries do you anticipate writing?

In addition to *Too Big To Miss* and *The Curse of the Holy Pail*, I have four more planned. Midnight Ink has bought the third book in the series, *Mother Mayhem*, and it is scheduled for release February 2008. I will know by book five if there will be more after the sixth one.

Where do you write your books? Do you have a cozy office? Or do you write on a laptop at lunch, or at your kitchen table while dinner is cooking?

Most of my writing is done on a PC at a desk in a corner of my bedroom, and usually both my cats are nearby. Raffi likes to sleep in a chair pulled up next to mine (and he'll whine until I do pull it close) and B likes to stretch out between the keyboard and the monitor.

Thanks for the interview!

Photo by Ivo Lopez

ABOUT THE AUTHOR

LIKE THE CHARACTER ODELIA Grey, Sue Ann Jaffarian is a middle-aged, plus-size paralegal. She lives in Los Angeles with her two cats, B and Raffi, and writes mysteries and general fiction, as well as short stories and occasional poetry. In addition to writing, she is sought after as a motivational and humorous speaker.

Sue Ann is the current president of the Los Angeles chapter of Sisters In Crime, an international nonprofit organization dedicated to the mystery genre.

Visit Sue Ann on the Internet at:

WWW.SUEANNJAFFARIAN.COM

WWW.MIDNIGHTINKBOOKS.COM

From the gritty streets of New York City to sacred tombs in the Middle East, it's always midnight somewhere. Join us online at any hour for fresh new voices in mystery fiction, book club questions, author information, mystery resources, and more.

Midnight Ink promises a wild ride filled with cunning villains, conflicted heroes, hilarious hazards, mind-bending puzzles, and enough twists and turns to keep readers on the edge of their seats.

MIDNIGHT INK ORDERING INFORMATION

Order by Phone
- Call toll free within the U.S. and Canada at 1-888-NITEINK (1-888-648-3465)
- We accept VISA, MasterCard, and American Express

Order by Mail
Send the full price of your order (MN residents add 6.5% sales tax) in U.S. funds, plus postage & handling, to:

> Midnight Ink
> 2143 Wooddale Drive, Dept. 0-7387-0864-X
> Woodbury, MN 55125-2989

Postage & Handling
Standard (U.S., Mexico, & Canada). If your order is:
> $24.99 and under, add $3.00
> $25.00 and over, FREE STANDARD SHIPPING
AK, HI, PR: $15.00 for one book plus $1.00 for each additional book.

> International Orders (airmail only):
> $16.00 for one book plus $3.00 for each additional book

Orders are processed within two business days. Please allow for normal shipping time.
Postage and handling rates subject to change.